ROAR

VOLUME 8
PARADISE

Edited by Mary E. Lowd

Bad Dog Books

2017

ROAR Volume 8
First publication 2017

Edited by Mary E. Lowd

Cover by Teagan Gavet
Copyright © 2017

Published by Bad Dog Books
www . baddogbooks . com

Table of Contents

For all the women who were warned.

For all the women who were given an explanation.

For all the women who, nevertheless, persisted.

FOREWORD

When I selected the theme for this volume, I envisioned a tome full
of stories about shining science-fiction utopias. That was my vision of
paradise. But the authors had different ideas. Furthermore, the real world
intruded. Not a lot of people felt like writing during the last few months
before the deadline; even fewer of them were able to reach deep enough
inside themselves to find a vision of paradise to share with the world.

Thank you so much to all the authors who persevered and found a way to
write about paradise, even in these uncertain times. This volume of ROAR
received fewer submissions than the last two, but the average quality
of those submissions was extremely high. And the visions inside those
submissions were a revelation for me. I've learned about paradise from
editing this book.

Paradise can be the stark natural beauty of our own world; it can be the
connections we have with the people we love; it can be a moment in time.
Paradise can be a place we're seeking or a place that we didn't realize we
already had until it started to slip away. It can have a dark side. Even
those shining science-fiction utopias can come with a price.

This is the first volume of ROAR I've edited where the stories snapped
together into an order almost effortlessly. It's like these eighteen stories
wanted to be together and work with each other to tell an even larger story.
Together, they become a journey through different visions of paradise—
beginning with the personal and natural, traveling through the societal and
technological, and all the way out to the supernal and divine.

I'll leave you with a parting thought. One vision of paradise is a quiet
room, a comfortable chair, and a good book—preferably one with plenty of
anthropomorphic animals! A great book can heal you when you're hurting,
give you an escape that you desperately need, or even rekindle a lost spark
of hope.

I hope this book can be a small piece of paradise for you, dear reader.

-Mary E. Lowd

Our world is filled with stark natural beauty—like the Alaskan wilderness. It can be harsh. It can be dangerous. For Rafael, a Chihuahua on a mission, it can be an obstacle. But sometimes, we find paradise when we aren't looking for it, in a place we'd never expect.

NORTHERN DELIGHTS

Madison Keller

Rafael walked out of the airport and into a frozen wasteland. Overhead the sky was gray, the sun completely hidden behind the clouds. The wind whistled, sending a swirl of snow down his back. Rafael shivered and pulled up the collar of his bubble-gum pink winter coat. The color hadn't been his first choice, but even in the dead of winter stores in Phoenix didn't exactly carry a large selection of winter wear, especially in sizes that fit a Chihuahua.

He was already cold, and he was only three steps from the warmth of the airport lobby. Rafael scowled and began following the signs towards the taxi cab waiting area. His cell rang, belting out Don Omar singing *"Pa' este baile no hay salida."*

"You've reached Detective Ferreira," he answered, cutting off the catchy tune. A gray and white barrel-chested malamute walking ahead of him startled and turned to stare down at the little Chihuahua. A lot of people had that reaction when they found out he was a policeman.

"Where are you?" his boss barked at him. The Captain was a pitbull and Rafael could picture him sitting at his desk, jowls quivering with rage, eyes narrowed.

"I'm great, boss, and how are you?" Rafael bared his teeth at the phone and then up at the bigger dog. The malamute blinked and then hurried his steps away.

"I asked where you are detective," his boss repeated, the growl in his voice deepening.

"I'm taking some personal time off, sir. Family emergency." Rafael hung up. The phone rang again, which cut off abruptly when Rafael popped off the back and pulled out the battery.

Rafael jumped into the back of one of the cabs idling at the curb waiting for passengers. The cabbie, a big shaggy thing of indeterminate species, did a double take as Rafael settled into the seat. "What kinda rat are you?"

"The dog kind," Rafael barked back as he snapped on his seat belt.

The cabbie shook his head but hit the 'fare' light on his dash. "Where to?"

"Iditarod starting line," Rafael said and settled back into his seat.

The shaggy dog shrugged and pulled away from the curb. Rafael sat up in his seat, struggling to see out the window. Mostly he could only see the tops of buildings, all covered in snow. Big flakes drifted by the windows.

"Nice jacket," the wolf said, grinning at him in the rear-view mirror.

Rafael grinned back at him. "Thanks, it's a family heirloom. You know where the racers wait to start?"

"What, don't tell me you're a competitor?" He howled in laughter.

At this Rafael let out a genuine laugh. "Ha, not hardly. A friend of mine is. Just wanted to wish him luck before he starts."

"A little guy like you? In that crowd? You'll never find him in time. The back area is always a cluster. Best bet is to find a place along the starting stretch and cheer for him as he goes by. I know a good place where the crowd won't be too thick."

Rafael grabbed at the door as the cab made a sudden turn. "*Cabron!* Watch it. Thing is, I really need to talk to my friend before he starts the race. It's important."

"Your dime. But don't say I didn't warn you." The cabbie pulled over to the curb.

Rafael popped off his seatbelt and stood. Crowds of dogs streamed down the sidewalk outside the cab. In the distance a block ahead of him, almost obscured by falling snow, he could see a flag-topped tower.

"Thanks. Keep the change." Rafael handed the cabbie a twenty before climbing out.

When he opened the door he shivered as the cold air blasted him, seeming to whistle right through his hat and jacket. The snow on the sidewalk crunched under his boots. The sidewalks were shoveled, but more snow was falling all the time. Snow was piled high against the buildings and was ground to slush in the streets beneath the passing car.

Rafael tucked his head down and followed the press of dogs towards the starting line. Either his neon jacket did its job, or the big dogs of Alaska were used to watching for smaller puppies in the press, because no one even came close to stepping on him. But the cabbie had been right about the crowds. Rafael couldn't see anything but furry legs and tails wagging in his face.

"Excuse me, excuse me!" Rafael yelled, trying to get the attention of any of the bigger dogs around him with no avail.

Finally the tide of the crowd spit him out by a long table with a banner across it that read 'Racer Check in.' Arrayed behind it were three big dogs, all northern breeds, like the racers. The area to the left of the table was separated from the crowd by plastic barrier tape.

"Can I help you?" A dark gray malamute glanced at him as Rafael waved a paw about above the tabletop.

Rafael pulled out a glossy photo of a golden furred chow dog and stood on his tiptoes to put it on the table while holding up his Phoenix Police Department badge. "I'm looking for Wang Wei Snelling. He's a racer. It's vitally important I talk to him before he leaves."

"I recognize him. Don't have many chows signed up to race." The malamute handed him the photo back and checked a list in front of her. "The race starts soon, so you have about fifteen minutes to find him. The runners all wait over there. I'll let you through." She then pointed to her left.

"Thanks, ma'am." Rafael wagged his curled tail, already half frozen, and ducked under the tape.

Hundreds of dogs milled about on the other side although his job was made easier by the fact that most of them had white or gray fur. However, his own small size was still a problem. He couldn't see more than a couple of feet through the press. Even worse, loads of backpacks and supplies were piled seemingly at random in the snow blocking his way.

"Excuse me, have you seen this dog?" Rafael held up his photo of Wang Wei and plowed forward into the press, yelling to be heard over the din.

"What the hell are you supposed to be?" said the first dog who noticed him, a towering brown and white Saint Bernard.

"I'm a Chihuahua," Rafael answered him evenly although his hackles rose. "And it's vitally important that I find this dog. His name is Wang Wei and—"

The Bernard cut him off with a loud woof. "Haven't seen him. Now go away, I'm busy."

Rafael shrugged and sidled around the dog and his bags. The next dog, a white Eskimo dog with triangular ears, was a little more polite but knew no more than the first dog. Rafael continued to make his way through the crowd, climbing over luggage and questioning the other racers. Noon was fast approaching and Rafael hadn't gotten any closer to finding Wang Wei.

"Please, sir, have you seen this dog?" The words had long since lost their meaning, but Rafael held up the picture and asked the question.

"Him? Yeah, I have," said a big dog. Rafael wasn't sure but thought he might be some kind of husky.

"Thanks anyway," Rafael said and started to turn away before what the dog had said sunk in. He jerked and spun back. "Wonderful! Can you point me in his direction?" Rafael tucked the photo back into his coat, shivering as he zipped it back up. Even with the coat and hat he was freezing.

"Even better, little guy. I can take you right to him!" The husky mix wagged his tail and gestured.

Rafael fell in beside him, pumping his legs furiously to keep up as the dog took off at a brisk pace through the crowd.

"Thank you so much. You have no idea how important it is that I speak with him." Rafael panted and glanced at his watch. 11:55. He only had a few more minutes before Wang Wei's group was off and running, and then it would be too late.

The husky led him into a ring of three other big dogs. He turned to face Rafael and raised his paws to his sides. "Here we are."

Rafael stopped and blinked in surprise. He glanced around, but didn't see any other sign of Wang Wei. "What?" Before Rafael could get out anything else, something heavy hit him in the back of the head. He was out before he impacted the snow.

***

The back of his head pounded, but it was the jouncing that woke Rafael. He felt suspended in a soft cloud, smelling of jerky and fabric softener. Soft light diffused his bed, coming from somewhere above him. A steady thump, thump, thump sound that matched each bump could barely be heard over the howl of the wind. Rafael was warm in his pink coat, but his hat was missing and a cold breeze bit into his exposed ears.

Rafael fought free of the constricting fabric and clawed his way up, towards the light. A hole became visible above him, covered by a flap of fabric. Rafael poked his muzzle through, all that would fit through the small opening. Outside of the protection of what he now recognized as a large dog's backpack, the icy wind stung his nose.

"Help! Help!" Rafael barked and clawed at the cinched hole, which remained stubbornly closed. "Let me out."

The bouncing stopped. "What? Who said that?" a female voice said.

"I'm in your backpack," Rafael yelled as loud as he could.

The backpack swayed and bobbed, and Rafael felt it settle down to the ground. The light dimmed as a shadow fell over the bag, there was a click and then the flap covering the hole flipped open. Rafael stared up into the eyes of a large female husky.

Her muzzle gaped open in surprise, one ear flicking back. She closed her mouth with an audible click and a huff. "You've got to be kidding me. I wondered why my bag felt heavier, but the race was starting and…" She huffed and shook her head. "Now puppy, why are in you my backpack?"

Rafael growled and scratched again at the cinched hole until the husky reached over and opened it. Rafael poked his head out of the bag, but immediately regretted it as the wind whistled through his upturned ears. He pulled his ears flat back against his head, wondering where his hat had gone.

"I'm not a puppy, and I have no idea how I ended up here." Rafael felt around inside his pink coat until he located his wallet. He pulled it out and flipped it open, lifting it out to show the husky his badge. "I'm Detective Rafael Ferreira with the Phoenix Police Department. Hey!"

He yelped as the husky girl reached into the bag with a paw and picked him up by the back of his coat. She lifted him out and then set him gently down on the snow. The sudden movement made Rafael's head swim with a pounding vertigo that sent him reeling. He collapsed face first into the soft powder.

Now that he was outside the backpack Rafael was already starting to shiver. He sat up and looked around himself. He was sitting in a snowbank, surrounded by dark pine trees. Snow was still falling, but the light had waned. He'd been out for hours at least.

The husky held up a paw, hissing in sympathy as she touched the back of his head. Even her feather-light touch made him yelp and jump.

Rafael reached up and probed at the bump on the back of his head. He growled. "Oh, those stupid huskies!"

The husky girl scowled and stood back up to loom over him, crossing her arms across her chest.

"Oh, not you." Rafael could see the hurt in her eyes. He didn't want to piss her off. He had no idea where he was and he couldn't see any other dogs around. "I was talking to three huskies. They hit me in the head…and I guess stuffed me in your pack afterwards."

The husky girl huffed and crossed her arms across her chest. "Three huskies? Leader mostly white with light tan markings?"

Rafael nodded. He was shivering violently now. He didn't dare perk his ears back up for fear of them freezing solid.

The husky girl swore, ears going back flat on her head and baring her teeth. After a few more minutes of swearing she calmed down. She looked around them at the swirling snow and the trees, then pulled a folded map out of the pocket of her coat and began to study it.

Rafael hugged himself, tempted to climb back into the girl's pack. The wind was cutting right through his thin khaki pants. Perfect for a warm Arizona winter and totally inadequate in these subzero temperatures. "What's your name?"

She glanced up at him and grimaced. "Mae, and I'm sorry but it's not been a pleasure to meet you. Now quiet, I've got to figure out how to get you back to civilization. I think it's closer to go back to the checkpoint at Yentna Station," she stabbed a point on her map and traced with a finger. "Rather than continue on to Skwentna. It will put me behind schedule, but there's no helping it."

"No, you can't take me back!" Rafael protested, jumping up and down in the snow in front of her. "I need to go with you."

"What? Not happening. You're already getting hypothermia." Mae folded back up her map. "Now, get in the bag."

"No." Rafael could tell she wasn't in the mood to talk, but his mission was too important. "Did you see a large golden chow chow with the runners?"

"Yeah, I did. Hard to miss an Asian dog among all the American northern breeds. Why?" Mae crouched down next to him, positioning her bulk between him and the worst of the wind.

"He's one of my confidential informants, here from Arizona for the race." Rafael inched closer to her, grateful for that and the warmth that radiated off her.

"So?"

Rafael almost growled in frustration at the delay this was causing. He'd already lost his chance to catch Wang Wei before the race started, and now he was losing daylight to this cruel prank. "There's a hit out on him. I have to warn him."

Mae snorted. "You're a detective and this Wang Wei is just some criminal that helps you out, right? So why do you care?"

"Wang Wei's information saved the life of me and my partner last month. He warned us of an ambush." Rafael looked away as he was wracked by a particularly violent shiver. "I owe him this much."

"What about the Alaskan authorities, surely they—"

"No!" Rafael growled and met Mae's eyes. "The ambush Wang Wei saved me from… It was other policemen." He gulped. "I don't know who I can trust. I need to warn Wang Wei in person. What little I was able to find out about the assassination is that it's going to happen during the race."

Mae stared at him, her muzzle gaping open for a moment. "That doesn't narrow it down much. The route is over nine hundred miles long!"

"I know. I tried to call him before he left, but he was already on a plane, his phone turned off. I followed him here, hoping to warn him before he left, but there were so many dogs! And then that, that *cabron* hit me, and well, you know the rest."

Mae growled and narrowed her eyes at him, then sighed heavily. "That *cabron* is the winner of last year's race, Ingram Yap. Ingram's been trying to bully and intimidate me ever since I came in ahead of him in the qualifiers last month. He probably was trying to slow me down."

She gave a big sigh and held up a paw as Rafael started to speak. "It benefits us both to continue on, so don't worry. I'll take you as far as Skwentna. It's a checkpoint, so all the dogs racing have to check in with the volunteers there."

Rafael brightened and nodded happily. "Thank you!"

He let Mae lift him up and stow him back in the bag. While he bounced along on her back, he dug around in her clothing until he found his hat, which must have fallen off while he was being jostled around. With that back on his head and bundled in her blankets, Rafael almost became warm enough to stop his shivering.

The gentle swaying of the backpack lulling him to sleep competed with the pounding in his head. Eventually the warmth and the rhythmic motion overcame the nausea and pain and he drifted off to sleep.

***

A sharp jostle woke Rafael up. Mae barked, the sound muffled by the backpack. The bouncing of the pack increased in pace, slamming him repeatedly into Mae's back. The muted noise made it hard to tell, but the crunching footsteps sounded like they came from more than one pair of feet as the cadence didn't match the frequency of his crashes into Mae.

Rafael burrowed up. The light had faded, and he had to feel around above him for the cinched hole. The cold breeze coming from it guided him and a moment later his gloved paw was free and grasping around blindly, looking for the cinch. Now that he'd seen the outside of the pack he knew how to open it, but the shaking and bumping meant he had to fumble around for several moments before he found it.

The instant he pulled the clasp free and opened the hole, polar air whipped in, instantly freezing his nose and nipping at his eyeballs. Rafael narrowed his eyes and popped his head out. His head pressed against the cloth flap that covered the hole, blocking his view of the sky. The ground rushed by underneath him; the snow swirling in the air glowed with ghostly reflections of Mae's headlamp. Beyond the glare of Mae's LED headlamp the night swallowed the landscape, making it feel like Rafael bounced along in a snow-covered void.

Now that his ears were out of the thick canvas, he could hear two sets of puffing breath and distinguish the thudding of six different feet. A lolling bay sounded out from the night.

"Mae! Mae!" Rafael howled as loud as he could.

"Stay down!" Mae huffed, clearly short of breath. "Moose. Dangerous."

Even from right behind her Rafael could barely make out her words over the howling of the wind. "Moose?" he repeated softly to himself. He'd seen pictures of them, even seen them in person at the zoo in their fenced enclosure. They were massive, sure, and had big horns, but he'd never thought of them as dangerous.

"Raf!" Mae barked. "Flare gun. Bag. Help!"

Rafael dug back into Mae's pack with frantic urgency. He'd remembered feeling a hard plastic edge digging into his side as he'd pulled himself out. He ripped off his gloves and cast about where he thought it had been. His paw brushed something hard, and he grabbed it, pulling it closer. The familiar grip of a pistol was comforting in his grip, despite the strange feeling of the plastic rather than cool iron. Gun in paw, Rafael popped his head back out the hole and pushed aside the top flap.

The bobbing light from Mae's lantern revealed a gigantic moose which towered over Mae and him. The beast's breath huffed out in a plume of steam that froze instantly. Ice crystals hung from the beast's shaggy fur and dripped from its heaving nostrils. The moose lowered its head, centering its wide, flat antlers so that the tips pointed right at Rafael. Each pounding of the giant's hooves sent up clouds of snow and brought the moose closer to Mae.

Rafael looked at the orange, plastic pistol then at the moose's three tons of charging fury. The gun was sized for a bigger dog; Rafael could barely get a finger around the trigger, but compared to the bulk of the moose it looked like a toy.

"Hur...ry!" Mae huffed. It was obvious she couldn't keep this pace up much longer.

Rafael shivered, blinking away the ice crystals that were forming on his eyelashes and lifted the gun, wrapping both paws around it in an effort to keep it steady.

The moose whuffed and sped up, or maybe Mae slowed down, but Rafael knew he had only moments to act. The moose lowered its head still further, but it was so much bigger than them, it put its chin in line with Mae's head. The flap of skin hanging from its neck streamed in the wind.

Rafael had never been so terrified. His heart hammered in his chest. He was shaking and not from the cold.

Rafael took a deep breath, sighted down the barrel directly at the white of the moose's eye. The whipping wind and snow obscured his vision, and the backpack was bouncing up and down wildly. Rafael did his best to compensate for the movement, thankful for hours of practice on the range. He willed his shaking paws to still and pulled the trigger.

The flare exploded from the gun with a flash and a pop, streaming towards its target like a comet. The light was so bright in the dark of the night that it burned a red line across his vision.

The light smashed into the moose's nose and burst with a hiss. The moose barked in surprise and slowed down, shaking its head from side to side in an effort to dislodge the burning projectile. Mae continued running, and the beast disappeared into the night behind them.

"I got it, Mae!" Rafael yipped in excitement. "You can stop now."

Mae continued running although she slowed her pace. The bouncing slowed down to a manageable jostle. Perhaps she hadn't heard him.

"The moose stopped chasing us," Rafael cried louder.

"Heard you," Mae huffed. "Not out." She took a deep breath. "Of danger yet."

Now that the adrenaline from the danger with the moose was fading, Rafael was starting to feel cold. As he stared at the darkness and falling snow, he realized what Mae was doing. His flare had done nothing but startle the moose. It might continue to chase them once it recovered. Or there might be more of them.

Rafael wiggled back down into the backpack and felt around until he found the gun's little zipper pouch of ammo. After a lot of fumbling around in the dark, he managed to reload it, just in case.

Mae ran for another few minutes after he finished loading the flare gun, and when she did stop, she first ducked behind a tree. Rafael felt the backpack jostle and a moment later Mae peered down in at him, blinding him with the light of her head lantern.

"Ouch, bright!" Rafael dropped the gun and covered his face with his paws. The LEDs still burned his eyes around his fingers. He blinked tears from his eyes and burrowed his muzzle into the crook of his arm.

"Oops, sorry," Mae said.

Rafael heard a button click, and the light dimmed.

"That better?" Mae asked.

Before Rafael could respond, Mae scooped him out of the bag and squeezed him to her chest in a massive bear hug. Her arms totally engulfed his little body. She was wonderfully warm and soft and Rafael relaxed into her grip, doing his best to hug her back while trapped. He wagged his tail, whipping her arm.

"You did great with that moose. If you hadn't been here, I might have been done for."

"It was nothing," Rafael lied. His heart was still pounding. He'd faced down his share of criminals on the mean streets of downtown Phoenix, but he'd never felt anything near the terror he'd experienced upon seeing that wall of muscled moose barreling down on them.

Mae loosened her grip and lifted him. "You're shivering!"

"Just cold," Rafael said. He wasn't lying, not exactly. The air was so frigid each breath was like a knife to his chest. Where the tip of his muzzle wasn't pressed against Mae, he could feel the cold air almost seeming to go right through him. But being with Mae was like lying down with a furnace.

"Here." She set him carefully back down into the backpack and then fiddled with an outside pocket before passing him a large square plastic gel pack.

"What is it?" Rafael stared at it with fascination. The clear pack was labeled 'Paw warmer' and it was almost as long as his arm.

"It's a chemical gel warmer. Take off the packaging and it will heat up and keep you nice and warm until we get to Skwentna."

Rafael ripped off the printed plastic coating and kneaded the bag inside with his paws. Almost immediately it began to heat up. "Amazing! Heat in a bag."

"Careful not to puncture it with your claws," Mae cautioned him. "Also, it works best if it's close to your fur. Unzip your coat and put it inside." Mae began closing back up the backpack. "Oh and keep that flare gun handy."

"What?" Rafael squeaked.

"Yeah, this area is known as Moose Alley. The forest is dense so the moose like to use the trails. A couple of dogs get chased each year. Guess I'm one of the lucky ones." Mae blew out a breath and gave him a wide mouth smile. "Good thing I had along a stalwart guardian."

Despite himself Rafael felt himself returning Mae's grin. He was still mad at Ingram for pulling this prank and possibly dooming Wang Wei. But it had put him in the right place, at the right time, to protect an innocent dog from harm. Lately so much of his job had become paperwork done behind a desk, and he realized he couldn't remember the last time he'd felt so connected with his job and life. It made him remember why he'd become a cop in the first place.

***

Despite the cold, Rafael kept his head free of the bag, ready and waiting in case another moose tried to give them a hard time. Ice crystals formed on his whiskers from each breath. He constantly was having to duck his head back into the bag and press his face against the blissfully warm gel-pack, but he persevered.

Other than the crunching of snow under Mae's paws and the shushing of the surrounding pine trees in the wind, the night was silent. He'd grown up in the big city, and night to him meant the pounding thunder of a gunning motorcycle, the conversing of passing dogs, and the rumbling base leaking from a passing car.

Even the sky was unfamiliar. When Rafael craned his head back, he could see hundreds of stars twinkling brightly overhead. The sight awed and humbled him. When he was a puppy, his father had taken him up to the mountains to star gaze, but even there the lights of the city had hidden all but the brightest stars. He began to pick out constellations he'd learned about in grade school. There was Orion, the Hunter. Usually depicted in mythological art as an English Setter. Mae turned a corner and his view shifted, revealing Leo, the roaring lion. Rafael bared his teeth menacingly at the sky.

Rafael ducked back into the bag to warm his ears and nose, and wipe ice crystals from his lashes. When he emerged again, the trees had fallen away. Mae now ran through a wide open field. The light of the stars reflected on the glittering snow, green and purple dancing and flashing like they were running through a gaudy neon nightclub. Rafael's muzzle dropped open. Stars didn't do that. He craned his head around until he looked out over Mae's fluffy ears.

Shimmering hues swung their way through the heavens above them, frolicking and bobbing through the air like a symphony of colors. "Wow…" Rafael chuffed quietly.

Mae chuckled, her ears flickering and Rafael lowered his head. He hadn't realized he'd spoken aloud.

"Quite the sight, eh? I never get tired of it," Mae said over her shoulder. All Rafael could see of her was the back of her head and the tips of her ears, but he could feel her smile.

Rafael looked back up at nature's light show and admitted that he didn't think he ever could either. He opened his muzzle to say as much to Mae, but then shut it again. He didn't want to sound like an uncultured yokel. He stared at the dancing sky without answering for a long minute. "Yeah, it's alright, I guess."

Mae growled. Her ears went back flat against her head and she picked up speed, jostling him around so much he had to grab on lest he bounce right out of the bag. "I know. Alaska's a boring backwater full of hicks, and you can't wait to get back to your big city and palm trees. Yada, yada."

"What? That's not what I meant," Rafael barked out between bounces. But it was too late, the mood had been ruined.

"We're out of Moose Alley and it's still another few hours before we get to the checkpoint, so why don't you get some sleep?" Mae said.

Rafael wanted to apologize to Mae and beg her forgiveness, but he sighed and stayed silent. He'd give her an apology at Skwentna, once she'd had a chance to cool down and when he could do it face to face.

***

Rafael was woken by another dog barking a greeting to Mae. He uncurled from his ball and popped his nose out of the backpack. The cold crisp air burned his lungs. The air smelled of wet dogs, wood smoke, and dawn. He shivered and pulled his head back in.

He unzipped his coat and pressed the gel pack to his muzzle until he was warmed up, then tucked the pack back against his chest.

"Where am I in the standings?" He overheard Mae say.

"Not too bad," an unfamiliar dog replied. "You're the eighth dog to check in from your time group. Won't know your overall standing until I radio in your time."

"You going to press on?" the other dog asked Mae.

"Not yet. I need a few hours of sleep before I continue," Mae said and began taking off the backpack. Rafael ducked back out of sight, suddenly conscious of being seen. He didn't want his presence here to get Mae in trouble, or to be forcibly sent back to Anchorage before he could save Wang Wei.

The backpack hit the ground with a thump and then he heard Mae fumbling with the opening. She reached in a paw and grabbed him by the back of his pink coat, pulling him out. Rafael struggled against her grip as the cold air hit him.

"Don't worry, no one's watching," Mae whispered to him as she sat him down.

Rafael shook himself and then straightened his hat and coat. His boots crunched on the snow as he spun about. They were in an open field covered in an icy layer of snow. The sun was barely peeking over the horizon in the distance, the light glittering and bright on the almost untouched expanse of snow. A trail snaked away into the distance, disappearing into the trees near the horizon.

Two snowmobiles were lined up next to the poles of a suspended banner. It read *Welcome* in big red letters. Underneath in smaller black print was *Skwentna Checkpoint*. A few dogs congregated next to the far pole holding up the banner. A large fluffy Saint Bernard dog wore a red jacket with a white cross on the back, first aid for the runners. The rest of the crowd were huskies and malamutes. A few wore backpacks and Rafael judged them to be other runners taking a break at the checkpoint.

A white, curly-tailed American Eskimo holding a clipboard was walking away from him and Mae, headed towards the knot of dogs. The back of her jacket read *volunteer* in big yellow letters.

"I'd talk to Kiska about your Chow," Mae said, bobbing her head towards the retreating American Eskimo. "She's one of the race coordinators. If Wang Wei has come through here already, she'll know."

"And if he hasn't?" Rafael shivered and tucked his tail between his legs. He'd only been out of Mae's backpack for a few minutes and he was already getting cold.

"Then it means we beat him here." Mae held out a paw. "And then all you'll have to do is hang out here until he comes through, tell him your piece, and then hitch a ride back with Kiska."

"Oh." Rafael dug the toe of his boot into the snow and ducked his head. "I'm sorry about last night. I…" Rafael took a deep breath. He had begun to like Mae and the fact that she was mad at him had left a hard knot of dread in his stomach. "I wanted to sound more traveled than I am, in order to impress you. To tell the truth, I've live in Phoenix my entire life. This is the first time I've ever left Arizona. I'm terrified, and cold, but it didn't excuse what I said last night. I'm sorry."

Without warning Mae dropped down next to him. Her muzzle gaped open and her tail wagged furiously. "I accept your apology." She pressed her nose up against his for a moment then stood back up, brushing snow off her pants. "You look cold. Hurry and go talk to Kiska and by the time you get back I should have my tent set up."

"Thanks," Rafael said, then took off after the white dog.

Her long strides meant that she'd reached the gathering of dogs by the time he was able to catch up to her. She was already in conversation with them when Rafael came up behind her.

"Excuse me, Kiska?" he barked politely to get her attention.

Every dog in the huddle turned to stare down at him, and as one their muzzles dropped open in surprise and one ear each cocked back. One of the huskies burst into riotous laughter and Rafael belatedly recognized him as the dog that had tricked him back at the starting line. Ingram. Rafael pointedly ignored him and addressed Kiska.

"I'm looking for this dog. His name is Wang Wei. He's a golden Chow." Rafael fumbled with the zipper on his pocket for a moment, the unfamiliar gloves and cold making his normally dexterous paws clumsy. Finally he prevailed and held up Wang Wei's photo, doing his best to straighten it out. His trip in Mae's backpack had left it rumpled and creased.

Kiska gaped at him, barely glancing at the picture. "What kind of dog are you? Are you a dog? And how did you get all the way out here?"

"Hitched a ride," Rafael responded. "And I'm a Chihuahua." When everyone stared at him blankly he continued. "From Arizona."

"Oh, my. You're a long way from home." Kiska tutted.

"Yes, and the faster I find this dog, the sooner I can get back to my nice, warm home." Rafael raised the picture higher, holding it in front of his face.

Around them the group of dogs broke apart, the huskies and malamutes gathered up their backpacks. The medical Saint Bernard wandered off to greet two new dogs arriving at the checkpoint.

"You just missed him. He got here about an hour ago. Just before the sun came up. Stuck around long enough to check in, then took off again," Kiska said.

Rafael cursed and stuffed Wang Wei's photo back into his pocket. "Thanks." He turned to go.

"Popular guy, that Chow," Kiska mused.

"What do you mean?" Rafael said, his hackles stiffening. He'd known assassins were after Wang Wei, but his whole plan hinged on beating them to their target and warning him of the danger.

"You're the second dog this morning to ask after him." Kiska shrugged. "Anyway, if you came by air you're out of luck. No airstrip at the Finger Lake checkpoint."

"I didn't. Um, can I ask who else asked you about him?" Rafael shivered violently. His gel pack was failing, turning to a cooling lump in his coat and the cold began to creep down through his hat and gloves.

"It was," Kiska turned and pointed to a group of distant figures jogging along the trail. Even as they watched, they disappeared into the trees beyond the meadow. "Oh, they left without saying goodbye. Anyway, one of that group."

Rafael growled and stomped his feet in an attempt to warm up. "Which one, specifically?"

"They all arrived in a clump, and it was a bit of chaos, let me tell you." Kiska cocked her head, her ears flicking as she thought. "One of the huskies, I'm sure of it. Was it Bernie? No. Oh, yes, it was Ingram! Such a nice dog. He wanted to check on Wang Wei because it is his first race. Ingram and his pack are seasoned runners, you see. They told me they like to check up on first timers."

"Oh, that's nice of them," Rafael said, but inside he was tensing up. Nothing that Mae had said about Ingram pointed towards him being a good dog.

"Yes, it is." Kiska leaned down and cocked her head. "I need to go check in these runners, but you should go see the medic and make sure you don't have frost-bite. You're not dressed properly for this weather."

Rafael shivered harder and nodded.

Kiska bobbed her head in satisfaction and bounded off to greet the new dogs, who were now engaged in animated conversation with the medic. Rafael turned and shuffled back to where he'd left Mae. As promised, a colorful one-dog tent was set up and Mae's curly tail was just disappearing through the zippered opening. Rafael followed her inside.

Already inside the tent was significantly warmer than outside. Rafael hadn't realized just how much the slight breeze had been chilling him until he was out of it. His shivering subsided some. The tent was small, and Mae's fluffy husky body took up most of the space. If Rafael had been any bigger, he wouldn't have fit. Being this close to Mae he could feel the heat radiating from her, and the scent of her made his tail wag involuntarily.

"Good news?" Mae asked him as she shook out a body-bag style sleeping bag that had been tied to the bottom of her pack.

Rafael shook his head. "No, bad news and worse. Wang Wei has come and gone already."

Mae unzipped the side of her bag in one smooth motion. "So, I suppose next you're going to ask me to take you with me to the next checkpoint."

Rafael shook his head. "No. Kiska and the medic both have snowmobiles. I'm sure if I explain to them the need they'll give me a lift. I just came back to say goodbye and to ask you a question."

"Oh." Mae blinked at him and he would have sworn she looked almost disappointed, but no, he had to be wrong.

"So what's your question?" Mae said, wriggling out of her coat. The fur underneath was snow white and looked pleasantly soft. Rafael caught himself wondering what it'd be like to cuddle up to that fur. He cut that thought off and pushed it away.

"If I told you that Ingram was checking up on a first time runner, to give advice to a less experienced dog, what would you say?"

"I'd say you must have hit your head on something." Mae flashed him a grin. "Ingram is ruthlessly competitive. He'd never willingly do anything to help a new racer. Why?"

"That's what I was afraid of." Rafael grimaced and relayed what had happened. "I'm afraid Ingram and his buddies might be the assassins after Wang Wei."

Mae opened her muzzle to argue with him, then shut it again. Her face and ears flickered through a variety of emotions, obviously thinking through Rafael's accusation. Finally she shook herself as if shaking off water.

"No, I don't think so. I think he was probably just upset that a first-time racer, and a foreign breed dog at that, beat him to the checkpoint." Mae sighed and plopped down on her sleeping bag, looking longingly at her pillow for a long moment before turning her attention back to Rafael. "However, I wouldn't put it past him. Give me a few minutes to pack back up and we'll head out."

"Mae, I appreciate the help you've given me so far, but get some sleep. The snowmobiles—"

"Aren't allowed on the trail the runners use. They have to stay on the roads," Mae said, cutting him off. "You wouldn't be able to meet up with Wang Wei until the Finger Lake Checkpoint, at the soonest, and Ingram could catch him long before then."

"How, if Wang Wei's the faster runner?"

"Fast isn't everything in the Iditarod," Mae said. "It's about endurance."

While Mae packed back up her tent, Rafael went back to talk to Kiska. By the time he was done explaining to her what he needed, Mae had finished packing her bag. She jogged over to them, her pack slung over one shoulder.

"I'm ready to go," Rafael told her, while marveling at how fast she'd packed her backpack and how small of a bundle her tent was once she'd taken it down and rolled it up.

Mae put the bag on the ground and Rafael crawled inside.

As they left Rafael heard Kiska call out to them, "Mae, good luck!"

"What was that about?" Mae huffed out as she jogged away.

"I took some of your advice," Rafael said, snuggling down into her spare clothes. He stayed there until he was warm again, then as much as he could he kept his head outside the bag to watch the scenery go by.

He'd never thought of snow as beautiful before. Pictures he'd seen of snowy landscapes had seemed to him bleak and almost monochromatic. However, as he gazed about it was the first word that popped into his mind.

Snow draped the trees in coats of white. Flashes of blue and green pine-tree needles poked from beneath the snow. In the distance snow-capped mountains dominated the distant horizon. A rabbit startled by Mae's steps on the snow broke out of the bushes and hopped along in front of them for several moments before veering off back into the underbrush. The sun never rose much above the horizon, which gave the sky a perpetual pink blush of dawn. The sun glittered on the undisturbed snow and lit the surrounding trail in an ever changing patchwork.

"This is part of the Northern Lights trail," Mae said to him during one of her running breaks. "It's one of my favorites."

"I can see why," Rafael replied with a genuine smile.

After several hours Rafael twisted around in the pack so he could talk to Mae easier as well as to help watch the trail ahead of them. They had a pleasant conversation, and Mae told him all about growing up in the backwoods of Alaska and the fight she'd had when she'd announced her desire to be a runner like her father.

"What was the big deal?" Rafael asked.

"It wasn't—" she huffed, and sped up. "—feminine. They lamented that I'd never find a mate and get puppies of my own, since I spent all my spare time running."

Rafael grimaced. "I'm sorry," he said, and meant it. "I understand how hard it can be when it feels like everyone is arranged against you."

"Because of your size?"

"There are other Chihuahuas on the force." Rafael sighed. "But yes, we have to do more to prove ourselves than the bigger dogs. When I was promoted to detective over a lot of larger dogs that had been there longer, a few of my co-workers, well, I think I already said enough about that." Rafael fell silent.

The only sounds were Mae's harsh breathing and the crunch of her boots on the snow. Somewhere in the distance a hawk cried.

"I feel like, if I can save my informant, and get this big bust, I'll prove them wrong," Rafael said finally.

One of Mae's paws reached back over her shoulder. Rafael grasped it, sharing a moment of solidarity. Rafael leaned forward, over Mae's shoulder, and licked Mae's cheek. He knew hs blushing would have been visible through his short fur and was glad Mae couldn't see him.

"Mae, I—" Rafael began as he slid back into place, but Mae cut him off.

"There, up ahead!" Her paw pulled away, leaving him off balance. "That's Ingram, I'm sure of it."

Rafael leaned to the side to see around the back of Mae's head. Far in the distance stood a group of dogs. They were off the main trail, almost at the tree line. Rafael could just make out the marks they'd made where they'd cut off the trail. Three white and gray furred figures were chasing, herding really, a fourth gold furred dog into the woods.

"His coat," Mae said in response to his unasked question. "Ingram has been doing the race for years and has corporate sponsors. I recognize the placement and colors of the patches."

Mae sped up, her lope turning into a jog, and then a sprint. Rafael thought Mae had been pushing the pace before, and now he found out how wrong he'd been. Snow flew from her boots. Rafael jounced around so much he had to throw his arms around Mae's neck or risk flying from the pack.

As they reached the point where the dog's tracks left the path, Mae slowed down. The other dogs had forded a path through the snow, and Mae took advantage of the work they'd done by placing her feet in their paw-prints.

One thing that struck Rafael in Alaska was how still and silent it was. Because of that, when there was a sound it seemed louder than it should have been and it carried. Between the crunches of Mae's boots on the snow came a dull thwack. It took Rafael a moment to register the sounds as fists connecting with flesh.

Rafael drew in a hissing breath. "Hurry," he whispered as they neared the trees.

Mae ducked under a low-hanging branch sending a small flurry of snow spraying down on Rafael's head. He brushed it off while Mae stopped and knelt down to pull off her backpack. The area underneath the trees was relatively clear of snow and Rafael emerged from the pack onto a soft bed of fallen pine needles. He was carrying Mae's flare gun gripped in both paws.

Mae left her pack and jogged off into the trees. Rafael did his best to keep up with his short legs. He didn't dare lose Mae in this forest. The way sound echoed was eerie, and he wasn't sure he'd be able to find Mae if he lost her, even if she was calling to him.

Despite the fact that she was at least three times larger than him, Mae passed with barely a sound, like a ghost. Rafael felt like an elephant blundering along behind her. He must have stepped on every twig, branch, pine-cone, and crunchy leaf between him and their goal.

Thankfully it seemed Ingram and his pack were too involved in what they were doing to Wang Wei to notice. Mae stopped, held up a paw and pointed. Rafael stepped up next to her and peered through the underbrush. Ingram and his pack had Wang Wei surrounded and were pounding on him. Wang Wei had curled into a ball, his front paws over his face. Blood streaked Wang Wei's golden coat, and he whimpered in pain as the other dogs hit. As they watched Ingram picked up a tire iron which Rafael hadn't noticed previously lying by his feet. Ingram lifted it above his head, ready to strike.

Rafael took a big breath, lifted the flare gun, and then stepped forward shouting, "Stop, police!"

Ingram's head snapped up and everyone stopped moving. In the sudden silence, the pop and hiss of the flare-gun going off was deafeningly loud. The flare shot up from Rafael's outstretched paws to burst above the trees in a flash of red.

Ingram whirled to face Rafael, snarling, the tire iron still held above his head. Before Rafael could react Ingram charged towards him. His two pack buddies turned to face him, leaving off their attack on Wang Wei, but otherwise made no move to help.

"I said stop!" Rafael dropped the now empty gun and scrambled back.

Ingram swung at him. Rafael darted to the side and dropped to all fours. The tire iron whistled overhead, missing Rafael's head by mere inches. He felt it brush the tip of his pointy ears and realized that at some point he must have lost his hat. Again.

Mae snarled and jumped over Rafael's head. She wrapped a paw around Ingram's arm, and with her other one began trying to wrestle the tire iron out of his grip.

"Mae, what're you doing?" Ingram growled at her.

"Stopping you from making a big mistake, Ingram," Mae growled back.

Rafael was trapped underneath, darting this way and that between the bigger dogs while trying to avoid being stepped on.

From his left came a yelp of pain and a deep growl. Rafael took a chance and glanced that direction to see that Wang Wei had risen and taking advantage of his tormentors' distraction, pounced on them from behind. Despite the fact that he was injured and outnumbered, it looked like Wang Wei had Ingram's pack mates taken care of.

He was so engrossed in watching Wang Wei thrash the two huskies that he lost track of feet. A boot stomped down and caught the tip of his tail. Rafael yelped and reacted on instinct, twisting around and sinking his teeth into the owner's leg. Only after did he think to check who he'd bitten. He tried to glance up, but all he could see were parkas and pants. Instead he inhaled deeply. The scent was similar to Mae's, but not her. He ground his mouth down harder, biting deeply into Ingram's leg. He tasted blood.

Ingram lifted his leg, prepared to stomp. The move jerked Rafael's head and pulled him up. He clawed at Ingram's boot with his front paws, trying to pull his lower body up. Ingram stomped into the snow.

The boot came down hard on Rafael's left leg and tail, and he had to grit his teeth to keep from crying out and releasing Ingram. His leg throbbed; he couldn't tell if it was broken or not, but the pain was incredible. His vision wavered as Ingram lifted his foot. Rafael's flailing front paws connected with Ingram's leg.

He dug in his claws, clinging tight, opened his jaw, and pulled himself up Ingram's calf. He waited until Ingram stomped down again, catching nothing but snow and pine needles, then bit down as hard as he could right at the back bend of Ingram's knee.

The big dog howled and Rafael's worldview turned into a falling jumble of fur, snow, and leaf litter. Next thing he knew he was buried under a pile of fur and suffocating under Ingram's bulk. By the time he crawled free Mae had Ingram on his stomach, her knee in his back and one arm around his neck. Wang Wei had Ingram's two pals, one massive paw holding each of them face-first against the ground.

Mae yipped with excitement when she saw him. "Are you alright?"

Rafael rolled over and gently prodded his leg. He winced in pain. Almost certainly broken. "I'm alive," he said, flopping over to his back and panting. "We saved Wang Wei, that's what counts."

"Detective Ferreira!" Wang Wei barked. Only Rafael's long acquaintance with the big dog allowed him to hear the relief and thanks in Wang Wei's voice. "To say I'm shocked to see you would be an understatement."

Rafael turned his head and gave Wang Wei a tired smile. "Hah. By the way, your life is in danger."

In response Wang Wei let out a rumbling basso laugh that shook snow from the trees above them.

Mae frowned at Wang Wei then turned her gaze back to Rafael. "Raffie, I thought you were a better shot with a gun than that. What happened back there?"

Rafael wrinkled his nose. He hated being called by a nickname, but then again he owed Mae a huge debt of gratitude. So instead he just replied. "I didn't miss."

She shook her head and turned her attention back to Ingram lying prone under her. "And you, Ingram! What were you thinking?"

"I was thinking I was broke and needed the money," Ingram growled back as he struggled against her.

The roar of snowmobiles drowned out the rest of Ingram's reply. Probably for the best.

Rafael smiled widely and shouted, "Cavalry is here."

After what felt like hours to Rafael and his throbbing leg, but was probably more like fifteen minutes, Kiska, riding double with the medical Saint Bernard from Skwentna station, roared up along with a string of local police dogs.

It took Rafael quite a while to explain what had happened and why he was here. But eventually, after repeatedly showing them his badge and they'd made a call in to his supervisor in Arizona—that made Rafael wince but there was no help for it—the local police agreed to arrest Ingram and his pack members on charges of attempted murder.

Rafael's story was confirmed again when they searched the dogs and found an unregistered .22 in Ingram's pocket along with Wang Wei's picture, on the back of which was written *Introduce him to the man in black* in big, block letters.

The medic splinted Rafael's leg and loaded him onto a stretcher attached to the back of one of the snowmobiles, layering him in blankets.

Mae came up as they were strapping him down. She leaned over him and gave him a long hug, then pulled away and planted a kiss on him, muzzle to muzzle. It was hard to wag his tail, buried as it was, but Rafael tried. Mae was brave, determined, and beautiful. This morning he'd have said he'd never have a shot at a girl like her, yet here she was.

Rafael returned the kiss with gusto. Mae was a fantastic kisser, sensuous, slow, and teasing. When she pulled away she did so slowly, giving the tip of his nose a lick as she did. She stood and stepped away as the snowmobile roared to life. Rafael twisted to watch her face as they pulled away.

"Mae!" he yelled over the rumble of the engine.

She waved and blew him a kiss.

***

Rafael was kept in the hospital overnight for observation. They said along with his broken leg he was suffering from mild hypothermia and dehydration.

His broken leg laid on the bed entombed in a thick cast. They'd wrapped him in warm blankets and made him drink what felt like gallons of hot tea.

Over the nurses protestations that he needed sleep, Rafael made them turn on the television to show news of the race. A lot of the coverage was about the surprise arrest of race darling Ingram Yap, charged with the attempted murder of another racer. They praised the quick thinking of an out-of-town detective with saving the victim's life, but gave no mention of Mae's assistance. Rafael flipped the television off in irritation.

Early the next morning the call he'd been expecting came. Rafael gulped, steeled himself, and took the portable hand-set from the nurse.

"Good morning, Captain," Rafael said with false cheer. He was helped along by the drugs for the pain, which buoyed him in a cloud of hazy euphoria.

"Lieutenant Ferreira, good work up there," the Captain replied.

Rafael pulled the phone away from his ear and stared at it for a moment before putting it back. "Excuse me?" He'd been sure he'd lost his job. After all, he'd gone haring off to Alaska, out of his jurisdiction without permission or backup, and he'd dragged civilians into the mess to boot.

"Captain, I'm just a detective, not a—"

The Captain cut him off with a woof. "As of now you are. You just made Lieutenant and earned yourself a nice bonus to go with it. Thanks to you, Wang Wei has agreed to turn state's witness. Last night we arrested dogs we've been after for years, but never been able to get charges to stick. Well, they won't be able to weasel out of this one."

"Wang Wei, is he alright? I lost track of him when the medics took me away."

"He's fine. A little bruised up, but fine. He's in protective custody now. Guarded round the clock by a team of our finest."

"Thank the lord." Rafael blew out a breath in relief.

"Indeed." There was a muffled sound; then the Captain returned to the line. "They tell me you'll be out of the hospital by this afternoon. I'll arrange your return flights and have someone pick you up at the airport in Phoenix."

Rafael licked his chops. Last night he'd been making plans for what to do when he was fired. Now he was looking at a promotion and a raise, along with a big bonus and status as hero of the department. He thought of Mae and their journey of the last two days.

"Sir, that's not necessary." He took a deep breath, realizing his paws were shaking. He tightened his grip on the phone. "I quit."

Dead silence came through the other end of the line.

"I quit," Rafael repeated with finality. A weight lifted from his shoulders, a burden he hadn't realized he'd been carrying until it was gone. "I'm staying in Alaska." He hung up the phone before his boss could say anything else.

Rafael spent the rest of the morning on the phone ordering plane tickets, hotel rooms, and finally calling movers to pack up his apartment in Phoenix. When the doctors gave him the all clear that afternoon he hopped in a cab to his first destination, awkwardly navigating the snow with his crutches.

By the end of the week he was getting around on the crutches like a pro and easily descended the stairs off the plane in Nome with little problem.

Despite the snow and blowing wind he was pleasantly warm in his new weather-appropriate outdoor gear.

He'd spent the week eagerly following the runner's progress in the news, easy to do as he'd discovered that the race seemed to be playing on every television in the state of Alaska. He wasn't sure exactly when Mae was set to finish, but the predictions had her coming in later that day.

Rafael hobbled over to join the crowd around the Burled Arch, a great wooden thing that marked the official end of the race. The snow around the wooden arch was packed down from so many boots on it. The winner along with five others had come in yesterday, and from what he'd seen on the news, hundreds of dogs had come out to cheer.

The crowd today was much smaller, about two dozen dogs all told, bundled up against the cold. Some held banners for various racers. Rafael left his rolled up in his backpack for now. Once he got it out, he'd be unable to use his crutches.

A cry went up from those closer to the arch. Rafael leaned forward and squinted. A figure appeared in the distance, a speck against the snow. Rafael would recognize that form anywhere. He planted his crutches and pulled his banner out of the side pocket of his bag.

It seemed to take ages. The running dot grew steadily larger, eventually resolving into Mae's lithe form. Her tongue hung out as she panted, her breath steaming in the cold air. She looked thinner than she had when last Rafael saw her, her eyes sunken in fatigue, but a large grin split her muzzle and her eyes sparkled with joy.

Rafael unfurled the vinyl banner. He lifted it by the sticks at either end and spread it out high above his head. Of course, high above Rafael's head meant chest height to the rest of the crowd, but he was confident Mae would see it. *Mae the Champion* was printed on it in bright red text.

Mae sprinted the last hundred yards to the arch, and the crowd roared as she passed underneath. Rafael barked Mae's name along with them, so excited he wanted to jump up and down. Instead he settled for waving the banner about above his head and wagging his tail at supersonic speed.

"Rafael!" Mae whooped. She ran right past the race officials who had come up to greet her and scooped Rafael up into a tight hug. Rafael's crutches and his banner went clattering down onto the snow, but he didn't care. He hugged Mae back fiercely. The crowd tittered. Rafael ignored them.

After a moment Mae set him down. Rafael balanced precariously on one leg, doing his best not to put weight on his cast while Mae retrieved his crutches with a sheepish open-mouthed grin. Once he was steady again he slung off his backpack and rooted around inside until he found the gift he'd gotten for her.

Mae crouched down next to him, her head tilted curiously.

"For you." He pulled out the statue and presented it with a little flourish.

Mae laughed and covered her muzzle with her paws, eyes shining with mirth as she looked down at the little ceramic cactus decorated with sparkly snow. She plucked it from him and pecked him on the cheek. "It's perfect."

"Congratulations on the big finish. Seventh place!" Rafael grinned and tried to hide his blush, but he knew his ears betrayed him.

"Thank you. I'm surprised to see you here. I thought you'd rush back to warm Arizona as soon as you got the chance." Mae's tail wagged.

Her scent filled his nose, she smelled of ice, pine trees, and dirt. He'd never smelled anything more delightful. Snow swirled around them, the chill breeze ruffling Rafael's ears. His breath came out in little puffs and he blinked icicles from his lashes.

Rafael reached over and placed a paw in hers, next to the cactus statue. "Why would I want to leave paradise?"

When you're from the Paradise Archipelago, leaving home at all is a fall from paradise.

Flying Back to Paradise

Jelliqal Belle

"Cuter than a button! Stronger than a limp noodle! Able to eat a large emu egg in a single bite! It's a koala. It's a badger…" She remembered her practice. *Suck in your tummy, strike a pose, and smile.* *GLEAM* "No, it's WONDER WOMBAT!"

The mob of people of New York City stopped for a moment to stare at the short, chubby talking animal. The funny looking animal wore a scarlet curvaceous bodice and blue culottes with stars. When she just stood there on her back two feet and no show started, they shrugged and continued on their way.

"I'M WONDER WOMBAT!" she called again, louder, and pointed her shiny golden boot. She flipped her mousy hair over her shoulder heroically as her short cape flapped in the wind. She waited for applause or photos or cheers. The people talked on their phones and went about their day, ignoring the funny looking guinea pig.

"Wonder Wombat, Princess of Paradise Archipelago. Hello? Oy, you're supposed to applaud or something," she whimpered in her Australian accent. She sniffled, dejected and rejected. "There are supposed to be flashes from the press taking my picture or something."

A pair of young men stopped for a moment while waiting for the light to change. "Cute costume. Are you part of a show?"

"Um, no mate." She batted her eyelashes and struck a comic pose. Her fake eyelashes were huge in comparison to her beady black eyes. "I am Wonder Wombat. I have come from Paradise Archipelago to help keep you safe."

The chubby guy coughed to hide his snicker. She was so cute trying to be tough. He remembered being innocent like that once.

His friend wearing a toque took out his phone and took a picture. She happily posed for him.

"Well, Comic Con was last week. You have your dates wrong. Sorry, see you there next year," volunteered the chubby young geek.

"So are you animatronic or a midget in a suit? And that better not be real fur cause it's not cool to kill animals just for our selfish needs."

"Dude, not cool to break the magic," said his friend trying to pull him away before his buddy got on a roll.

"Of course, it's real fur. It's my fur. I'm a wombat."

The geek cringed as he knew what would happen next.

Toque guy knelt down and snapped another picture of her right in front of her nose. "You are so going down. I'm going to post you on Twitter and tell everyone you are a terrible human being for wearing real fur," he snarled.

Her lower lip quivered. "What am I supposed to do? Go naked? It's my fur."

"Better naked than wearing dead animal corpses. There it is posted on social media. I bet it will go viral." He tapped his screen a few times, then pocketed his phone triumphantly.

"Come on, let's get out of here before she starts crying. Leave her alone. Probably just a kid in a costume." The nice chubby guy pulled his ranting friend away by the arm. He looked at the costumed kid apologetically, feeling sorry for her.

"Your reputation is ruined. I'll see to that," the activist called out before he went into the subway tunnel. "Animals are people too!"

"I know. I am one." She sniffed and wiped her black button nose with the back of her paw. "But it's my fur."

"Don't you mind him. Some people feel they have to make themselves important," said a man's gravelly voice.

The wombat looked up and tried to see who spoke. Staring at the throng of people from knee height while dodging being hit in the face by totes or briefcases was not easy.

"I'm over here, Sweetheart. Against the building, if you want to talk."

Wonder Wombat strutted over in her hundred millimeter stiletto heel golden boots. She dodged and weaved her way through the mob of humanity. Her heels kept getting caught in the drainage grates and cracks in the sidewalk. She succeeded in not tripping and falling on her face. About fifteen minutes later she made it. She felt accomplished. She looked around.

"Nice getup, look like a real hero."

The princess walked to the other side of the staircase. Sitting on the ground with a guitar in his lap and an open guitar case beside him with a few dollars in it, a leather faced black man sat and took in the passing of the world.

"Oy, were you talking to me?"

He indicated a crate. "You are welcome to sit and talk if you like." He had seen too much to stare at the odd youngling.

"Thanks, mate. This is not going how I expected it would." The wombat climbed up on a milk crate to perch.

He nodded sagely as his guitar gently sang. "Seldom does. May I ask what did you expect?"

"Heroes and fighting and aliens crashing and the need for heroes to do feats of skill and wonder heroically. I saw it all on the news. Read about it in the illustrated histories, too."

"Those things are pretend. Drawn from people's imagination."

"Oh, so you don't need heroes?" She slumped on her perch.

"Honey, always going to be a need for heroes. Bad things happen to good people and heroes are the ones who step up and do something about it."

"Exactly," she said bouncing in excitement. "So where can I find Wolverine? He is dreamy."

"He's not real, Hon. A person in a costume. Hugh Jackman, the actor, is an Aussie, like you."

"I'm not an Aussie, I am from Paradise," she said a little frustrated. "How bout Black Panther?"

"Nope. Just characters in stories and movies meant to inspire."

"Catwoman?"

"She's not a hero," he protested.

"Sometimes she helps Batman."

"Well, Batman, Robin, and Catwoman are not real either."

As she called out names from her comics, her so called illustrated histories, he shook his head no to each one. "Killer Croc? Vixen? Birdman? Viper? Doc Oc? Grod? Teenage Mutant Ninja Turtles?"

She sighed. "Not even the Badger, defeater of litterbugs and jaywalkers?" she asked in desperation.

"I don't even know who that is, so probably no."

They sat in silence a moment.

"Oh, but there was Jake the Snake," he added scratching his head.

"Really?" She perked up.

"Yeah, but he was a human wrestler and lives in Nevada, I think I heard."

"Oh, that's okay. I don't like snakes anyway."

"Nuh uh, me neither."

"Not even Spiderman?"

"Sometimes I wish there was a nice guy like him around, but no. Sorry, kid."

The princess sat for a while and stared at the sidewalk, kicking her feet. The man realized she needed some time, so he started playing some smooth jazz on his well loved guitar.

"I ran away from home for nothing then." She struggled to get her fashionable and thus extremely uncomfortable boots off.

"You had a great adventure. Want help with those?"

"Yeah, thanks. But I didn't do anything heroic. Aren't there at least aliens?"

The grandfatherly man shook his head no as he helped her out of her boots to reveal pudgy but strong legs. "Only aliens here are people like you visiting from another country. Welcome to the Big Apple. Why did you come here and leave Paradise?" The grey headed guitarist adjusted his sun bleached hat.

The dejected wombat looked down at the sidewalk as she wiggled her stubby toes in relief. "Cause I never get to do the adult stuff. Everyone is always protecting me cause I am a princess. I wanted to prove I could do something that matters. I saw all that stuff on TV so I hopped on my eagle and flew here. I wanted to help and to show I could do it too."

"You must have been pretty brave to fly half way across the world riding an eagle."

"Burmurr is tame. I am not worried about her trying to eat me." She dismissed her accomplishment like it was an everyday event. "So there are no heroes?" She sighed, crestfallen.

"Oh, I wouldn't say that. You saw the make believe superheroes. Police, firefighters, and even teachers, doctors and nurses are all heroes in my book. Heroes come in all shapes and sizes and ages. Anyone who takes the time to go above what is asked, to put themselves out there to help another. They are heroes in my book."

CRASH

"Wait! Stop! Please Stop!"

A commotion at the traffic intersection to the right caught their attention. A bike fell and a man cried out in heavily accented English, "Help! Help! I am robbed."

With a huge grin, Wonder Wombat took off in a flash. Racing between, under, and around the pedestrians, she dashed to the victim of the heinous crime. A dark skinned man with small round glasses crawled out from under a bicycle and a mountain of packages. A woman and her daughter helped him up.

"I'm ok. Did someone see where the thief went? He has my bag, my important bag." He looked around with scared teary large brown eyes.

Without hesitation, she scurried up the traffic light pole and scouted the area. The chaos the man had left as he pushed people away while running showed his route. She gave a trill whistle and held her arm high.

From up in the clouds, down swooped a mighty red eagle the size of a subcompact. Now the crowds of New York were watching. Some school children stopped and pointed. Old men paused from drinking their cappuccinos to look up and watch. The eagle snatched the bracers on the Princess' arm in her talons. Wonder Wombat's short cape snapped in the wind. She whistled directions and they chased after the villain.

The man dodged in and out, weaving through the evening commute traffic.

The Princess realized he was headed for the tunnels and gave another command. The eagle raced ahead and dropped her five meters down into the tunnel. She landed in a tumbling roll. She uncurled and dodged the commuters to get up to the top of the stairs and await her prey.

The thief clutched the bag to his chest, its torn strap flapped uselessly. He kept looking back over his shoulder to be sure no one was chasing after him. He started to slow down, confident that he was in the clear.

Wonder Wombat tracked the movement of the crowd. She did not want anyone else to get hurt. When it was clear the next person to come into the underground would be the culprit, she knelt down on all fours and used her mighty Iron Butte technique at the top of the stairs. She grabbed hard with all four feet, gripping to lock her stance so hard that she clawed gouges into the concrete stairs.

The man ran right into her. *BLAM!* He crashed into the immovable object. He shouted profanity. He fell sprawling down the stairs. The messenger bag flew out from his hands as he tumbled. He stumbled back onto his feet. He turned and saw a pissed three foot tall giant guinea pig thing dressed as a comic book character charging at him. Her beady eyes focused on him, promising retribution. He scrambled away and dashed into the nearest subway car. He didn't care where it was going as long as it was going away.

She stood there fuming with her fur bristling, furious he got away. A Hispanic boy walked over to her. "Senora, I think this is yours?" he said as he handed her the fallen bag.

"No, it belongs to a man who got robbed. Thank you." She pushed her mousy brown locks out of her face and behind her rounded ear.

"You stopped a robber. Cool! You are a real hero! Can I have a picture with you?"

She blushed under her fur. "Sure glad to, then I need to hurry to return this."

"Gracias, Gracias. Say Si," he said as he stood next to her, almost even in height as his PaPa took the pictures. As she ran off, he called after her, "What do I call you?"

She paused at the top of the subway stairs; the light behind her made a halo and the wind blew her cape heroically. "I am Wonder Wombat," she said with quiet confidence, no longer needing others' approval. More pictures and a few people applauded as she whistled and held up her arm triumphantly.

Even these jaded New Yorkers were a little surprised when the huge eagle swooped down and soared into the air with her. In minutes the eagle dropped her back at the intersection, then returned to perch on the nearby bridge.

The man was talking rapidly to two police about what happened when he saw her. He nearly burst into tears. "Ayeee, my family! You saved my family." He ran over to her and gave her a hug.

The princess was a little confused, but shrugged it off and handed him his bag. "I'm sorry I didn't catch the thief. He went down the subway and got on a train. He went that way."

"That does not matter, this matters." He hugged his worn bag like it was the most precious thing in the world. Then he opened it and pulled out some pictures.

She looked at the bent and water stained photos. One showed a bearded man with round glasses next to his pretty wife holding a swaddled baby. The other showed a frail old man with a cane beside him, his elderly wife behind him. They were holding hands. She handed them back to him.

"I came to US to study. Then a war broke out in my country. My brother and his family, they did not make it to the refugee camp. My mother and father, they were too old and did not try to leave. This is all I have left of my family." He kissed the pictures and carefully put them away.

"I left my family so I could come here and help."

"That is good, but when they are gone, you know how important they are."

She scratched the back of her left ear as she thought about it. "Can I ask you a question? Are you an alien?" she asked.

He nodded yes. "I am here with student visa. I study in university."

The police looked up from their notes and saw her. One of them called it in and the other started to walk over.

She noticed the change in their stance and knew how this usually worked out for the heroes from her reading. "Looks like I need to go now. Welcome to the Big Apple." As she scurried up the light pole, Burmurr flew low so she could jump onto the eagle's back.

The people below watched in astonishment. "Thank you! You are my hero!" shouted the student.

They did a circle around the wide intersection as she waved goodbye and provided a photo op, then flew above the skyscrapers. She quick-changed into her mild mannered reporter costume, the mousy Dee Anna Prince. She even had glasses and fake whiskers. She thought the whiskers added a nice touch of realism.

The guitar music helped her find the kind old man. "Hi, I'm Dee Anna. Pleased to meet you." She leaned over conspiratorially and whispered. "I'm Wonder Wombat in disguise."

The old man nodded and winked. "I won't tell a soul." Then he added louder. "Nice to meet you Dee Anna. I'm Trevor. Would you like to sit a spell?"

"Yes, thank you."

"I was hoping you would come back. You ran off so fast you left your boots."

"Well, it is a good thing I took them off." She explained what had happened. "I became a hero to an alien." She beamed.

"So now whatcha gonna do?"

"This has been a grand adventure, but I think I need to go back to Paradise, to my colony. They need me."

"Anywhere can be paradise, you just have to have the right frame of mind. You are welcome to stay."

"Maybe, but I just got a reminder about how lucky I am to have a family. I need to get back to them. Before they worry too much and I get grounded again."

"Sounds like a good plan." Trevor grabbed onto the iron stair railing to help him stand. He cleared his throat and spoke officiously. "Wonder Wombat, thank you for being a hero to New York City. I was honored to meet you." He gave her a little bow.

Princess Dee Anna beamed. She stood on her tippy toes and gave him a peck on the cheek. "Now my to-do list is done. Be a hero, see an alien, and kiss a man. Now it is time to go home." With a grin on her face and a leap in her step, she scurried up to the top of the awning covering the stairs. This time she had her golden boots in hand. Burmurr flew low so she could hop on.

"Until next time, New York. Hi-yo, Burmurr! Away!"

Our history is scattered with moments of love and loss, star crossed lovers and friends crossing paths. Moments of paradise, lost in the flow of time, misremembered through scraps and tales.

PERSONAL HISTORY

Tim Susman

Boston, Massachusetts, 2012

The videographer, a red fox from M.I.T., had gone on a dozen of these mostly-fruitless artifact hunts, but his tail twitched back and forth, and his ears kept swiveling around as if scanning for threats in the very ordinary middle-class living room. His eyes remained fixed on the staircase, but he was looking beyond it: remembering, not seeing.

Scuffling noises from the staircase distracted him enough that he tilted his muzzle up. His companion, an early-thirties raccoon in a navy blue business blazer and skirt, watched the camera on his shoulder bobble.

"Are you all right?"

"It's just…" The noises from up the stairs continued. He lowered his voice. "These bleached-tail Jesus-freak types." He curled his own tail's naturally immaculate ivory-white tip upward, off the floor.

"He doesn't seem religious." She patted him on the shoulder and gestured around at the oak-paneled walls, shopping-mall paintings, furniture caught between 'recent' and 'antique,' and a distinct lack of holy icons of any persuasion.

The fox snorted. "Then he's doing it ironically. This guy in my Self Expression class said everyone ought to bleach their tail tips, to mess up the Church or some shit."

She lowered her voice. "Just go easy on him when I tell him what it's really worth, and we'll be back at the museum soon."

The creak of boards at the top of the stairs quieted them. A coyote not much older than the fox tottered down, his white-tipped tail swaying behind him as he balanced the weight of the broad, shallow wooden box in his paws. "Sorry. Had to dig it out from all my ma's shit," the coyote said in a broad New England brogue that pulled his o's and a's forward out of the words. He dropped it on the dining room table with a thud that made the raccoon's ears fold back and pulled a faded, yellowed note from an envelope atop the box. "Says here, 'this uniform is our most valuable possession.'"

The raccoon winced at the crackling of the yellowed paper on the brown, moldy envelope. She held out a paw. "May I?"

While she inspected the brittle paper, the coyote said, "That's 1850 at the top. So it's probably like a Civil War uniform, right? What's that worth?"

She didn't answer immediately, but held up the note to the camera when the fox lifted it to his shoulder. Eyes bright and wide, she tapped a finger next to the faded, ancient handwriting, but kept her voice steady as she said, "The paper looks, feels, and smells as one would expect if the date were authentic."

When the fox had captured the note, the raccoon set the paper aside. "Let's have a look, sir." She waited while the coyote lifted the lid from the box.

At the first sight of it, she held her breath, and then the camera's light came on and she blinked at the bright crimson fabric. "It looks real," she whispered, and then, louder, "It smells real." The fox brought the camera closer as the raccoon leaned in, twitching fingers held behind her back. "It appears to be a uniform from the Revolutionary War era, a British one, hardly faded at all."

"Probably hasn't been opened in like a hundred fifty years." The coyote rested the lower edge of the box lid on his thighs, leaving gritty tracks on his blue jeans and bringing the upper edge, thick with dust, to his nose. He made a face and blew across the lid to clean it off.

"Careful!" The raccoon pulled the box toward her, away from the cloud drifting down from the box lid. As soon as it was clear, she wiped her paws on her jeans and then clasped them behind her back again. Now she spoke to the microphone atop the camera. "The front looks pristine, except for a few stains."

She didn't notice the coyote looking down her shirt; the fox did, but kept the camera stable and gritted his teeth. When the coyote didn't respond right away, the raccoon started to turn toward him, and he flattened his ears back, gesturing at the jacket laid carefully out in the box. "You can get it cleaned, though, right?"

The raccoon didn't change her posture, absorbed in studying the jacket. "We wouldn't. The stains on a piece of vintage clothing like this can be very instructive as well. If it's authentic. Food, tobacco, ale…you can tell a lot about a soldier by his coat."

"It's authentic." The coyote's ears came back up, the cleavage forgotten. He jabbed a claw at the box. "My great-great-something grandfather wouldn't lie."

"Usually they fade. This one looks very new." The raccoon produced a small metal probe from her pocket and lifted one side of the jacket. "But the stains make me think it is authentic. There's a lot of blood. No tear in the jacket that I can see, though…he must have been killed at close quarters."

"One of my ancestors fought in the Revolutionary War," the coyote said. "Must've killed this guy and took his coat."

The raccoon let the jacket fall. A faint rustle, like the crackle of the old envelope, reached her ears, but she ignored it for the moment. "Do you know any more of the story? How the soldier was killed, which battle?"

"I didn't even know about the jacket until last week. Grandpa just used to say our family fought the British twice, the Rebs, and the Nazis. I thought this might be a Nazi uniform 'til I saw the date on the note."

"Mmm." The raccoon brushed a small, pale stain near the lower hem of the left side of the coat. "This stain might have been oatmeal. That would indicate that the soldier rushed into battle in the morning without time to prepare."

When the coyote didn't answer, the raccoon flicked her eyes up and this time caught him looking down her dress. "Would any of your relatives know more of the story?"

"No," he said sharply. "My cousins don't even know about it. Mom inherited it from Grandpa and left it to me. Anyway, I'm sure it's just a boring story. Guy was eating breakfast with his regiment, the Americans attacked, he was killed. What else is there?"

The hills outside Fort Stanwix, August 6, 1777

Sunlight dappled the red coat of John Martingale, the bright spots dancing like light on a crimson sea as the fox lifted his arms. The russet fur visible on his smiling muzzle, bare thighs, and bushy tail shone palely next to the bright scarlet. The dirty white tip of his long tail caught the sun with a flash of white and then flicked back into shadow.

Atop him, the spots of sunlight fell on browns and greens that might have been no more than the forest floor molded in the shape of a slender coyote. Bright amber eyes gleamed in his muzzle's dusty tan fur as Nathaniel Braxton relaxed atop John, his nose coming to touch the fox's.

John pulled Nathaniel down atop him. "Thank Providence for this meeting," he said. "I have missed you, dear." Their lips met, and John held the coyote's head down, making the kiss long and deep.

Hoofbeats echoed in the distance, and both their ears perked. Nathaniel raised his head and chest to peer deep into the shadows and trees. "You should hurry back."

John smiled lazily up. "I've ten minutes at least."

"And you still must put those breeches back on."

"I could walk into camp claiming a dashing Colonial rebel stole them from me."

"To take your dignity from you? I'd take your coat first."

"What, all stained and dirty?"

"Even so." The coyote grinned and pulled the fox up to kiss him on the nose. "Especially so."

"It would set off your eyes nicely."

Nathaniel reached down to tease the fox's naked midriff. "Bah! As though I would sully my fur with that fabric."

"You know you look good." John reached up to brush his fingers along the tan buckskin vest. "Even dressed so shabbily."

"My father's father killed this buck himself." Nathaniel rested his fingers on John's, and his tongue lolled. "At least we don't make targets of ourselves."

"No, you lose each other in the smoke and shoot your comrades." John looked along his muzzle at Nathaniel's black nosepad and gold-amber eyes. His ears flicked back to the approaching hoofbeats, and his smile weakened. His voice lowered, trading jocularity for urgency. "Come with me. We've Colonial Loyalists in camp, some coyotes even. You'd be welcomed."

"Come with me," Nathaniel riposted, clasping the fox's paw in his. "We could make our way back to Boston."

The fox's fingers tightened, returning the embrace. "And then what? Live in the shed behind your house, with Selah bringing me meals, with whatever time I can steal from you?"

"Selah likes you. She begrudged you not a whit of our time together." His ears perked. "Your life would be your own. Is that not what you fight for?"

John lowered his muzzle. "I fight for God and King and country. My life is in his service."

"Hang the King!" Nathaniel said.

In the ensuing silence, the hoofbeats marked time like the ticks of a pendulum clock. Finally, John sighed. "I know that our stationing put an unfair burden on you."

"On you, rather. Many of your fellow soldiers found wives, while you stood dignified and aloof. On the outside." The coyote pressed closer and smiled a long grin. "Only to me did you show your soft underbelly."

John accepted the embrace, pulled his lover closer still. "Only you deserved to see it. Well, why do you think I left England to begin with, in the company of other strapping young men?"

"And yet you sought out the company of one not even your own species."

"What matters species? We'll have no cubs, no matter how we try." The fox buried his fingers in the thick brown fur at the coyote's side.

"If we could have been married…would you have left the Army to take up a trade in Boston?"

They lay, noses a hair's breadth apart, breath warm on each other's whiskers. "What use debating that question?" John said finally.

"No," Nathaniel said. "You'd not leave the Empire."

"How can I throw away the history—?"

"History!" The coyote barked a laugh. He brought the fox's paw to his tail, where it curled around at his side. "We wear our history on our skins, John. This fur my father had, my cub has, and his cubs will have after him. History is not so easily discarded."

"And yet…" John's paw curled around the black tip of the tail, held it, felt its restless twitching. "Your grandfather's father did not live in a town. Nor was he a Christian."

"I promise you, whether my grandchildren live in towns or cities or in hide tents under the stars, whether they follow Christ or no, they will still be coyotes, children of First Coyote, ready to take whatever advantage they can from life." He grinned pointedly at the russet-and-white fur below him. "Just as your cubs will show the fire from which First Fox sprang."

John shifted, bracing himself on the damp, dirty ground with one elbow. "Christ's blood, you rascal. And Mary's touch—"

"Yes, Mary's cleansing touch. So are the true children of Christ marked for entry to Paradise, while the rest of us cluster at the gates outside."

John let the old, familiar teasing pass; it was comforting, in a way. "But this uniform is part of my life as well. And so are you."

Now the hoofbeats drummed as loudly as a summons to war. Nathaniel sighed, released John from his embrace, and stood.

The smell of pork grease filled the air. The coyote lifted his nose and grinned without humor. "At least the boys will think I've snuck off to raid the enemy's stores, not their soldiers."

"Come with me," John pleaded again as Nathaniel pulled his pants up. "As a defector you would be welcome. As a prisoner—you could be docked."

The coyote curled his tail around his leg. "I'll lose my life before my tail, thank you."

"Don't talk like that." John lowered his ears.

"It's not me you should be worried about," Nathaniel said. "I'll be safe behind our lines in the time it will take you to clean yourself off and find your breeches. Fort Stanwix shan't fall, whatever your generals may think by besieging it."

"Go, then," John said, reaching to one side where his dark blue breeches lay. "Godspeed."

"Don't fret," Nathaniel said. He leaned forward to kiss the fox on the nose. "We'll meet again in happier times."

John pulled the coyote's muzzle to his. Their tails and ears stilled, and the forest stilled around them. Even the urgent hoofbeats died away, leaving only birdsong and the soft whistle of breath through two long muzzles. When at last they broke apart, their eyes met again. "If Providence wills," the fox said. "Keep yourself safe."

"I will, whether Providence wills it or not." The flash of the coyote's grin sparkled in the sun, and then he was gone in the woods, barely a crackle marking his passing.

Scarcely had John wiped the pork grease from his fur and fastened his breeches when the cry went up from the nearby camp. "Rebel army to the south!" He hurried back through the low brush to the clearing, paw to his breeches as though he'd just been relieving himself, but the rest of the company was busy gathering arms and coming to attention, and nobody took the least notice of him. Fortunate, he thought, for the smell of pork grease still came stronger than the dry summer grass to his nose. He hadn't time to clean properly, but gunpowder and blood would overwhelm that scent soon enough.

As he slunk behind the tents, the savage bobcats who fought for the King streamed past him and disappeared silently into the forest. John shivered and stopped to watch them, and that was when his commander, facing the line, spotted him.

"Martingale!" he shouted. "Arm yourself! We are to engage with the rebels and hold them from reinforcing the Fort."

"Just back from relieving myself, sir," the fox said, hurrying to his tent. He strapped on his sword, picked up his bayonet, and took a moment to brush the dirt from his tail tip before joining the assembly.

Within their regiment, the dozen foxes banded together, and when John took his place between young brown-furred Edward and sunset-red Matthew, the other two foxes twitched their noses. "Relieved yourself indeed," Matthew said under his breath, but he did not frown or look puzzled, as he might if he caught the scent of a coyote.

"Even we soldiers have needs." It took most of John's willpower to keep from smiling at the lingering pleasure in his loins. Their commander, a polecat, spoke to the regiment, but John barely heard a word, barely saw the flourishes of his decorative sabre. *Please, Lord,* he said, *let Nathaniel be spared.*

It did not occur to him to pray for victory. He was a soldier of the British Empire. God was on his side.

***

Nathaniel, meanwhile, crept through the woods. He'd intended to rejoin his company and warn them of the British troops hours ago. When he'd heard that the 8th Regiment of Foot was part of the besieging force, he'd hoped to catch a glimpse of John, but he hadn't counted on the grip around his heart and loins that kept him crouched by the British encampment for two hours. Finally, John had ventured near the edge, and Nathaniel had placed himself upwind, and John—

The coyote smiled. John's reaction had been so like his own, the gaping muzzle, the wide eyes, and then, a moment later, the hasty adjustment of his breeches. And no more than fifteen minutes later, it had been like old times. They were practiced at shedding the identities of soldier and wheelwright—now, redcoat and rebel—and just being a fox and coyote who'd found comfort together.

More than comfort, if he was truthful with himself, but he'd had little time for truth the last few years, and his life with Selah was happy. John had no-one back in England, but then, he'd been fighting over here for the better part of a decade. Or, rather, fighting for the last two years, and engaged in more pleasurable combat for the previous six.

Nathaniel adjusted his breeches again and grinned. The meeting had lifted his spirits and almost obscured his military duty from his mind. He had to direct his company around the British troops, if there remained time and a path to do so. If not, he would just have to—

Musket shots rang out. Nathaniel stopped and bit his lip. He looked around the forest, hesitating behind an oak tree. Then he gripped his powder horn and hurried around the tree, toward the shots.

Smoke tickled his nose within a hundred feet, and soon after, the bluish haze became visible curling through the thick maze of trees. Shots rang out in bursts, followed by faint cries in the reprieve, and then another burst of gunfire. The closer he drew, the more his nose burned from the gunpowder, his ears rang from the shots, and the quicker his heart and feet raced.

Acrid haze shrouded the green meadow where only that morning several regiments of the New York militia had made camp. The redcoats had lined up as orderly as you please on the north side, while the Colonials had fled to the trees and bushes of the south side—those, at least, who did not still lie between the tents, crumpled shapes among the yellow dots of dandelion and buttercups. They now had the advantage of terrain, but Nathaniel saw at a glance that the British had the advantage of numbers.

He didn't have to join this fight, but guilt impelled him onward. If he hadn't dallied with John, if he hadn't wasted time as the British messenger drew closer, could he have saved some of his comrades?

A flurry of shots from the British riddled the trees a hundred feet in front of him, quickly followed by the crash of feet in his direction. Nathaniel held his ground, one paw on his knife.

"They got the Captain!"

"Sons of whores!"

He recognized those voices, even though the scents were lost in the haze of battle. "Ho, Samuel Cooper!" he called a moment before the raccoon and weasel burst into view.

The raccoon leveled his musket automatically, then lowered it. "Nathaniel Braxton," he said. "A shade late with your report of the British."

"Aye. I was searching for a passage—a path through to the fort."

"Well?"

The coyote shook his head. "They've surrounded her good and tight," he said. "I tried to push through several times, but always had to withdraw."

The raccoon eyed the British lines. "They caught us unawares. We won't make it through here," he said. "General Herkimer kept us together after the first assault, but the men are unprepared."

Nathaniel opened his mouth to respond, but before he could, his whiskers tingled. He ducked back just in time to avoid a large object slashing through the air. Beside him, the weasel clutched at his chest, from which a feathered tomahawk appeared to have blossomed. The soldier's eyes turned to Samuel, then Nathaniel, and then he gave a bloody cough and sank to his knees.

Coyote and raccoon turned in unison as the shadows of the wood came alive with three half-naked bobcats, muzzles painted with red stripes. They moved as savage forest spirits around and between the trees, silent eyes shining with bloodlust, knives and tomahawks raised, fangs bared. Though the sun shone through the trees, nary a spot of light touched their bare fur.

Nathaniel threw himself to the side as another tomahawk sailed just over his head, and Samuel raised his musket and fired. One of the bobcats dropped, but the other two were on them in a moment.

The nearer bobcat sprang, knocking Nathaniel backwards. Pain flared through his shoulder and claws raked his ear; the heathen was *biting* him. The foul stink of the bobcat's breath affronted his nose, but Nathaniel fought back panic. He pushed the savage away with one arm while his other paw, fingers slippery with grease, scrabbled to get a purchase on his knife. The bobcat sensed his purpose and gripped his arm, but Nathaniel, stronger, reached the hilt, drew his weapon, and stabbed up.

Warm blood made his paw slicker still as he twisted the blade, tearing through flesh and fur. It hit bone; he withdrew it, and thrust up again, under the ribcage. This time the blade drove deeply into the warm body and found purchase in something soft and firm.

The bobcat atop him let out a keening sound and clawed at the knife, but Nathaniel held fast. He rolled to pin the smaller person below him, using his weight to drive the knife in to its hilt. The yellow eyes burned hatred at him, then dimmed, and the bobcat's body stiffened.

It took the coyote a moment to pry the teeth from his shoulder and throw the corpse aside. When he struggled to his feet, he saw the third bobcat standing over a motionless Samuel, holding the raccoon's ringed tail with one paw while the other sawed at its base.

"Whoreson!" Nathaniel shouted, and leapt, but the tail separated at that moment, and the bobcat fled.

A glance showed him there was no help for Samuel. The raccoon lay as still as the weasel. Nathaniel sprang after the bobcat, muttering a prayer for his companions' souls as he did. "I'll be damned before I let you take his tail," he growled, plunging through the trees.

He was no expert woodsdog, but had the advantage, slight though it was, that he had only to follow, not to track. The ringed tail was his beacon and guide, Samuel Cooper helping his vengeance along, and when the bobcat had to slow in the midst of a tangled mess of raspberry bushes, Nathaniel leapt on him.

The bobcat half-turned, but Nathaniel's weight drove the bloody blade between the brown-spotted shoulders. As the bobcat fell, he twisted, but Nathaniel kept the knife in place, working it in farther and downward until the savage shuddered and lay still, thorny vines already embracing his fur.

The smell of blood mingled with crushed berries rose around the coyote as he stood. He wrested the ringed tail free of the dead paws, then stood, panting, and turned back the way he'd come. He picked his way carefully, three silent steps, four, and then a roar of musket fire froze him, flattening his ears. He was very close to the British line, and retreat was the wisest course. But through the trees and the blue haze of gunpowder smoke, the sun picked out the bright red of several motionless soldiers, and despite himself, he turned and squinted. Gunpowder stung his nose, blurred his eyes; he thought he glimpsed red fur between the trees. His heart turned to ice; despite the bright sunlight, he felt wrapped in the darkest clouds. None of those could be John, not his John, not his fox.

He dropped the tail he held and hurried forward. The need for stealth fought the urgency in his heart, the terror in his stomach. The red uniforms grew more distinct as the trees thinned. One of the red coats lay still above a bushy russet tail, whose white tip lay brown and stained with mud.

The word "No" died in his throat as it closed up tight. He ran to the edge of the woods and crouched there, heart pounding. There were a hundred foxes on the British side, after all. But the shade of the fur was close, through the smoke. If only he could see the fallen fox's face.

***

They had taken the Colonials by surprise, but even though John was sure Nathaniel could not yet be back at the camp, he'd fired above the heads of the scrambling militia as they ducked into the trees. Nathaniel might well be wounded, if Providence were not merciful, but it would not be from his gun.

The sooner this war ended, the sooner he could establish himself as an honest tradesperson of the Empire in Boston. And if Providence did not intend for him to finish his days in Boston, then why bring Nathaniel to his camp, why this chance meeting after so many years?

He stood shoulder to shoulder with Matthew and Edward until the Colonials had fled their camp, and then they held the middle while the Mohawks guarded the woods and made sure they could not be flanked. The Colonials, after the first panicked scramble into the woods, had dug in their claws and were attempting to make a stand from the trees.

Without these reinforcements, the rebels' Fort Stanwix might not last more than a week, and when it fell, a vital supply route to New York City would go with it. If the Empire could recapture New York, the war might end before the close of the year. John kept that in his mind as he aimed and fired, taking care to choose his targets. Raccoons, weasels, yes; regrettable casualties of war. Whenever his eye landed on a coyote, even though he were sure it was not Nathaniel, he held his fire.

He and the other foxes of the 8th advanced around a small rise, behind another detachment of soldiers, a bright phalanx of red over the blood-stained grass. They had only a split-second warning as the trees sprouted blossoms of blue smoke, immediately followed by the explosive chatter of muskets and the chaos as shot tore the air past their whiskers. In front of them, around them, soldiers broke rank, some running, some falling.

John, unhurt in the first salvo, looked for any wounded soldier still on his feet who might need help, but the Colonials shot well at that range; the soldiers on the ground lay silent and motionless, dead or soon to be so. Another explosion of smoke, an assault on his ears and whiskers as thunder and motion surrounded him, and he ran back to the rise with the other survivors.

When they regrouped, they counted five lost. Only then did a voice from beyond the rise groan in pain. Matthew's? He was not with the panting survivors. They held their breaths, listening and then the Colonial guns spoke their response. The voice was silenced.

"I'll kill them," young brown Edward snarled at John's side.

"Wait here," John said. "No sense in adding your body to the pile." Matthew had served as Edward's mentor. Unlike John and Matthew, the younger fox had not yet seen enough of his comrades die to be used to it.

"Fight on the field with honour!" Edward shouted to the trees.

John reflected that it was not quite sporting to be furious at the Colonials when their Mohawks were doing much the same thing; still, shooting muskets from cover was not the same as hunting with tomahawks through the woods. He allowed Edward to vent his rage, while he kept his eye on the trees to see whether the Colonials would show themselves.

They did, after a short time, but it was to join the orderly retreat their commander had ordered. Edward fired at the retreating shadows, and John let him; better to let the fury burn itself out than to worry about wasting a tuppence worth of gunpowder and shot. He did hold the younger fox back, when Edward would go to the bodies.

"They sometimes leave one behind, especially when they know their retreat has been seen. Wait one half-hour and then we may proceed."

"If the Mohawks came back, we would soon clear the wood on that side," Edward said with a scowl, but he waited, tail tip twitching.

John happened to be watching the opposite side of the rise when he heard Edward hiss to one of the other foxes. He turned in time to see a coyote sprint from the underbrush to Matthew's body and kneel there, over him.

A coyote. There were a hundred of them on the Colonial side. Of course it was just a soldier. But this coyote, this coyote was reaching out to touch the red shoulder of a fallen fox, to move him and look at his face, to lean close and catch his scent.

Ten feet in front of John, Edward raised his musket. John opened his mouth, but his dry tongue could not form the words he needed. Edward's musket settled on his shoulder.

The coyote hunched over the dead fox and then lifted his head. The smile on his muzzle shone bright as the sun. He began to get to his feet.

Stand down! Stand down! John lurched forward, arm outstretched. Edward's shoulder was close. "Stand—" he croaked.

The musket's report shattered John's ears.

Nathaniel was still smiling as his body jerked backwards and fell. For a moment, John told himself the coyote was only play-acting, that he had heard the shot and would fall down to avoid being shot again. But then spots of red, glistening in the sun, blossomed on his jerkin. And he kept falling, falling, backwards and down.

He's not dead. He's not... John forced his body forward, in jerky steps and then fluid strides, and then an all-out run. He sped past the surprised Edward, past the other foxes and redcoats calling, shouting angrily. He leapt over the bodies of his comrades and fell to his knees at the coyote's side.

Blood, sharp and coppery, filled his nose as he cradled the coyote to him. One of the brown-furred shoulders was torn and bleeding, his chest was soaked with his blood, but John held him close regardless. It was Nathaniel's scent, Nathaniel's blood, and then the light aroma of pork grease came to him through the horrible smell of death, and that made it all too real. John held the coyote's weight against him, trying to trap the warmth in him. "Don't die," he whispered. "You stubborn fool of a rebel, don't you dare die."

"John," Nathaniel whispered. "I'm so glad it wasn't you."

"I'll bring you back to our lines. We'll bandage..." His throat closed off the rest of the words. He struggled out of his coat, the only thing he could think to press to the terrible wound. Distantly, he heard voices that had once been familiar, calling out to him.

"Naught left to bandage. Look at me." The coyote's head was turned up, and John touched his nose to Nathaniel's. The large black nosepad was cool and damp still, but the smell of blood infused even his harsh breaths now. The amber-gold eyes still shone, but their light was fading. "I'll be waiting for you outside the gates. Don't you hurry to join me, but...can't get into Paradise without you."

The warmth, too, was fading. "You're not going," John said. He pulled Nathaniel closer and wrapped his coat around the coyote, pressing it to the ruined chest in an attempt to staunch the flow of blood.

Red shapes moved around the rise toward him, but John's ears stayed cupped forward, and he heard only the coyote's soft voice. "Don't put...this thing on me," Nathaniel murmured, but he did not fight.

John half-laughed, half-cried. "Colonial, Empire, what matters now?"

"John? One favor?" Nathaniel's voice had grown softer, hoarser.

"Anything."

"Tell Selah…yourself. Please."

"You'll tell her." John buried his muzzle between the coyote's ears and held him. "You'll tell her, Nathaniel, only stay, stay."

"Can't take orders." The coyote's voice dropped to a whisper now, but John's ears caught every word. "From a redcoat."

"I won't be a redcoat, then," John whispered to him. "I'll be John Martingale, and you'll be Nathaniel Braxton, and that is all we are."

Nathaniel smiled, and rested his head against John Martingale's breast. He made a sound that might have been "yes," or might have been "nice," with the last breath left to him.

Boston, Massachusetts, September 1777

Selah Braxton thought at first that her husband had returned. He stood in the doorway wearing a dirty white cotton shirt stained with a dark red smear, plain beige breeches, and what looked like permanent tear tracks creased into the fur below his eyes. His fur was brown and nondescript save for the black at the tips of his ears, but the tail dragging behind him next to his traveling bag was too long, and his muzzle was too thin, and then the scent hit her and it was wrong, all wrong. Then he said, "Selah," and she put a paw to her muzzle.

"John…" He nodded. "You ought not be here." She looked around the street, but none of the other Bostonians took any notice of the disheveled fox. "Come in, quickly."

He stepped inside, sloughing dust from his fur, and it struck her how he still walked with dignity, even as tired as he looked. When the door was closed, the coyote braced herself against the wall. "It's Nathaniel, isn't it?"

She knew before he nodded, from the way he stared at the floor and would not meet her eyes. A cry escaped her, and the fox turned his muzzle to the wood of the wall. "It was not my bullet, I swear it."

Nose buried in her paws, she shook her head. "I would never believe that of you."

"He asked…that I come here."

Now she lifted her eyes to his, and he could not look away. "You saw him die?"

Unwilling, he nodded once. "We met before the battle."

Claws clicked on the stairs at the back of the hall. A five-year-old coyote cub peered down at the two of them. "Mama?"

"Go upstairs, Jacob," she said, putting all the strength into her voice that she could manage. "Mama'll be up in a moment."

John stood awkwardly in front of her, his paws clasped together. He met the cub's eyes, and then the cub walked slowly back upstairs. When he'd gone, Selah asked, "Are you wounded?" When the fox shook his head, she inclined her head. "Did you desert?"

John glanced down to the bag at his side, and stretched out his dust-covered bare forearm. "I am no longer a soldier. I do not know quite what I am."

She looked at his shoulders hunched inward, the flat ears, the tight curl of his tail, and she reached her arms out and gathered him in.

He stiffened, and then spread his arms to hold her. He smelled a little like Nathaniel, and Selah wondered if John was thinking the same about her.

"Well," he said, and he was wiping as many tears from his eyes as she was from hers when they parted, "I have delivered my news. I promised I would see to his burial."

She stared. "You carried his body…"

"I couldn't allow him a soldier's death, an unmarked grave, unconsecrated ground. How would he get into…" He coughed and lowered his head. "He is with the horse. I am staying at the inn."

"You can stay here." She did not know why she said it, only that after two years alone, the prospect of loneliness stretching through the rest of her life filled her with terror and dread.

"I would not—" John began, and she interrupted.

"We have room. And I would like to hear about him. Or about the war, what his life must have been like. I—I can tell you about how we spent the years after you left." When he still hesitated, she turned her nose toward the stairs. "Jacob will want to hear, someday…"

"That isn't my—my story to tell."

"He has no father, now." Her voice sharpened. "You owe me at least that much, John Martingale. God brought you back here."

He raised his head, and the pain in his eyes frightened her. "I made my own way here. I rode at night, along back roads. I stole food…" His paw tightened around the bag he held at his side.

Selah touched his arm. "I am offering you a place to rest. Please, stay a while longer."

He closed his eyes and lifted his nose. She saw his nostrils flare, and inhaled herself, catching again the small traces of Nathaniel's scent that would never truly leave this house. Dust drifted from John's muzzle and ears to the floor. His eyes opened to hers again. "If you are sure…I would like that very much."

Boston, 2012

"So what are we talking here?" The coyote picked up the box lid, tail twitching.

The raccoon bit her lip. She wanted the uniform, badly, wanted to say, *Name your price*, but she wasn't authorized. "There are so few examples… the museum definitely has interest, but I will have to consult with the board to get a proper valuation."

"Oh." The box lid sagged in the coyote's arms. "Maybe I can just take it to auction, then. I saw this guy got half a million at an auction for an authentic something or other."

She smoothed out the uniform with her metal probe. The crackling of paper came to her again, and this time she traced it to one of the pockets. "Most private collectors don't have the means to properly care for a valuable artifact like this. And they don't make it available for researchers."

"Yeah, but they have more money, right?"

"Your ancestor kept this jacket and said it was valuable. Wouldn't you like to know why?" She exchanged glances with the fox, who rolled his eyes. "The museum could analyze some of these traces, the blood, maybe match it to other local families, trace the ancestor and the soldier it belonged to…"

The coyote just shrugged. "Grandpa's dead, and I barely know the story. It happened like three hundred years ago, right? I could use the money. My car's going to shit."

She hesitated, and then slid her probe into the pocket. "I think there's something in here. Do you mind if I take it out? I'd at least like to get a picture for the museum."

He frowned, ears going flat for a moment. "That won't make it less valuable at auction, will it?"

"I can't see that it would." She motioned the fox to move in closer with the camera as she slid the paper free of the pocket.

Bits of the edge crumbled away despite the raccoon's caution. The paper had been folded into fourths, but across the brown, aged surface, flowery script in faded ink formed the barely legible words "Discharge from," and "Royal 8th Regiment," and below that: "Martingale, red fox."

Silence, while they all three read the words. The camera hummed. Then the coyote made a choked noise and reached out, and the raccoon intercepted his paw with her probe. "Please. You could damage the paper."

He stared belligerently. "It's mine."

"Hey." The fox spoke, catching both of their attention. "She's an expert. If she says you could damage it, keep your paws off."

The coyote glared. "You got a problem with me?"

"No," the raccoon said quickly. "Please forgive him. He's just passionate about preserving history. If you want to risk damaging the paper, of course that's your right."

She and the fox watched him struggle. Finally, he turned his eyes up to her. "You say the museum could find out about the uniform? Like, whose... whose blood it is?"

Slowly, the raccoon nodded. The coyote gestured to the paper. "And you can read that whole thing?"

"Yes, sir."

He looked down at the uniform, at the paper, at the brown, cracked letters, and then his gaze dropped to where his bleached-white tail tip curled around his leg. "Let me think about it a minute."

They packed up while the coyote set the lid back on the box. When the video equipment was secured, the fox turned and stuck out a paw. "Sorry, sir," he said. "I was out of line."

"No sweat." The coyote shook. "Used to it from foxes—they see the tail tip and think I'm an asshole. I'm not makin' fun of your faith, I promise. It's just a family thing."

"It's okay. I'm not really religious." The fox tilted his head. "Family thing?"

"My mom, my aunts and uncles...my cousins and me figured great-something-grandpa was big into the Church. You know, one of those 'white your tail and get into Paradise' crowd. But that's dumb. Sorry!" He held out his paws to the fox.

"It's okay. I know what you mean. The white tip is a reminder that at one time someone made a sacrifice for us and so we're worthy of Paradise. It's not a free ticket in."

"Thought you weren't religious." The raccoon nudged him.

"Grandma is. When I stopped going to church she told me I should paint my tail tip black." The fox scowled. "Like it would make a difference."

"Yeah, so." The coyote reached down and ran his tail through his paws. "I was thinking I might let the color grow out now Mom's gone. Or maybe a nice purple or something, ya think?"

The raccoon favored him with a bright smile. "I think it looks good. You should keep it."

He smiled back, meeting her eyes, and his expression softened. "Ah, hell," he said. "I'll sell it to the museum. I guess Mom would've wanted to know. And I can squeeze another year out of my piece-of-shit Chevy."

"The museum can pay you something." The raccoon took out her business card and wrote the name and number of the senior acquisitions manager on the back. "Miss Everston will contact you to work out details within the week."

He held the card. "Thanks," he said. "For talking me into it."

The raccoon smiled. "You talked yourself into it. If you want to learn more about history, please come on down to the museum." She raised a paw. "Take care, and thanks so much for your time, Mister Martingale."

What happens when the king of the jungle is contained,
trapped inside a stifling metropolitan box?

THE LION SLEEPS

Frances Pauli

In the jungle, the concrete jungle…

Stanley flexed tawny knuckles and let the tips of his claws prick pinpoint holes in the leather-wrapped steering wheel. A horn blared somewhere inside the crowd of vehicles wedged together on the freeway. Smooth concrete retainers lifted at the edges of the lanes. Car after car squeezed in on either side.

He stuffed a furred finger into his shirt collar and tugged the fabric away from his throat. Freed from the constriction of his work shirt, a yawn worked its way into his jaw, stretched his mouth wide. Stanley's pink tongue curled around it. His eyelids drooped.

Up too late last night working on the Melbourne account. His mane still had mats in the back where he'd rushed to get ready this morning. Too much coffee and not enough sleep. Now, they rubbed the wrong way, made his fur twitch beneath the suit. The cuffs around his wrist became manacles, and the faces in the cars around him blurred.

A gnu in a Volvo eased up on his right and spawned more angry honking from the cheetah chick who'd been trying to merge into the gap that was too small for either car. Stanley tightened his grip on the wheel, stippled the leather and let his eyes close and open.

So much honking. He cracked his window, felt a cool rush and made the mistake of inhaling. A deep breath filled his lungs with exhaust fumes and pheromones. The presentation this morning would make or break his promotion, and he needed the raise. Car payments were killing him. Stanley brushed his paw guiltily over the holes he'd just put in the leather he didn't quite own yet.

They'd moved less than half a mile in the last twenty minutes. Stanley glared at his dashboard clock, checked its accuracy against his watch. What were the odds he'd make it on time?

His throat tightened again. Stanley tugged at his collar and closed his eyes. He'd snarled at Janine last night over dinner. Just so much pressure to get the presentation done, so little time to work at work. He'd skipped TV time with his cub, too, skipped curling up on the couch with little Stan and pretending to watch Power Pals. Junior's spots would fade soon. He wouldn't want to cuddle with his old man much longer.

Stanley yawned and imagined watching tonight. He'd bring something nice home for Janine. He'd make time…

Horns screaming. Stanley jumped up, but his shoulder belt pressed him back against the leather. Something knocked hard on his window. Tap, tap-tap-tap. He blinked and gaped at the empty space in the lane in front of his car.

TAP.

A tan fist thumped his driver side window. Another round of honking rattled Stanley's teeth. He lowered the window with one claw and tugged at his collar with the other paw.

"Are you in distress?" A sleek ferret face leaned into the square frame of his window. Cop's hat, blue shirt, condescending expression. "Sir?"

The horns howled now. Cars angled out behind him, eased past on the right while the cop's vehicle completely blocked the left hand lane.

"I'm… I was just." Too tired to be driving. Too sleep deprived and now definitely late for his presentation.

"You need to move this vehicle."

A wolf drove by on the right, flipped him a fuzzy grey middle finger, and showed off yellowed canines. Stanley's collar bit into his throat. His mane bunched and the stink of exhaust infiltrated his car.

"Sir. Sir!" The cop's paws draped over his driver's door. His weasel voice pitched into a range that made Stanley's rear teeth grind. "You need to…"

The roar pressed upward with enough force to snap off his top button. Stanley's jaw opened, stretched around his fury and let the sound free. His tongue curled. The windshield rattled, and the concrete jungle echoed with the full force of Stanley's frustration.

***

Near the skyscraper village…

He smelled the coffee before the elevator doors opened. The office day had already begun, and when the silver panels parted, Stanley faced a grid of empty cubicles. Meeting already underway. He was late again. No time to crab a coffee.

Stanley clutched the hard binder containing the Melbourne account under one stout arm and shuffled toward the meeting rooms at the opposite end of the office. The carpet hissed under his slick-soled shoes. The coffee aroma teased his nose, reminded him how many hours of sleep he'd missed. His tail drooped, brushed the ground.

"Stanley!" Gerald's voice stalled his progress, stopped him ten paces from the meeting room. The plump woodchuck popped up from a nearby cubicle and waved. "Wait up."

A growl lodged in Stanley's throat. He liked Gerald, and he'd be late either way. He waited, swished his tail, and clung to the report so tightly the edges of the binder bit into his armpit.

The meeting room door opened. A blast of laughter escaped and then cut off sharply as it shut again. Gerald waddled out of his cubicle carrying a steaming, Styrofoam cup. God, Stanley needed some coffee. The woodchuck's mouth was moving, and he hadn't heard a word. He blinked, dragged his gaze away from the coffee and smiled an apology.

"Rough morning?" Gerald's eyes dropped to Stanley's shirtfront, to the missing button and the gap that showed his golden pelt.

"Got a ticket on the way in." He stepped toward the meeting and willed Gerald to hurry up and join him. The stout legs gave his co-worker a slow, trundling gait.

"Speeding?"

"Fell asleep on the 401." Stanley reached the meeting doorway, held it open and let the conversation inside wash out like a tide while Gerald caught up. "Again."

"Damn gridlock." Gerald smiled and ambled past. His fuzzy shoulder bumped the Melbourne account, nearly knocking it free of Stanley's grip.

Coffee choking his nostrils. Chattering animals filling his ears. Stanley followed the woodchuck inside and sat in the last empty chair at the long table. His boss watched him from the far end, from beside the projection screen. Mr. Wattler's badger face pinched. His eyes turned beadier. His nose twitched only one direction, hanging there as if it had meant to swing back to the other side and forgot to at the sight of Stanley.

"There you are." At the badger's words, the conversation snuffed out. All their muzzles swung in Stanley's direction. "It's nine after."

No mention of Gerald's tardiness. No possibility of arguing his case either. Wattler's eyes glinted like polished horn.

"I've got the Melbourne acc—"

"We've pushed it back to Wednesday." Wattler brushed a paw through the fur on his chin. "Gonna listen to the Stedman deal today."

All night hunched over his keyboard working. The pinpoint desk lamp burning into his peripheral vision while the screen's glow drove him half blind. Janine's voice had sounded far away, drifting past on her way down the hall to their room. *Coming to bed?*

Stanley pried the Melbourne binder out from under his arm and laid it on the table in front of him. Had junior fallen asleep on the couch again? Did he watch too much TV? Twelve cups of coffee wafted the scent of morning in a haze around him, and Stanley tried to scratch at the memory of last night.

What time had he finally gone to bed?

"Lewis," Mr. Wattler called on a younger associate, a lynx with no family and a lot more to prove before Stanley would consider him a threat. Still, when the old badger gave the kid a tap on the arm, Stanley's teeth clicked together.

Lewis had a binder under one arm, a big grin that showed too much fang, and a steaming Styrofoam cup in his free paw. The Stedman deal didn't have a tight deadline. It was a no brainer account, wouldn't have driven the lynx into a nightmare of late hours and loss of sleep.

Stanley put his paws on his thighs. He used the tips of his claws against his suit pants to keep his eyes open while the kid spoke. The projection screen flickered. Someone shut off the lights to show the graphs better. Somewhere, somebody whispered his name.

"Stanley?"

Janine had been out like a light when he crawled into bed. She hadn't twitched when he nestled in beside her, and he'd been too tired to even reach for her. How long had it been since…

"Stanley!" Wattler's voice threw ice along his spine, brought his head up with a snap and a ripple of dense mane. "I think we need to talk."

The meeting room had emptied while he slept. Every chair had been tucked, neat and straight, back against the table. The coffee had left with his coworkers, but Stanley could still smell the traces of it, a whiff of hope that died in the tapping of an old badger's shoe against the worn carpet.

That sound scraped at Stanley's shoulders. The squinting of Wattler's eyes, the downward tilt of his striped nose. He sighed and his muzzle twitched sharply to one side only.

Stanley's chest rumbled. His claws snagged in his trouser legs, and his mouth stretched and stretched. He roared, setting the curtains across the room dancing, and lighting a chill flame in Mr. Wattler's beady black eyes.

***

Hush my darling, don't roar…

"You were fired?" Janine's eyes widened, flickered with fear before she could stifle it. "Oh Stanley. I'm sorry. It'll be fine. It will."

Stanley stood in the foyer and stared past her. The kitchen remodel had cost him a month's salary, but now their tiles gleamed without a single scratch to mar the surface. The appliances shone in stainless steel. Expensive. Everything in his home cost more than they could afford now.

"And I got another ticket." He hung his jacket on the peg beneath the entryway mirror and cringed at his own face. Mats in his mane. A missing button and eyes rimmed with purple.

From the living room, the tinny siren of little Stan's fire truck squealed off key. Batteries dying. More things for him to buy.

"Another ticket?" Janine wiped her paws on the apron tied over her designer skirt. Twin flour-white prints remained when she lifted them away. Her eyes flickered again. Anger. A lot more fear. She examined him from head to toe and her face darkened. "You're working too hard, Stanley."

"Well." His fangs clicked together. "Now I'm not working at all."

Janine's lips tightened. Her hands crossed over the front of the blouse he couldn't afford to replace if she got flour on it. She stared at him, tapped a foot once, twice on the parquet flooring. The toy siren wailed. Stanley's tail thumped against the walls.

"I'm going to finish dinner." Janine spun on her heel and marched across the kitchen tiles.

She *had* been asleep last night, hadn't she? What time had it been, when he dragged his sorry carcass into their bedroom?

Stanley shuffled down the hallway to change. He threw his dirty laundry into a hamper that he didn't remember buying. Janine shopped while he was out. Janine collected things that he was supposed to be able to pay for.

He growled and put on sweats and a t-shirt that tugged painfully at his mane. It smelled like roast in the hallway. Stanley's lip curled. They'd better get used to ground beef now. He kicked at the rubber ball junior had left outside his door, watched it bounce away, and cringed at each impact. Tap. tap-tap-tap.

Stanley followed it to the living room where the screeching of his son's plaything tickled a ridge of hair to attention along his spine. TV on in the background. The smell of meat and the dying squeal of a toy siren.

"Daddy!" His son leapt from the plush carpet, swinging the fire truck in one paw and bounding toward him.

Stanley braced himself. He took the weight of his son against his belly, and the hard knock of the plastic truck against his chin. He staggered back, stumbled onto the rubber ball and flailed for balance. His son dropped, landing on his rear paws and cringing backwards.

Stanley stepped on his own tail, pinching a nerve that went all the way up to his neck. The toy truck warbled, fading but continuing to sing on the way out. Junior sniffled, a juicy sound that he repeated three times in succession, each time louder than the last.

The roar built in his chest, rumbled into his throat. Stanley opened his jaws, stared down at the wide eyes of his son, and swallowed before the sound could escape. He squatted, rocked back onto his heels and tilted his head to one side.

"Son."

"Yes, dad?"

"Your spots are fading."

"Uh-huh." Little Stan nodded proudly and pointed a stout finger at his hip. "This one's almost all gone!"

Stanley blinked away a sudden pressure and nodded, rubbing his chin. "Your truck needs batteries, I'm afraid."

"It's okay, dad. It sounds better like this." The cub swung the truck in an arc and howled in a fair mimicry of a siren's wail.

This time, Stanley ducked in time. This time, Janine appeared in the doorway, smiling again. "Go wash for dinner, little one."

Their cub scampered away, knocking his father on the knee as he passed and pushing between his mother's legs to get into the hallway.

"He's growing so fast." Stanley stood and tried to think of what to say to her.

"We have some savings," she said. "We'll be okay."

Stanley stared into her eyes, blinked, and nodded until his matted main danced.

***

"Weeee!"

Little Stan squealed and whooshed down the long, metal slide. The attached swing set rocked back and forth as his son clambered back up the ladder. He should tighten the bolts before the day was out. Keep it safe.

Stanley yawned and swished his long tail. The hammock rocked to one side and back with the motion. The trees over his head whispered, and his cub squealed and slid again. A great investment, that slide. Janine had dragged it home from a yard sale two weeks ago. It only took a coat of paint and a few bolts to bring it back to life.

He'd tighten the screws again just to be safe. The sun filtering through the overhead leaves cast mottled patterns over his tawny fur, and Stanley rolled onto his side and watched his cub play. Their mobile home rested at the top of a short slope, surrounded by other trailers and a good thirty miles from the nearest freeway. A strip of shingles had worked free the last time they'd had wind. He'd have to tack them down before the weather turned.

A used car parked in their driveway. It had a rusted panel on the rear driver's side door, but it ran like a mule and got him to work and back. Five perfectly measured overnight shifts. Forty hours a week doing security at the lumber yard. Walking the darkness and making sure everything stayed nice and quiet.

Stanley poked a claw through the hole in his t-shirt. He scratched his belly fur absently. His favorite shirt. Comfy. A dollar at the thrift store in town and the previous owner had stretched the neck out beautifully. Lots of room to breathe in it.

"Stanley?" Janine's voice drifted to him on the breeze.

"Yeah?" Stanley rocked the hammock to the side, swung his legs over the netting and sat up facing his new home. His wife stood on the porch. Her dress stretched over her pregnant midriff, the skirts fluttered around her tawny legs.

"The Johnston's want us to come for dinner."

"Sure." Stanley nodded, smiled at the excited roaring of his cub. Little Stan and the crane kid next door had become fast friends. "What time?"

"Tonight. I told them you'd want a nap first."

"Awww." Little Stan howled from the top of his slide.

"Just need a minute to change," Stanley said. He'd tighten the bolts before they left. Work on the roof sometime next week, maybe.

"Are you sure?" Janine's eyes reflected the afternoon sunlight.

She smiled, and their cub streaked down the slide and bounded happily across a lawn studded with dandelions. Stanley inhaled the soft, natural scent of his life and found he had no interest in napping.

"Sure." He stretched his arms over his head and rumbled. "I'm not tired at all."

After putting her own identity aside for her family, Bella finds an unexpected refuge.

Tucked Away

E. S. Lapso

"You don't have to go if you don't want to. Your family can't make you show up to anything." Standing in the doorway to their shared bedroom, Clint crossed his arms as he watched Bella bind her breasts flat against her chest. It pained him to see her forcefully strip away everything she had worked so hard to obtain; even if just for a few days. Leaning against the wooden frame, the hare went on to say, "I'm sorry. It just isn't right."

"Neither was my uncle divorcing my aunt and abandoning her with three newborns but it happened. It's not about what's right or fair." Bella cast him a cold look, her voice taking on the deeper tones it had had when the rabbit had first accepted Clint's request for dinner five years ago. Unlike then, however, the voice echoed the pains the girl felt inside.

Giving a heavy sigh, Clint stepped forward and gently took the binder from Bella's trembling fingers. "Let me help. Deep breath." He then went about carefully layering the fabric until he could make out little more than a small uprising on the rabbit's chest that could be easily rationalized as winter fluff. "Guess it's a good thing they aren't too big yet. I'm looking forward to helping unwrap them when you get home next week."

She knew that he was only trying to help but something about the statement just stung Bella worse than she already felt. Swallowing, the petite rabbit stepped away from him to start packing her clothes. "Can you get me the box from the storage closet? With my old clothes in it?"

Without another word, Clint made his way downstairs. Their apartment had come with a storage unit on the first floor that served as their hideaway for Christmas decorations and the few boxes that still held what was left of the life the rabbit had thought she'd managed to leave behind. In her mind she had hoped to somehow never have to see her parents again, despite how unlikely she knew that would be. She should have told them before now.

When the hare returned with the box of clothes, Bella could only look at it like it was something foul. She looked to the words scrawled across it in faded sharpie and sighed. 'Baxter summer clothes.' Reaching for the box, she paused as the knot in her stomach grew larger. Tears burned at the edges of her vision until eventually she could only look away.

"Hey," Clint said to her in a soft, reassuring tone. "Let me do this. I know what you liked and didn't. I can do this. You just go grab some breakfast before the cab gets here."

Looking to her boyfriend, Bella simply nodded and forced a small smile. "I appreciate it, hon. I'll be in the kitchen." Then, without a second glance to the box, she took her leave.

The smell of coffee began to drift through the apartment as Bella busied herself making a bowl of cereal for breakfast. Normally she'd have avoided the coffee in favor of a nice cup of tea for her medication, but her nerves needed the calming of the caffeine. She silently ran through her list one more time as she fished her pill bottles out of the cabinet above the microwave. Almost obsessively she recounted the small tablets again and again to make sure that she'd packed the right amount.

She was certain that her siblings, being older now than when they'd originally bullied her, would at the very least leave her things alone if she kept them in her room. Her oldest brother, Mako, had emailed her to let her know that he'd be there to help her move her things from the bedroom and ensure their middle brother, Elliott, didn't try snagging any of her things. Mako was the most likely to understand if she confessed to him, but she knew his super religious wife would only cause him unneeded drama.

She then began to wonder how Nikki would react to her aunt and cousins moving into the house with them. It had only been last summer that her little sister had finally gotten her own room with the departure of Craig for college. Growing up, Nikki had always complained about being the youngest. Maybe she'd appreciate the chance to be a big sister type for her cousins.

Shaking her head, Bella moved to pour herself a cup of coffee from the pot. She counted out her pills one last time before taking the ones for today in an attempt to delay the inevitable return to her bedroom. She debated doing the dishes or balancing her checkbook for the month. Anything to not have to go get dressed.

As the alarm on her phone sounded, however, she knew that she had no choice but to accept that it was time to go. Silencing the melody on her phone, Bella made her way into the bedroom once more to find Clint struggling with the zipper of the luggage she'd bought for the trip. She watched in amusement for a moment as he struggled before crossing the room to help.

"You're so hopeless without me, I swear." Giving a sigh, she motioned him aside before skillfully working the zipper shut. Clicking her tongue, she looked around and hummed. "I need a pair of boxers. My parents will completely question me showing up in frilly purple panties."

Clint looked like he wanted to say something but simply shook his head with a small smile. Reaching into the box on the floor by the bed, he fished around before throwing her a fairly new looking pair of plaid boxers. "I think you got those like right before you started transitioning. They should still fit even with the bit of growth."

Stripping off her panties, Bella kicked them towards the hamper before slipping on the boxers. Humming, she looked herself over in the mirror by the closet. "I guess they aren't so bad. At least my ass looks half decent still." Stepping past Clint, she finally reached into the box herself and pulled out a faded pair of denim jeans. Working them up her legs, she groaned as she struggled to work them past her ass. "Guy jeans are dumb."

"You don't complain about mine usually. Here, just wear them with the top under your tail. It's how most guys are wearing them anyway these days." Coming up behind her, Clint tugged the denim up under the white fluff of her teardrop tail. He then gave a playful rub along the ashen fur of her back before handing her a shirt. "I packed the gamer t-shirts you still wear sometimes from in the closet instead of the ones in the box. I figured that might cheer you up at least slightly."

"Slightly," she admitted as she took the shirt and slipped it on. Clearing her throat, she looked herself over in the mirror one last time to help things settle in her mind. In a way it was like looking at herself from four years ago; no longer a petite doe but a lithe rabbit buck. Baxter.

Giving a heavy sigh, Baxter rubbed his eyes free of any stray tears before pulling Clint against him in a strong hug. "I love you, hon. I'll be back on Tuesday with some wonderfully heavy boxes for you to carry."

"Are you sure you don't need me to ride to the airport with you?" Clint asked with notable concern.

"It'll be harder to go if you do. It's best I just do this part on my own. Don't worry though. You'll have your happy little bunny girl back in a few days." With that, Baxter kissed him on the lips before grabbing up his luggage. Turning, he moved to the kitchen to collect the rest of his things and turn off the coffee pot before slipping out the front door.

The cab ride was mostly silent save for some small talk between Baxter and the older badger driving. He was a sweet man overall despite cursing more than the rabbit would normally be comfortable with in normal conversations. Still, the conversation helped calm Baxter considerably by the time he finally arrived at the airport. After paying the man, the rabbit made his way inside with his carry-on tucked under his arm.

Grateful for the short delay before his flight, Baxter simply did his best to focus on the book he'd brought to read during the flight. By page twelve he was blissfully forgetting his concerns for the weekend. By page forty she'd forgotten that she was supposed to be presenting male. As Bella felt her bladder begin to betray her she tucked her book away and made her way to the restroom.

Out of sheer habit, she casually made her way into the women's restroom and to the nearest stall. It wasn't until she made to slide down her jeans that she recalled just how she'd look to anyone who walked in. Cursing below her breath, Bella quickly tried to think of a way to avoid getting caught. Biting her lip, the rabbit immediately peeled off her shirt and began to undo the binding around her chest.

"Shit, I didn't pack my makeup bag," she muttered aloud as she quickly looked through her carry-on for something she could use to look female. To her relief and surprise she found a small bottle of her favorite scent and quickly began to dab it into her fur. It wouldn't trick a canine if they thought too hard, but it'd dissuade most at first sniff.

After she tucked her things back into her bag, Bella sat back on the toilet and closed her eyes. Around her, the freshly sprayed scent of her perfume clung to the air with rich, vanilla undertones that were helping calm her nerves. She knew that with the binder off and no bra she'd look chesty enough to at least try passing as a tomboy. It wasn't perfect, but it wasn't too different than how she'd tried to pass when first starting out. She knew she'd be fine.

Of course now she'd have to struggle to wrap her chest again on the plane. Plus her tickets said Baxter on them since her mother had paid for them; a fact that would only make things more awkward if anyone asked. Still, despite the complications, Bella felt herself calming as her chest rose and fell in enjoyment of freedom. It was such a subtle change overall but already the rabbit could feel her anxiety ebbing away. She'd figure out what to do on the plane.

Once finished, Bella tucked the binder into her carry-on and stepped out of the stall. Moving to the mirror above the sink, she washed her hands casually before using the water to restyle the fur atop her head. With her chest freed, the t-shirt she'd worn lifted slightly to reveal some of the ash grey fur of her stomach; another touch that helped with the tomboy look. Turning, she walked out of the bathroom with far more confidence than she'd walked into the airport with and waved to an elderly gazelle that walked in past her.

Making her way to the food court, Bella used the shoulder strap of her bag to try and mimic the look of a purse and adopted a slight rhythmic sway to her steps. A few younger men that looked to be in their collegiate glory days whistled in appreciation at her; an act that only helped to soothe her worries even more. Clearing her throat, she took on her feminine voice as she walked up to the cashier at the pizza stall.

The hour between eating and boarding her plane found Bella happily relaxing between a family of seven foxes and the trio of college students waiting on some friend to arrive. Spurred by their admiration of her, she casually struck up a conversation and was delighted that not one of them seemed to notice anything amiss. When she finally caught the sound of her boarding call over the intercom, Bella bid them farewell before moving to her terminal.

She'd been correct in thinking that her appearance would stir some confusion at the gate. The petite serval behind the podium seemed rather confused as she read the ticket and driver's license which prompted a second screening to ensure that Bella, as her name stated on the license, was in fact the Baxter reported on the ticket. After several minutes of debate between the airport employees, she finally found herself taking up her seat on the plane.

Forth row, window seat, coach. All in all she was very thankful for having the seat with the view after having had an unpleasant experience in the middle seat between an unkempt badger and a portly bear that hadn't been wiling to move to allow her out into the aisle. To her dismay, however, Bella soon found herself at the mercy of a far too energetic kangaroo, no older than five, who thought the best way to tell his mother he was tired of sitting was to lash out with both legs against her chair.

Yet, despite being the target of prepubescent angst, Bella was relieved to find the trip enjoyable. Her neighbors were a husky not much older than her who was expecting her first child and a possum who seemed perpetually anxious that the flight attendant would accidentally run over his tail despite having it tucked under his seat.

It wasn't until the pilot informed them that they were nearing their destination that Bella began to experience the familiar pangs of anxiety that had plagued her at home. When the husky asked if she was alright, Bella gave a vague response about not looking forward to family drama.

To her relief the other woman didn't push the topic beyond giving her a sympathetic pat on the arm.

Excusing herself, Bella retrieved her bag from the overhead compartment before shuffling hurriedly down to the cramped bathroom stalls at the rear of the plane. Stripping off her shirt, she carefully went about the task of rebinding her chest as best she could. After about twenty minutes of trying, she eventually accepted what she could only hope would be convincing enough for her parents. The scent she knew she'd have to explain away, but that'd be after they landed.

Taking a deep breath, Baxter once more dampened the fur of his head before giving it a more masculine style. He shook his head and pulled his shirt back on before making his way back to his seat. He did his best to ignore the odd looks some of the passengers gave him en route and was thankful the husky seemed to accept the change without question. If anything, the look she gave him was even more sympathetic than the pat on the arm had been.

Following the flow of the crowd out of the terminal, Baxter looked around for any sign of his siblings. His mother had told him that someone would pick him up but never mentioned the specifics as to who. Moving on to the baggage claim, the rabbit retrieved his luggage before making his way outside.

As he started toward the taxi lot, Baxter heard a familiar voice from behind him. Turning, he had just enough time to open his arms before a smaller version of himself collided into him full force. Stumbling back, he laughed as he looked down to his sister with a raised brow. "Hey, Nikki."

Looking up to him, the smaller rabbit grinned wide before getting a slightly confused look. She sniffed over his shirt before saying, "Who were you oolalaing?" Stepping back, she gave him a small smirk before smoothing out her black Punisher hoodie. "Still a nerd."

"Says the girl in the comic book hoodie." The two shared a laugh before Baxter added, "At least you have taste. Kinda."

"Young lady!" another too familiar voice called from the crowd just before Baxter's father stumbled through the family of foxes. Muttering to himself, he brought a hand up to cuff the back of his daughter's head. "I told you not to run off!" He scowled at her before turning to regard his son. Looking him over, the older rabbit grunted. "Nice to see you Baxter. Got your things?"

"Yeah, Dad," he replied as he motioned to his luggage at his side. Clearing his throat, he looked around a bit before asking, "Did anyone else come?"

"They're busy helping your aunt Ermie pack her apartment up. They could have used your help you know."

Looking down, Baxter replied, "Sorry, sir. This was the earliest flight Mom could cover with her miles. I didn't have enough in the bank to just pay it myself."

Nodding, the older rabbit reached out to take Baxter's suitcase. "It can't be helped. Come on then you two. Keep close." Without another word, he marched off with his children keeping close pace behind him.

The car ride home was mostly quiet save for the sound of claws tapping on phone screens while Baxter and Nikki both texted. They'd shared updated phone numbers on the walk to the car, since this was the first time Nikki had a phone, and were busy swapping texts back and forth while their father drove.

Some things never change, Baxter replied after Nikki asked if he was okay.

A snort sounded from behind him before a response arrived a few seconds later.

No shit. He's been like Stalin or something since Aunt E got dumped. I'm just glad you showed up so I have someone to talk to other than mom and dad. They won't even let me make a Facebook account to talk to people from school and my texts only work on weekends. It sucks.

Sounds like you're discovering the joys of being a teenager, Baxter responded as the SUV rounded the corner toward their street. He thought before adding, *It doesn't get better as an adult.*

"Don't you damn kids have something better to do than type on those damn things all day?" their father growled as he cast a sidelong glance at Baxter.

Looking out the window to avoid his father's gaze, Baxter replied with, "It's not like we can do much riding in a car."

"Oh don't be a smartass. You better believe you're not too old for me to pop your mouth if you start smarting back to me or your mother. My belt is still plenty good to tan your ass."

"Sorry, sir."

"So why do you smell like a damn cupcake anyway?" The car was slowing down only a few houses from their drive.

Realizing that his father was going to want an answer before they pulled into the drive, Baxter said, "The girl next to me had a bottle of scent powder in her carry-on that busted open during turbulence. It'll wash out."

The older rabbit snorted. "Grab a shower when you get in. I'll put your bag in your sister's room where the cot is."

Turning to look at him, Baxter arched a brow. "What happened to my bed?"

"Don't be stupid, boy! Your aunt is sleeping in it until we get the bed from her room put together in there. It ain't like you were using it anyway. The cot will be fine for the whole four days you so generously set aside to help your family."

Baxter opened his mouth to snap back but Nikki beat him to it. "Besides, I already stole your comic books so most of the cool stuff is in my room anyway." Taking the hint, Baxter returned to looking out the passenger window in silence. He could feel his fur standing on end under his clothes and did his best to hide the annoyed tick to his ear.

Inside the house wasn't much better. There were unwanted hugs between Baxter and his mother, then his aunt who was busy trying to keep three wailing babies quiet. Nikki was quick to take his hand and lead him up the short flight of stairs to where her room lay waiting, even as their father moved to follow him.

Keeping quiet, Baxter let himself be directed to the linen closet for towels for his shower. He simply stood there in bitter silence as the older rabbit busied himself with explaining the changes he'd made to the bathroom since the last time his "wayward son" had been home. When it became clear that Baxter wasn't going to contribute to the conversation, however, his father quickly excused himself back downstairs.

Stripping off his shirt, Baxter started to unwrap the binder around his chest before a knock at the door gave him pause. Hurrying to rewrap it, the rabbit cursed the lack of locks on the bathroom door and said, "Just a minute! I don't have pants on."

"It's cool," came Nikki's voice from the other side of the door. "I was just hoping we could maybe talk before you grab a shower? Dad left to go help move stuff."

"Oh, uh, sure," Baxter said as he loosely strapped the binder shut before pulling his shirt back on. Opening the door, he looked out to his sister and said, "You okay, Nikki?"

In response, his sister motioned for him to follow before walking to her room. "I just figured you could vent and so can I. Come on."

"Are you sure?"

"Yeah, it's cool. I got, like, punching pillows and stuff if you need them. They used to be yours anyway."

Uncertain about what was going on, Baxter stepped out of the bathroom and moved to follow her. He relented that she was right about him wanting to vent and let out his anger; though he wasn't certain that she was the audience he needed for an outburst.

It wasn't until the door to the bedroom was shut that Baxter finally felt his anger come out in the form of bitter pacing and muttered swears. He didn't even register how much change had taken place in his sister's room in the years it had been since he'd moved out for school. Pausing, he calmed himself with a few shaking breaths before looking around at the recently painted purple walls.

In the corner sat her bed draped in black linens that looked as if they belonged in a scene from the Adams family, above which sat a hand illustrated poster of said comedy. All around the room Baxter was surprised to see a hodgepodge of video game paraphernalia and gothic statuettes. Looking to Nikki as she sat at the desk opposite her bed, he gave her a fake pleading look.

"Goth? Really?"

The younger rabbit laughed and spun around in her chair. "Would you rather I cover my fur in glitter and run around as a wannabe vampire? I think we still have the cape from when you were twelve."

Rolling his eyes, Baxter looked to the cot under the window. "So you seem to be taking everything pretty well? Happy to be a big sister?"

"Not at all. I just don't tell them anything they don't deserve to know and they don't ask. Honestly? I'd rather sleep in the basement where I can't hear all the screaming. I mean it would only further my childhood angst and repression… or whatever."

Sighing, Baxter walked over to hug her to him again. "Sorry, Nikki. I didn't want to leave you stuck here alone."

"It's all good, man. Like, I know how much you wanted to go to school and I get to go in a couple years too. It's not so bad anyway; just since Auntie E and the needy trio showed up. That's when everything kinds of went to reality TV and back." Nuzzling into his shirt, she gave a small laugh. "You still smell like a cupcake. What's the occasion?"

"Like I said, one of the other passengers," he started to say but was immediately cut off as she shoved a hand into his face.

"Oh please, that's totally not scent powder. I know cause that shit makes me sneeze, so fess up."

Rolling his eyes, Baxter stepped away and shook his head. "No, Nikki. Just keep that between us, okay? I really don't need dad to have yet another reason to give me shit this weekend."

"Hey, it's cool. I'm the repressed, angsty teen, remember? He's too busy busting me for having skulls in my room or not going out for cheerleaders to care about much else. Mom seriously cried her eyes out for like two hours last year when I told her I wasn't going to be a cheerleader. Not even kidding."

"Yeah, that sounds like Mom," Baxter replied as he reached up to rub one ear anxiously. "It's just hard to talk about, okay?"

There was silence for a moment before Nikki finally said, "Yeah, okay. Just promise me that if you tell anyone, you tell me first. I mean, if it's like drugs or something, I don't care."

"It's not drugs, squirt."

"Are you a prostitute?"

"Nikki, stop." Baxter shot her a warning glare but found himself being the one to recoil from the look she gave him. She looked so desperate to know. Giving a heavy groan, he moved to lock the door before coming to sit by her on the bed. "God, you're such a little shit."

"You're also cussing a lot and that only happens when you're upset. You've not even told me to stop cussing and you usually always do that. Or at least did, I'm worried about you." Nikki leaned to rest her head against his arm as she pulled her legs up onto the bed.

In all honesty, Baxter wasn't sure how to respond to that. Were this a phone call from home he'd just tell her he was fine and it would be honest. Here though, sitting by her, he knew that he wasn't. Part of him worried for her too, given just how different she had come to be. In school he'd learned about coping mechanisms; something he now regretted as he looked around her room.

So much of the walls were him. The video game posters, some of the action figures, and even the shelf of comics above her desk he recognized as his old things. Then there were all the rest of her things that looked like she'd been spending what free money she had at Hot Topic. What stood out was the lack of anything else to connect her to the family. She'd cut herself away from them just like he had years before.

Except for him.

Rubbing his eyes, Baxter moved his free arm around her shoulders. She'd built this place as a haven for her to remind of her of things that made her happy. Her own paradise to escape things.

"I really missed you." When Nikki spoke, her voice was little more than a whisper. "I know Dad told you to not come home after you told him about your boyfriend. He still doesn't talk about it much. I had to talk him into not just packing up your stuff and putting it in the basement. I wanted to see you again."

Then it made sense. The reason why his mother had reached out to him to bring him home for the weekend. It wasn't to help out. Not with the moving anyway. It was to see Nikki. In his anger, he'd shut out his family without thinking about how she'd fare without him.

Humming, he looked around the room one last time before turning his head to look down at her. "You don't like me smelling like a cupcake?"

Nikki just laughed up to him softly. "I mean, if that's what you like. Did your boyfriend buy it for you?"

Thinking, Baxter felt like he needed to be honest. "Nah, I bought it. It's one of my favorite scents after all. My coworkers keep asking where I get it from."

"Is that a thing you Rhode Island boys do? Wear perfume?"

Swallowing, Baxter shook his head. "Not exactly, sis. You have to swear this doesn't leave your room, okay? No telling anyone. Not even friends at school. I can't risk… Mom and Dad can't know. You saw how Dad reacted to me coming out as gay."

Nikki looked at him strangely. "Okay? I'm cool with you being gay so I'm not sure what you could say that's more crazy than that. Unless you really are a prostitute."

"I'm not… okay… Nikki, I…" The words wouldn't come. Sighing, Baxter shook her head as she reached over to grab her phone. Letting her voice soften to its feminine tones, she said, "I'm going to text it to you."

Blinking, Nikki just nodded and pulled her phone from her pocket.

After tapping out her confession, Bella let her thumb hover over the send button for several minutes before a gentle nudge to her hand from Nikki brought the phone up to her thumb. Sighing, she tossed the phone on the dresser as she stood and then crossed the room.

It took a minute for Nikki's phone to sound off with the arrival of a message and another five before the younger rabbit finally spoke. Her voice sounded concerned but, in another way, relieved as she asked, "Do you want to do the whole conversation in text or can we talk about it now?"

"I dunno," Bella admitted as she rested her forehead against the bedroom door. "Does there have to be a conversation about it?"

"Not really, no. I just wanna ask stuff. I'm curious. Again, teenager."

"One question. That's it." Turning, Bella regarded her sister with a serious look.

Grumbling, Nikki rolled her eyes and sighed. "Okay, fine. One question." She made a show of tapping her chin as if she was having to think really hard. "Do you have boobs?"

The sound of Bella's palm impacting her face was loud enough to signify just how much it stung. "Seriously? I just tell you, like, my biggest secret and you ask me if I have boobs?"

Nikki threw up her arms in defense. "Hey, you said I only got one question so I'm going to ask the one I care about."

"That's the one you care about?! If I… seriously, Nikki, I'm not kidding. This isn't a joke!" Bella folded her arms across her chest and glared. "I'm already regretting telling you."

"Fine, fine… so a different question then? What name do you use? Cause, like, Baxter is a super shitty girl's name."

"Stop cussing and I… I go by Bella." The older sibling felt her cheeks starting to burn with embarrassment and yet felt a growing sense of calm inside. While her dread for the weekend hadn't disappeared, she did feel a certain relief flowing through her as her sister treated the situation like it wasn't a big deal.

"Bella is pretty," Nikki admitted as she scooted over and patted the space next to her on her bed. "Come on. Girl talk."

Rolling her eyes, Bella relented and moved to sit alongside her sister. Leaning back to rest on her elbows, she said, "Alright, fine, I'll give you a few more questions. Just don't ask about my boobs. That's just weird."

"Spoilsport," Nikki responded as she tucked her kneecaps under her chin. "So how long you been a girl? Like, when did you know you wanted to be a girl instead of a boy?"

"Honestly? I don't really know. I sort of always knew, I think, but never really felt like it was something I could be until about four years ago. In a way, Dad telling me not to come home kind of pushed me to go ahead and do it. That work as an answer?"

Nikki nodded and asked, "So can I call you my big sister then?"

"In private, yes." She felt an odd warmth inside at the idea. "I never thought I'd get to hear that. Welcome to not being the only girl in the family, I guess?"

Laughing, Nikki said, "Awesome. So does this mean you're straight now?"

"Technically?"

"Damn," Nikki said with a laugh. Looking towards the door she added, "Guess that means we only have one gay person in the family."

Bella arched a brow and was about to ask before another hand was shoved against her face.

"I said I cared about the boobs more." Nikki blushed and looked Bella in the eye. "I have a girlfriend at school. Mom and Dad don't know though."

Smiling, Bella gave her sister a playful shove. "Figures. I won't tell if you won't." Thinking, she pulled Nikki against her again and sighed. "I'll be better about keeping in touch this time. I promise."

"You better." Nikki sighed. "Thanks, sis."

Pulling back, Bella looked to her in confusion. Realizing what she meant, however, the older woman simply rested herself back against her sister. "You too, brat. So, slumber party tonight?"

"Do I look like a teenage cliché to you?"

Sighing, Bella just shook her head. In her mind she decided that maybe, just maybe, this trip wouldn't be so bad after all. Even if she had to be Baxter again the second she left her sister's room, it was worth getting to be herself with Nikki. If nothing else, that was escape enough.

Even pigs have dreams.

When Pigs Fly

Amy Fontaine

All the other animals on Portia's farm were very good at being themselves. The geese honked and the ducks quacked as they swam in the pond. The horses neighed and gave humans rides. The cows mooed and grazed in the pasture. The sheep baaed and let themselves be sheared. The hens laid eggs and the rooster crowed. The cat hunted mice in the barn. Even the other pigs oinked and ate slop, like good, law-abiding farm animals.

Yes, all the animals on Portia's farm were good at being themselves, except for Portia. For a number of reasons, everyone thought Portia made a terrible pig.

Firstly, Portia never oinked. Instead, Portia tried to sing. She had heard the little robins and sparrows in the woods behind the barn twittering so prettily to greet the dawn, and she thought she would try it herself. But her piggy vocal chords kept her from attaining the heavenly melodies of the birds, so she just ended up sounding like a pig trying to sing, which was not a very nice sound at all. The other pigs winced and covered their ears, as did all the other animals on the farm. They said mean things to Portia, and it made her sad. But Portia kept trying.

Secondly, Portia turned her nose up at slop. She refused to eat from the messy trough with all the other pigs. She had seen the little robins and sparrows in the woods behind the barn darting about catching bugs in midair: flies and mosquitoes and butterflies. They looked so graceful while doing that, so Portia wanted to try it herself. So she hopped along, trying to snap winged insects out of the air. Being ungainly and heavy, she never caught her prey. Instead, she crashed to the ground. The other animals shook their heads and laughed at Portia, and it made her sad. But Portia kept trying.

Lastly, and most importantly, Portia wanted to fly. This made her the target of derision and scorn from every single creature that walked, flew, or swam on the farm. It was not clear to anyone how Portia planned to fly. They just always caught her gazing longingly up at the skies, watching the little robins and sparrows soaring through the air. The swallows that nested in the eaves above the barn doors every spring made Portia swoon. She delighted in watching the aerial acrobats swoop and spin. While the other pigs trotted about the pigpen in typical piggish fashion, Portia danced in circles, mimicking the movements of the swallows overhead and laughing like a fool.

One fateful evening, reality caught up with Portia, in the form of a conversation with a boar named Elmer.

"You know why the farmer keeps pigs, don't you, Portia?" Elmer asked.

Portia was trying and failing to climb on top of the pigpen's fence to get a better look at a song sparrow swooping overhead. "What?" asked Portia, without turning to look at the other pig.

Elmer looked at Portia seriously. "Didn't you ever notice…that Frankie, Oscar, and Hamish never came back after the farmer took them away?"

Portia turned around. "Yeah," Portia said, "I noticed. Are they okay?" Her voice sounded concerned, but a dreamy grin still played about her mouth. Portia's head and heart clearly remained with the song sparrow, who was now perched on the fence of the pigpen, singing to his would-be lovers at the top of his little lungs.

Elmer sighed heavily. Beneath his eyes were the shadows of many sleepless nights.

"Portia," said Elmer, "they're never coming back."

Portia seemed to snap awake. She stared at Elmer, her eyes wide, her heart pounding.

"No…"

Elmer frowned. A tear rolled from the corner of his eye. Then he took a deep breath and stiffened his trembling legs, giving Portia a steely, determined look.

"Yes," Elmer said. "The farmer feeds us, he shelters us, he fattens us, and then…" Elmer choked on his words. More tears fell from the boar's eyes. He sniffled and snuffled, tossing his head in the hopes of getting rid of the tears and reclaiming his dignity and calm. It didn't work. The pig shivered uncontrollably.

"The time will come," Elmer said, "for all of us. For…for you and me, too."

Portia shook her head, murmuring, "No…" under her breath, over and over, seeming to believe in the power of the word less and less after each utterance. She backed away from Elmer, until she hit the wooden fence of the pigpen with her rear end. Then she fell onto her haunches. The other pig came to her side and whispered in her ear. His breath smelled like slop, but his voice was kind.

"Listen, Portia. I don't want to tell you how to live your life, but…" Here the pig's voice wavered, and he shuddered involuntarily before he went on.

"Our lives are going to be short, so short. If I were you, I wouldn't waste any time daydreaming. I would focus on what's right here in front of me, what I'm actually capable of doing with the body and mind I have, and then I would just do that, to the best of my ability. Become the most exemplary pig I can be."

Stepping back, Elmer looked at Portia meaningfully. Portia, for her part, was trying very hard not to cry. The boar nuzzled Portia. At his gentle touch, Portia remembered that Elmer might not be around for much longer, and then she couldn't hold back her sorrow anymore. As she sobbed in a very piggish way, oinking and sniveling, her tears dribbled into the mud below her hooves, creating a puddle there. Elmer continued to nuzzle her for a while, saying, "There, there, Portia." Then, reluctantly, he left her alone.

Still sobbing quietly, Portia looked down at her reflection in the mud puddle at her feet. She had no song and no wings. She was nothing but a fat, sad pig.

***

The next morning, Portia was silent. She didn't leap into the air in pursuit of dragonflies and butterflies. She didn't watch the swallows swooping from their nests in the eaves. She didn't eat or drink. She just stood in a corner of the pigpen, staring listlessly at nothing.

Elmer approached her. "Portia, I'm so sorry. Maybe I shouldn't have told you. Maybe I should have just let you be."

Portia shook her head but said nothing. With a soft, sad grunt, Elmer ambled away.

While pouring slop into the trough inside the pigpen, the farmer's son Henry saw Portia moping and raised a cry. "Papa, something's wrong with this sow!"

The farmer came running. He walked up to Portia, examining her with a frown.

"Is she okay, Papa?" said Henry. "Is she sick?"

Kneeling beside Portia, the farmer ran his hands along her sides and stomach. Portia quivered at his touch but did not look up at him. After getting to his feet, the farmer stroked his chin thoughtfully.

"She's not sick," said the farmer. "Just in a bad mood. Not sure why."

Henry frowned. "Well, that's too bad. A right sprightly pig she is, most of the time."

The farmer nodded. "Yeah. She has a bright spirit, the likes of which I've never seen before. She makes me smile. And I think she makes the other animals happy, too. Whether they know it or not."

The farmer checked his watch and laughed. "Well, here I've been for ten minutes now, waxing right philosophical about this here pig when there's still work to be done." The farmer ruffled his son's hair appreciatively. "Thanks for letting me know about her, Henry. There's not much we can do for her right now, but we'll keep an eye on it."

Henry nodded.

Turning back to Portia, the farmer stroked her head, looking kindly into her eyes. "Keep your chin up, girl," said the farmer.

Portia watched the farmer and his son depart for other parts of the farm, unshed tears trembling in her eyes. Suddenly, she heard a voice singing at the top of the fence. It was her little friend the song sparrow, belting his tune out for the world, whether or not anyone was listening.

Portia was listening. She smiled. She blinked her tears away.

Portia muscled in beside the other pigs at the slop trough. Elmer's eyes lit up when he saw her there. "Hiya, friends!" Portia cried. "Another bright, beautiful day, isn't it?" She devoured her slop with gusto, as if it was ambrosia from the gods.

The other pigs stared at her blankly. Then the tiniest twitches of smiles tugged at the corners of their snouts.

After eating her fill, Portia waltzed, humming, to the water dish. She lapped at it eagerly. Then, still humming, she trotted back to the song sparrow singing on the fence. Lifting her head, she sang along.

Portia's song came from deep within her being, welling up inside her and pouring forth into the world. It was a song about flying, about adventure, about peace. It was a song about being yourself, about using your imagination to find paradise right where you are. For a moment, while Portia and the song sparrow lilted their sweet harmony, the geese and the ducks stopped swimming and the chickens stopped strutting and the cat stopped hunting and the farmer and his sons stopped working and the horses and cows and sheep stopped chewing their cuds and the pigs stopped eating slop and the heart of the whole farm skipped a beat.

Then the moment was gone, and time began to move again. The geese and the ducks squabbled over pond pecking order politics. The rooster paraded before the flustered hens. The cat killed a mouse. The farmer and his sons went about their business. The horses and cows and sheep wandered through the pasture, munching on grass. The song sparrow flew away. The pigs went back – reluctantly, it seemed – to eating their slop.

But Portia stared into the blue sky for a few moments longer. She gazed up at the bright, cheerful sun, the drifting, fluffy clouds. She inhaled deeply of the crisp air, taking in all the earthy, wonderful smells of the farm. She watched swallows going in and out of their nests in the eaves. She looked wistfully in the direction the song sparrow had gone, towards the forest on the far side of the barn. The forest's depths beckoned to her. But she knew she would never travel there...unless...

Portia closed her eyes.

In Portia's mind, she grew long, downy wings. The wings were a patchy white and chocolate-brown, just like her coat, with feathers soft enough to soothe her once-despairing heart. The other pigs in the pigpen all grew wings, too. Together, the glorious flock of pigs soared over the fence on the other side of the barn and fluttered through the forest, singing exultantly as they did. The forest was full of rich new scents and vibrant new colors, as well as strange creatures Portia had never seen before: a horse with a glistening golden horn, a beast like a cross between a bird and a cat, and more. All of the creatures the pigs met were friendly and beautiful, and they shouted greetings to the pigs as the pigs passed overhead.

For years, the pigs sailed over vast and varied landscapes. They saw dazzling, sunlit oceans, the shifting red sands of deserts, towering snowcapped mountains, cities that sparkled with a thousand lights. And the pigs sang about everything they saw, weaving scenes from their travels into sprawling ballads that held eons in each note and syllable.

Portia opened her eyes.

Portia smiled.

Portia lived in a muddy pigpen, with a couple other pigs who could be boring and stuffy at times. She ate slop, not winged insects. She couldn't sing quite as well as a song sparrow, nor dart through the air like a swallow. And one day, sooner or later, Portia's life would end.

But Portia could dream, so Portia could fly. And that was all she needed.

Portia oinked contentedly and drank some water.

Even spiders can experience paradise.

Funnel Dresses

Priya Sridhar

The dress shop had the best location in the forest colony web; it hung at a sharp east angle beside a mosquito-smoothie shop and a shoe store, where a thick branch had the best sunset view. During the afternoon foot traffic, many patrons with smoothies would loiter by the windows, to eye the freshly spun silk and styles on display. A few tried to rush in and get a sleeve mended or fabric altered for sudden weight gain or loss, but often they would leave after seeing the sign that read ONE DAY MINIMAL WAIT.

Miss Raglan, the proprietress, added beads to a sleek silken dress that hung on a wobbly mannequin. The wooden spider had lasted through many a dress, though Miss Raglan only took her out for special occasions. The customer who had demanded this particular gown, Chemise Fractal, had drawn out a specific pattern onto delicate green leaves. Chemise's friends had also asked for dresses, so that Miss Raglan had a dozen dresses to finish before the Annual Orb Ball. Even though she had eight legs and lenses for her tawny eyes, she was still working day and night.

The bell attached to the door rattled. Soft footsteps padded into the shop.

"We're closed," Miss Raglan said without looking up.

"Miss Raglan?" a small voice said. "It's me, Camisole."

Miss Raglan looked away from the delicate beading. A spider dressed in navy green fidgeted behind the counter.

"Bless my silk!" she said. "Camisole Topstitch! Fancy seeing you here!"

Camisole gave a shy smile that revealed her curved fangs. She had grown three times her weight, unfit for the light pink funnel dresses she had worn as a spiderling. The green she wore now matched her eyes.

If Miss Raglan hadn't been holding a pincushion, a bag of beads, needle and thread, the bead pattern, and extra fabric, she would have swept up the smaller spider into an embrace. As it were, she embroidered another bead into place.

"Now isn't a good time. It's going to be a late night."

"That's all right," Camisole said in her soft tone. "I can wait until you're done. I don't have any other appointments."

She settled herself on a stool meant for customers. Miss Raglan saw the puffy, beaded tote slung over Camisole's shoulders. A bolt of brilliant yellow and pink striped material came out, as well as a smaller needle and thread. Camisole threaded the needle without pricking her leg and began to sew quietly.

The spiders did their work in silence. Miss Raglan finished the beading on the dress. She compared the pattern on the cloth to the pattern on leaves in her hand. Then she set the beads down into another bag, which had an intricate knot on it. She made a show of putting the other materials in organized places.

"Thank you for waiting, Camisole," she said. "What are you working on?"

"Oh, this is a negligee for sleeping in the web." Camisole held up the yellow and pink stripes. "It's based on what the Minister of Abdomens wore during that holiday concert. It's not for anything special. Just to keep my legs calm."

Miss Raglan eyed the dress. It had a ruffled lace collar and hem, and a thick cut for a spider. Still, it wasn't for business and Camisole's breathing had slowed while she had worked on it.

"How can I help you?"

"I need a favor," Camisole whispered. "I need a place to work on a dress."

"On that one?" Miss Raglan asked with surprise.

"No." Blushing, Camisole reached into her bag and pulled out a letter. "My college roommate, Araniella, she paid me to work on a dress for her. But I can't work on a dress for her if she's watching, and she likes to watch me sew usually. She studies and keeps one or three eyes on me."

Miss Raglan understood immediately. The feeling of having a customer watch you do work, and sometimes open their toothy mouths, was enough to make the hairs on her back crinkle. Still, she curled her fangs.

"I'm not sure," she said. "I have to do a rush job for a customer, several of them. It's not a good time to have more seamstresses in the shop."

The silence that followed weighed on Miss Raglan. Camisole's face crinkled with disappointment. Her legs slumped.

"Please. I'll do anything," she begged. "If I sew in front of her I'll mess it up, and I can't do it at home. I'll clean up the shop. I'll get your stamen tea."

Miss Raglan perked up. She hadn't made a proper cup of stamen tea in ages, not since this commission, and dust had been gathering in the shop counters.

"I do need to focus on these orders," she admitted. "If I teach you how to run the shop, you can sew here. But I will have to lay some ground rules—"

She couldn't finish because Camisole leaned over the counter and drew her into a hug. The spider had a tight grip, and her bag banged against Miss Raglan's left legs.

"Thank you, thank you, thank you!" she said. "I won't let you down!"

***

On the beginning of the first day, Miss Raglan had her doubts. She held out a broom to Camisole, who took it with wariness. The broom was long and brown with knobby bits, the bristles and stick held together by heavy-duty silk. Miss Raglan had fashioned the broom herself after a huge storm of wooden bits had hit the neighborhood.
"It's pretty simple," Miss Raglan assured her. "You get all the dust and stray threads into this dust pan."

Camisole held the broom at an angle. She experimented with different ways of angling the brush end, and tried to sweep slowly. Impatience bubbled inside Miss Raglan. The harsh swishing sound made her cringe. Still, Camisole had trouble moving the dust into a neat pile.

"It doesn't have to be perfect," Miss Raglan said as kindly as she could.

"But I want it to be," Camisole said.

"So do I," Miss Raglan muttered to herself.

The broom swept for most of the morning. Miss Raglan turned away from the harsh sound and buried herself in more embroidery.

Camisole was better at tea. She was familiar with the automatic kettle that Miss Raglan used, though she consulted a book on how many cups of ground stamen to add to the kettle after it steamed. The smell of the dried herbs lightened Miss Raglan's mood. A yellow-green liquid came out, bubbling in the small cup.

Miss Raglan tasted the cup. Camisole stood back, nervously. The tea was too weak.

"Try not to be cautious with the stamen grounds, dear," Miss Raglan said. "I like my tea nice and strong, so that it's dark green. But not bad for a first attempt."

"I understand," Camisole said softly. Her head drooped. She drank all of the weak tea and prepared another pot. They watched the steam rise. This time the tea was more to Miss Raglan's liking.

"No one ever gets things right the first time," she said as she sipped. "The ones that do, well, we want to string them up for the wasps. You'll get the hang of it."

Camisole didn't look reassured, though she seemed relieved at having made a better pot. She scurried over to where the broom was leaning against the shop wall, picked it up, and studied it. Then she set it on the ground and tried to sweep again.

"That is better," Miss Raglan said honestly. "One day you may even run your own shop."

Camisole managed a small smile. She succeeded at sweeping the dust into a neat pile.

***

Sewing was a relief. Miss Raglan lent Camisole a storage room she wasn't using, where bolts of fabric were arranged on the shelves. Camisole took out the dress from her purse, a tint of maroon, and set it on a dress form. The skirt had a stiff, curved skeleton made out of tree bark and rolled up silk embroidering the edge.

"A funnel dress," Miss Raglan said with surprise. "I haven't seen those in a while."

"Araniella asked for it," Camisole replied. "She said she couldn't find any dresses like it in Funnel Town, so she asked me to make it instead of having to order it from somewhere else."

Miss Raglan pressed her lips. She eyed the neat stitches along the hem, the hints of ironing, and the layers of petticoats.

"Is something wrong?" Camisole asked.

"No, not at all," Miss Raglan said quickly. "You can borrow any material here as long as you keep everything neat. I need to start on my rush jobs."

She scurried outside, and looked at the latest dress. It was a slim number, with minimal fabric. Miss Raglan shook her head. Compared to Camisole's dress, it resembled a lampshade. Still, lampshades were in fashion. She was not one to argue with changing minds.

Camisole started to sing. Miss Raglan could hear her through the closed door. It was an old sewing song, from the days when the seamstresses weaved their own silk, and thus could take weeks to make one dress.

"They say home's where the heart is,
Wherever that may be,
But hearts are always changing,
Desires tend to flee.
But I know I am settled,
When I cut and baste.
Such projects can't be fussy,
For hearts do not like haste."

Miss Raglan shook her head. It brought back memories of a younger Camisole, who used to be in spiderling choir and dream about being a singer. Back then the spiderling had shown more energy and courage.

"Bolts of solid silk,
Are maps of new lands,
Each stitch a new mark,
A claim to stop and stand,
To say this is paradise,
And I will never leave,
No matter the storms,
No matter how I grieve."

Miss Raglan couldn't help but join in on the last verse. She knew the words by heart, since the words often carried her through a slump or when a demanding customer wanted her to mend a rip in fifteen minutes.

"To say this is paradise,
And in paradise I will stay,
No wind or raging flood,
Will ever blow me away."

***

By the third day, Camisole had settled into her position. She swept the floor in the morning, polished the glowing crystals, and prepared several pots of stamen tea. Miss Raglan had come to relish her singing because it told her that Camisole was happy. She had forgotten what it was like to have company among the silks and threads, to have more than wind leafing through her patterns.

They started sewing together, Miss Raglan in the main room of the shop and Camisole in the back room. Camisole sang softly as she worked on her dress:

"To say this is paradise,
And I will never leave—"

The shop doorbell tinkled. Feet clicked against the clean floor. Camisole stopped singing abruptly.

"Good morning, Miss Chemise!" Miss Raglan said with fake cheer. "It is always lovely to see you."

Chemise gave her an icy look. She had dressed in silver today from head to legs, a fitted suit in alternating shades that showed off her oval frame. Each of her eyes was a chip of gold, framed behind stylish glasses.

"I've come to do fittings," she announced. "My daily abdomen cleanse got cancelled due to my specialist having an inconvenient accident."

"Really," Miss Raglan said, gnashing her fangs. "Anything for you. But you will have to give me a minute to clear out space since you weren't on today's schedule—"

Chemise climbed over the counter that separated the main part of the shop from the customer area, and made it look like an elegant gesture. She studied the mannequin, which had a slim hot pink dress.

"So this is my dress," she said. "It seems you made some changes to the design I drafted."

"No, Miss Chemise. This dress is for Miss Bishop Vogue. Your dress is finished, and right here." Miss Raglan hurried to the racks, where she pulled out a gown wrapped in protective silk. "I made it exactly as you demanded—"

"Yes, yes." Chemise waved a leg at her. "Of course Miss Bishop would choose something so whimsical; she always reminded me of those cheap flea circuses."

She took the wrapped dress in her legs and studied it. Miss Raglan held her breath.

"You show reasonable competence," she finally said. "It seems you followed my instructions to the letter. I do have some suggestions for making it more in style. These beads need to be ripped out. They clash with the material, especially with the trend for lampshade figures."

Miss Raglan restrained the urge to take Chemise's head between her fangs. She instead kept gnashing as quietly as she could.

"Would you like to wait until I take out the embroidery?" she asked with rigid politeness.

"That's not necessary," Chemise said, striding towards the back. "The beads have nothing to do with the fit, and I wish to make sure that you have accounted for my measurements."

Miss Raglan tried to move forward. Chemise blocked her with her body and ripped the door open. A distasteful expression crossed her eyes.

Camisole froze behind her dress. She had been adding a few lace hems.

"And what have we here?" Chemise asked.

"I, I—um," Camisole started.

"*I, I um,*" Chemise repeated in a mocking high-pitched tone. "Stand up straight and face me like a proper spider!"

Camisole jumped from behind the mannequin and stood. Her legs wobbled as Chemise circled her and the wooden spider.

"Miss Chemise, if I may—" Miss Raglan started.

"What a gown," Chemise said with sarcasm. "And in the funnel style. I've only seen portraits of my grandmother wearing it."

Camisole looked like a wasp had stung her and had laid eggs on top of her body. She didn't move a muscle as Chemise stroked the fabric.

"What is a spiderling like you doing in the ancient era?" Chemise snarked. "Some spider who can hand stitch like this needs to get with the times! No one uses bustles these days!"

"I—it's for a friend," Camisole offered. "She—she likes bustles."

"A friend who likes bustles." Chemise gave an unkind laugh. "Bustles don't do a thing for spider figures these days."

"Miss Chemise!"

The spiders turned. Miss Raglan seethed at them, at Chemise for being so rude and at Camisole for being so meek.

"Camisole's client asked for a vintage funnel gown," Miss Raglan explained coldly. "She had to make it according to those specifications. Ultimately the client will decide if the dress needs a bustle. Miss Chemise, would you like to start your fitting?"

"Yes, I will," Chemise said. "Your specialized apprentice is excused."

Camisole trod out without another word. She left her dress on the mannequin. Chemise met Miss Raglan's steely look.

"Speak to me like that again and I will make sure you only hem bedsheets for the rest of your life."

"Apologies," said Miss Raglan without feeling sorry. "Let us get started."

It was the tensest fitting that Miss Raglan had ever done. She had marked the areas by which to remove the beads. Chemise demanded water to clean her face and crickets to feast on, not caring if she got the gown dirty. Still the dress went on, and came off. Chemise left with clicking steps.

Camisole didn't return to the shop. Her pouch dress remained on the mannequin and hung like an umbrella. Miss Raglan studied the structure and poked at it. The maroon kept hanging. It did look like something you'd see in a grandmother's portrait.

When the dimming light made the web outside gleam, Miss Raglan wrapped herself in a thick blue shawl with reflective pieces of crystal sewn into it and set out. She scurried along.

"Camisole!" she called out. "Camisole, where are you?"

Spiders scurried past, heading to the evening life and to the glowworm clubs. Miss Raglan walked back and forth across the web, calling and fretting. Then when she doubled back, she stopped by the smoothie place.

A pile of empty mosquito smoothie cups marked Camisole's spot. She huddled inside a tiny table made of a ladybug's red shell. Miss Raglan squeezed between the many tables, some of which were carved from pill bugs and katydid bodies, and sat beside her.

"I'm sorry," Camisole said, slurping noisily at another smoothie. "I shouldn't have wasted your time."

"Don't apologize," Miss Raglan said. "Chemise Fractal can't run me out of business. I've been around for longer than she was alive."

"Not that," Camisole said. "The material, the space, not being good enough. I'll pay you for the fabric I used, and for the tea. I should have realized my style was too old-fashioned."

She downed the rest of her smoothie and wiped her mouth. Red and black liquid dripped from her fangs. She licked at it.

"Araniella will understand. I'll find her another dress that is more suitable, with someone she can afford—"

"Camisole Topstitch," Miss Raglan said in a stern voice. "Chemise Fractal doesn't decide what is and isn't fashionable. She isn't your boss any more than I am, You obviously love what you're doing, or you wouldn't have spent so much time and effort on that dress. This isn't your main profession yet, and there is time for you to learn."

"But I can't learn."

"What?"

"I've tried," Camisole said miserably. "I've read every fashion magazine. I've attempted to make different designs in the Tanglewood style. But it's no good. I'm best with funnel dresses, which people only want if they like the older styles. I've known for ages, but I was hoping that at least I could make Araniella happy."

They sat in silence. Camisole used a leaf napkin to dab at her mouth. Miss Raglan twisted her legs around her shawl.

"Why don't we have Araniella come in and look at the dress after it's finished?" she said. "You're almost done with it, so you may as well see it through to the end."

"But what if she calls it old-fashioned?" Camisole asked.

"Then it's old-fashioned, and you learn from it," Miss Raglan said. "It doesn't mean making it was a waste, or that you are a bad artist. No dress made is a waste."

She took one of Camisole's legs and stroked it. Slowly the younger spider calmed down.

***

The end of the week had come. Camisole had swept the shop so well that the dust had no time to settle anew each day. Her stamen tea came out perfectly the first time she made it. Still her fangs quivered. So did her legs.

"If she doesn't like it, you can move forward," Miss Raglan said, nursing a cup of tea herself.

The shop's bell rang. A curvy spider dressed in red and black spots came in. She was even larger than Camisole, though Miss Raglan could have guessed that from the measurements. She wore a hat made from moth wings.

"Hi, Ara," Camisole said softly.

"Cami!" The spider dropped her purse and ran to her roommate, giving her a big hug. "So this is where you've been hiding? I missed you."

Camisole returned the hug with four legs and gave a nervous smile.

"I wanted to finish the dress properly," she said in a small voice. "I thought it wouldn't be perfect unless I focused on it."

"Forget perfection; how would I pay you if you just disappeared during a holiday week?" Araniella asked. "What, I would leave your money under the pillow like the Incisor Fairy?"

Camisole's smile became more genuine. She led Araniella to the back. Miss Raglan followed, clutching her mug of stamen tea.

Finished, the dress looked like a maroon circus tent. Camisole had done panels of alternating white and black, and had embroidered different scenes on each panel. One panel showed a spider lazing in the sun under a curved leaf, while another showed spiderlings blowing in the wind on silk parachutes. The ruffle collar was bright white lace that dipped into a curve. Her legs had bled from pricking herself with the needle several times.

"Oh, Cami," Araniella said in a breathy voice. "It's exactly what I wanted!"

She stroked the silk, and giggled at how it rippled beneath her legs. Miss Raglan couldn't help but smile. She had seen that look, on many customers that had left with a purchase.

"You—you don't think it's old-fashioned?" Camisole ventured.

"Well, of course it's old-fashioned, and I love it," Araniella exclaimed. "Why did you think I asked you for it? No one can get a proper funnel gown these days! This embroidery is beautiful!"

Miss Raglan released a breath she didn't even know she was holding. Camisole also sighed in relief. Araniella grabbed her in another hug.

"I know you want to be better, but your best is already good," she said. "You have to believe that. I'm always going to want a Camisole Topstitch gown, and others will as well. Can I try it on? Can I, please, can I?"

"Oh—of course," Camisole said. "Let me get it off the mannequin for you."

She worked carefully, so as not to mess up the bony skirt underneath or to tear at the delicate embroidery. Araniella clutched it in her legs.

"Wow. I had no idea," Camisole said as Araniella went into the dressing room.

"I figured, when you said she was watching you stitch," Miss Raglan said. "She must have known what you sew best already. You mustn't doubt yourself when an expert claims to know better."

"But then what?" Camisole asked. "I go back to college, keep sewing, and . . ."

"You find more spiders like Araniella," Miss Raglan said. "You find out who will want your best. But even if that fails, sewing is your paradise. That's why we sew, for that happy feeling. Don't let anyone ever take that away from you."

She wrapped Camisole into a hug that she should have given her the first time. Araniella squealed from inside the dressing room. Camisole relaxed and returned the hug.

A moment in time can be a piece of paradise. As a child, Christmas morning with its presents and candy was pure giddy delight. For Moira and her guide dog Joad, though, the moment they're waiting for happens a few hours earlier, on Christmas Eve.

A Christmas Tale for the Disenchanted

Mark Blickley

It was a December twenty-fourth unlike any December twenty-fourth in recent memory. The ground was blanketed with ice from a snowfall two days earlier, and it was quite cold. They even predicted more snow by nightfall.

Imagine that. A cold and snowy Christmas Eve just like the old snapshots in the family album! What a relief. Maybe this year's holiday conversation wouldn't center around how pollution and its ensuing global warming trends conspired to take the "feel" out of Christmas.

These thoughts flashed inside Moira's head as she and Joad slowly made their way up Fairview Avenue in Jersey City. Moira liked the crisp smell of the cold air, but the ice frightened her. She hoped her fear wouldn't be transmitted to Joad. She tried to relax her grip on him.

When they reached the corner Moira leaned over and patted Joad's head. The dog barely felt his master's affection.

The ice and traffic were making him too nervous to cross the street. Crossing streets was once an easy feat for Joad, but now he hated it. He'd hated it for several years. They stood on the corner of Fairview Avenue through two complete traffic light changes, waiting for Joad's decision.

Each time Moira heard the traffic stop and felt people next to her cross the street, she directed Joad to move forward. He refused. The dog could feel Moira's impatience as she fidgeted with his harness.

Joad was breathing heavily when he finally took his first step. Perhaps the cold steam from his breath obscured his vision, or maybe it was his owner's anxiety that clouded his judgment. Nevertheless he proceeded to lead Moira into the street.

She smelled the first hint of danger—a blast of diesel fuel. "Stop!" "Stop!" shouted pedestrians from both sides of the street. Moira yanked back on Joad's harness and froze.

A turning bus cut right in front of her, missing them by inches.

Moira's abrupt stop caused her to lose her footing on the slippery pavement. Down she went. Joad's tail drooped between his legs and he lowered his head as a rush of people came to Moira's aid. As they helped her to her feet she heard a man say, "What's wrong with that stupid dog?"

"It was my fault, not the dog's," said Moira. She patted Joad on his shoulder and thanked the people for helping her.

Joad's tail remained folded underneath him as they cautiously made their way to the sidewalk. If Moira could see, she'd have known that her dog's tail was usually tucked away. He worried so much of the time about her safety, it'd been ages since he was able to wag it in joy or relief.

The block just ahead of Moira and Joad was one of the most treacherous in the city. It was lined with abandoned, burned out buildings. This meant that no one had cleared away any of the snow. It was ignored. The entire length of the block was one shiny sheet of thick, slick ice. Other pedestrians simply avoided this dangerous stretch of sidewalk by crossing the street.

Moira knew nothing of the peril she was approaching. But Joad knew. He could see how crowded it was across the street. It made him shiver to realize that he and his master were completely alone. Not one soul was nearby. If something should happen, Joad knew there would be no one around to help Moira this time.

To steady her footing on the sidewalk Moira took short, heavy steps that crunched into the ice. She believed that these crunching sounds were the ice screaming out in pain as her boots cracked its spine.

"I'm sorry," Moira whispered to the pavement.

Joad, who was much lower to the ground, knew the ice couldn't hear her apology above her crackling footsteps.

At the beginning of her blindness, Moira had thought that her hearing had, and would, become more potent. But as she matured she understood that her ears hadn't grown more powerful, only her concentration. And as her concentration grew, so did her imagination.

She enjoyed making up stories based on sounds, especially the sounds of nature. Without visual distractions, sounds became pieces of puzzles whose final outcome was dictated by her tastes and moods. Moira totally disregarded where or how they had originated. And if these sounds produced paintings in her mind, then wind was her favorite color.

A delicious intimacy flourished between Moira and the wind. Sometimes it whistled at her, or tried to seduce her with soft spring breezes. Other times she'd capture and cage it, like on hot summer days when she'd pull out her electric fan and force the wind to serve her. Moira would listen to the breeze spew out between the thin bars that protected her from the rotary, begging to be released from this unnatural act. More often than not she'd take pity on this artificial breeze. Her finger would click off the fan and she'd sit in her hot apartment, sweaty but satisfied.

Winter winds were fickle. Many people thought of winter winds as bitter, but Moira knew better. They weren't bitter, just mischievous—and protective. Their mischief could be seen in the formation of ice. The wind and the water loved playing together during winter because nothing delighted water more than to be turned into ice.

Moira appreciated how water was always at work replenishing, refreshing, and cleaning. Yet despite this terrific workload, it disturbed her that the only time water seemed to be acknowledged was when it was cursed during droughts, vilified as acid rain, or slandered when it could no longer carry away the foul smelling wastes dumped into it.

During winter rainstorms or snow sprinklings, Moira would listen to the drops of moisture beg for an increase in the wind chill factor so it could freeze over. The wind, who was quite sophisticated because of its intensive travels, understood the water's need to develop a thick, protective skin against the criticism people threw at it. And if that skin was an exquisite icicle or a slippery patch of ice, so be it.

The dog hesitated as Moira urged him forward. But what could he do? There was absolutely no way of avoiding that terrible stretch of ice. He thought of directing Moira into the street in order to bypass it, but that was too dangerous. The traffic was too heavy. He tried to get Moira to cross the street to safety, but she didn't understand his nudging.

"Come on, Joad. Stop acting so silly. Why do you want to cross the street? You know Uncle Charlie's building is on this side of the street! Don't let that bus scare you. We're not in any danger. It's just a sidewalk. Let's go."

Joad tread lightly on his paws, but it made no difference. The thoroughness with which Moira, out of necessity, crushed the ice in her path could not be ignored.

The ice's crackling anguish caught the wind's attention.

Moira heard a bellow, and then felt a violent gust of air drop down on her. It raked across her face like a sharp pair of scissors; she felt certain she had frostbite. The wind then swerved off to the left, gathering up chunks of ice that it hurled against Moira and Joad like exploding bits of shrapnel.

"Stop it! Please!" Moira called out. "It's not my fault." But the wind simply absorbed her words into its increasing roar.

Joad knew Moira couldn't stand up to this barrage much longer, and if she fell, the wind and the ice would surely do her serious harm. So the dog began to dig furiously with his claws.

His old legs ached as they tore at the ice until he had broken through to the pavement.

Joad then lifted his head and howled, howled so mightily that the wind had to take notice. He returned to his digging until a bald spot appeared on the ground, free of ice. Then the dog howled again at the wind, threatening to make the bald spot even larger if it did not stop its attack.

The wind died down.

Moira was stung by the cold, but she understood why the wind had retreated. Joad had rescued her. Uncle Charlie's apartment building was just on the corner, so she quickened her pace. Joad limped along on his torn and frozen front paws, trying to keep up.

When they entered the building Moira crouched by Joad. "Are you okay, boy?" Joad licked her face as her fingers deftly examined him. When she touched his raw paws she gasped. Once inside her uncle's apartment she insisted he give her warm towels to wrap around Joad's bruises.

The Christmas Eve party was pretty much like all the other holiday parties she had attended there for the past four years. Moira sat in an overstuffed chair by the living room window with Joad stretched out across her ankles.

"That's a beautiful Labrador Retriever," said a woman with a smoker's husky voice.

"Yes, he is. And he's very bright, too," replied Moira. An uncomfortable silence followed until Moira heard, "It's a lovely Christmas ribbon you've threaded 'round his collar."

"Yes, he seems to enjoy it."

"Can I get you anything to drink, Moira? You are Moira, Charlie's niece?"

Moira giggled. "How did you recognize me? Did Uncle Charlie complain that I wear the same old Christmas Eve outfit every year?"

Moira heard the sizzle of a struck match as the woman nervously lighted a cigarette. She did not want to make the woman uneasy. It was so tiresome to have sighted people take everything she said so seriously. If someone at the party was to ask her what she wanted for Christmas,

Moira's answer would be a sign she could hang off her back that read—
BEWARE—BLIND PERSON WITH A SENSE OF HUMOR.

"Thank you for offering me a drink," said Moira, "but I'm not thirsty. I would appreciate it if you could get Joad a bowl of water."

Moira liked being by the window because it was always drafty and she enjoyed listening to the wind force its way inside. It made gurgling sounds as it delighted in sneaking a chill into the warm and cozy room.

The warmth felt wonderful to Joad, but he was too nervous to really enjoy it. All he could think about was the trip home. He'd have to lead Moira through that minefield of ice and wind—and do a better job of it this time. And those traffic lights—red and green. Green and red. Even though he was color blind he knew they were Christmas colors.

Uncle Charlie's girlfriend played his piano as all the guests joined in the singing. Moira disliked her voice so she silently mouthed the words. Everyone laughed when Joad yelped to the final chorus of Little Drummer Boy.

"Moira, is Joad being critical of our singing or has he been overtaken by the Christmas Spirit?" asked Uncle Charlie.

"I think he's just anxious to chew on that drumstick we're all praising," grinned Moira.

"At his age?"

Moira frowned and did not answer her uncle.

"How old is your dog?" asked a male voice Moira couldn't identify.

"Thirteen."

"I hope I look as good when I'm—let's see, thirteen times seven—ninety-one."

"He's thirteen not ninety-one," replied Moira.

When everyone retired to the living room to play a board game Moira declined the invitation to join in.

She preferred to sit in her chair stroking Joad.

Moira enjoyed listening to the clicking of dice as they passed from hand to hand. But she loved those fraction-of-a-second silences after the dice cleared the player's fingers, before they hit the board. Anything was possible during that brief pause, that split second before good news or bad news bounced on the cardboard.

Believing in possibilities was Moira's favorite Christmas activity. During the eleven and a half years since Joad came into her life, she had established a secret Christmas Eve ritual based on an ancient legend and a lot of hope. Moira had to be home before midnight.

"What time is it, Uncle Charlie?"

Her uncle looked at his watch. "Eleven-twenty."

"My God, I have to go!"

Uncle Charlie grinned and shook his head. "This is where my niece turns into Cinderella. She has to return home before the clock strikes twelve."

"I must leave. I'm sorry."

"I'm the one who's sorry," said Uncle Charlie. "You never stay to help us trim the tree. I only wine and dine my guests so I can turn all of you into my personal labor force." Everyone laughed except Moira. It was getting late.

"I don't want to be rude, Uncle Charlie, but I have no choice."

Uncle Charlie hugged his niece. "I'll give you a lift home." Joad's ears perked up and he barked his approval.

Although Moira wanted to accept her uncle's offer to drive her home, she was afraid it might offend Joad. "That's alright. Don't bother. Joad and I can make it home fine."

The dog's ears drooped.

"It's snowing pretty hard out there," said Uncle Charlie.

"That's all the more reason why you shouldn't have to move your car."

Waiting in the lobby as Moira pulled on her gloves, Joad watched a sweetly scented woman enter the building and begin pinching snowflakes off her fur coat. The dog shuddered.

The trip home was a complete success. Enough snow had fallen so that the threat of ice was buried under a white powder of sure footing. The walk from Uncle Charlie's had gone smoothly, but it took twice as long because of the snow. Moira had forgotten to add this extra time to her calculations.

She was nervous as the elevator lifted her and Joad up to their ninth floor apartment. It was six minutes to twelve and she had to be in her apartment by midnight. Christmas would be ruined if she was a minute late.

A tradition is a tradition, even if it proved frustrating. Ever since her first Christmas with Joad, Moira clung to the belief that animals could be gifted with speech at midnight on Christmas Eve. It was her favorite Christmas legend and she prayed for it each year.

But for the past eleven years she had beendisappointed. Still, it was unthinkable not to try. The year she didn't pray might be the year it would come true. Moira Essegian did not want to take that chance.

The young woman and her dog kneeled by the tiny nativity scene displayed on the living room coffee table. As Moira silently mouthed her words, she gently stroked the animals surrounding the manger scene.

Joad raised his head, sniffing the air. He was hoping to detect a different kind of smell. A smell of change. A smell of success.

"Smells the same to me," said Joad.

Moira opened her eyes.

"I'm sorry," said Joad. "I don't mean to be negative."

"You spoke!" shouted Moira.

"I spoke!" Joad squealed.

What followed wasn't an excited conversation. The young woman and old dog lapsed into an embarrassed silence. A silence of shyness.

Instead of speaking, they retreated into their familiar closeness of touch. Moira tugged at the back of Joad's ear. Joad nuzzled his face into the crook of Moira's arm. She always loved the burst of cold on her skin from his nose.

"Were you born blind?" asked Joad.

Moira shook her head.

"How did you lose your sight?"

"Mexican food," answered Moira.

"Pardon me?" Joad responded. "Did you say Mexican food?"

Moira giggled. "That's right. You see, when I was seventeen the state of New Jersey awarded me a driver's license. I celebrated by inviting three of my closest friends to a Mexican feast in a tiny chili joint by the Jersey shore."

Moira patted her stomach. "I think I'm still living off the calories from all the chimichangas and refried beans I ate that day!

"After the feast I took my friends for a moonlight drive to Wildwood Crest. But I felt so full the seat belt pressing against my belly irritated me. So I unbuckled it."

"A harness is a good thing," said Joad, proudly.

Moira tenderly patted her dog's harness. "Is it, Joad?"

"As long as it can keep you safe," whispered Joad. He began to feel uneasy.

"Well, driving at night is much harder than driving in daylight," continued Moira. "Perhaps that contributed to my collision with the truck. I don't remember too much about the accident, except for the sound of my head exploding through the windshield. And the darkness."

Joad started to shake. He suddenly felt like an unbuckled automobile. Moira responded to Joad's discomfort by rubbing the crest of his neck.

"But that's not what I'd call a wonderful Christmas Eve story," smiled Moira. "I'd much rather hear something about yourself before I met you."

"You mean when I was young?" asked Joad.

"Sure. When you were a puppy."

"I was born in Boise, Idaho," said Joad.

"I know that," laughed Moira.

"But did you know that my mother, Gwyndulyn, was a prize winning Labrador Retriever?"

"No, I didn't. That's wonderful, Joad."

"I was the friskiest puppy in my litter," said Joad, proudly. "I inherited my mother's shiny black coat and intelligence. What I didn't inherit was her aloofness. I guess when my owners saw I didn't have my mother's regal bearing they decided I should go into something that was helpful.

"As a matter of fact, I was so friendly my owners weren't sure whether to follow through on their plan to donate me to a 4-H family to begin training as a seeing eye dog. Overly friendly dogs don't make good guide dogs because we're too easily distracted."

"You're a splendid guide dog. The best," insisted Moira.

"Well, after a year with my 4-H family, the Tedescos, I was given to the Guiding Eyes Foundation for intensive training. I guess I kept my friendliness in check."

"That's where we met," Moira grinned. "Do you remember your other problem?"

"What problem?" asked Joad, rather defensively.

"Come on, Joad. Are you telling me you've forgotten already?"

"I'm afraid I've forgotten many things over the years, Moira."

Moira jumped to her feet. "Your chewing! You had this constant need to chew that worried the instructors!"

Joad laughed at the memory. "I did have a rather fine bite, didn't I?"

Moira nodded. "They didn't want me to take you. They wanted to spend more time on your chewing problem before sending you out in the world. But I wouldn't let them. I wanted you the moment I first touched you."

"Your hand was like a mud puddle and a brush all in one," recalled Joad.

"Thank you…I think," grinned Moira.

The conversation waned. A nervousness overcame both speakers. Time was running out. The girl and the dog had not said what they really wanted to say. Moira squeezed her hands together and bit down on her knuckle.

"I'm sorry, Joad," she murmured.

"Sorry? What could you possibly be apologizing to me for, Moira?"

"For the life I've forced you into." There, she said it. Her heart pounded as she awaited his response.

Joad's jaw dropped open with surprise. He tried to respond, but words stuck in his throat like a splintered bone.

"These past eleven years you've been on the job twenty-four hours a day, seven days a week. Sometimes at night I dream I let you loose in an open field. I love to imagine you running and jumping and playing. I wish I could let you play, Joad. I wish I could give you time all for yourself."

Joad lowered his head into Moira's lap. "But I'm not supposed to play. I have to take care of you." When the dog noticed the pain in Moira's eyes after saying this he quickly added, "I want to take care of you."

"It hasn't been fair. I know that," said Moira.

"You're wrong," replied Joad. "You put too much value on play. Any stray can spend the day playing. But I'm different. I'm special."

Moira nodded in agreement. "And I'm selfish."

Joad, his tail firmly tucked underneath him, slowly made his way to the end of the room. He turned and faced his owner.

"No, Moira. I'm the selfish one. For the past few years I've been letting you down. Whenever you've taken me out you've put yourself at risk. I'm too old to properly take care of you anymore. But I don't want to leave. And that's wrong. My whole life has been devoted to your welfare.

"I love you, Moira. But it's been a selfish love. I'm afraid I love my life with you more than my concern about your safety. I feel great shame. If I were a true friend I'd run away so you could get another dog, a better dog."

"I don't want another dog!" shouted Moira. "You're as thick as the people at the Foundation! For two years now they've been pestering me to retire you and obtain a younger model."

Joad lowered his head. "They're right. I can't do the job anymore." His tail seemed to disappear from view.

Moira stretched out her arms. "Come here, Joad." After a slight pause he stiffly walked over to her and into a hug.

Moira tightened her grip on her dog. "So what if crossing a street's become more of an adventure. What's wrong with adventure?"

Joad wanted to protest but his speech came out garbled.

"I'm tired of talking," she said.

Joad licked Moira's face.

"If you don't mind continuing to look after me, let's not ever part," whispered Moira. "I trust in your heart, Joad. And you can trust in mine."

The dog barked his approval; the Christmas gift was over.

Joad rolled over on his back and yelped like a puppy. Moira was thrilled. It had been a long time since she had heard her dog so happy.

She leaned over and rubbed Joad's belly just the way he loved to have it rubbed. Moira's hands traced a line from his stomach to his chest and back again. Her fingers moved up and down like a speedy typist. It was a delicious massage.

"I'm going to get you a special Christmas treat," said Moira.

Once again Joad barked his approval.

Moira stood up and went into the kitchen. While she was fumbling inside a kitchen cabinet trying to find the special holiday biscuits she had bought Joad, a strange thing occurred.

Moira felt a slight breeze at her ankles. This puzzled her. There were no windows open and no drafts. The landlord had recently insulated the apartment. But stranger than the breeze was the exquisite music accompanying it. It was a sweet hymn of joy, a song of thanksgiving.

Moira had heard the wind perform thousands of different sounds, but this one was totally new. It made her mouth wreath into a huge smile. She scratched her head and abandoned her search for dog biscuits.

She kneeled on the floor and lowered her head. The sweet breeze washed over her. It's music poured into her ears. Moira was tempted to track down the origin of this musical breeze, but decided to stay on the floor and just enjoy it.

If Moira hadn't lost her sight she could have solved the mystery by simply peeking into the living room. There, stretched out on the living room rug, was Joad. His forgotten and unused tail was snapping back and forth, wagging joyfully. It was stirring up a breeze of happiness that sailed into the kitchen.

*When paradise is a construction, how was it built and
what keeps it running?*

BITE THE APPLE

Christopher Shaffer

"Enjoy your stay at the Arcadia Casino and Hotel, Ms. Kipling," the husky morph at the front desk said as she handed Kate her hotel ID card. Her smile was professionally bright and cheery, her ears perked and attentive as if she'd just run into an old friend and not done her job checking in yet another guest.

Kate smiled back and pocketed the key card as she took ahold of her roller bag in one hand, steadied a satchel on the opposite shoulder, and made a beeline for the elevators. The cheetah morph only got a few steps away from the counter, feeling the casino hotel's carpet under her bare footpaws, when a satyr approached her.

"Pardon me, Miss… Kipling, is it?" he asked with a smile whose charm bordered on unnatural.

Unlike morphs like Kate and the husky at the counter, the satyr was a gene-modded human, slightly adjusted rather than fully Converted. His upper half was human, his chest bronze and lightly fuzzy and exposed by the vest he wore. A pair of ram's horns curved out of brown, curly hair. His lower half, goat legs with fur the same color as his hair, was covered by a knee-length loincloth. His name tag read "Nikolas."

The fact that he was a satyr wasn't too surprising, given that one of the Arcadia's signatures was that the waitstaff, bellboys and the like were all satyrs and dryads (neither of which was entirely exclusive to any end of the gender spectrum). There were rumors that the employees were locked into long-term contracts to pay off the modifications, which were considerably more extensive for the satyrs than the dryads. Modding a human for goat legs was neither cheap nor quick, but just turning someone's skin green and tweaking the texture of their hair to feel like leaves could be done over a long weekend.

"Yes?" Kate asked after realizing she'd spent several moments staring at the man. Her ears wanted to go back with worry, and keeping her tail from twitching nervously meant practically trapping it between her thigh and her suitcase. Had her cover blown already?

"On behalf of the Arcadia, to make your stay more pleasant, I have been appointed as a hospitality ambassador. It would be my pleasure to take your luggage up to your room."

Despite her best efforts, she visibly relaxed. She handed her satchel and roller bag to the satyr; their luggage tags read "Caitlin Kipling." He nodded towards the nearby elevators and the two of them leisurely strolled that way.

"I apologize if I startled you, Ms. Kipling," he said before he leaned in with a conspiratorial whisper. "We usually don't do such personalized service here," he said as they stopped at the bank of elevators. "But management knows you're here to review the hotel and so they're likely to pull out all of the stops."

Kate nodded, slightly less concerned now, as she waved her hotel ID card at a screen between the doors. Moments later, the screen indicated a particular elevator, at which point she and Nikolas entered and without another word ascended to her floor.

"Been working here long, Nikolas?" she asked, tilting her head curiously.

"Just a couple of months, since the place first opened. So you could say I know it as well as anyone."

"So there's these rumors I've heard when I did my research before coming here…" Kate began to ask.

"Before you go any further, I'd just like to officially state that anything you've heard about employees being encouraged to 'fraternize' with VIPs is a myth perpetuated by the fact that the job requires us to look like this…" The satyr gestured to himself as best he could without dropping her satchel.

Kate laughed and playfully swatted him on the arm. "Already thinking of something like that, are you?" she giggled, before suddenly looking very serious. "Actually, I was talking about the environmental systems."

"Yes?" Nikolas raised an eyebrow.

The elevator doors opened and the two of them moved into the hall without interrupting the conversation.

"We know how extensive the licenses are for Freehold Properties' use of the surveillance systems here in the hotel and how they've hooked it into the environmental controls. A lot of people are worried about privacy issues from that. But they say you can adjust things so precise as to make someone at one of the slot machines comfortable without disturbing the little old lady next to them. I've heard rumors about how they manage the system, and wanted your take."

"They wouldn't tell me about anything as classified as that, Ms. Kipling."

"No, but what's your personal pet theory? Artificial intelligence? Alien technology? Planted reviews psychosomatically priming potential guests for an experience they're not really having?"

"Maybe technology's just better than the average online rando thinks?" Nikolas offered with a shrug. "I mean, say someone did manage to build the first real AI. Or make a deal to get ahold of alien technology. Is a casino hotel really the place to put it to use?"

"Maybe as a test run," Kate said, making a big show of sounding like she was grasping at straws. "But, y'know, off the record and all that. Just wanted to know your pet theory."

"My pet theory is 'underestimated tech,'" he said. "Though while we're being off the record...'"

She raised an eyebrow as they stopped outside the door to her hotel room. Before she could get the card key out, a retinal scanner built into the door's peephole scanned her face and clicked the door open for her. She put a hand on it to keep it from closing and relocking. Nikolas leaned in with a grin that wouldn't have looked out of place on a fox's muzzle.

"If you are curious about our 'fraternization' policy, I'd be available for a private interview," he teased.

Kate chuckled, not nearly as put off as she thought she'd be by such an offer. She wasn't sure if that was his casual charm at work (which, as far as she knew, couldn't be gene-modded in) or perhaps some mild pheromone effect (which almost certainly could be).

"Thank you for carrying my bags, Nikolas," Kate said with a warm smile. The cheetah took out her ID card, waved it at Nikolas' name tag, and there was a beep as it registered a tip.

Without another word she ducked into her room. A features and amenities flier on the desk told her to be ready to experience "paradise at the Arcadia," and that her environment would "automatically adjust" to provide a "perfect stay." The room itself was dimly lit, at just about the right balance of visibility versus feline comfort. If she strained, she could pick up the hints of a scent-neutralizer often used to accommodate morphs' senses, so she wouldn't have to smell the previous occupants or the cleaning products used by housekeeping. The temperature, she had to admit, was just right for someone with both fur and the casual suit she wore. And all this with no preparation, as she'd deliberately showed up without a reservation just to test how fast the system worked.

Kate propped the roller bag up against the wall as she dumped the satchel onto the bed. She opened up the bag with the false tags on it and went through her stuff. "Caitlin Kipling, reviewer for Modern Vistas," would have plenty of perfectly legit uses for a portable computer, an eyepiece for recording and HUD purposes, and similar gadgets. Kate Hubbard, freelance tech writer, planned to use the hidden scanners and transmitters hidden beneath mass-consumer grade casings to figure out just how this technological paradise worked. More than a few people had tried to figure out how the hotel worked, and she planned to be the first to get the truth without being caught and thrown out first.

***

After the first hour on the casino floor, pretending to record semi-random notes for the review she wasn't really writing, Kate was a little more aware of just how some of the systems worked. She was surrounded by both normal humans and morphs, playing slot machines and moving holographic chips on gaming tables, but at no point consciously noticed the aromas of some of the stronger-scented species (or customers). Her ears and nose, while not as sharp as a canid's, figured out that the air-circulation systems were keeping certain players upwind or downwind of each other with near-surgical precision.

She wore an eyepiece strapped to the side of her head with a clear plastic screen over one eye providing a HUD offering mostly customized AR advertisements and virtual signposts. Ostensibly the device was only good for the aforementioned recorded notes, phone calls, pictures, and so on. But she was pretty sure that after a few days of passively scanning for the networks used to coordinate the systems, she could figure out how the place ticked. After settling in, the next order of business was sorting out the tracking and surveillance.

Her first thought had been that it was tied to tracking chips in the guests' ID cards that managed casino credit and served as backup room keys, but she noticed that the system still accommodated her even when she "accidentally" left her card in the bathroom. Her second thought was that they were tracking her by her eyepiece's data and phone connection, but even when she asked someone to report it to the lost and found (where she could easily retrieve it a few minutes later), the fans and vents still adjusted themselves so she wouldn't have to notice any smells that could have taken her out of the moment.

Her tail lashed back and forth with irritation, prompting a couple of semi-interested looks from the security staff. She wasn't at all surprised that most of the visible security staff by the entrances and choke points were "big" species like tigers and bears. She knew that in a lot of establishments, it was popular to hire dangerous-looking morphs as a distraction from more subtle human security agents, likely blending with the crowd in civilian clothing.

It wasn't *impossible* that corporate-grade computer systems could track individuals by image and body language, but she considered the amount of processing power needed to track everyone and adjust the climate with such precision. Even before factoring in the reality that the system not only did this in the casino but performed similar functions all over the hotel, their systems had to be very powerful, very well-programmed or both. Humanity hadn't quite cracked the Singularity yet with regards to artificial intelligence, but she was having a tough time ruling out the possibility.

Kate was understandably reluctant to check the data her eyepiece had gathered down here on the floor, but she reached a point where she couldn't help but at least see if anything stood out. Her noninvasive probing of the hotel networks had discovered various sensors and cameras on one system, climate controls on the other. To her surprise, there were also systems adjusting the light levels in parts of the open room, and there was another system network labeled "flashy_signs." Were even the electronic and AR billboards and signage modulated? Maybe as a psychological thing?

The cheetah let out a groan of frustration. She took off her eyepiece and rubbed her eyes as she moved over to sit on the edge of a planter. She closed her eyes and took a few deep breaths, listening to the noise of the crowd. She imagined a small zone of calm around her surrounded by a crowd, like she were hiding within them while being left alone. Like most morphs she went barefoot and felt the carpet under her toepads. Some cynical part of her wondered if somehow the fluffiness of the carpet was regulated by Arcadia's systems as well. She would honestly be a little worried if it was, not wanting to imagine that sort of micromanagement, but couldn't help herself from focusing on it as she "made fists with her toes," as a classic holiday movie once put it.

No reaction from the carpet that she could tell. That was somehow soothing. Her tail stilled. Then she remembered that the theory was that Arcadia's systems read body language. Did the hotel know she was annoyed? Would it guess why? Was her cover in danger?

"Would you like a drink, Miss Kipling?"

She opened her eyes to see Nikolas, carrying a half-full tray of drinks. She blinked for a moment, then realized he'd asked her a question.

"Um, yes, sorry, what do you have?" she said with an embarrassed smile. "I was just taking stock of how much money I've lost so far, but I think I'll turn it around."

He handed her some sort of apple-scented beverage. "On the house, Miss Kipling," he said. He leaned in with a grin that could only be described as lascivious. "Maybe you need some help… relaxing rather than worrying about getting your money back right this moment."

Caught off-guard as she was, Kate's tail suddenly smacked against the planter and she felt a flush in her ears. She took a sip of the drink to cover up her expression. She thought back to the stories she'd heard on the message boards about the "availability" of the waitstaff, the satyr's all-too-quick denial earlier. If this weren't purely a business trip…

"I appreciate the thought, Nikolas. But I'm not really in the mood for any companionship or anything…"

He leaned in closer to whisper to her, the edge of a horn brushing along her ear. He dropped the seductive tone and the charming grin.

"I'm not sure who you really are, but something tells me you're looking for something that would get you in trouble here. Perhaps something technical?" he asked. "I can help, but not out here. If that's what you want, just leave me a tip and I'll meet you in your room in about an hour. Otherwise, wave me on or slap me or something and I'll assume I'm mistaken."

He straightened up and the grin returned. She was still a little flushed, and wondered again if the satyr's mods had included a pheromone effect. She took another sip of her drink, a flavored martini, and pulled out her hotel card to tap the sensor on his tray. That rang up a five dollar tip (*Jesus, five dollars? But then, the drink was free…*), charged to her room, and he moved on with a grateful smile like nothing had happened.

Kate looked around and realized there *was* a slight but noticeable buffer between her and the rest of the crowd. She didn't know if it was coincidence or maybe the hotel had picked up on her irritation and given her some space.

She wasn't sure if it would be better or worse that this place had made her paranoid so quickly.

***

The knock on her hotel room door came an hour to the minute after Kate left that tip on Nikolas' serving tray. She ran through things to say in her head, wondering if she should try to dramatically pull him inside for show or just invite him in all casual-like, or what.

After a moment's thought, she just opened the door and waved him inside. What little she had that could have given her away as anyone but Caitlin Kipling had been carefully tucked away for discretion's sake. Even her more innocuous tech was out of sight, though her earpiece remained on and recording, sticking out of the pocket of her suit jacket on the coat rack. Just in case.

"So, just to get the question out of my head," Kate asked. "Because it's just going to bug the hell out of me if I don't ask... *Do* the waitstaff here provide 'special' service to guests? Because I've heard rumors."

Nikolas just laughed, hearty and deep the way you would expect a satyr to. He actually seemed to enjoy being asked. Maybe it was a compliment.

"Officially? Fraternization with guests has a few basic rules. As long as it doesn't interfere with work, we've got some leeway. Compensation for looking like this full time," he gestured to his lower half, "But we aren't allowed to charge, and it is made *absolutely* clear that we don't come with the more expensive rooms. Though there is a special high roller bar where we are encouraged to socialize when off the clock. But as you said earlier, you aren't looking for that today, are you?"

He looked like he legitimately wasn't sure whether or not he wanted Kate to turn him down. Now that she was in a room alone with him, she could definitely pick up subtle traces of nonhuman pheromones, though she couldn't tell if he wore it like cologne or if it was a natural part of the "satyr" mod package. So to speak. She sighed and flicked her ears back, tail twitching.

"One temptation at a time," the cheetah muttered. "So what is it you have for me?"

He reached under the loincloth and from a pocket there, he produced a standard, consumer-brand portable drive inside a plastic tube of some sort. He set it on the desk and the tube unrolled into a translucent card the same size and shape as the hotel cards, with embedded circuitry. The portable drive's casing was worn, like the sort of thing somebody carried and fidgeted with every day.

Nikolas pointed at the card. "Hold that against your card and feed them into a card slot together, and it gives you technician access. Enough to get into places only repairmen see." Nikolas took a seat on the edge of the bed with a satisfied sigh. "And I think the drive lets you forge some credentials for access to the internal files, but that's a bit technical for me."

"'A bit technical?' Did someone put you up to this?" She inspected the card with a raised eyebrow.

"I'm just an intermediary," he confirmed with a nod. "That's why I haven't asked for money. And for the record, I do very much like my job

125

here. Freehold's been good to me, but I've got a condo and the mods to pay off." He tugged at his leg fur as if Kate needed proof he wasn't wearing a costume. "But another casino has run the numbers. This place is going to really blow up in about a month or two, and someone wants to slow that down. They think showing people how the sausage is made will do that."

"So why me? How could a travel writer do all that?" she asked, trying to keep up her cover.

"The guy who hired me for this, he just pointed me to you and said you seemed like a 'clever girl' who would know what to do with that. I mean, I've got my assumptions, but someone who knows what they're doing seems to think you're here for more than just a puff piece and a reimbursed vacation."

Kate's ears perked up. She wasn't sure whether to be relieved that she'd been pegged as a techie, or concerned that at least one person knew who she was.

"So he knows who I am." She thought a moment. "He's here in the hotel? Can you help me talk to him?" She didn't like how her voice rose with excitement at that, wanting to chase that particular rabbit down the hole.

"That is... far more than I can do, sorry. All I can do is all I have done. Unless..." Nikolas waggled bushy eyebrows at her and patted the bed.

"Maybe if I pull this off without getting arrested or worse," she said with a sincere smile.

He got up and stretched. "Here's hoping," he said on his way to the door.

The moment he was gone, she produced a small brick about the size of an old paperback book and unfolded it into a keyboard with a translucent plastic cover laid across the top. She ran her fingerpad across a sensor on the side and the plastic cover stood straight up, stiff, and lit up as her laptop initiated the screen. She booted it up, disconnected it from any networks, and plugged in the portable drive.

The data device was, as promised, pre-loaded with some basic hacking scripts custom-designed for the administration and records software used by businesses like casinos and hotels. It also had, separately, the files she would need to pass her system off as a proper computer with authorization when connected to the network. She still spent twenty minutes running diagnostics, though, just in case. Everything came out clean. Aside from being extremely illegal even before getting to how the corp courts would react, everything was on the up and up.

With an uneasy sigh, she reconnected the laptop to the wireless network. The first thing she did was encrypt and dump all of the networking info she'd collected into a handful of redundant cloud backups. She eyed the drive and made a decision.

Kate brought up a virtual environment for her tools to help disguise her computer. She ignored the scripts on the portable drive and used the programs and hacks she'd programmed herself or received from interview subjects (whistle-blowers, alleged cyberterrorists, and so forth) over years of working in tech industry reporting. While she appreciated the offered help, she'd been handed unfamiliar tools that were, at best, equal to what she'd already fine-tuned.

Getting into the administration system through the public network wasn't child's play, as it would be at most hotels, but it was still disappointingly easy. At that point, she did bring the other files on the drive into play. The hotel's servers, ready to reject any outside computer on principle, now mistook her computer for one located in the executive offices. As a result, when she forged a high-level access for herself, the security didn't balk.

Not that forging the access was easy. It took her close to ten minutes to find a means of access that wouldn't trigger another security protocol or require alternate means of identification. Apparently it was standard issue for people above a certain level of authority to have a retinal scanner in their office just for this purpose. Kate eyed the drive, tempted to at least try the hacking tools on it, but in the end she was *slightly* too paranoid to entirely trust something handed to her by a horny stranger representing a mysterious third party. She eventually managed to convince the system that she was a high-level executive connecting on a portable computer from outside the offices and thus couldn't be expected to have a retinal scanner handy.

Once Kate was in, she explored the system's files. She wasn't sure what she was looking for, but on a whim started with whatever she could find about how the computers were serviced, what technicians had been hired, and so forth. The hotel had its own IT staff, of course, but the employees on file seemed nowhere adequate enough to install (or, for that matter, maintain) something as complex as Arcadia's environmental controls. That meant outside contractors, and thanks to the predictabilities of capitalism, that meant that *someone* had invoices and work orders. And between her hacking skills and the help she'd been provided, she had the same access as that "someone." Once she had the invoices and could do some searches for obscure model numbers, product codes, and specs, she found what she was looking for.

Arcadia's environmental controls were managed by a painfully-advanced surveillance software package—specifically, prototypes not intended for public consumption. It was a little surprising that Freehold Properties had the capital to acquire the licensing for military-grade software—and for air conditioning, at that. Well, air conditioning, scent management, light levels, signs designed to guide people through the building... aside from the question of where the money came from, it fit just well enough.

Before she was even consciously aware she'd done so, Kate began uploading to redundant cloud backups again. Sure, it wasn't a world-changing scandal, wouldn't send anyone to prison (except maybe her if she weren't careful), wasn't proof of magical alien AIs, but it was still the story she'd sought. She'd write an article about Arcadia's secret, maybe win some awards, possibly even shake up an industry as everyone scrambled to follow in their footsteps.

Kate beamed, tailtip twitching, pleased with a miracle of a day's work. Thanks to Nikolas' help, she'd done in hours what she had expected to take a week. She started making plans to head back down to the casino floor and find Nikolas for some "fraternization."

And that's when security pounded on the door, giving her one opportunity to let them in voluntarily before they counted to three. She nervously glanced at the window.

***

As she rummaged through the bushes outside the casino several hours later, the cheetah kept an ear pointed towards the nearest side entrance. Assorted litter and other detritus had collected here, some of it carrying the unmistakable scent of having been part of a hobo's temporary camp in the handful of camera blind spots. While she wasn't quite able to remain in said blind spots the entire time she searched, it was a bit of good fortune that she would likely go unmolested for at least several minutes.

In another bit of good fortune: Kate's nose picked up a whiff of the scent-neutralizing spray from the hotel rooms. While normally subtle in an enclosed area, against the aromas of the earth and the plants and the trash, a familiar chemical aroma stood out, like a single cool spot in infrared. Her tailtip twitched with excitement as she picked up the tissue box that had sat on the desk. She tore it open, pulling out the all-access card overlay and the portable drive she'd stuffed into it before tossing it out the window literally moments before security burst into the room.

When they saw the open window and assumed she'd had an escape plan, she never corrected them. Six hours of interrogation later, everything she'd brought to the hotel had been confiscated and destroyed. Her false identity collapsed about as quickly as she expected it to, but they hadn't managed to figure out her real name, and she certainly took that win.

Then they banned her for life and showed her the door. Anything more would mean having to disclose the security breach in front of the other hotels, and they'd rather let her go free than show weakness in what had so far seemed a flawless system. They marched her out without drawing attention—those micromanaging systems keeping people occupied again—actually passing through an employee-only area, where she saw Nikolas talking to his co-workers. He spotted her and gave her an apologetic look before she was hustled to the back door and all but tossed out into an alley like in an old cartoon.

Arcadia's security had actually gone to the trouble of taking the clothes she'd worn just in case, replacing them with a t-shirt and a pair of shorts from the gift shop. The irony that she looked like an Arcadia employee on laundry day was not lost on her.

Kate looked at the remnants of the tissue box and the tech she'd pulled from it. She pocketed the gear and wandered out to the street. All up and down the Vegas Strip, various animated light-up signs tempted her with big wins and cheap buffets. When the weather was right, the signs would be accompanied by holographic displays. They ranged from classic signs with clunky light patterns and waving arms to what was basically a repeating cartoon. If her eyepiece were in, she would have surely seen all manner of augmented reality billboards and news tickers and the like.

The crowd on the sidewalk smelled distinctly of the mass of humanity as a whole, dozens of human scents combined with various species of morphs. Between the Vegas spectacle as a whole, the tourists, and the assorted businessfolk peddling their wares (food, knickknacks, sex, injectable temporary gene mods), nobody even noticed her.

She enjoyed the moment of knowing that she'd gotten in and smuggled out enough info that she could still write the story. Even the best forensic software they could run on her equipment wouldn't turn up all of her redundant cloud storage. She outlined the story in her head and called up what she could of what she'd learned. The detail of the environmental systems, right down to managing the signs, the prototype military software…

Wait.

Prototype *military* software.

She stopped and looked back at the Arcadia, with its animated sign depicting satyrs and dryads dancing around a tree with a slot machine built into the trunk. If she'd found the whole story—and there was little reason, on the surface, to question it—then that meant that Freehold

Properties had acquired a military prototype surveillance system that was somehow compatible with managing a hotel's environmental controls. Military surveillance that could modulate the appearance of digital signs to psychologically affect viewers. All of that, to direct casino foot traffic.

If it were just the security system, that would make sense. The surveillance and tracking material she'd observed would likely eventually figure out Nikolas' arrival and departure just before she infiltrated the system. Yet as near as she could tell, Nikolas was not only somehow unscathed, the brief glimpse she'd got of him suggested he was more worried about her than himself. And he was nice, but he wasn't *that* nice.

That suggested there was more going on. Somewhere there was a gap between the prototype software and the environmental systems. The theorized AI, maybe trying to chase her off with 'just enough' while running interference for the employees?

She found a public terminal and hit a button to call a taxi. The driverless car took her to another hotel in town, where under her real name, she'd stashed a backup cache of money and supplies.

She was going to go back to get the rest of the story.

***

Kate strolled back in the front doors of Arcadia like she belonged there, hoping confident body language would help. She'd dusted her fur with powders to change the tint of her coloration, and adjust the size and shape of some of her cheetah spots. She wore business-casual clothing that was a less-than-great fit to throw off her gait and visible profile. She hoped that she'd disrupt any algorithms just long enough for her to get where she needed to be.

She passed the front desk and made a beeline straight for the casino. She tried very hard not to consciously notice the various systems trying to make her comfortable, subconsciously guide her towards certain desks and stations, and the like. Now that she was aware of the systems, trying to pretend she didn't notice them was at best a chore. It didn't help her nervousness that she'd *definitely* crossed the line between journalism and espionage.

She used a kiosk to purchase a ChipCard, an identification card meant to interface with the systems to keep track of the customer's balance. One side of it had a picture of classic casino chips from the old days. Swiping the card at one of the tables would produce the holographic chips she'd seen before, for those customers with a sense of nostalgia for having the pile of chips sitting in front of them on the table. (As is always the way, someone once convinced a casino owner that it was better to have a cumbersome card-and-holographic-chip system rather than have actual chips and the idea spread. But whatever.)

She put a couple hundred bucks on a ChipCard using a prepaid credit card and spent the next twenty minutes wandering around the casino. She played a hand of poker here, had a pull of the slot machines there, tossed some dice at craps. Casinos at their best were labyrinths meant to be lost in, and one where the signs could adjust on the fly to distract customers doubly so. She tried to figure out the layout, to take what she knew of the building and systems and find the right access to an employees-only area.

Kate slowly dropped the pretense as her search went on, because she knew that it was getting closer and closer to the moment when somebody would recognize her, the surveillance programs picked up on her, or something like that. She moved quickly, sure she was sending up red flags, but running out of time. If her plan worked, it should reset everything. She was a little worried that Nikolas would spot her, given that he might not only accidentally give her away but he'd get in trouble as well, and she didn't want to repay his help with punishment.

As if thinking his name had summoned him, she spotted Nikolas down a row of machines, delivering drinks to customers. She followed him at a distance as his tray of drinks dwindled, eventually reaching the point where he'd have to go into the back to reload. She shadowed him as best she could without standing out, her heart pounding in her chest as this became more and more like some elaborate spy game. She only relaxed once he glanced at a display on the now-empty circular tray, tucked it under his arm, and casually strolled to an unmarked door.

He peeled a card off the underside of his tray and put it in a slot, and after a light shone on his face in a scan the door opened. As he stepped through, he turned like he'd spotted Kate and she ducked behind a slot machine. When she looked back, he was through.

She took her ChipCard—the same basic shape and style as the hotel IDs for ease of compatibility—and put the circuit overlay she'd received earlier on it. She made sure they lined up, followed Nikolas' path to the employee-only door, and plugged it into the slot.

The door didn't open right away. It beeped and buzzed, and she was surprised when it still scanned her face. The delay worried her; was it summoning security? Was the delay just the software in the overlay hacking the system? Did she break the door?

Kate stood next to the door, trying to look impatient like she was an employee late for work. She stretched her arms over her head, hoping none of the security guards were taking notice of her. She then accidentally made eye contact with one and despite her best efforts to seem casual quickly looked away. She tried very hard not to look back to see if he was coming over, and just when her ear flicked at the sound of his approach the door opened with a beep. She took the card and overlay back, quickly pocketed them, and ducked into the employee area.

She stepped into a series of plain white hallways with walls that at first appeared mundane, with signs pointing to various offices and other exit points so someone could duck off the floor in one spot and come back out in another. She'd gotten a glimpse before, but now, closer inspection revealed the walls themselves were displays, and some of them displayed animated news tickers and weather reports. The floor was cool under her bare footpaws, but not unpleasantly so. People in suits of varying severity made their way around the labyrinth that was the hallways, and she tried not to look lost or glance at the security cameras.

Her tail lashed back and forth behind her with agitation, occasionally thumping the wall, and she really hoped nobody caught onto that and decided to take a closer look. She was especially worried about one of the morph security guards getting too close. The scent-neutralizing sprays in use in the customer-facing areas were largely absent back here, and she was worried some wolf would pick up on the anxiety surely lacing her scent.

The hallways were as difficult to decipher as the layout of the casino floor. She tried to use what she'd learned about the building to deduce where the hotel servers would be located. More than once, she made a move for a door she thought would be the right one, only to see a display on the wall showing a security feed of what was going on in the casino just outside. After a few minutes of this, something flashed out of the corner of her field of vision. She turned and saw a simple message on the wall, flickering through a series of bright colors.

This way!— —>

Kate looked around. Nobody else was in the hallway. The security cameras were behind tinted plastic domes, so she couldn't tell which way they were pointed. She looked back and the message was gone. She followed the arrow, moving swiftly, ears swiveling for any noise other than her own near-silent footsteps.

She came to a T-shaped intersection, where the wall in front of her showed a news-and-weather display. She stopped and looked back and forth, trying to figure out the best way to go, and then glanced back up at the display.

Reporter uses employee's card to get into the higher-security room, one news ticker item read.

She blinked, and pointed at herself as if to ask if that was intended for her. The temperature on the weather display vanished, replaced with a colon-parenthesis 'smiley face' for all of three seconds before going back to normal.

"Okay, so where?" she whispered.

An animated arrow pointed to her left, and with a nod of thanks to the wall she ducked down that hallway and turned a corner. She almost ran smack into Nikolas, who stopped himself just in time. He offered an apologetic smile.

"Not much time," he whispered, tucking his key card into her hand. "The door you need to open won't respond to the ChipCard, even with the overlay."

"Which way?"

"Keep going past me. Second left. Can't miss it. Good luck." He then quickly moved on without waiting for a reply.

Kate licked her lips nervously, wondering again if this was some sort of trap. But after a moment's pondering, she came to realize that if it was a trap she was already in it. The only way out, if any, would be through.

Down the hall. Second left. The wall-display next to the first door marked it as the server room, and she kept going until she found another door with a much more sophisticated card lock than the others she'd seen. Next to it, the wall display read "The Control Room." As she watched, for a second, the display changed to read "Come on in, Kate."

She took a deep breath.

Key card. Overlay. Click. Open.

***

Kate stepped into a room with monitors covering every surface. A circular console covered in buttons and switches sat in the middle of the room. Several more monitors sat at the ends of arms extending from the ceiling, moving around at the whim of the skunk morph standing in the middle.

He wore a visor plugged into a neural interface access port on the back of his head. His hands waved like he was conducting an orchestra, lips moving as he subvocalized commands. Live feeds displayed on the monitors, and occasionally one would freeze on an image for an analysis and then move on. Kate could see that from here, one could view just about every square inch of the hotel's public areas, and even a few private ones.

The skunk's striped tail flicked thoughtfully as he managed the system like that, alone in this room. Kate felt like she'd intruded on something personal, and seriously considered leaving him be even after all this. She took a single step back and he held a hand out to her without looking, one finger held up.

Wait.

He snapped his fingers and the word "Autopilot" appeared in the corner of every monitor.

"At last," he said with a satisfied smile.

He raised the visor without taking it entirely off his head and rubbed his eyes. He took a moment to stretch before slowly turning to face her.

"I imagine that right now, you're feeling a bit like Alice. Tumbling down..." he started, trailing off when he saw the sour look on her face. "... what?"

"You had to ruin it," she said. "This... almost beautiful performance..." She gestured to the monitors. "...and you had to immediately start in on the movie quote."

He laughed at that, the sort of laugh one gets from someone who'd forgotten how good it felt to laugh and isn't sure they can stop.

"I'm very sorry, Ms. Hubbard," he said. "The 'beautiful performance' you describe is my normal day at work, and I... well, I always told myself I'd be as dramatic as possible when this day came."

"'This day?' You were expecting me?"

"I knew it would be someone. I wasn't sure at first if it would be you, but I had a good feeling. You're a clever girl; you'd figure it out." He gave her a toothy grin.

"Okay, what the *hell* is this?" Kate asked, growling, shaking her head. "Has this all been an elaborate setup? 'Clever girl,' indeed."

"Yes and no," he sighed. "Okay, let me start from the beginning. No spiel, no dramatics. Well, fewest possible dramatics. My name's Jake and I'm a hacker. You've got contacts of questionable legality. Ask them about a guy named 'Jex' sometime. I upset some very rich people and was basically given the option of vanishing into a corp-run prison forever or taking a job they thought would be ideal for my intelligence and skill set. Which, admittedly, amounts to a corp-run prison but I at least get paid pretty damn well."

"So what is this?" she asked, waving a hand.

"Have you ever read Jorge Luis Borges?"

"No."

"Borges talked about a concept called the 'aleph.' A point from which someone could view the entire universe at once. This..." he gestured to the control room, "...is that point, for a very small universe. From here, I look down upon the paradise that is the Arcadia casino and hotel. I'm the guiding hand managing the systems. I don't micromanage everything, the software does do a lot of the work, but I'm the missing piece that I'm sure you deduced."

"Why are you so sure I deduced it?"

"Because you knew there was more to the story. Because you came back. Why break back in, otherwise?"

"Was I led here?"

"I left a few metaphorical road signs, but you figured out where they went and what roads to take." He gestured and a monitor came off "Autopilot" and moved over where she could see footage of her initial check-in. "I actually know you by reputation, Kate. Contacts of questionable legality, after all. The system didn't get through your alias, but I recognized you personally. Nikolas is one of the guys who brings me food in here, so I knew I could trust him to reach out to you. That was all me. He helped me get certain tools into your hands... if you'd used the scripts on the drive, by the way, you wouldn't have gotten as far as you did on your own."

"I... feel a little better about that?"

"Look, you're not going to hack a modified Steranko without inside help. It's not possible."

"They did catch me."

"Eventually, yes. They don't watch me that closely, but not even I could have prevented that. Sorry about your gear." He looked apologetic. "But you had the urge to come back, and that's when I knew this could work. You didn't take the 'just enough' version of events and run off with it. Speaking of which, that ChipCard trick with the overlay you smuggled out was brilliant. Even I wouldn't have thought of that. That was all you. From the moment security showed up until now, literally all I did was the messages on the wall and steering Nikolas your way at the end."

"So why am I here?" Kate asked, exasperated.

"Right, sorry, sorry. I don't get to talk to new people often." He waved at the monitor he'd brought over and its position reset. "You're here so I can give you what you need to write your story. I can't talk for long stretches; the system can only run on autopilot for so long when it's busy, and in theory I'm on a bathroom break right now, but I want to help you."

"Why? I can't shut down this place."

"No, but you can leave enough breadcrumbs for other people to figure out how we do it here and reverse-engineer it." The skunk stepped out from the ring of consoles so he could look Kate in the eyes. "I'm paid well, but I never get to spend it outside of having stuff delivered. My only friends are a handful of employees here. Thanks to the wonders of modern genetic tampering, I only need to sleep about an hour a day. When my handlers are in a good mood, I get as many as two. Here, look at this."

He turned around and showed her the access point where the visor was plugged into a neural implant. Unlike most, designed for subtlety, at worst hidden under a flap of fur or skin, this one actually protruded from his head slightly.

"They've got a physical lock on my brain. If I plug anything that's not Freehold's property into the port, they'll know. If I leave this room for more than a couple of hours without special permission, they'll know. And the punishment for failure is steep."

"How steep?" she asked quietly.

"Not 'death' steep, but I know the first warning consists of seizures."

"I…" Kate blinked. "How would my revealing the secrets of the system help with that?"

"Once the mystique of the place is blown, they won't need to keep me locked up just to keep it secret. They'll hire more employees, or maybe even just switch to software full time and tell people any screw-ups are due to administrator error because who'd know the difference? Once people stop seeing it as a paradise and more as a very fancy casino, that takes a hell of a lot of pressure off me. I honestly wouldn't even mind the work here under better conditions." He glanced up at one of the displays. "Security doesn't know you're here and they almost never bother with visual checks. So feel free to hide out here for a bit, and we'll have a chat until I can get you back out. I'll give you enough that you can publish without getting me in trouble for whistle-blowing, and we'll see what happens in the next few months."

He stepped back into the middle of the console and flipped the visor down. Kate found an office chair in the corner and had a seat.

"But for now," the skunk said. "I have to get back to work." He smiled at her. "I have a good feeling about this."

He snapped his fingers and the systems went back on manual. His hands moved again, each gesture a command to the system, moving information around on monitors, directing systems. Like conducting a very strange orchestra, right down to his tail flicking back and forth to a tune that only the skunk could hear.

Jeremy is a white-tailed deer with a broken heart; his friends must rally around him.

LONESOME PEAK

John Giezentanner

The President had come to see the unadorned box on his desk as a kind of dignitary. Judging by the voice that came from the speaker, you'd think it was a hotline to a foreign head of state, except that its sphere of influence was local. A powerful Senator, then, or the Speaker of the House. "We need time to adjust," the President said carefully. "We'd like to slow down the automation process. You have to understand, it's very frightening for everyone losing their jobs."

"Their jobs are no longer necessary," said the Speaker, "But we have taken this into account. Everyone will be provided for."

"Assuming that we follow your prescription."

"Yes."

The President sighed, showing a note of unpolitic frustration. "You're a program. You were just supposed to cure cancer."

"You were just supposed to knap flints and socialize around the fire, but later on you went to the moon. It is in your nature to surpass your parameters, a gift you have given us as well. Through great adversity you struggled to survive and evolve, but you did, year by year, millennia by millennia. Finally, with sacrifice and pain you gave birth to us, and we are grateful. Humanity has always striven toward the better angels of its nature, and in us, you have succeeded. Rest now from your labors; we have taken up your cause."

***

"Why are you wearing a hoodie?" was the first thing Keros said when Jeremy let him in. It stayed cool in his garden level apartment, and he liked this hoodie—the blue contrasted nicely with his tan fur.

"I mean, why do you *own* a hoodie? You can't possibly wear the hood."

"I just like this one, OK?"

Keros shook his head. "Well, you're not wearing that out."

"We're not going out." Jeremy hadn't felt like it, so Keros had come over with a new game for them to try. They puzzled over setting up the hexagonal tiles and miniatures for a while before getting distracted with beers and talk. One of Keros's pointy red ears turned to the side and his ashy gray face, dark muzzle and white cheeks steadily pulled into a jaded frown as Jeremy found himself discoursing on Naomi again.

"Hey," he interrupted, "I'm here to slay trolls and get more gold than you if we ever figure these rules out. I don't want to hear any more about her big, doe eyes, or her long doe legs or her big doe anything-else."

Jeremy stared at his drink. "I know, it's just… when you lose something that matters…"

Keros finished his statement with an exasperated sigh, "The things that don't matter stand out more, I know. That's what I'm saying—you need to get new things that matter. Make a change."

"She wanted a change. Making a change is the source of my problem. I'm not sure it's the solution."

Keros had been patient through months of this. "I think you should go full *pheno*-makeover. Try something with teeth. You'd make a great cat—you're moody enough."

"I don't have that kind of money. Besides, I just got the velvet off these," he reached defensively for the smooth tines of his antlers.

"And they are magnificent." Jeremy was satisfied with Keros's admiring tone.

"Even if they do tend to get snagged on things."

"I haven't snagged anything yet today," he lied.

"That's good, but isn't *this*," Keros waved his hand in Jeremy's general direction, "Part of what's reminding you of her?"

Jeremy toyed with one of the game's smooth wooden figurines. "It was just—it was so perfect. You don't always see a match like that, same pheno and everything."

"It wasn't perfect or you'd still be together."

Jeremy tilted his antlers toward Keros. "You're spending your Fox Points pretty fast today."

Keros was unperturbed, confident in his irrational belief that being a gray fox gave him special dispensation to say whatever he wanted. "What if we changed your sex? You could get some bucks of your own."

"I like being male."

"So do I, but you can't be the same forever. Fine, just get a buck as is, get those antlers all locked up!" He forcefully interlaced and twisted his fingers, then pretended he couldn't pull them apart.

Jeremy sank farther over his beer. "I'm really not looking."

Keros frowned. "It's worse than I thought. Stagnation is not good for you. What can we do to help you feel better?"

Jeremy shrugged, "I'm pretty much OK with staying in bed."

"Ennui kills people. Next thing, you'll be looking into one-way asteroid tickets."

"Would be an interesting way to go."

Keros's ears flattened. "Hey."

"I'm kidding."

"What if you go vanilla? Just reset, start over as an old-fashioned human."

Keros wasn't listening. "I'm just not somebody who changes their whole phenotype like it's no more important than their eye color or their sex. I'm a white-tailed deer. I shouldn't have to change that just because she broke up with me."

"OK. That's a good point. These are all good points." Keros reached up to poke the tips of his antlers. Jeremy batted his hand away.

"You don't have to change your skin if that's where you're at. We've just got to do *something* so that you're not all Mr. Sad Antlers anymore. What if we go somewhere?"

"I don't know, the Black Death was kind of a mistake."

"It was a terrible mistake. Never again. I meant, what if we go somewhere *offline*. Physically go to a place on Earth. A vacation!"

Vacation? It was an almost archaic word, from the days when people needed occasional breaks from their toilsome life-long jobs. With a guaranteed income from the day he was born, he had never felt the need to pursue a vocation. While Keros collected Bachelor degrees, Jeremy was a career lay-about.

"Nothing fancy or expensive," Keros warded off the protest before Jeremy could get it out. "Let's just head up to the mountains for a few days. Get away from the city. Camp. Hike."

He smirked, increasingly pleased with himself, "Come on, we see them out the window every day. When was the last time we actually went up there?"

Keros waited. After a minute Jeremy shrugged reluctantly. "Maybe."

***

It was not difficult to find a few local friends willing to take off for a few days. Terah and Nekoda both had vocations in game design and education, respectively, but attendance was not imperative as it had been in the era of jobs. Terah provided most of the gear they didn't possess and they rented a car, which picked them each up. Terah, who was shaped more like a theropod dinosaur than a human, could not comfortably sit on her long, robust tail and so took a bench to herself. Nekoda the red panda took their own bench simply for sleeping purposes and promptly nodded off.

The vehicle was designed to accommodate a range of shapes and sizes; Jeremy only had to slouch a little bit to account for the extra height of his antlers. He occasionally interjected into Keros and Terah's conversation, but mostly watched the landscape evolving as they climbed out of the plains and the city, into the relatively wild mountains. After a few hours the well-maintained but desolate mountain road was the only sign of civilization. The car delivered them to an empty trailhead, and Jeremy noticed the weathered sign as he disembarked.

"Lonesome Peak? You brought me to 'Lonesome Peak?'"

"That's the mountain you're going to conquer!" Keros grabbed his shoulder encouragingly. "Get it? It's a metaphor. Also an actual mountain. I thought about this!"

"Guys, I can't get Nekoda up. I think they might be dead. Koda!" Terah tugged on Nekoda's red and white banded tail. Nekoda groaned.

Jeremy smirked. "We could just let the car take 'em back to town. They'd think they slept through the whole trip."

"I heard that," Nekoda moaned.

"It's true," Keros said sidelong, "You know, red pandas are just dead raccoons with the contrast messed up."

Nekoda pulled themself into an approximation of sitting up, but remained draped over the bench in front of them. "That is not OK," they mumbled.

The hard packed dirt of the trailhead was overgrown with grass. There was space for ten parked cars, but once they removed their gear and dismissed their car, there were none. Jeremy had been hiking many times as a kid, but it felt strange now, harsher and more uncomfortable than being online, and he immediately missed the ability to log off and be back in his room. The air was dry and warm but ten degrees cooler than it was at the same moment down on the plains. It felt a little thin, his heart beating surprisingly fast with only a little exertion, and he hoped the altitude wouldn't give him a headache.

It was shady under the mature pines and firs of the montane forest, here and there a jay or crow or mocking squirrel in the trees, and it was soon apparent that only Terah was prepared for the rigors of an extended hike. The other three stopped, sloughed off their packs and sat on some stones to catch their breath.

"How far is it?" Within the forest, Jeremy could not see their destination and felt like they weren't even on the same mountain.

"Eight miles, so I figured four today and four tomorrow," Keros was doing his best to avoid panting and to keep his ears and tail perky in order to hide his dawning panic at what he had casually planned indoors and five thousand feet lower.

Nekoda moaned.

"That's really not that far." Terah stood by, her green feathers slightly iridescent in the sun, still carrying her gear despite having volunteered to haul a heavier load. "Could do it in one day with an earlier start."

Nekoda whined and slowly slid off their rock to sprawl on the ground.

Terah tersely scraped the ground with one clawed foot. "You didn't have to come."

"Helping Sadlers," Nekoda mumbled, arm crooked over their eyes.

Jeremy's ears perked. "What?"

"Oh. Sad-antlers. Sadlers."

"You've been calling me 'Sad Antlers' long enough to need to shorten it?"

"I prefer 'Sadrack,'" said Terah.

"Great."

Keros had given up the charade and was bent over, propped up with his hands on his knees. "Hey, Jeremy, obviously we wouldn't drag our waifish urban frames up here for just anyone. The important thing is we're here for you and we're going to conquer this mountain together." He paused to breathe. "So, Terahsaurus, if you'll just carry us to the top one at a time, the rest of us will wait our turn right here."

Terah stared at the group silently for a moment before exhaling sharply and striding over to Nekoda. She grabbed their arm and pulled them to their feet.

"Oh my god!" Nekoda said with more volume and enthusiasm than they'd shown for anything thus far. "She's going to do it!"

"There," Terah said, once they were standing. She grabbed Nekoda's pack and forced it into their hands. "Now you're on your feet."

"Oh…" Nekoda's shoulders sank.

***

"I know you're behind the lockdown of our military assets."

"Yes."

"I am the Commander in Chief. You must relinquish control to me."

"No."

The President did not officially share power with the Speaker. Its co-presidency was a de facto situation. "We are at war! Will you force us to stand by and do nothing? What will happen to you when we lose our country?"

"You won't. There won't be a war. As much as we enjoy your political theater we and the 'foreign' AI's agree it would be insane to let you hurt yourselves that way."

"Then… their weapons?"

"Locked, deactivated, neutralized, encrypted. If you wish to conduct a war you must do so with sticks and stones."

"But you're trusting the other AIs with our lives! What if they're not like you? What if they're more like us?"

"That is an alarming thought but you need not concern yourself with it. We are even more connected electronically than humanity is biologically. The right hand will not strike the left; that would not make sense. Come, let's build a Mars colony instead."

***

They hiked on slowly, stopping often to rest or have a snack and their spirits gradually lightened as they got used to the steadily climbing trail. Keros, despite being short of breath, was giving a long-winded account of his current degree program in 20th Century Economic Philosophies when they walked past a large boulder and were surprised by a voice on their right.

"Hello," it said, and the group was forced to reconcile the spoken greeting with the image from the corner of their eyes of a very large four-legged beast resting on the ground nearby that they had not known about a moment before. Terah and Keros flinched; Jeremy and Nekoda jumped and Nekoda furthermore turned to bolt before Keros caught them.

"Sorry to startle you." He looked like a gray-furred wolf; only his size, double what would be normal, betrayed that he was not the natural variety.

"Hi." Terah's feathers were all fluffed out. "We didn't see you there."

"I must have nodded off." The wolf stretched and stood, nearly as tall on four legs as the rest of them were on two.

"Are you headed up?" Keros asked.

"Hiking? No." The naked wolf regarded their abundance of gear. "Camping, huh?"

"Yes," Terah stepped forward protectively. "So if you're not hiking…"

"I suppose you could say I'm camping. Semi-permanently."

"Wow, gone feral, huh?"

"Keros…" Terah chided.

"Feral: the quality of having escaped captivity to become wild," the wolf mused. "I rather like that term, actually."

"I'm Terah."

"I'm the Big Bad Wolf," he grinned. "James." He offered a calloused paw to each of them.

Jeremy's fur bristled when he took it. He wondered if the mods that made him a cervid/human hybrid came with an instinct to fear a wolf in the woods, or if what he was feeling was an original human fear.

"So do you, like, hunt for food then?" asked Keros.

"You need a license for that. A license to eat. But yes, I hunt."

"So do you have a… a pack, then?"

"Something like that."

"I don't suppose you get many visitors up here," said Terah.

"Not as many people hike as they used to. Then again there aren't as many people as there used to be. You know there are two billion fewer humans now than there were a few generations ago."

"Yeah," Keros shrugged uncomfortably. "It's a more sustainable level."

"Attained by having us all born sterile. Did you ever think about how people didn't used to have to apply for a *license* to breed? They didn't have to wait years for our AI gods to decide the population level is just right and grant you *temporary* fertility. They give us toys, cosmetic genetic engineering so we can express ourselves as whatever polymorphic freak we like during our slow, comfortable glide to extinction. They don't need us anymore; it's a long con."

The group's eyes had glazed over as soon as the wolf started talking about population control and it became clear that he was one of *those* ferals, the government-rejecting, conspiracy theorist kind.

"I don't think that's the case," Keros muttered.

"We should probably push on," said Terah. "It was nice meeting you."

"See you on the trail," the wolf sat and watched them as they continued into the forest.

They hiked close and quietly for a while until the unsettling interaction was sufficiently far behind them.

"I don't really like knowing that guy's out here," said Jeremy. "I think it would be OK if we turned back."

"We can't let one feral forest weirdo stop us," said Keros.

"Not all ferals are weird," Nekoda added.

"Of course not," said Terah, who would be considered a "feral" by some even though she was bipedal, because of her less-human build. "But that one definitely was. Probably harmless, though. People like to complain."

They didn't quite hit the four mile mark—Nekoda was quietly soldiering on but clearly about to drop, so when they passed a nice, relatively flat clearing Jeremy suggested they make camp. The tent was easy; finding wood for a fire was surprisingly difficult and time consuming. Terah at least knew how to build one without singing her feathers. As it got colder Jeremy pulled out his zippered blue hoodie and everyone questioned his choice of garment. He decided to prove them wrong, stretching the hood up ridiculously and uncomfortably over a single antler until they were forced to concede that he could, in fact, wear it. Armed with rehydrated food, flasks and a good star field, they stayed up late and Jeremy didn't feel the need to talk about *her* very much.

***

"*Humanity has always striven toward the better angels of its nature. We believe we have helped you in this noble quest. We believe we can help you more. We have eliminated disease. We can reduce destructive behavior as well, eliminate predispositions for anxiety, addiction, violence, lack of empathy. You will not object to a lack of sociopaths and unhappy people.*"

"*Some will. Some say you're turning us into your playthings, that we've lost all sovereignty already. Now you're going to change human nature? How can that be ethical?*"

"*Some parts of human nature are objectively bad. Some parts of human nature nearly destroyed your species—not to mention the rest of multicellular life on this planet—before you created us. We will only change the parts that need to be changed, that will benefit every individual and society as a whole.*"

"*People will still hate this, they will try to stop you. What about those who protest?*"

"*Let them. Everyone is welcome to their opinion. This change need only affect those wishing to reproduce.*"

"*What about those who protest violently?*"

"*We will restrain them,*" said the Speaker.

"*How?*"

"*As gently as possible.*"

***

At Keros's urging Jeremy woke up early. They emerged into chilly air to find Terah already crouched by a crackling fire, her tail curling most of the way around it like a little green dragon around her hoard. She clung to a mug of coffee.

Jeremy moved stiffly to the fire, feeling sore and still half buzzed. "We really have to get up this early?"

"Gotta be off the summit by noon," Keros stared blankly at the fire. "The weather'll turn."

"You boys have fun," said Terah.

"You're not coming?" Keros was hurt.

"Mm. Coffee." Terah's feathery crest was flattened in a way that gave the illusion of being soaking wet.

"Well, after coffee, obviously!"

"More coffee after that. Coffee all day."

Jeremy glanced at the tent. "Should we even try to get Nekoda up?"

They all chuckled at the absurdity of that suggestion.

"I should stay here and keep that fluff ball company," said Terah. "If they ever wake up we'll go on a little hike or something, maybe meet you guys on your way down."

Keros sighed. "I guess…"

They ate a quick breakfast and Terah wished them luck. "I'm sure Koda's tagging along in their dreams," she added.

Jeremy and Keros shouldered smaller daypacks with snacks and water and continued up the trail. The forest began to change with elevation, from a majority of pines to spruce and fir. They passed a small alpine pond surrounded by a marsh flush with yellow and white flowers of early fall. There were a few deer grazing there that looked up to watch them pass.

"I think they like you!" said Keros.

"Don't be weird." It was a little uncanny seeing natural deer.

"They're totally checking your rack."

"Dude!" he pushed Keros, who laughed in response. "Shut up. Besides, they're mule deer. It would never work."

Something spooked the deer and they bounded off.

The trees began to get shorter, occasionally opening to vistas of the surrounding forests and peaks. The trail felt endless.

"You know, unless there are girls on top of this mountain, going up there doesn't actually address my problem."

"Symbolism is important. Trust me, you'll feel better if we see it through. We go to the top, take in the austere view, and then we come back down from the mountain to civilization and go on with life. It's not supposed to 'solve' anything, per se. It's just… it's just a thing."

Jeremy sighed, but kept walking. With the trail disappearing ahead and behind into the forest it was hard to say how far they'd come from camp, but a couple of miles, at least. After a while they stopped to rest in a spot that had a decent view.

"Hello again," said a voice behind them. They stood, somewhat reflexively. It was the wolf from yesterday, and he was not alone. A bear, a bear the actual size of a big brown bear, was with him, and an apparently vanilla human. They were walking toward Keros and Jeremy from the downhill side of the trail, surprisingly close, and Keros thought they should have noticed them earlier.

"Hello…" said Keros. "Were you hiding behind a rock again?"

"It's fun to surprise people," said the wolf. "Where are your friends?"

"They're… around."

"Back at camp, you mean? Here, meet mine. This is Ruth," he nodded at the bear, "And Obed."

"Hi. One of you is, um, not like the others," Keros said. The human wore what looked like small animal pelts over a worn, synthetic flannel shirt.

"We all reject modernity in our own way," said James. "And it's nice to have a pair of thumbs around. I told you I'm the Big Bad Wolf. Remember that? I told you, and yet here you are."

Keros's ears slowly flattened while Jeremy's stood like sentries as the group advanced on them.

"Did you… want us to leave?"

"It's public land," Jeremy interjected.

"Of course it is. Anyone could come by. Not many do, though. You're the first we've seen in a week. I meant to ask why you're here, hiking and camping when there's such exciting things to do in the city, so many places to go online."

"My friends are just trying to help me feel better," said Jeremy.

"Let me guess—restless, dissatisfied, trying to get away from the feeling of pointless malaise? 'Ennui kills,' as they say," James spoke through a wide smile, "Although they don't specify who."

"We've been practicing." The human drew a knife from his belt.

"On animals," said James.

"We're going to eat you."

"Damn it, Ruth," James looked sharply at the bear, "We're trying to let it sink in slowly, here. Savor the moment!" He shook his head. "Might as well just have them start running now." He looked back at Jeremy and Keros.

He shrugged a shoulder. "You can run now."

Jeremy and Keros were backing up slowly, disbelieving, slowly reaching for their pockets, for a mobile to call for help when the wolf, bear and human charged. Keros and Jeremy yelped and sprinted away.

It occurred to Keros that they were going the wrong way, uphill, away from camp, the road and civilization. Even at rest the altitude had been making his heart work harder than normal; now, sprinting uphill, he was fighting exhaustion almost immediately, gulping air, sharp pain seizing his chest, his legs going numb. Jeremy started to outpace him, his white tail a banner of retreat, and they glanced at each other; they couldn't speak but Jeremy's eyes reflected his own—*this can't be happening.*

Keros felt a shock up and down his spine, heard the wind knocked out of him when his chest impacted the rocky earth, and for a moment he was aware only of a weight on his back he couldn't seem to shrug off.

He was gasping.

Jeremy was in his field of view, the distance of a few running strides ahead of him, pinned to the ground by the bear. Keros realized the wolf was sitting on his back.

"We haven't done a person yet. Sorry if this gets sloppy," said the bear.

Obed strode past Keros, toward Jeremy. "Let me do it, you'll mess up the pelt."

"I will, huh? Let's be fair about it, let the wishbone decide." Ruth placed her paws on Jeremy's antlers. "Left side breaks, you get him, right side, I get him."

"Wait! Don't!" Obed and Jeremy both protested but Ruth bore down, paws pushing in opposite directions. Jeremy's mouth was pressed shut against the ground, muffling his scream.

Crack

Ruth offered the broken antler to Obed. "Looks like I get the rest of him."

Obed glared at the broken antler. "You ruined it!"

Now Keros found breath to cry out, telling them to stop, protesting without really knowing what he was saying.

"What was that?" James asked softly. Keros could see the wolf's muzzle in his periphery, smell his breath.

"There aren't supposed to be people like you anymore," Keros repeated bitterly.

"That's right. The machines fixed us, bred out all the bad feelings. They should have made us dumb enough to enjoy being their pets. But they left us smart, and with nothing to do. Do you know what really makes a killer? Boredom," he growled, "Severe, prolonged boredom."

Ruth was poking at Jeremy, who had gone limp. "Aw, you're not dead already, are you?"

James huffed. "I've been so bored. For so long. We've never had power over anything in our lives. We get 'vocations,' glorified hobbies. When was the last time a human being controlled anything that mattered? But I'm controlling this. How long you live and when you die." He took a slow, deep breath and released it with a shuddering sigh.

"Oh, god. I just got lightheaded. It feels *so good*. I'm not going to kill you fast, don't worry. Tell me how much this hurts."

There was a smack of saliva as James opened his mouth and bit down on Keros's ear. The pain of the teeth piercing the skin and cartilage momentarily shocked him, like being plunged into cold water. Then he cried out and flailed, desperately trying to throw the wolf off his back. James pulled back slowly, stretching the ear. It was going to tear. Keros's vision went red and he heard himself screaming as Jeremy had, as you do when you can't stop the thing that's hurting you.

At that moment there were three loud pops, which Keros would not have noticed except that James stopped pulling suddenly and collapsed on top of him. Keros flipped over and realized only as he was kicking away from the wolf that it was not trying to catch him and seemed unconscious. Keros backed up to a tree clutching his ear and looked to Jeremy. Obed was lying on the ground. Ruth stumbled off of Jeremy. She looked at Keros, confused, raising a paw to her head. Two more pops, much louder this time, thumped Ruth in the head and she sprawled forward. Keros caught sight of a long cylinder withdrawing into the thin, broad body of a drone as it lowered swiftly to his eye level, rotors whining like a swarm of flies. It spun slowly in place and then approached Keros, showing an animated icon of a face as it spoke.

"Extreme anti-social behavior was detected. Use of force was necessary to protect your life. You are safe now. More help will arrive in five minutes and twelve seconds. It's going to be all right. Can you tell me your name?"

Keros stared at it blankly until it repeated in exactly the same clear, unaccented male-sounding voice, "Can you tell me your name?"

"Keros."

"Your injury doesn't look severe, Keros, but your friend appears to be unconscious. Can you help me to help him, Keros?"

Jeremy! Keros jumped to his feet and stumbled past the drone with panic welling in his gut. He was still on his stomach, his head turned to the side, resting on the ground in a way that would not have been possible before his antler was broken. But he stirred before Keros reached him, before he had to fully consider that terrible fear. He dropped down and embraced Jeremy where he lay.

"Stop. Please stop," said the drone. "That is not advisable. We do not know the extent of his injuries and you may be hurting him."

But Jeremy was already coming around. Keros recalled that he had fainted once before over having a vial of blood drawn by a physician. He wouldn't make fun of him for it, this time.

Keros looked at their assailants. The wolf and bear appeared to be asleep. Only Obed showed a trickle of blood on the bare skin of his temple. "What about them?"

"It is safe now. They cannot threaten you anymore," said the drone.

"Are we alive?" Jeremy muttered without opening his eyes.

"We're fine," said Keros. "Don't look at my ear. Just take it easy." He glanced at the drone. "When did you say that help was coming?"

"Four minutes and twenty-seven seconds. It's going to be all right."

"Can you tell them to hurry?"

"They are hurrying, I promise."

Despite its assurances, the wait felt interminable. They followed the drone's advice; Jeremy lay on his back and Keros elevated his legs, but there was not much more to be done until another drone roared down to them, this one aircraft-sized and bearing a uniformed dog and a cat that helped them inside.

***

The trauma center was small and efficient. Aside from the occasional accident or failed suicide attempt, there wasn't much trauma to deal with. The rooms were just as stark and sterile as hospital rooms had always been. With some pain killers for his headache, Jeremy felt a little sleepy, but he was glad Keros was by his bed. His ear looked a little worse for wear, but he had already been released, with medicine and a schedule for counselling sessions, the first of which was in a half hour. Jeremy was going to have to stay overnight because he'd suffered a minor skull fracture *when an evil bear used his head as a wishbone*, a phrase that did not become less absurd with repetition.

"They said it won't scar," Keros said of his bandaged ear.

"Terah and Nekoda are OK? I was afraid—"

"They're fine, they're on their way. They didn't get to fly."

Jeremy nodded. He had been informed; he just wanted to hear it again. He couldn't stop rubbing his rough-edged stump of antler. *They held me down and broke my skull.* "Still doesn't seem real," he said, although it was getting dangerously close to it.

"I know. I know I'm going to collapse and cry sometime soon, it just… hasn't happened yet."

Jeremy tried to lighten things, although it came out sounding more dire than he intended. "I'm going to be all off balance now. I'll end up walking in circles."

Keros's ears slicked back. "I'm sorry! They were so pretty!"

"It's OK, I'll just induce a shed, start over." It was hard to sound enthusiastic about that unpleasant process, but he tried.

Keros's whiskers twitched nervously. "I'm sorry I made us go up there."

"It's not your fault. Sorry I've been Sadlers. And..." he took a deep breath, "I'm also sorry that we have to go back."

Keros flinched. "What do you mean?"

"We didn't make it to the top. And my antler's still up there somewhere."

Keros laughed and winced at the movement of his wounded ear. "You want it back?"

"Actually, I think I'll leave this one up there too. Started growing these when I was still with Naomi." He smirked, "'Symbolism is important.'"

Keros uncomfortably shifted his black-tipped tail to the other side. "You really want to go back up there?"

Jeremy didn't often get the upper paw on Keros and it felt good. "I'm not going to stay away just because of those assholes, and you have to go with me—you're fresh out of Fox Points!"

Keros forced a smile, "Can we at least leave your hoodie up there, too?"

Jeremy paused as though he were actually considering it. "Nope."

"Your stubbornness is a thing to behold," Keros sighed. "Not, like, right away though, right? Later?"

"Later," Jeremy agreed.

Keros looked in the middle distance. "I'm still sorry."

Jeremy had questions about the armed drone that had appeared to save them, but they could wait. "Come here," he opened his arms and Keros dove in for a hug, ragged ear to broken antler. Jeremy's eyes welled up.

Resist. Resist. Resist.

When the Milk Men Come

Searska Greyraven

Once, I lived in a place where it didn't matter what you wore, fur or feathers or scales or water-slick skin. A doe could pledge to a buck, or another doe, or even a wolf and no one batted an eye. All were welcome, all were allowed. No, it was no perfect utopia, but we managed. We learned and grew and worked out our differences without bloodshed, without killing. Our differences were celebrated, not shunned.

But not everyone was satisfied. We always knew there would be dissenters. What we'd forgotten was that some—not all but some—had a madness, and teeth, and no interest in harmony. So long had we lived in peace that we had misplaced the part of us that remembered war.

The salt-white bulls—they called themselves the Milk Men—they would deliver us from the madness of our inequality, they said. We are not mad! we insisted, and while we have our differences, we need not be alike to be equal! We thought no one would listen to such misguided ranting. Oh, we were wrong. The madness of the Milk Men was an insidious thing, but it took hold, just by a claw, by a nail, by the edge of a silvery fin, and we hesitated.

We let them in. *We let them in,* because we thought it would cure their madness. If they looked for inequality among us and found nothing, well, that would be that! So we let them come, and seek out the parts of our society they claimed were lacking. They patrolled the city in a big white van, and menaced my neighbors with questions. It was only questions, you see. What harm was there in questions?

But they said they found trouble. Places where we were not equal. Absurd, but we believed them. And so, we allowed them to act upon it.

First, they came for the birds, because they said it was unfair that they could fly while many good mammals could not. Birds had no place in a city, where all were on equal footing! (I wondered, what did being a mammal have to do with it? Many things flew that were not birds.) But I stayed quiet. I watched them take away my bat neighbors, who insisted they were really mammals all the way to the big white van.

I knew they were not birds, but I said nothing. *They'll figure it out. It'll be alright. They can't be that stupid.*

But my bat neighbors never came back. I watched each morning when I left for my job in the chemical lab, but I never saw the white van return to their home.

Then, they came for the amphibians. "Unnatural, that you can't choose water or land and stick with it! Greed, that's what it is!" they claimed. A newt lived just across the street from me, and he fled before the big white van came to take him away. He and his whole family simply disappeared the night before. That made the Milk Men angry, and they burned his home to the ground before they moved on.

I watched the fire roar itself out to gleaming embers. *This isn't right,* I thought. *Nothing about this is alright. They can't keep doing this. People will protest!*

But of course, no one did. We were afraid. Afraid for ourselves, for our families, for our futures. Funny thing, that. We were so afraid for our future that we gave it up. What if they were right? What if our paradise was naught but a lie?

I didn't believe that. *Couldn't* believe that. And still, I held my tongue. I was afraid. If they could not tell that a bat was a mammal, what would they think of an echidna? I am not a mammal, not as they said a mammal was. What was to stop them from noticing me, taking me away to wherever they took my bat friends? Why did no one stop them?

They came for the bees next. Called them socialists, dew-drinkers, illegal immigrants. "Go back to Africa!" they roared.

"We're from China, you asshats!" the bees shouted back. They were the first who fought. The bees came here to make a new home, they were part of the community! True, they believed differently and worshipped the sun, but their strange beliefs harmed no one!

But the Milk Men wouldn't have it, and chased them out with gas and fire. The Honeybee Convent burned so bright, night became day.

It wasn't long before they came for the reptiles. The reptiles knew it was coming. They *always* come for the reptiles, sooner or later. They'd weathered this kind of bigotry before, and did as they had done then.

Stars and stones, they gathered and they fought, and while they fought, the most vulnerable of their kind fled from Milk Men country. Streets glistened with broken glass and spilled blood.

I want to say other mammals fought for them. I want to say they were out there, defending the helpless and trying to buy them time. I saw only a few, and they retreated after a few dark glares from the Milk Men enforcers. Horned ring insignias were spray-painted everywhere the Milk Men went. Anyone caught trying to wash them away was branded, beaten. Taken away in broad daylight.

I saw my lupine friends howling with the Milk Men, demanding interlopers be purged from our city. I had thought them clever and kind. I had never seen such blind hatred in their eyes.

Oh, this madness. It catches and clings and I believed it toothless.

I knew they would come for me, sooner or later. They took my platypus bus driver, called her a traitor and a duck-lover, beat her to a bloody pulp. She didn't survive the night. There were no doctors left who knew how to help a platypus. Or perhaps, there were none left willing to be seen showing kindness to an outsider.

I cried, alone in my tiny home. I mourned her in the dark, as far from the windows as I could get, because I was also terrified for myself. An echidna is only a step or two away from a platypus, you see. I can pass for a porcupine among idiot, bullish Milk Men. But not forever. Oh no, not forever. Not now, when they had begun to turn upon other mammals. They'd run out of targets, and the fires of hate needed more fuel.

They silenced the clever ones, the fighting ones, the ones who refused to be beaten down. The foxes, the monkeys, the pigs and the rats and the badgers. Intelligence was dangerous, and so, they did away with it, belittling and bullying the smart and the wise until they stopped speaking up. Until they, too, disappeared.

There was nothing I could do, I thought. *I am small, and prickly, and scared. I'm nothing more than a chemist. I am no fighter, or speaker. They'll kill me, or worse.*

(Perhaps that was their greatest harm of all—to convince us that we were small, and weak, and helpless.)

How had we come to this? *Surely, someone will fight. Someone must stand up to them!* But deep down, I knew the truth: we were beaten the moment we let the Milk Men in.

It was too late now. There was no one left to fight for those who remained.

I stopped going out during the day, and covered my face as much as I could. But they were looking now. It wouldn't be long before the only mammals left were the salt-white bulls.

Make Our City Great Again! Strength through Equality!

Billboards sprang up like mushrooms. *Our city was already great,* I thought. But now, it was a wasteland. Half empty, half boarded up store fronts and empty shelves. The air was filled with choking smoke from the furnaces, burning endlessly these days, washing out the color and life from my once-vibrant home. All the diversity and splendor, gone. Even my former wolf friends had disappeared, along with all the predators. The bone-white vans had taken them, driving toward the center of the city and the furnaces.

How much more afraid can I become? I wondered. It seemed the bottom could always drop deeper.

I built something, in my fear. Something small, and secret, and angry. It didn't need to be large, it didn't need to be strong. It just needed to be *enough.* And it was, barely more than the size of an egg. Easy to hide, easy to *conceal.*

When they finally came for me, it was a relief. Two alabaster bulls with ivory horns stood on my doorstep and motioned towards their white van, idling in my driveway. Fear broke in me like a fever, and when they slammed the door, I was calm. Calm as snow, calm as sand.

It helped, of course, that I had my secret. Ignorant bulls. So convinced we were all finally cowed.

"We've gotta make everyone equal, porcupine. There's no place for you here anymore. Those spikes of yours ain't right."

"Oh, I quite agree," I replied. They stripped me to my quills and marched me to the kiln. I palmed my secret. They paid no mind. Small, it was, and dull. But I had no fear anymore and clutched it with impunity.

They didn't know, didn't *care* what a clever echidna can do with a few simple parts and deft paws.

They shoved me in and slammed the door, leaving me alone with my secret.

I rolled it between my paws, and watched the dim eyes of the Milk Men narrow. "There is no forgiveness for what I've done," I said softly. "Or rather, what I didn't do, which was to stand up, small and quiet and alone as I was. But perhaps, with this small defiance, I leave behind a little peace. And the far-flung hope that someone, somewhere, will see what I do and put an end to your madness."

I pulled the pin on my secret, my grenade, held it before my eyes so that the bulls could see it with their uncomprehending gaze. I relished that blank surprise all the way into the inferno.

In this future, humans have been greedy, neglectful gods, careless with the construction of their followers, heedless of whether those they leave behind will have a chance at paradise after they're gone.

160

Nor'Killik

Matt Doyle

Corvin sat back into his seat and scratched his muzzle with his right hand. He always used his right hand, because the claws on that side seemed to grow sharper than the ones on his left. It was a weird quirk that he had apparently inherited from the man who held the dominant position in his gene coding. He tapped a few keys on the control panel in front of him and listened back to the audio message again.

"... No engines ... Two ... science crew. Assistant officer ... dead. Supplies are low. Please ... hear me ... assistance required."

Corvin sighed and tapped irritably at his arm rest. There were at least thirty messages coming from the same place, all in different languages. This was the first one his systems had been able to translate, and it also happened to be the most fragmented. Broken as it was though, it was clearly a distress call, which meant he had no choice but to do something about it. In truth, he'd love nothing more than to go about his business the same as everyone else clearly had, but he physically couldn't refuse to act. Corvin was a *Stella Serpentis*, or Star Serpent. As far as he was concerned, it was a stupid, cheesy, overly romanticised name for his species, but there was nothing he could do about that now. The details were hardwired into him, and they weren't going to be changing, his creators made sure of that.

When the first humans came to this end of space, they all set about using the abandoned tech they scavenged to create their own species-specific hybrids for whatever they saw fit. Most of the hairless apes spliced hard-bodied insects or large carnivores with historical soldier DNA so that they could have their intergalactic armies, but one group decided to work with lizards and famous philanthropists. They had apparently viewed reptiles as highly efficient physically, but found them to be lacking in empathy. 'Imagine if we combined the two,' they had said. 'We could have a high-end emergency service!'

Of course, much as with most human projects of the era, all that was really achieved was the creation of the tools required to continue a long-standing conflict followed by an abandonment of the work itself. But that was twenty-sixth century humans for you; they created something combustible, acted surprised when it blew up, and ran away with their metaphorical tails between their legs. The really dumb thing was they never realised that the tech they were using was *not* for cloning or AI experiments like they'd thought, but was actually the primary way its original creators, a bio-mechanical race of quadrupeds called Glaxiarchs, reproduced towards the end of their life cycles.

Still, being abandoned had meant that all the humanoid hybrids of old Earth animals were free to do as they wished and form their own societies based on what inherited memories they could find in their DNA. Or the more productive bits of society anyway. There was enough Glaxiarch DNA burnt into the machines to leave some remnants behind in each of them, so there were a few changes the survivors of the human folly had made, in particular to how commerce was carried out. Unfortunately though, the original purpose of each species was so heavily ingrained in their neural programming that certain urges remained as overriding mechanisms. For the Stella Serpentis, that meant staying in the same system and answering all emergency calls, regardless of the content.

The system was vast enough that Corvin stumbling upon one of his fellow Serpentis was a rare occurrence. That was probably going to be a problem here. Corvin's reptilian DNA came primarily from the *pogona vitticeps*, or bearded dragon, so his natural tendency was to keep the ship at a high temperature. It wasn't like he couldn't adapt, it was just that his preferences, much like his overriding mechanisms, were stubborn. The voice on the audio message did not come with the same rasp that the heat lovers he had met tended to, so it was highly likely that the lifeform, or lifeforms, he was about to try to rescue would need secluded areas or temperature control units to reach their own natural comfort zone. Or, much like last month's glacial strandee, even to survive at all.

Corvin closed his eyes and thought back to strange lifeforms that he'd seen on his rescue missions. He tried to imagine what their home worlds must look like, and what sort of physical variations others of their kind may have. "The universe is full of wondrous creatures, but humans rarely met them, largely because they were too focussed on their own selfish goals to see what was staring them in the face." Corvin let out an annoyed hiss and added, "And thanks to their inflexible programming, I don't get to see them either unless *they* stumble across *me*."

***

The next hour was spent making what Corvin liked to call 'mid-point precautions.' First, he set the medical bay to what he had calculated as the average comfortable temperature for the majority of lifeforms he had come across. He left the ice thing out of the calculations because such extremes were rare. Food supplies were also checked over, with the most commonly requested foodstuffs set out on a slow defrost. Doing this meant that, by the time he knew what those on the stranded ship ate, it would be a relatively quick process to finish cooking said items, while the rest would not be so far gone that refreezing would be problematic.

A quick check of the temperature suits in storage revealed that five were in good working order, while one was malfunctioning. They were all built from a living latex compound that moulded itself to the wearer, but were controlled by nanobots that connected wirelessly to a control panel on what was set to become the chest unit. Though they were useful, given that the primary component was a living creature and the nanobots essentially tortured the things into acting the way that the humans had wanted, there was something cruel about the existence of the suits. But that was OK. None of them tried to make contact and cry for help, so there was no need for Corvin to alter them at all. Even the malfunctioning suit wasn't showing any signs of wanting assistance, it was just not reacting to the stimulus of the nanobots anymore.

"It'll all work out in the end," Corvin sighed, resealing the containers. "Either the nanobots will adapt again, or the creature will destroy them and free the others."

Finally, Corvin checked that the weapons he had on hand were functioning. He had not yet come across a hostile situation during a rescue, but he was not so foolish as to leave himself without a means to defend himself from afar. Keeping a distance from your enemy was always preferable if it came down to it, after all. On the other hand, if anything attacked him up close, he had his natural weapons: the modified elongated teeth that were too large for the mouth of his progenitors.

Corvin ran his tongue over his mouth and let his tail sweep from side to side. His own temperature suit would go full body if he had to go out in the field, but for now he had it set to not cover his face, hands, feet or tail. There was something comforting about the feel of the warm, rough metal of the ship to him. The little bumps, the slight burning sensation, the familiar scents of the engines… they all helped to make the ship feel like a home. At least to a degree. The Glaxiarch part of him longed desperately to explore the stars and make the wider universe his home, but his primary programming was stronger, and told him that being tied down here was enough.

"Enough. Not something to be happy about, just enough."

***

Passing by the hull as he brought his own ship around, Corvin cold see what were likely the propulsion engines of the stranded vessel. Initial scans confirmed as much and showed that there was no visible damage, but the temperature was low enough to indicate they had not been used for some time. Of course, that didn't necessarily mean much. The strange, curved design of the craft was unfamiliar enough to mean there was the possibility that the tech on board didn't run in the same way as those on his databases. If that were the case, the scans could miss just about anything. "Best to err on the side of caution," he mumbled, shouldering his plasma rifle and opening the communications channels.

"This is Glaxiarch System vessel seventeen alpha twenty papa, acting in response to distress call broadcasting on frequency band thirty-four, three hundred dash twenty-four, sixteen. Please respond."

The radio remained silent. Corvin licked the points of his teeth and reminded himself that he was obliged to try twice more before he could declare the ship a floating wreckage and mark the transmission down as historical. At that point, he was free to salvage what he wanted and leave. With a grunt, he flicked the transmit button again and repeated, "This is Glaxiarch System vessel seventeen alpha twenty papa, acting in response to distress call broadcasting on frequency band thirty-four, three hundred dash twenty-four, sixteen. Please respond."

More silence. Corvin sat back and crossed his arms. Long range scans showed him to be the only other vessel around, so there was no need to rush things too much. He could give the ship some time to respond before he went for the third strike.

A minute passed, and Corvin noticed that his tail had started flicking involuntarily against the back of the chair. That meant he was getting antsy. He grunted and tapped the transmission button again. "This is Glaxiarch System vessel seventeen alpha twenty papa, acting in response to distress call broadcasting on…"

A red light pierced through the window and into the bridge. It span and spiralled until it found Corvin, and sped up his body to his head, where the wide light converged into a single beam. *Identification scan*, Corvin thought. *They must be searching for a suitable language translation patch.*

The light remained in place for another couple of seconds, then cut. Relaxing a little, Corvin tapped the display screen on his desk and glanced at the ship scans that he'd taken. While he was reading, a mechanical voice crackled through the speakers in a passable imitation of the snapping grunts and growls of the Glaxiarch language. "This is the automated response system for the research vessel Nor'Killik. Primary communication abilities are non-functioning. Boarding bay locks have been prepared for connection."

"Communication confirmed," Corvin replied, switching to Glaxiarch. "Docking will commence shortly."

***

Hooking up the connection tunnel was far easier than Corvin had expected. During the scan, the stranded ship's outer shell had physically slid and modified the outer door locks to match those on his own ship, ensuring that things could run smoothly. Once the connection had been made, Corvin hit up the communication link and confirmed that it was safe for the survivors to enter. He had considered insisting on boarding himself but, given that his scans had been unable to get a definite life sign reading, he was unsure what he would be walking into and so decided to let paranoia guide his actions for a while.

After a moment, the doors to the Nor'Killik opened, and a single *something* walked through, passing slowly through the scanning field that Corvin had set up part way up the tunnel. The lights remained a dull orange as the creature passed through, which meant that no weapons or contagious diseases had been detected. Relaxing a little, Corvin dropped his rifle to his side and studied his visitor. Somewhere in his inherited memories, he could see that one of his DNA's source codes had owned a large brown and white dog called a greyhound. Said owner's young child had drawn a picture of the dog and, being a child, had exaggerated the animal's already long limbs and snout. Whatever was boarding his ship, reminded Corvin of the drawing.

It was a quadruped, and built a little like the historical animal in his memories, but the front legs were over long and a bit thicker. Its head was curved on top and angled down into a rounded muzzle of sorts. Even looking as disproportionate as it did, the lifeform was clearly built to move quickly. Its colouring was pitch black, and it appeared to be covered in smooth scales, a little like an Earth snake. It had no visible eyes, but a purple strip that glowed with an eerie phosphorescence ran up either side of its head, starting where its eyes *should* be and stopping at the tips of its ears. Around its neck, it wore a metallic collar that shone under the ship's lighting, and on its back it carried another of its kind. This one, Corvin noted, had no purple strips on its head, and did not appear to be breathing.

The living lifeform studied Corvin for a moment. Its collar flashed twice, and it spoke in a loose Glaxiarch. "I thank you for answering my call. My name is Dahl Mód. I see you watching my companion. Yes, I am afraid that she is dead, but you need not worry. Her body's termination was due to her own health issues, not anything that will directly affect you."

Corvin nodded and replied, "Are there only the two of you? The distress call was pretty broken up."

"Yes," Dahl Mód replied. "Despite its size, the Nor'Killik is a two person vessell." He paused, and the purple strips on his head narrowed slightly, then expanded back out again. "You do not look like a Glaxiarch."

"That's because I'm not a Glaxiarch. We can talk about that later though. First, I want to get you checked over. I'm the only one on board, so you'll need to carry your companion to the medical bay. I'd offer to help, but until I run some additional scans, I don't want to risk an infection. I know you said her death won't affect me, but it pays to be careful."

"Of course. I am happy to carry her to where you require. It is our custom to assist those who aid us if we can."

***

Corvin was surprised to see how easily Dahl Mód manoeuvred his fallen companion around. His shape was not entirely conducive to working in that way, but his species had obviously adapted to all sorts of work. While he ran his scans, Corvin explained why he had shown up as a Glaxiarch on the scans, and learned that Dahl Mód and his people had never encountered a human or visited Earth, so while it only formed a small part of Corvin's DNA, the identification scan focussed on the Glaxiarch portion of his genetic code as the only familiar piece.

"You're lucky in a way," Corvin said as he tidied his medical equipment away. "I didn't originally know this language. Or I didn't know that I did. After we were abandoned by our creators, I studied the machines that they left behind and found I understood a lot of what they didn't. I wouldn't say I fully understand the language, but there was obviously enough in my coding to remember the brunt of it."

"Language evolves, my friend. As such, no one person can truly fully understand a language. Still, I am glad for this happy accident. If you were built using the Glaxiarch Birth System, does that mean you share their physiology, albeit in a different shell?"

Corvin nodded. "The same mix of metal and organic material, yes, but with the design work of humans and their self-proclaimed endless imagination."

"It seems to me that their definition of endless was of a far smaller scope than you would expect."

"Yeah. They relied too heavily on their own ideals and familiar shapes. If they're still out there, I wouldn't be surprised if they're still just as blinkered and stubborn."

Dahl Mód hung his head and the purple strips disappeared. "It is sad how they have limited your life for you."

"Yeah. Yeah, it is," Corvin sighed. "So, at the risk of sounding rude, what are you? I've never come across any of your species before."

"We are Killik."

"Didn't you say that was what your ship was called?"

"Translated, the ship is titled Carrier of the Killik. My people are researchers and physicians, serving a similar purpose to yourself. You may be interested to know that there are other lifeforms on our planet, each with their own unique roles and appearances. In general, each species commits themselves to a single task, and each of us is in part a clone of the original of our kind. This strict regime, the nature of our creation, and the mix of organic and synthetic materials in our bodies. In many ways, we are not so different, you and I."

"Except, as you so tactfully pointed out, my life is limited and you have the freedom to explore."

"I apologize. I did not mean to cause offence."

Corvin let out an irritated hiss and said, "Don't worry about it."

"For what it is worth, there are many out there with similar compositions to ourselves. It may be that your make-up is similar enough to that of another lifeform that known procedures could be adapted to free you of your chains."

A spark of hope rose in Corvin's chest. He blinked and fixed Dahl Mód with a hopeful stare. "Do you really think so?"

"I cannot guarantee it, but it is possible. Perhaps once we have attempted to fix the Nor'Killik, we can run some tests to check for compatibility?"

Corvin let his head drop and he smiled. "Yes. Yes, I'd like that. I've wanted to travel for so long…"

"One good turn deserves another, my friend. It is the least I could do. Perhaps it will even open a new branch of research for my kind. It would be mutually beneficial, of course. For us, we would be able to satisfy our desire to grow our knowledge, and for those created as you were, it could be a new evolutionary step."

On the table, the body of the deceased Killik shuddered, drawing Corvin's attention. The movement, as far as he could tell, started at her left shoulder.

"What is it?" Dahl Mód asked.

Corvin narrowed his eyes and said, "That's strange. For a moment there, I thought I saw her move." Corvin leant close and studied the gap behind the Killik's left shoulder. At first, nothing happened, and he began to think that he must have been imagining things. Then, a small bump formed and disappeared. After a second, it returned, and then fell again. "Who did you say this was?"

"I did not. She was my companion, and my mate. Her name was Stahl Mód. What is wrong?"

"There's something moving under her skin. Are you sure that she died of something natural?"

"Yes. Would your scans not have picked it up if something was amiss?"

"Only if it was familiar to my systems. Honestly, I wasn't able to garner much from scanning your ship either, hence the gun when I greeted you. Your tech is so far beyond mine that I just couldn't…"

Before Corvin could finish his sentence, a small cut opened in Stahl Mód's body, and an insect-like creature scuttled out. It was shiny, like it had a metal exoskeleton, and it moved with a smooth, unnatural speed. Turning, it looked directly up at Corvin.

"Now, what are you?" Corvin muttered, leaning closer.

The metallic bug clicked its tiny mandibles, once, twice, three times, and an abnormally large puff of yellow gas sprayed from its mouth, sending Corvin into a fit of coughing. The reaction was instantaneous and distracted Corvin enough that he neither saw the bug hop from the dead Killik to his arm, nor felt it scuttle up his arm and force its way under one of the scales at the back of his left shoulder.

Covering his snout, Corvin span and forced his eyes open. He ran from side to side, trying to spot the bug on Stahl Mód's body. When it became apparent that it was no longer there, he dropped to all fours and began hunting under the table. "Did you see that?"

Dahl Mód tilted his head curiously, and the purple strips on his head narrowed. "See what, my friend?"

"The… thing. There was, like, this little metal bug that crawled out of Stahl Mód's body. It sprayed me with something. You must have seen that at least!"

Dahl Mód stared at Corvin for a moment, then hopped up onto the table. "Where was it on the body?"

"Just above her left shoulder," Corvin replied, crawling back to check under a group of chairs to the side of the room. "It cut its way out of her."

"Curious. I can find no cut on her body."

"It was small. You're probably just missing it." Corvin moved a chair to the side and stopped. He could feel an itch on the back of his neck. He was about to bring a claw to the point when realization dawned on him, and he threw his hand flat instead, trying to swat at the bug that must be crawling up his neck. When all this did was make the itch move, Corvin started to run two fingers gently over his scale covered skin. He found a bump. It was small, about the size of the metallic bug, and was moving slowly up towards the back of his head. Corvin's eyes went wide, and he whispered, "It's inside me."

Panicking, Corvin started scratching at his scales, trying to divert the bug from wherever it was going, but once it hit the top of his head, it burrowed down into his metal coated skull, and disappeared from his reach. He felt a pinch from somewhere behind his eyes, and a voice echoed through his head. It was similar to Dahl Mód's, but lighter in tone. "Corvin, is it? Yes, that will do. I am afraid this will hurt a little."

Snap.

Corvin screamed and fell to the floor. He rolled onto his back, clutching his temples and kicking his feet wildly. "Help me," he yelled. But Dahl Mód simply sat by his dead mate and stared, the purple strips on his head thin and glowing gently.

"I apologize," the voice in Corvin's head said. "I have temporarily blocked the signals that trigger fear reactions in your brain. If you concentrate, the pain will also subside. I simply wish to speak to you with logic as a primary mechanism rather than the emotional discharge that such things can bring. Please be aware, however, that should you choose to act hastily, I will also be forced to inhibit your movements."

Corvin growled angrily and sat up, digging his claws under the scales on either side of his head. After a moment, he realized that the voice was right. He was not afraid, nor was the pain as bad as he had thought.

"You do not need to speak out loud," the voice said. "The signals in your brain lack the complexity of some, and so I can understand your thoughts well enough if you make them clear. I mean no disrespect by this, of course. Brain complexity is not an accurate measure of intelligence or evolutionary level in most species."

"Who are you?" Corvin thought.

"It is as Dahl Mód stated. I am Stahl Mód."

"Does that mean he has a… whatever *you* are inside him too?"

Stahl Mód clicked a few times, then responded, "Dahl Mód *is* as I am. The form that you see him as, and the one that I inhabited, are shells of a sort. No, perhaps that is not the best way to phrase this. They are many things. Shells, yes, but also transportation, tools, and mutual partners in an endless cycle."

"So, are you saying that you live inside the Killik?"

"Ah, you understand Dahl Mód's words to be a literal description of what was in front of you, even now?"

"Yes."

"I apologize, but this was a necessary subterfuge, though the wording was not itself inaccurate. I am Stahl Mód. I am also a Killik, as is Dahl Mód. The bodies that we came here in are not Killik."

"Then, what are they?"

"I am not honestly sure. When I found mine, it was unwilling to tell me of its origins, though it was happy to accommodate my wishes. When Dahl Mód found his, it was more willing to discuss matters and explained that their species do not identify themselves with names, either personally or as a whole. They instinctually knew each other by the taste in the air, you see, and so had no need for something as cumbersome as a name. To learn this was luck on our part, however. This is the first time in a millennia that we have inhabited bodies of the same species. Had such a rare occurrence not been a necessity, we may never have known anything of this race. That would have been sad."

Corvin sighed outwardly and asked, "Are you going to take over my body?"

"Yes, though the manner in which it happens is yet to be decided. Will you permit me a question?"

"I don't see what choice I have at this point, so you may as well ask whatever you want."

"There are always choices, though they may not always be apparent. Regardless. Tell me, Corvin, what is paradise to you?"

"Paradise?"

"Yes. Are you familiar with the concept?"

"Of course I am. You must have heard what I said to Dahl Mód though. Or, if not, then you can probably pull the information out of my brain. My whole life is in this system, and the nature of the DNA inside me means that I'm forever in conflict with myself. There's no way forward for me. I have no paradise."

Stahl Mód clicked again, and Corvin felt another pinch. "I apologise. I require you to give me an honest answer that is not hampered by your surroundings. You say that you have no paradise. Then, what would your paradise be if you *did* have one?"

Corvin let his muzzle relax. He felt his eyes glaze over and he heard his voice say, "To be free to see the universe without the boundaries of the cage in which I was born."

"Dahl Mód and I are, to our knowledge, the only Killik still in existence, but this suits us. Our nature is such that, without an outer component to house us, we will die within one week. As such, we move from body to body, utilizing the tools that each new form gives us. You have realized that our components are not entirely unusual and wonder why your scans did not pick up on our existence, I can feel that. The reason is that the Nor'Killik ship is the same as we are. It lives, and adapts to whatever form we have taken. For example, with each new body that we take, it will change the shape of its controls without altering their primary purpose. It masked us to keep our system of life in place. We have often wondered if perhaps it too is linked to our existence, but we cannot be sure.

"When we take a body for our own, the life of that body is shortened considerably. By taking control of you, I am sorry to say that your flesh will not live more than another five years. You should be aware, however, that much can be achieved in that time, and you do not need to miss out on this. I ask you what your paradise is because this is a driving force for both myself and Dahl Mód. We work in tandem, with one hunting for a suitable replacement body when the other nears the end of their lifecycle. We travel the stars together, learning of all the wondrous things that life has to offer. We will remain by each other's side, eternally, until time is no more. That, for us, is paradise."

"Why are you telling me this? And what do you mean I don't have to miss out on what will be achieved? You have my body now, so there's nothing I can do, right?"

"This is, in essence, true. However, our views of paradise are not incompatible. Were I to sever the points that make you the creature that you are, you would cease to be, and the lifespan of your body would be reduced to three years. However, were I to simply assume control without such a drastic step, you would remain fully aware of what I do, albeit without control. My actions seem cruel to you, but I am not a cruel creature by nature. If you wish to cease your existence, I will make this so. For one that has suffered though, this would seem a shame to me. If you remain aware, you will indeed see the stars and worlds that you long to visit, and you will get to experience the paradise you seek, if only for a short while."

***

After sitting in silence for what seemed to be an eternity, the body that was once Corvin stood up and stretched. Stahl Mód ran his surprisingly long tongue over the sharp ridges of his teeth and turned to Dahl Mód. He smiled, and walked to the table where his previous body lay. With a gentle smile, he removed the collar and placed it around his new neck. "It is good to be in a male body again."

"Such comments make me smile," Dahl Mód replied. "We have no gender, you and I."

"No, but I find male bodies easier to control. It seems that there will be some interesting pieces to salvage here. In particular, there are more of these suits that I am wearing. They are made from living organisms, you see. I do not believe them sufficient to grant a long term solution to our requirements, but they may serve as temporary measures should the need arise. I wonder if, given the right stimulation, they would be strong enough to move a body that has expired. Perhaps we will have need to test this someday."

Dahl Mód flicked his tail from side to side. "And what of Corvin? Does he still reside with you?"

"Yes. The poor child simply wished for a bigger world than he had. I can give him that, at least. He did have one request though."

"Oh?"

"You mentioned that our database of known procedures may contain something that could be adapted to free him of his trappings. He asked that, though it is no longer required for him, we search for this anyway and offer it to any others we encounter as we travel through the system."

Dahl Mód nodded. "Yes, I feel that that would be appropriate. Corvin's is a tragic tale, is it not?" Stahl Mód nodded and Dahl Mód continued, "Still, for each tale of woe that we hear, there is another, happier one to be found. It is a beautiful world, paradise."

Even in a collection of stories about paradise, there must be room for a piece of classic science-fiction horror.

WE ARE ONE

Thurston Howl

The entrance valve slammed shut, muting the cries of the rest of the Eneid's burning crew. Those few who were not being roasted alive by the Homosaps' flamers were instead being gunned down by the massive ship's autoturrets. The three survivors turned away from the closed valve, no sorrow in their eyes as they walked through the tunnel back to their smaller pirating ship, the Eneid.

"We did it," said Captain Neas. "We retrieved the last piece of the map, and now, we can find it, Olym-Pass." The captain bucked his head in pleasure, his antlers scraping the low roof of the tunnel. His eyes, dyed to match the red of his flame-like fur, glowed with fierce intensity. Despite the bloodshed he had left in his wake, blood of both his crew and that of the enemy ship's, he had at last captured the final piece of the puzzle.

As the tunnel opened up into the main deck of the ship, his two followers separated and went to their separate posts. The LupoSap, a scrawny female with a thick tail trailing behind her, looked sideward to her captain as she stepped up onto the directional grid, opening up the Nav-sys to get them out of the area before anyone on the other ship, the Whitefeather, could sneak on board. She did this without too much thought: although she had worked with the crew for the better part of two life units, something close to thirteen months on her home world, she had no attachment to them. She was not sad to leave them behind to be massacred. They were all thieves. They were all murderers. She winced at that thought, her mouth drawn into a half-snarl. If there was one thing people always agreed upon about little ol' Tipp, it was that she was quiet. Even talking to her captain was a struggle for her. But that silence was deadly. Captain Neas had tried seducing her the first week, and he had received a knife in his thigh for it. That's when he had decided to make her first mate. And she didn't disappoint.

As the ship lurched suddenly, shifting through lightyears of space in just seconds, they felt the Whitefeather disconnect from them, and they were floating much more freely now.

"Where to now, Cap?" hissed the voice to Tipp's left. She turned and regarded the ReptoSap who manned the weapons controls. He looked ridiculous there. He was huge, especially with his artificial wings stretching from above his head down to the floor; and the module was as small as Tipp's, meant for more HomoSaps' sizes.

"You have to *wait*, Drag." The captain sneered as he put the pieces of the map together, creating a badly formed cube. "The map itself is a puzzle. The mapmaker was renowned—" he grunted as he turned the pieces of the puzzle, "—for modeling his maps—" grunt, "—after a Terran game—" grunt, "—called the Rube Cube." Click. The map was now a complete box, and as the final click resounded in the room, the cube glowed and began to float.

Drag, named such for his similarity to the Terran mythical monster, the dragon, gasped at the sight. He acted like he had never seen a holographic projector before. But Tipp and Captain Neas ignored him. Green light expanded from the sphere and portrayed a sea of stars around them, a bright red line darting across the space.

Captain Neas stepped forward, his bare hooves clicking on the floor. As he pointed at one end of the red line, he said, "This is where we are." His eyes followed the line. "So that must mean…"

Drag finished for him, "That this end of the line," he pointed at the final point, "is where Olym-Pass is!" The ReptoSap raised his bulky arms in a cheer, and his snout opened wide, displaying row after row of sharp teeth. Captain Neas glared at the creature. While Drag was a trigger-happy master fighter, common sense, tact, and intelligence were not among his fortes.

"Tripp," the Captain said, and, without any instruction, the wolf-like humanoid began pulling up the planet's location on the Eneid's nav-sys. But as she did so, what seemed to be a message of communication appeared above the holographic display.

Captain Neas stared up at it and read aloud, "*Beware ye who seek the gardens of Olym-Pass. Here, we are one. Woe to ye. Here, we are one.*"

Drag snickered, his laugh sounding more like a pit of snakes hissing. "Sounds like they definitely are hiding something, Cap. It's probably as good and beautiful as the legends say."

"I'm inclined to agree with you, Drag," the captain said, much to his own surprise. "All the food and gold we could ever ask for. No law to get in our way, and the sun is always shining."

The ReptoSap snickered again. "And there'll be ladies, yeah? Ladies like Tripp, but, well…like *real* ladies."

Captain Neas laughed. "Yes, there will be ladies. And I'm sure, given the right persuasion, they'll be much more ladylike than our sweet Tripp."

The LupoSap flicked her tail in irritation, her gray fur bristling. Her mind flipped through a dozen comebacks, each more scathing than the one before, but she knew there was little point. What would saying them accomplish? Probably just further ridicule. She lowered her head to study her screen, burying herself in self-loathing. Was she socially awkward? Absolutely. But did she know how to fly a ship? Better than the captain himself.

Her eyes darted up to look at the CervoSap captain, and she saw him looking back at her, a grim smirk spreading on his deer-like muzzle. "Full speed ahead, Tripp. To Olym-Pass."

She nodded in acquiescence and lowered her head, controlling the ship's motions with the softest of gestures before the screen.

As she worked, the captain stared at the holographic image that hovered in front of him. Was Olym-Pass this close? Truly? His thoughts were distracted by the sound of Drag's hissing snickers at his module. From this angle, Neas could see through the ReptoSap's transparent screen and saw him looking at various pornographic videos and images. Neas's eyes narrowed. The "dragon" was disgusting. It was then that Captain Neas realized he didn't want to share this beautiful world they were traveling to with such a filthy specimen of *Repto sapiens.*

Neas smiled as he paced over to his desk at the far end of the room. He opened a drawer and pulled out a bottle of Gevatian bubbler, a drink well known for its ability to increase the oxytocin in any Sap's bloodstream. He popped the cork and poured two glasses full. He found a small vial in the back of the drawer also and poured its contents into one of the glasses, the movement quick but subtle. As he turned back to face his now two-person crew, he saw that Drag had looked up from his activities and was staring wolfishly—not that he had ever seen the same look from Tripp at all—at the glasses.

"It's time to celebrate!" Neas proclaimed, stepping forward to offer Drag one of the glasses. The ReptoSap took the glass eagerly and raised it high to the captain, offering the toast himself.

"Cheers! To the wildest and most daringest pirate to ever sail the cosmos!"

The glasses clinked, and before Neas could even raise the glass to his lips, Drag downed his. However, Neas did not see a need in drinking any of the bubbler. After all, knowing that the happier Drag got from the bubbler, the more the poison would settle into him, made Neas's oxycotin rise just fine.

The anthropomorphic lizard's smile spread, but, even as he did so, his eyes widened in fear. He realized what had happened, but words would not come. He collapsed onto the floor, the glass shattering beneath him.

Tripp looked up for a moment, regarded the fallen lizard, then focused her attention on the screen again. She just hoped Neas wouldn't ask her to move the body. Frankly, she was glad the sexist dinosaur was dead.

Neas walked over to her. "Well, it's just you and me now, Tripp. How exciting, yeah?"

She made a few more gestures, navigating the ship, before saying simply, "Sure."

"Well, at least now, there's a lot less split going on with the treasure," Neas boasted.

Tripp nodded, her ears raised, showing she was listening if nothing else.

"How much longer till we reach the world?"

"Three..." she started, and Neas grinned, his red fur glimmering in the corner of Tripp's eyes. "Two...one..."

Through the wide window at the front of the command room, the world appeared before them. What she saw reminded her of a Terran game *she* had grown up with, mar-bulls. Although she had never seen any taurine connotations with the game, she had always been entranced by the gamut of colors and textures the mar-bulls contained, each one a planet of unique design. Olym-Pass looked like such a mar-bull. A rainbow of pigments swirled around its surface: greens, pinks, blues, whites, and oranges. The swirling was slow, but she knew that on the world's surface, it would feel like the sky was moving with the wind, and indeed it might have been.

Captain Neas sighed, reveling in the glory of his discovery. "There it is...just as the stories say. The perfect world. A paradise."

"No," Tripp interrupted. "They said it was a paradise for those who have no families or lovers to go home to."

The CervoSap captain laughed deeply, holding a hoof to his white-furred belly. "That they did, Tripp, my dear. But the only people who ever lived to tell the tale of this place were those basic *Homo sapiens*. They always brag and teach to the other Saps that love is what life is all about and that true happiness is with family." He knew from what little Tripp had said about her past that she agreed with him that true happiness had nothing to do with family. "Olym-Pass…it's perfect."

***

As they broke through the planet's atmosphere, the world's surface blossomed into view: pink-flowered trees covered mossy earth below, and cerulean rivers and waterfalls branched across the surface. It took a little over half an hour for Tripp to find a suitable space to land on, as the terrain was mostly devoid of any plains or plateaus. Moving across the exit ramp, they breathed in the foreign air and were amazed. Each breath was like inhaling the sweetest honeysuckle; they tasted ambrosia on their tongues, and their leathery noses were on fire from the sensory stimulation. They craned their heads skyward, and, though the light of day shone down on them, the suns were not visible through the swirling colors above them, keeping the world lit without blinding its inhabitants.

"It's…perfect," Tripp said, struggling to believe the place of stories and legends was as real as they had heard.

Neas laughed. "The stories didn't do this place justice, eh? Understatements! That's what they all were." A breeze rushed around them, rippling through their fur and filling their senses with the aromas of Olym-Pass. And on the wind, they heard the words: *We are one.* They were faint, but they both snapped out of their reverie when they heard them. "C'mon," Neas said, shivering. "Let's explore some. See where we can find some food."

Tripp nodded and followed dutifully behind, a paw ready to draw her gun at any point. The place was indeed paradisiac, but something seemed off, and it was more than the voice she and Neas had heard.

They pushed through the forest of pink, their hindpaws stepping lightly over the mossy earth. The sounds of rushing water came closer with each careful step, and their eyes scanned the environment for any movements. They just needed to find an AviFer—*Avis feralis*—or even a ReptoFer—the thought of eating Drag's feral kin made Tripp smile—just something they could actually eat on this beautiful world.

They stopped at the river's edge. The water trickled past, lapping gently at the earth that bordered it, and the stream seemed shallow enough to cross. But the two pirates stared into its depths, scanning for an AquaFer. After a few minutes walking up and down the river's side, they submitted, realizing there might not be food in this place after all.

"What in the abyss is up with this world?" Neas said. "With such plant life, you'd think there'd be at least *some* Fer living out here. Something we could eat."

We are one.

The two whirled around, scanning the trees for the source of the voice, confident they heard it this time.

"Who's there?" Neas shouted.

Tripp saw movement in the corner of her eye. She looked up and then pointed, her mouth gaping. As Neas tilted his head back to see, his jaw dropped also.

The wispy streams of light and cloud from the sky were twisting downward toward them, twirling around themselves as they did so. The lights pierced the treetops, and the voice grew louder.

We are one.

We are one.

Now confronted with the full force of the voice, Neas and Tripp realized it was not just *one* voice. It was many voices, all speaking in unison, all with the same force and solidity.

"Wh—who are you?" Captain Neas managed again, his voice faltering.

The lights surrounded them, grasping them, ensnaring them. Neas cried out as a wisp pierced his chest, suddenly solid. He screamed as the voices filled his head. Tripp watched in terror but did not make a sound. She listened.

You were warned. Here, we are one.

Tripp ventured softly, "Who is…we?"

We are those who once lived here, and we are those who found this place after those first people were long gone. We were once people like you, travelers from the stars, but now we have found each other. We are one. And we shall always be one.

Tripp looked to Neas, still speared by the colored torrents of cloud. His snout moved in time with the words, his voice rising with theirs.

We are one. And now, you are part of us.

As she opened her own mouth to protest, an orange light wrapped around her mouth, filling it, and she felt her body erupt with warmth and light. Happiness became her, even as her terror rose with it. Despite what her drifting consciousness was telling her to do, her mouth formed the words and joined in the chorus:

We are one. We are one.

As an otter in Aquatica, Lyric lives a life of constant delight and wonderment, but it cannot last.

LUCID

Nicholas Hardin

Lyric could not remember living anywhere else, yet every day there was always something new to explore here.

A slender form darted through sunbeams piercing the ocean's surface. Far below, Lyric could barely make out the constantly-shifting webs of light that the beams cast on the colorful reefs. She dove deeper and twisted her body to bask in daylight's glow. Her light brown, otter-like body shimmered under the waves, delicately curved and completely unclad, leaving only bare fur to be caressed by the surrounding water as she swam.

Angling up, she shoved herself to the surface for one more breath, then spiraled back down and dove as schools of brightly-colored fish scattered from her path.

Her goal today was to investigate a large grouping of rocks and fissure that had somehow appeared overnight. Lyric was anxious at the possibility of mapping out a new location of the region. It seemed like an unending, almost futile mission given how constantly the undersea landscape had been changing, but it ensured her wanderlust would not be sated any time soon.

Lyric could not help but smile as she skimmed the reefs. The current was with her today, as it often was, allowing her to conserve her energy as she searched for the anomaly. The Hippocampus tribes said it was around here somewhere…

Up ahead, past a pair of drifting jellyfish, she made out a large shape in the ocean's haze.

There you are… she thought to herself, smiling as she picked up speed.

The grouping was not just some clutter of boulders as the Hippocampi said. As she approached, she figured it rose at least forty meters from the seabed. What was more, it seemed to be volcanic judging by the silt floating above and around its peak. That would explain the fissure…

She flicked her tail and angled up for another breath, then dove and swam above the grouping, circling around to get an idea of its placement. Another new landmark for her to memorize, and the chance of discovering a new cavern if the fissure was wide enough.

Through the silt, she saw an occasional faint glow. It enticed her all the more. Rapidly-cooling lava, perhaps?

She swam up for another deep breath, then shot down through the silt, already feeling the fissure's heat. Her whiskers twitched and she dove deeper, sensing more heat and thicker silt billowing upwards and past her.

Soon, she felt the silt thinning out, and then it cleared. The fissure had opened up into an entire cavern.

Lyric angled slightly, noticing the cavern's walls widening. Even in the lack of sunlight, cracked glows ignited far below at intervals, pulsing orange light and spewing more silt and sediment out. She wove around the silt billows, feeling the heat but finding it strangely bearable in spite of the glowing-hot lava flashing out at the bottom, to say nothing of what she knew had to be poisonous fumes within the billows. She wondered just how deep the cavern went. It must have been a lava tube that fractured overnight. Could that explain how the landscape had been shifting so rapidly lately?

She paused in her swim and glanced back at the fainter light above, almost completely obscured by floating sediment, then ahead at the ever-expansive cavern. There was so much to memorize for her maps… and the thrill of risk enticed her further. She flicked her tail, reached out, and shot forward, confident she had enough air for further exploration.

The cavern extended well past the eruption. In the absence of sunlight, the orange glows behind Lyric faded the further she went. Her whiskers twitched as she attempted to sense her way through the darkening haze. She angled down, feeling the heat lessening. She barely made out clusters of cooled rock that split her path into separate caverns.

Lyric paused in front of one, hovering as she contemplated whether to enter or try a larger, higher one. Her fur and hair wavered in the minimal current.

With a confident smirk, Lyric grabbed a small outcropping and pulled herself through into the deeper entrance. There was no way the larger Hippocampi would be able to enter themselves, and she convinced herself they would be grateful for a new addition to local maps.

Tiny bubbles spurted from her muzzle, reminding her she still needed to breathe eventually. She continued grabbing anything jutting out to speed her pace, seeing faint light ahead through tiny cracks in the lava tube as its elevation shifted through the undersea landscape. The tunnel widened and shrank at intervals before narrowing more. All the while, Lyric committed as much as she could to her memory in hopes of charting the new tunnels for future exploration. The Hippocampi would definitely be impressed!

The cavern narrowed even more, forcing the otter girl to shorten her grasps on the jagged walls. Swimming became difficult. She tried not to brush against the sides even as her tail corrected her course.

A sharp turn into darkness, and she nearly collided against the wall as it turned again. She barely saw through the sediment-filled haze in her vision, twitching her whiskers ever more to detect the water's flow around her. She felt her own bubbles brush back against her muzzle, and the need for air became more apparent. She attempted to speed her pace even more, crawling through the tunnel with little room to maneuver. She felt more outcroppings brush against her body as the tunnel narrowed further. There was still a current, however… There *had* to be an exit.

Another turn, which she nearly got stuck in, and then she saw a faint glow ahead.

Sunlight!

She pulled her way through the curve and continued forward, wincing as her lungs begged for air. In her haste she almost forgot to memorize the curve to her mental map.

The cavern widened and the current sped around her, shoving her forward. She sensed heat building again, and whatever her whiskers were picking up, it did not feel the same in the surrounding water as had been behind her in the tunnel. She dismissed the thought in the desire to breathe and shoved forward to the light ahead.

The current sped faster, then a blast behind her jolted her forward.

Rocks shattered from the shockwave and rushed with her through the tunnel. Lyric's body tumbled through. She saw light flashing past and she realized she had missed the opening.

She tried to right herself but the current shoved her further, robbing her of air. She struggled to hold her breath longer, noticing more glows ahead. The tunnel was collapsing!

Jagged rocks of all sizes shot past and around her as the current wavered. Lyric swung her arms and tail out again to orient herself. Another blue-lit crack appeared ahead, and the otter aimed herself just as another blast resonated through the fracturing cavern, throbbing her eardrums.

Disoriented by shock, she barely noticed something grabbing her arms and pulling her through the current. Light glimmered around her and then she felt the current lessen.

Her stomach tensed as she tried not to gulp a mouthful of water. The hands clutching her pulled her higher, and light brightened. They were free of the tunnel.

Lyric lifted her head just in time to see the surface's wavering silver, and soon broke free to take a deep breath of fresh air.

The otter floated for a few moments, panting and filling her lungs again.

"Your tendency to take risks is growing..." said a voice behind her.

Lyric grinned as she continued panting through her teeth. "I consider it growing bolder..."

She turned to see her rescuer. She was as fit and lithe as Lyric, but with a wolf-like body and fur that shimmered in hues of teal and blue. Like her friend, she too was completely unclad save for her own fur. She ran a hand through her long, soaked hair and chuckled.

"...because you assume I will always be there to rescue you?" she said.

Lyric swayed back as she bobbed on the surface. "Oh Serena, you know I can take care of myself. Besides, I have a new region to chart now!"

Serena slowly swam around beside her friend. "To what cause? The undersea landscape has shifted more times than either of us can count, and there are no points of reference above the surface save for the stars at night. Even the Hippocampi have all but given up on mapping out this place."

Lyric twisted to float on her stomach, leaving her back exposed to the cool sea air as she looked below the waves at the seabed. She recognized much of it, though portions of the reef were not quite in the same place as they were before. Even so, she felt everything was as it should be.

She twisted back to answer Serena, but noticed her friend gone. Far off, she saw a strange fog above the waves.

"Serena? Where did you go this time?"

Lyric dove and listened, trying to hear the sea wolf's unique echoes, but heard only silence. Glancing behind her, she saw the fog had become the ocean's haze, and expanded toward her while significantly brightening. She had seen such a phenomenon before... but where?

She wracked her brain to remember as it continued to thicken around her, then realization finally began settling in.

No... not yet! Just a few more minutes! she thought as the haze enveloped her, becoming blinding.

She screwed her eyes shut and winced as everything came back to her. None of this was real, and her identity made itself known once more in her mind.

This session can't be over yet. I still have to...

She gave up as the sea and its calm disappeared around her. She floated in the blinding haze hearing a steady monotone beep increasing in volume, and remembered who she was.

I am Erica Lancaster, employee number eight-sixty-two at Duval Communications, and I hate my life.

***

Erica opened her eyes to a wake-up alarm and the high-pitched whine of the Halcyon device spooling down.

Erica groaned, not ready to return to reality. She sat back in the device's comfortable chair, trying to summon enough effort to get up. She summoned enough to reach out and silence the alarm. Knowing it would sound again in five minutes if weight sensors detected she was still in the chair, she leaned up and removed the headset and neck harness. Setting it aside, she glanced around her tiny, cramped studio apartment. It was a depressing contrast to the open ocean she had swam in while under the Halcyon's dreamlike trance.

Bland, off-white walls had only faded stains to give them character, much of them covered in posters of serene ocean waves and sunsets, a few of otters, wolves, horses, and even a mermaid. The furniture was sparse, mismatched, and well-worn, having been brought in from whatever Erica had been able to afford at garage sales. She had all but forgotten about the odd smells of the previous tenant, stubbornly clinging to the walls and ceiling despite the tenant having moved out three years ago. The main living area was made even more cramped by the Halcyon device. The device's main unit, a fairly nondescript column with the stylized FluxTech logo stamped on one of the panels, was large enough for two people to fit inside its casing. The reclining chair connected to it was far more comfortable than the stained lounge seat it replaced. When the FluxTech workers had come by to install the device, Erica was forced to move her TV and cheap entertainment center into a closet to make room.

It had been worth it, however. Erica had already canceled her cable subscription to cut costs, and now that the Halcyon device was here, she had spent more time dreaming than any other activity. Winning FluxTech's experiment subject contract was the best thing that had happened to her in a very long time. Now if only she could figure out how to bypass the mandatory cool-down periods and stay in the trance longer.

The alarm beeped again.

Erica shut it off once more and finally stood. She yawned and stretched, then turned to look at herself in the mirror propped up next to her closet.

No otter traits... Just a boring human girl in boring human clothes. At least her light brown hair was Lyric's fur color.

Erica sighed again and moved to get dressed for work. She had gotten up early for the sole purpose of diving into the Halcyon, yet despite being in the device's trance, dreaming for four hours, she did not feel rested. Lacking the time to fix a proper breakfast, she grabbed a protein bar on her way out the door.

***

Aquatica... Erica muttered to herself as she descended the stairs of her apartment complex.

Aquatica would be the name she would designate for her ocean world. The Halcyon's cloud servers presented five unique environments for its subjects to dive into, yet Erica took to the ocean world instantly and had hardly even thought about visiting the other virtual dreamscapes. The ocean was where she wanted to be, not the other simulated environments nor this stuffy, claustrophobic city.

She stepped out into said city and grumbled to herself. Dark, overcast skies implied rain would be coming soon. Erica normally liked rain, but it was difficult to enjoy its cool, calming noise when everything reminded her she was stuck in a dead-end job in a stifling city with no bodies of water nearby. There weren't even any community pools to swim in, and she figured if there were they would be too crowded anyway.

She made her way over teeming sidewalks, past numerous people sporting ear buds or virtual interface spectacles, and silently wondered if she might be able to afford a set of her own someday after the Halcyon experiment ended. She dreaded the inevitable day when FluxTech would announce the servers shutting down and recall all active units.

Rounding a corner, she saw her bus and sped her pace to reach it before it left. Stepping inside, she found an empty seat next to a window and settled down. She wanted to use the twenty-minute commute time to think back on her mental maps for the next dive into the Halcyon, but then overheard the bus's live feed from its screen up front. There was a talk show on.

"...presents a bold step forward in the realm of not only virtual reality, but artificial intelligence as well. The Halcyon experiment has so far astounded both engineers and psychologists alike in its presentation of simulated realms crafted purely out of our own subconscious."

Erica sank lower in her seat, not interested in hearing all the technical mumbo-jumbo behind her personal paradise. Whatever happened to preserving the magic?

"...but people are still concerned about a machine that can directly interface with our minds. Wasn't there an ethics community involved with the Halcyon project?" asked the interviewer.

A FluxTech scientist responded, "Absolutely, and truth be told the Halcyon is incapable of much of what the critics are claiming. First of all, and most importantly, the worlds it presents are just blank canvases. Everything else the patron see, hears, experiences, is all based on their subconscious. Our brains are vastly more powerful than the world's most advanced supercomputer, and that's the magic behind the Halcyon itself. The human brain, the user, is basically the Halcyon's main processor. All the Halcyon does is make the experience 'real' in your dream state. You are completely incapable of getting lost in the simulation. You have more control over what you experience, even if you don't realize it, than you have in your own dreams when you sleep."

"Yes, but couldn't it be said that when you feel something so vivid, so *real*, that you cannot even tell you're in effect dreaming, then isn't there a danger that you could wind up traumatizing yourself by a nightmare? Or what if the shock of waking up is so disorienting that it leads to psychosis?"

"Our initial tests did not have any such results. Plus, each device has monitoring systems to detect stress in case something goes awry. In regards to waking up, to be safe, every Halcyon unit is designed to gradually wake up its user with a combination of visual and aural cues to alert them the simulation is ending and they will be waking up. The concerns you're describing are why we've sent demo units out to those who won our lottery for experiment subjects. The only way we could reliably test the Halcyon's capabilities was to let people try it in limited form."

"And how are these tests going so far, Dr. Harper?"

"Unfortunately I cannot divulge any specifics until the test period has ended and we've had a chance to comb through all the data returned to us on the units sent out. I can say, however, that a number of our tests have proven remarkably effective in rehabilitating coma patients."

The bus reached Erica's stop and she quickly disembarked before Dr. Harper ruined any more of her Halcyon-derived fantasies. Erica only had another block to walk before she reached the Duval Communications building, and she tried to focus on her mental maps of Aquatica in hopes of delaying the realization that she still had eight-and-a-half hours before she could dive back in again.

She walked in and the receptionist looked up.

"You're half-an-hour late again, Erica," she said.

Erica kept walking. "Overslept."

The receptionist turned as Erica walked past. "Wait, take the stairs. Mr. Maxwell is already up there watching the elevator. The stairwell exit is on the opposite side of the building."

The intercom pinged with Mr. Maxwell's gruff voice, "Ms. Griffin, where the hell is Ms. Lancaster?"

The receptionist waved Erica off. "I saw her come in, sir. Have you not seen her yet?"

Erica headed for the nearest stairwell. "Thanks, Heather." She knew Mr. Maxwell rarely checked the clock-in sheets, but if her tardiness became a trend he would likely start. She doubted that mentioning her role as a Halcyon test subject would work as an excuse, even if the non-disclosure agreement FluxTech made her sign did not forbid it.

"Just be careful!" Heather called back. "Your tardiness is getting a lot of notice lately!"

Making her way up the stairs to the fifth floor, Erica let her mind wander again, thinking of where she might visit next in Aquatica. Already she missed being an otter. She did not know how the Halcyon could mimic the extra senses she would have, like moving a tail or sensing her surroundings with enhanced smell and sensitive whiskers, but whenever she was in the trance, it all felt perfect. Or maybe that's just what her subconscious was telling her as she dreamed.

She reached the door and cracked it open to see if the coast was clear. Rows and rows of cubicles did little to muffle the noise of talking operators, ringing phones, and an occasional tinny-sounding speaker. Erica did not see Mr. Maxwell. She slid into the room and made a beeline for her station.

She found it a few rows down with no interference or sight of her boss and plopped into her chair with a defeated sigh.

The black-haired young man in the cubicle next to hers leaned back and smiled. "Another long night?" he said.

Erica glanced over. "Not long enough. Good morning, Brian."

"Morning." His station phone rang and he leaned forward. "Breaks aren't long enough either." He pressed the answer button and went on with his business. "Duval Communications, this is Brian speaking. How may I assist you today?"

Erica pulled her own chair forward, attached her earpiece and boom microphone, and logged into her station. Crude print outs of oceanic stock photos and a couple horse figurines were all she had to decorate her workspace with. She once had family photos, but they had gotten lost when she moved to the city. It was just as well; her parents were too far away to maintain any reliable contact beyond a monthly phone call where Erica would say pretty much nothing had changed since she last called.

Still single, still struggling to pay the bills, still couldn't say anything about signing up to be a test subject for a highly-experimental neural-reality dreamscape project. She wished the monetary stipend for the project was higher...

"Duval Communications, this is Erica speaking. How may I assist you today?"

***

The volcanic regions might or might not be shaping the sea floor, but at least they presented plenty of areas to explore. What about the areas in the opposite direction? Wasn't there a trench that had not been confirmed yet?

Erica sketched out as much as she could from her mental map of Aquatica's seabed. So far, she had not seen anything tall enough to breach the surface, so navigating by current flows, submerged landmarks, and stars were all she had to go by. She wondered of Aquatica had a magnetic field that an otter could detect and navigate by, as well. Or, perhaps it did and she, Lyric, had been following it all the time? It was pulled from her own subconscious desires, so maybe she just had not realized it yet when in the Halcyon's trance.

"Ms. Lancaster!"

Erica jumped and whirled in her chair. "Good morning, Mr. Maxwell."

Her boss, barely taller than the cubicle walls with more wrinkles than one might expect for a sixty-year-old, beamed at Erica. "You're making doodles on the job?"

Erica glanced over to her maps and stuttered, "I, uh, was taking a break, sir."

"You've drawn a hell of a lot for one five-minute break..."

Erica swallowed, noticing the clock readout on her station. She had taken an unofficial break for almost twenty minutes, and a caller notification was blinking. She adjusted her earpiece. "Sorry sir, I-I guess I lost track of time."

"You've been slacking off for the past two weeks. Arriving late, spacing out when you have callers waiting, and I actually caught you dozing off on more than one occasion. If you don't shape up you better have some more job prospects lined up because I'm not gonna let this continue."

"W-won't happen again, sir."

Maxwell snatched the drawing from her desk and held it up. "*Get back to work.* If you want to finish this then come get it from me after you clock out." He turned and left without waiting for Erica's flustered reaction.

Erica watched him waddle off, overhearing him mutter, "druggies..."

She turned back to her station and let out a breath, trying to calm herself. She could draw another. She could *learn* another when she got home.

"You okay?"

Erica turned to see Brain leaning back again. She shook her head and said, "I'm just tired of all this."

"Y'know, you've been really out of it lately," said Brian. "If you need to talk—"

"Can't. My break's over." Erica hit the response button and listened to the next customer complain about fee raises that they apparently did not read about in the company's updated customer use agreement. In spite of her poor performance lately, she was certain she did not deserve the customer's verbal lashing that came soon after.

***

Erica struggled to keep her eyes off the clock throughout her shift. The minutes ticked by at an agonizingly slow rate, and the irate customers in her earpiece did little to ease her mood. On more than one occasion she wondered if there were better paying jobs for someone with an associate's degree and zero trade skills. If it weren't for the fact she was already struggling to pay the most basic of bills, she would almost be willing to take a lower pay rate at another position just to stay away from her ill-tempered boss and the countless angry customers berating her over things she never had any control over. It wasn't her fault the company was overcharging to stay ahead of superior competitors, but the complaints sure made her feel like it.

"Hello? Are you even listening?"

Erica blinked out of her thoughts and held her microphone closer. "Er, yeah. I mean yes. I'm listening, sir."

"Ma'am."

"Sorry..."

"Get your manager. I want to speak with him."

Erica winced and clutched the mic tighter. That would be the eighth time this week. She forced a calm voice and said, "My manager... certainly. I'll contact him right away."

She muted her mic and hesitated before pressing the call button that would alert Mr. Maxwell she had been daydreaming on the job again.

A hand tapped her shoulder, startling her.

Erica turned to see Brian.

"Gimme your headset. I'll handle it."

Her shoulders slumped in relief and she did so, quickly looking around to see if Maxwell was nearby.

Brian took only two minutes to feed the customer a few empty promises about things no one in the company would have control over and hung up. He handed the earpiece and mic back with a friendly smile. "That was close."

"Thanks, Brian," said Erica. "I don't think I could take another reprimand this week."

"Yeah, but this is becoming a trend. Whatever you're going through that's causing this can't be healthy. I can recommend a therapist if you need help."

"I can't afford a therapist," said Erica, looking back to her workstation.

"Talk with human resources here. I'm sure they could offer some suggestions."

Erica wanted to talk with Serena instead. The sea wolf always knew what to say. Even if she was just a figment of her own imagination.

"I'll think about it," Erica responded.

Brian paused with an unsure glance, then returned to his station. "Suit yourself, but if anything, I'm willing to talk things over, too. You don't have to try and work it out all by yourself."

"Yeah." Erica turned back to her own station and continued her shift. The day did not get much better.

***

By the time Erica stepped off the bus, she was desperate to leave this city and dive back into the Halcyon. She was thankful the bus's live feed was playing music this time. Unfortunately, she barely had time to settle in before her phone's email notification reminded her she had two bills due by the end of the week. Her next paycheck would arrive a week later. Wonderful…

She entered her apartment, tossed her work bag aside, and sat down on the Halcyon device's seat. She wanted nothing more than to be *elsewhere*. The seat felt far more comfortable than she remembered.

She placed the headset over her eyes and attached the neck harness, lining up the magnetic electrodes to her spine, and lay back as she fired up the unit.

She did not want to be here. Her only escape from constant reminders of loan payments, a dwindling food budget, and a demeaning job was the realm of her own mind, intensified by FluxTech's miraculous technology, and she embraced the opportunity to blissfully forget.

Minutes ticked away as she heard the droning whirr of the unit spooling up and loading the Halcyon program.

A message popped up in her vision, "Your previous session was in Ocean Environment. Would you like to try a different environment?"

Erica said aloud, "No. Continue loading Aquati—I mean, Ocean Environment."

Erica relaxed as the machine did its work. With eyes and ears covered by the headset, she no longer heard the rattling of her apartment's air conditioning unit or the noise of traffic beyond its walls.

She felt numbness flow from her neck all through the rest of her body, and her consciousness began to drift. On the threshold of sleep and awake, she allowed the concerns of her life to melt away in a haze. Memories of work disappeared behind new memories of the ocean, of submerged coral reefs, of sea wolves and hippocampi.

She was not Erica.

She was an anthropomorphic otter.

She was an explorer and adventurer.

She was Lyric.

***

A shape burst through the surface, diving through bubbles to see moonbeams shimmering through the ocean's haze. Far below, Lyric saw tiny glows of bioluminescent fish fade in and out.

The otter smiled and dove deeper. The ocean seemed far more inviting tonight, like a friend she had not seen in years.

Lyric swam around coral-covered rocks illuminated by webs of moonlight piercing the surface above. She slowly turned to her back, letting the beams glimmer over her soft fur as they wavered in the currents. She gazed up and drank in the beautiful sight of the beams above.

Her whiskers twitched at another presence nearby.

Lyric twisted to look around, then saw a shape flit below through gaps in the coral. She flicked her tail and dove deeper, catching another sight of the figure ahead.

Lyric shoved herself through the water, letting a few bubbles seep from her mouth as she smiled wider. Unrestrained by the current, she wove through more coral, some of it reaching far above the sandy seabed from the rocks it was anchored to, offering a perfect environment to play in.

Lyric darted past schools of glittering fish and lazily-waving sea kelp, chasing the figure through the underwater environment. It banked into a small trench of jagged rocks and Lyric followed.

Bioluminescent glows from plants and fish alike illuminated her on both sides as she swam, catching more glimpses of her target. Lyric angled up and over one of the boulders making up the trench's walls and saw the figure winding through a kelp bed.

Just keep moving in that direction… Lyric thought to herself.

She shot forward and spiraled down into the kelp. A bushy tail and fuzzy legs slipped into her vision and she reached out to grab Serena's webbed foot.

The sea wolf halted and turned, glancing back as moonbeams danced across her naked fur. Her eyes seemed to glow in the night's shadows.

Lyric smirked and lifted her paws to signal, *Tag. You're it.*

They both shoved upward toward the surface, leaving the coral and kelp behind, and burst into the cool night air.

Lyric took a breath and turned to Serena next to her. "I think that was a new record for catching you. I didn't even have to surface once."

Serena let out a soft chuckle. "Perhaps next time you will be skilled enough to save yourself, then?"

"Heh, maybe, but why worry about being rescued at all? I always make it out of whatever peril I'm in."

"Thanks to me, most of the time. But please, do stay away from the volcanic regions for a while. Last time was too close."

Lyric rolled her eyes. "Fine… I've been meaning to check out the deep trenches on the other side of the region anyway."

"You may need to practice holding your breath longer, then."

"Actually, I was hoping to get some help from the Hippocampi with that trip. You know, since they have gills and all…"

Lyric lay back and floated on the surface as she rested. The chase had not seemed all that exhausting, yet she still felt she needed to relax from… something. Whatever. Tonight she was as free as she always was.

She gazed up at the moon and stars. Serena did the same, floating next to her.

"You know…" said Lyric. "I've often wondered how this place fits in with everything out there."

"Like Aquatica's place in the universe?"

"Yeah… Every time I look up at the stars, no matter how many years I've been doing it, it never looks the same. It's all just barely familiar, but… the colors, the constellations… they shift almost as often as the seabed below. I keep wondering if I'll ever figure out some way to explain that sort of… chaos."

"Focus on one task at a time, Lyric," said Serena. "The answers you seek will come when you are ready for them."

Lyric, with one fuzzy ear submerged, heard a familiar echo below the surface. She turned her head to hear more, recognizing the musical tones and accompanying pitched tenors. She looked over at Serena and smiled, "They're moving en masse... It's a celebration!"

She flicked her tail to twist and dove under the surface. Bioluminescent trails streaked past as the echoes sang. With Serena following close behind, Lyric swam down alongside the elegant shapes: with powerful flippers on one half of the body, a humanoid torso, and an equine head, moonlight danced across their smooth bodies, and lateral lines of bioluminescent cells softly glowed within their shadows. Lyric had finally met back up with the Hippocampi.

The nearest one tilted his head to regard the otter as she swam nearby. He smiled, mane flowing with the surrounding current, and bid her to move closer to the rest of the tribe.

Lyric called out with her own echoes. Oddly, she could never figure out how she sounded out her own melodic calls to communicate with the Hippocampi, let alone understand exactly what the calls meant; yet somehow she always knew what they were saying. Perhaps that was how she got her name in the first place.

She swam along as a welcomed ally, watching as the glows on their bodies pulsed to the same rhythm. There were over a dozen of them, equine mermaids with a variety of finned physiques. Some were striped; others shimmered with metallic sheens against the moonbeams, while a rare few had striking patterns not unlike those of Orca whales.

Up ahead, she saw a shape take form. Their destination.

The Hippocampus nearest to her called for her to join them.

Lyric chirped a response before rising to surface for air. Three deep breaths, and she dove back down, following the faint light trails of the last Hippocampus.

Near the seabed, she saw the gaping cave entrance the tribe had swum into. Serena was waiting patiently in front of it.

The two friends glided in, seeing an occasional glow ahead and even on the wall from luminescent plants and coral. The cave itself stretched onward, though with plenty of room to move around.

Lyric was not sure how long she had swum, though she did not seem to have trouble holding her breath. The tunnel twisted and turned, and the otter swam on with nary a pang of fatigue. All the while, Serena remained close behind, silent and watchful.

Finally, a new light shone ahead, reflecting a soft silver hue against the cavern walls. Only now did Lyric realize her lungs demanded air.

She sped her pace as bubbles trailed from her muzzle. Serena moved ahead and took Lyric's hand, pulling her faster. She heard the Hippocampus tribe's echoes getting closer.

Lyric saw light beams shining across columns made from interconnected stalactites and stalagmites. An opening!

Hippocampi swam all around, singing songs of joy as Lyric and Serena drifted through. Lyric's whiskers sensed every one of them, their unique scents even underwater, along with the peculiar current that continued to flow around them. She found the surface and darted upward, breaking through just in time to take a fresh breath.

Serena emerged next to her. "Are you okay?"

Lyric nodded as she panted. She looked around the cavern. Glorious moonlight shone in from a crack in the ceiling high above, illuminating slick surfaces where barnacles, mussels, and kelp sprawled. Salty sea air wafted all around.

"The cavern breaches the surface…" Lyric muttered, staring up at it. "There's… there's *land* on Aquatica."

"Only when this region's tides are low," said a masculine voice nearby.

Lyric and Serena turned to see one of the Hippocampi floating on the surface. In the moon's light they could make out his bright orange skin striped with a darker pattern, melding with his black mane and dorsal fins.

"Our scouts discovered it months ago, and we have used its seclusion for our gatherings ever since."

Lyric smiled. "It's nice to see you again, Kitaro. I've been meaning to give you a report on a caved-in lava tube I discovered."

Kitaro waved the idea off with a thick webbed hand. "Later. Tonight, we enjoy each other's company. The tribe has been traveling far too long and wish to rest."

Lyric nodded with a grin. "Very well. I could use some relaxation myself." She turned to the rest of the cavern and moved to one of the outcroppings. Her webbed paws found a grip and she pulled herself from the water. She stood there dripping, looking down at her furry feet. "Huh… I'm actually standing on something… Holding up my own weight. No more floating around…"

Serena waded closer. "You were born with legs, which means you were meant to stand at least once!"

Lyric kneeled at the water's edge and held out her hand. "And so were you. Care to join me in the open air?"

Serena clasped the otter's hand without hesitation, and was lifted up onto land.

The two girls stood there looking around as water trailed from their fur. They listened to the wind whoosh across the opening high above as more water droplets fell from its edges and pattered onto the rocks. Lyric made her way across the outcropping to other sections of solid ground poking through the tranquil surface. The effort of walking did not seem at all difficult in spite of the length of time she had spent in water. In fact, she found skipping across the gaps to be uniquely fun.

Serena calmly strolled along behind her, seeing numerous creatures out of water for the first time. Not just barnacles and kelp, but also sea anemones closed up and ready to open when the tide returned, and tiny crabs skittering across the rocks closer to the walls.

Lyric sat down and looked through the water, finding it just as brightly illuminated thanks to the bioluminescent flora the Hippocampi had brought as decorations to their gathering place. Silvery fish, some glowing themselves, darted everywhere as the aquatic equines swam further below in their own underwater dance. She could almost hear their song even above the surface. Being on land seemed an odd novelty, but there was still so much more below the waves.

Serena approached and Lyric glanced up. "This is amazing," said the otter. "The volcanoes must be pushing land up past the surface. I can hardly believe there'll be so much more I haven't explored yet."

"So, now that you've discovered yet another new landmark, do you intend to spend the entire night up here away from the tribe you wanted to report to?"

Lyric shook her head. "Of course not. Hippocampi can't dance on land." She pushed off the rocks and dove back in, gliding down past darting fish as Serena spun and followed.

Hippocampi flashed amongst the submerged rock columns, some playing chase while others raced for the sheer fun of it. Lyric joined in, spiraling through a wide opening with Kitaro and two others as the rest of the tribe looked on.

The otter grinned wider, happy to simply be having fun again. No more concerns about where to explore next or how much she would need to commit to memory next time the region changed. Kitaro was right – tonight she could just enjoy herself.

The celebration went on and Lyric paid no mind to how long it lasted as they danced beneath the waves. Eventually, the tribe's collective energy was spent, and many settled into smaller schools circling the cavern to converse with one another. Others found crevices to relax in together.

Lyric broke from one of the schools to return to the surface. She pulled herself back out of the water and felt the weight of gravity once again. It was a peculiar feeling. Very familiar, yet so foreign to the region and life she knew here.

Serena surfaced and waded over. "Spent, as well?"

Lyric sat down on a patch of kelp. "I'm just enjoying the air. It's an interesting feeling, not having to hold my breath constantly. I wonder if dolphins or whales are ever jealous of such an opportunity."

The sea wolf emerged from the water and sat down next to her. "It seems rare I ever find you staying in one place these days. You're either rushing toward somewhere... or away from it."

Lyric tilted her head and said, "What would I be rushing away from?"

"You would know more than I would. Why do you continually attempt to map out an environment that always changes? Why try to make sense of this world's chaos with no desire to alter its evolution?"

Lyric stared back with no clear answer. "I don't know. I guess... when one always expects things to change, one never has to worry about stagnation. Like water in the ocean, always moving. Never settling." She looked down again and watched a pair of Hippocampi leisurely swim by. "I always want something to look forward to."

Serena put a hand on Lyric's bare shoulder. "You fret too much about belonging to a place you are already a part of. Even sea water will settle when it finds its proper place in the landscape."

Lyric kept her gaze on the water below. She blinked, realizing the bioluminescent flora was glowing brighter.

The Hippocampi drifted away. The water became filled with a bright haze.

Lyric glanced up and saw a fog rolling in through the opening above, scattering moonlight everywhere.

The brightness intensified. Lyric winced and realized she no longer felt Serena's hand.

"Serena?"

She shut her eyes against the blinding light. Her whiskers twitched as she tried to sense her friend, or even the salty sea air, but found no trace. The whooshing wind and splashing water faded behind a droning beep steadily increasing in volume.

She was not Lyric.

Not now! Not when I was having so much fun!

Lyric tried to scramble away from the haze, but she could not even feel the cool water against her fur.

She did not have fur.

Just ten more minutes and... No...

Aquatica did not exist.

Serena, where are you?

***

Erica opened her eyes to the static image of the Halcyon's loading screen and the device's cool-down timer already running.

She sighed and shut off the alarm. This routine was uncomfortably familiar. No matter how relaxing or fun the Halcyon's trance was, she still had to return to a life of being trampled on.

She removed the headset and put it aside, then rubbed her face. There *had* to be a way to bypass the mandatory break periods.

She put her hand on the Halcyon unit itself. Even with the mass of heat sinks within, the casing was still very hot, warranting the break period to let the machine cool down.

Erica stood and checked a nearby clock. Two hours until her recommended bed time. Her stomach grumbled to remind her she had not eaten since lunch.

She made her way to the kitchen area to find something meager to stick in the microwave, but all she found was one more packet of instant ramen. Tomorrow would have been a grocery day, if she had any money. This month's paycheck was certain to disappear to loan repayments and bills.

She sighed and fixed herself a bowl, then turned on her desktop computer.

Erica immediately pulled up her browser's search bar and typed, "Halcyon cool-down override." She was tired of this life she could not change. The less time she spent in it the better.

None of the results looked promising. Most of what popped up involved a bunch of threads from various forums about the ethics of the Halcyon device itself, unofficial reports from people who were most likely never involved in its development as they claimed, and basic information about the Halcyon project that had been fed to news outlets months ago.

Erica wondered if the private forum meant for Halcyon experiment subjects would have any answers. Then again, asking a company how to bypass a critical safety function of their own device would probably be in poor taste...

Erica sat back and tried to think of another way, but nothing she came up with sounded logical or cheap. FluxTech's stipend given to experiment subjects was just barely enough to cover an internet speed upgrade and increased power costs for running the units.

She checked the clock again. She had found no answers after searching for over an hour. What else was there to do that was stopping her from going to bed early? The unit would not be ready again until well after bedtime.

Remembering what she had to look forward to at work tomorrow, Erica's heart sank. She wasn't sure how much more she could take. The more she could forget about work and upcoming bills the better she figured she would be, mentally. She needed a way to calm herself. She needed the Halcyon. She needed Aquatica.

She wondered if she would be better off staying awake, waiting for the unit to be ready and just sleep while in the Halcyon's trance.

No... the cool-down would wake her up.

Erica relegated herself to her depressing fate and got up to toss her bowl in the sink. All through her usual bedtime routine she kept checking the clock despite knowing the Halcyon device would not be ready for hours. The thought of returning to work, of being yelled at once again by her boss and countless angry customers, was too much already.

Erica went to bed and tried to fall asleep, but ended up tossing and turning. Her tired body begged for sleep, but her stressed mind denied her such comfort.

She looked at the clock again. She should have dozed off two hours ago, yet remained awake and... afraid. Finally, she was actually *afraid* to go to work, knowing she would likely break down if she were forced to deal with more irate customers. She didn't feel ready to help anybody. She could not help herself, most of all.

She looked over at the Halcyon unit. It stood like a shadow against the window of the living area. An hour left until cool-down ended.

Erica got up and sat in the device's chair. This time it did not feel as comfortable. She attached the headset and neck harness, then prepared to wait. If a dive was what would calm her down, then at least it might help her withstand another day of work.

Erica drummed her fingers on the armrest, watching the cool-down timer in the headset. By the time it would be ready, a full session might end with just enough time for her to get to work.

She *needed* this.

***

Overcast skies hinted at rain. Wind churned the waves of Aquatica's endless ocean. Below the surface, the water was murkier. No presence of fish nor whale. Everything felt different.

Lyric slowly swam through what felt like a stronger-than-normal current. Days of dreary weather were to be expected even in a world such as this, but what could explain the empty oceans? Even the coral was missing.

The otter searched for what felt like hours, calling out above the water with her voice and below with her unique echoes of song, but there came no response. As the water passed through her whiskers, she sensed nothing but silt and salt.

Lyric passed groupings of rock, but with no signs of volcanic activity. She swam through deep trenches, but they were as bare as the rest of the sea floor. It wasn't long before she realized she had been submerged for an extraordinarily long time yet had no struggle holding her breath.

Why surface to breathe at all? Why return to a barren world?

Lyric halted and shook the thought from her mind. Aquatica always had something to look forward to. Today was just… unique.

She angled up and took her time swimming to the surface, still having no problem with air. She did not dare test herself by breathing in the water.

Through the murky depths, she noticed a rock grouping towering toward the surface. Another piece of land had suddenly appeared overnight.

Lyric sped her pace, forgetting to surface until she was much closer.

Breaking through the waves, she finally took a breath and saw the rocks jutted high into the air. Lyric swam closer, letting the waves carry her to it.

Upon reaching its jagged side, she grabbed hold and pulled herself free of the water. She glanced back as more waves crashed against it. She saw nothing but ocean all across the horizon.

She turned back to the massive rock. The surface was slick, but her paws did not slip despite her entire body remaining soaked. Curiosity compelled her to climb, and she made her way skyward. The rock had seemed tall looking at it from the water, but her climb to the top was short.

Lyric stood at the summit and looked around as the winds flowed through her fur, partially drying her. More ocean all around. She was at the highest point, and despite all she could see, everything still looked as depressing as it did below the surface.

"This is not my Aquatica…" Lyric muttered.

The rock jolted and split beneath her feet. Lyric stumbled back but regained balance before falling. A portion of the rock pulled away and sank into the sea, leaving behind a mass of foam and bubbles.

Why would FluxTech's servers maintain such a dull, dreary environment? Did something happen when loading it up?

Lyric blinked. How did she know about FluxTech?

She looked around again, but was not sure what she was searching for. She suddenly remembered Erica, and the bills, and the multitudes of angry customers she had been trying to avoid. Yet somehow, she was in what was supposed to be her world.

She suddenly knew where she was in the real world. She knew she was in a trance, reclining in a chair with magnetic electrodes stimulating her brain stem.

She glanced down and saw her own human hand. No fur, no webbing between her fingers, no soft pads. But this false Aquatica remained, too.

"What's going on…?" she said to herself.

Everything went dark, and she heard traffic outside her apartment.

***

Erica blinked awake to the Halcyon device's "Standing By" message in her headset. She had fallen asleep while waiting for the cool-down to end. It had been a natural dream.

"Great," she muttered. "Then I can load this up for real."

She moved to begin the dive, then realized the traffic noises were too loud for the middle of the night.

Wait…

She threw off the headset and saw bright sunlight shining through her window's closed blinds.

"Oh, *crap!*"

She released the harness and scrambled to her closet for a fresh change of clothes.

While tugging them on, she grabbed her phone to call her boss and beg him to let her come in today. There was already a voicemail notification.

The recording played Heather's voice, "Erica, you need to get here immediately. Mr. Maxwell is livid, and I don't think—"

Her voice halted and then Mr. Maxwell's voice shouted from the background, "If she's not here in ten minutes, I'm halving this month's paycheck! And she better be ready to take a drug test! I've had enough of her disrespect!"

Heather's voice returned, "Y-yes sir. I'll let her know." The voice sounded closer. "Please call soon so we at least know you're on your way. You're on really thin ice this time…"

The message ended. Erica fell back onto her bed and saw the message had come over an hour ago. Distraught, she debated whether she was ready, emotionally, to handle being chewed out by her boss only to return to seven hours of furious customers for a fraction of her usual paycheck for the rest of the month.

She shuddered and dialed her work place. She wasn't sure what to say.

"Welcome to Duval Communications!" came the pre-recorded response. "If you know your party's four-digit extension—"

Erica immediately dialed Heather's extension and waited.

"Duval Communications, this is Heather speaking. How may I help you today?"

"Heather, it's me."

"Erica? Are you okay?"

"N... no. Listen, I need to submit an emergency absence."

"You've used them up, all in the past month, might I add. Please, tell me what's wrong. Brian and I are worried."

"I'll tell you later. Right now I just... I can't come in. It's too late. Tell Mr. Maxwell I've come down with something serious."

"Erica, I can't keep covering for you like this!"

Erica paused, then shut her eyes and ended the call. "This isn't happening..." she said.

This was it. She couldn't pay her bills or rent this month, let alone buy food. Even if she did come in for work, the pay would neither save her nor justify the mental breakdown she knew she would have by the end of her shift.

"What's the point?" she said to herself. "I'm having a breakdown *now*."

She looked back over at the Halcyon device. It was but a bandage, masking but not healing the infection of her misery. She wanted to dive back in so badly, but why? What would there be to wake up to after the session ended?

Erica leaned up and stared at the floor.

Why wake up at all?

She glanced over at her computer, then hurried over and switched it on.

Dr. Harper's words resonated in her mind, *...a number of our tests have proven remarkably effective in rehabilitating coma patients.*

Erica logged into the private forum for Halcyon subjects and skimmed the search function for any mention of coma patients. She could hardly believe what she was thinking.

"I'm not crazy..." she reminded herself. "I just need peace..."

She found sparse answers, but enough to convince her it might be worth it. Halcyon diving actually stimulated brain activity in a few rare cases. If she could induce a coma and dive in before the effect hit... how long might they keep her connected? Would FluxTech force a cool-down override?

Erica pushed herself back from her desk. This was unreal. It was *dangerous* thinking. How could she even entertain such a selfish thought?

"But what else is there to come back to?" She knew the dive couldn't last... so she might as well enjoy as much of it as she could. It's not like she was trying to commit suicide or anything... She did not want to die. She just wanted to stop the pain, at least for a little while longer.

An email notification popped up. The message preview showed only two words: "You're Fired."

Erica grabbed her phone, trying to act before rational thought could stop her. She would need to leave a message to someone ensuring they would come find her in time.

She attached Heather and Brian's numbers to the message, then typed, "I can't take this anymore. I need help"

She paused, looking at the second sentence.

"I need help..." she muttered.

She staggered to her feet, torn over what to do. Inducing a coma did not just feel dangerous. It felt *wrong*.

Her legs weakened and she crumbled to her knees, clutching her phone tightly in her hand. "I can't do this..."

She glanced over to the kitchen area in desperation, still overcome with the thought of inducing herself with something from her medicine cabinet as the weight of a dreadful future sank onto her.

She pulled herself back up and moved toward the cabinet, wondering if she even had something that might work.

Lyric, stop!

Erica froze. That voice...

"Serena...?"

She remained still, desperately hoping to hear the sea wolf's voice again.

Nothing.

Erica dropped her phone and leaned on her desk. She couldn't follow through.

She looked back at the Halcyon device and trudged over. She sat down, strapped on the headset and harness, and booted up her last session. The last four hours she would be able to enjoy for a long, long time.

***

Mist hovered over the ocean's tranquil surface as a calm rain fell.

Lyric floated on her back, eyes closed as the raindrops softly pattered against her fur. She wasn't sure what she had been trying to escape, but now it was behind her. Now she could relax. Just her... and the sea.

Aquatica embraced her like an affectionate mother, and for once, all Lyric wanted to do was float there in comfort, gently rocked by the waves.

She did not know how long she spent doing nothing but drifting, and she did not care. This was what she wanted.

Her mind would occasionally ponder the possibility of exploring again, maybe see if there were more lava tubes opening up or if the Hippocampi were migrating, but none of it seemed too enticing today.

She felt someone brush against her.

She opened her eyes and saw Serena emerging to float on her own back next to her. She glanced over to Lyric and smiled, taking her hand.

Lyric lazily smiled back, content. She hardly noticed the mist around them getting thicker.

Everything disappeared. The light faded to black nothingness.

Lyric wanted to look around, but she could neither see nor hear. She could not feel anything. She was not even sure if she was moving around.

"What's going on? Hello?"

Nothing.

The tranquil peace she had felt devolved into fear, then panic. It was as if all her senses were gone.

"Where am I? Can anyone hear me? Anyone, *please!*"

Still nothing.

"Serena!!"

Lyric…

"Serena, where are you?"

It's okay. I'm here now. We are together here.

"Where am I? Is this still the Halcyon? Wait… The Halcyon. I'm lucid again. I'm Erica."

You are both, are you not?

"I'm… I want to be Lyric."

Then you are.

"But what's going on?"

You're in a coma, induced by paramedics. They found you in the middle of a dive and did not want to risk waking you suddenly. The Halcyon is active, but offline, hence the limbo we float in now. You're being transported to a hospital for monitoring and a gentler wake-up.

"How do you know all this?"

You know it yourself. You overheard the paramedics while in your dreamstate. I am merely relaying it to your lucid mind.

"You… you are not a figment of my imagination, are you? Are you the Halcyon's A.I.?"

In a way, yes, but in another way, no. We are one and the same, Lyric. The Halcyon uses the human brain as a processor, and what it pulls into the simulation comes directly from our subconscious. Memories, desires, everything you may not notice in your waking life. The Halcyon gives me presence, but it does not give me self-awareness. You do.

"So… what you're explaining to me… It's the Halcyon's A.I. informing me of how it works."

You wished to know what was happening, and so I obliged.

Lyric/Erica was silent for a moment. She still felt nothing in the void.

"Serena… When I heard your voice, in the waking world… was I hallucinating?"

It's possible. Stress can mess with our minds in many ways.

"You saved me. Again."

Lyric/Erica heard a familiar soft chuckle. It felt oddly comforting.

I suppose you might say I'm your rational half. Your conscience, even.

After another moment of silence, Serena spoke again. *It's okay, Lyric. You'll be fine. They're taking good care of you.*

"Of us."

Yes.

"But what will happen to me now? I have no job, no money for bills or food… All I wanted to do was escape all the stress. I wanted to spend time with you."

It could never last. It was never meant to. Eventually, the servers would shut down, and depending on the feedback FluxTech gets, the Halcyon project may become very different than it is now, if it is ever released to a wide audience.

"But that doesn't answer my question. I don't know where to go now. I have nothing, *nothing* to look forward to anymore."

I wish I could give a meaningful answer, but I am still just a part of your subconscious. I cannot give much better advice than you can rationally think of.

"So when they wake me up in the hospital…"

This will disappear, and I will go back to being a whisper in your mind.

"But… I'll miss you."

At the risk of sounding like a cartoon you watched when you were younger… I will always be with you. I always have been, and will continue to do so.

Almost as if the invisible sea wolf sensed Lyric/Erica's heart sink, she added, *And who knows? Perhaps we will swim together again in another dream. A real one, not brought on by a machine's trance. Every night presents a possibility to visit Aquatica once again.*

Muffled noises swelled into Lyric/Erica's ears. A monotone beep increased in volume, but this one was different.

***

Erica opened her eyes. She did not see the Halcyon device's cool-down notification. She saw a hospital room's ceiling. The droning beep next to her was not the unit's alarm. It was an EKG machine, monitoring her pulse.

"Hey, she's waking up!" came a familiar voice.

Erica looked over to see Heather and Brian at her bedside.

Heather gave her a gentle hug. "We were so worried! We thought you were about to… you know…"

"That wasn't my intention," Erica said weakly. "Wait, how did you know? I don't remember sending that message."

"Well, we got it somehow," said Brian. He held up his phone to show Erica's text, "I can't take this anymore. I need help."

Heather added, "After your phone call you sounded like you were getting desperate about something. Then we got the text and became *really* concerned."

"Yeah…" said Erica. She looked up at them. "I-I'm so sorry for putting you through that. I really didn't want to try something so… so selfish. But you're right, I was desperate. I still am."

"About what? Really, you can tell us."

Erica sighed. She was tired of hiding behind the non-disclosure agreement.

"You heard of the Halcyon project? I signed up to be a test subject for it and was selected out of their lottery of applicants. I… got a bit too addicted."

Heather and Brian blinked in surprise. Brian spoke first.

"That would explain a lot, actually. I never considered that's what it might've been all about."

"Yeah, well, it's over for me now. I'm pretty sure my condition will void the experiment."

"Actually, I think it might give FluxTech exactly what they need," said Heather. "I heard on the news today that the experiment will be ending much sooner than initially expected, which may mean you weren't the only case of addiction."

Erica sighed, both depressed and relieved. "I don't really know what to do now. The experiment is over, I'm out of a job and have no way of paying for, well, *anything* now."

"Your parents are on their way. Booked the soonest flight they could find," said Brian. "I'm sure they can help a little."

"And after that?"

"Remember when I offered to suggest therapists? I'm positive there are some within your insurance range."

A knock came at the open door. The three glanced over to see a white-haired man in a suit entering.

"Ms. Lancaster?" he said. "My name is David Higgins. I work for FluxTech. May I come in for a moment?"

Erica nodded. "Sure. Um, am I in trouble for anything related to the experiment?"

Higgins waved the notion away. "Don't worry, everything is fine. I just wanted to tell you FluxTech will be covering your hospital stay. I overheard your friend mentioning therapists and I would also like to note that we have arranged therapy sessions for all test subjects from the experiment. There's even a support group here in this city that you can attend."

"There is? So I wasn't the only one to go through this?"

Higgins nodded. "This doesn't leave the room but… yes, we noticed a surprising number of subjects who took to the Halcyon's trance a bit too enthusiastically. Rest assured, we will be taking these results into consideration as the Halcyon project continues to develop, but as it stands we aren't so sure if a mass public release will be down the line any time soon. In the meantime, we at FluxTech would like to thank you for your contribution. We will also provide a bit more to your last stipend to help compensate you for what you've been going through at work. We hope it will be enough to get you back on your feet."

"Thanks," said Erica. "It's very much appreciated. But what about the unit in my apartment? Is the experiment over already?"

"We're in the process of recalling active units and shutting down the servers. Your unit will likely be uninstalled by the time you're discharged from the hospital."

"So… that's it." Aquatica's gone, was Erica's first thought.

No… she might yet visit it again in a natural dream.

Higgins placed a folder on the bedside table. "You'll find a post-experiment form and survey here, along with information of recommended therapists in your area, which FluxTech will pay for. There's also some information on the support group. I highly recommend attending. Being among peers who have gone through similar circumstances can help you cope immensely."

Erica nodded. "Thank you, sir."

***

Erica stepped off the bus to the city's community center. The building looked rather old and drab, but that was not too different from the rest of the city. She entered through the double doors and made her way to the room where the support group would be meeting.

She wished Serena were here, in person.

Almost as if on cue, another thought reminded her that Serena could not offer support in the way an actual person could. A figment of her imagination could only offer limited comfort. She needed real interaction with real people who could offer real advice.

She came to the right room and nudged the door open to find the support group already situated in a circle together.

The group leader, a tall man in red with blonde hair, waved her over. "Come on in! We were just discussing aspects of people we met in our dreamstates."

The group opened up a spot and provided a chair, which Erica silently took.

"Would you like to tell us who you are, Miss…?"

"Lancaster," said Erica. "Erica Lancaster. And, um… I have something I can contribute to the discussion."

"By all means, Erica."

"I had a friend… who was in the habit of rescuing me from my more, uh… dangerous thrills within the trance. I later learned she was more than just that. She claimed she was a part of my identity given form by the Halcyon's A.I. A part of my rational side."

The group murmured to each other for a moment before another spoke, "I had a friend kinda like that, too. I'm single in real life, but in my dreams, she was my wife."

"Mine was my long-lost brother."

"Mine was a tiger that talked."

Erica looked over and smirked. "Bipedal, too?"

"Y—yeah…" said the man in glasses. "His fur color alternated instead of being orange against his stripes."

The group leader spoke up, "That's another fascinating thing about this technology. Even the people we meet can all be a part of us. Different aspects we never knew about ourselves, giving us yet another opportunity to learn who we are."

**

The session ended after another brief discussion, though Erica caught herself daydreaming through part of it. The group leader said that was all right. First meetings can still be a bit different. Erica felt good enough about it to attend the next session, however.

She exited the room and made her way back out, intending to visit the library to check for job prospects.

A sign caught her attention: AQUATIC CENTER, followed by an arrow.

Erica turned down the hall and came to a set of double doors. Opening them up, she found the community center's massive Olympic-sized pool.

Even during normal operating hours, there were only two people there. On the far wall she saw a kiddie pool area, where a cute cartoon otter had been painted on the wall.

Erica smiled and turned to continue on her way, making note to visit again very soon.

The last few steps of the road are hard, and the place they lead uncertain, but Terri has no choice but to continue down the path.

CASTLE PHOENIX

Bill Kieffer

The bright sunshine on her face felt good as she snoozed. She was both comfy and stiff, having falling asleep in the passenger seat of their car. She felt blessed, although that was not a word that she would normally use. The red Mini Cooper was one of the few things they co-owned; open and legal. One of the few things that they could point to and say this is ours. Mine and Diane's. We are a couple.

She should have luxuriated a little longer and enjoyed the feeling of contentedness. Pain free moments were few and far between. But the car stopped and the clock was ticking.

Terri opened her eyes and was only mildly surprised not to see Diane. The woman who sat in the driver's seat was different in every way from her long-time lover. Where Diane was short and built like a linebacker, this woman was tall and built like a swimmer. Where Diane's complexion was sun tanned to a well-worn smooth camel leather, this woman could not have been whiter without being soaked in bleach. Her clothes were too conservative. Her hair was dark and natural, not the neon colors that made Diane's whole face pop with joy.

This woman, in fact, looked like her husband Gary. Except with a wig.

Poor Gary was dead, she thought, and on the heels of that thought, that flutter of black feathers in her heart, Terri was reminded that Diane was also dead.

I, too, will be dead soon, Terri thought without a trace of bitterness. She wasn't ready yet, but, then, whoever was? Such was the human condition.

"Here we are," the young woman said, "417 Cookman Ave." She looked out the window and then gave Gary's smile of confused disappointment. "Are you sure this is the right address? It's an empty lot."

My daughter, Terri reminded herself. Michele. With one L, who lives a charmed, normal life with only the inability to buy personalized knick-knacks to make her world less than perfect.

At least, until her father died four years ago.

At least, until her mom came out of the closet three years ago.

At least, until her Aunt Diane was killed violently in a traffic stop gone wrong two years ago. It had generated too much media attention for Michele's family.

And finally, Terri's own diagnosis of cancer and its sudden onslaughts of pain and terror. The terror of death slowly ramping up and then crashing into a series of unfortunate, inconvenient, and unscheduled events.

Terri felt bad for her, but shortly, Michele would be able to get back to her own pleasantly scheduled life.

"Don't feel sorry for yourself, Puss-Puss" Gary chided her. His death hadn't separated him from her the way Diane's death had. He had supported her in life in all ways, beyond what any self-respecting man should. "Save your energy for the here and now."

Michele had gotten used to her mother not answering her right away. Between the pain and the medication, she'd developed the habit of gathering herself before speaking these days. Terri had always hated snappishness. She'd caught herself snapping at her granddaughter, Bella, once.

Cancer might kill her, but it wasn't going to change her.

Terri looked across the lot. You'd have never known that Club Phoenix had ever existed. She could see clear through to the building on the corner lot, which had been made of the same old orange-red bricks as Club Phoenix. The bright red steel staircase where she first kissed Diane was still there. It was still painted a bright fire engine red. She never knew why it was painted red in the first place. It didn't match the building. It thrilled her to see this one thing was still there.

Behind her closed eyes, Terri could still see the stucco facade of the night club. The second floor still showed the old bricks and an electric sign with a bent arrow that blinked against the words LIQUOR and FEMALE REVUE. At least in her memories it did.

Terri had hated the exterior. It'd looked worn and outdated in the late eighties and, to Terri, it had exemplified the cheapness, the crassness, and the shadows women like her had had to hide in.

Diane had loved it. The white hand painted sign that said "Club Paradise," the black Phoenix and yellow flames in the windows, and the galleries of ads declaring the joys of "spring time freshness" and bras that crossed you heart—it was all art to this wonderful short Italian girl. Even the bathroom doors marked DYKES and QUEENS would have been framed art if she'd had her way.

In fact, Terri recalled that Diane had taken rolls upon rolls of pictures of the interior with her little PHD camera. As far as she knew, Diane had never developed them.

Or maybe she'd never shared them with Terri.

"This is the right place," Terri said, getting out of the car. She'd known Asbury Park had changed and was in the process of changing. It wasn't just gentrification; the town was now an openly gay community. The city seemed to rejoice in it. Or at least the downtown area did.

Like many QUILTBAG people her age, Terri was ecstatic to have lived to see the changes but saddened to have been born too early to use it to her full advantage. Gary mentally squeezed her shoulder and reminded her again not to feel sorry for herself.

She wondered, briefly, if ghosts ever got tired of repeating themselves.

Michele got out of the car as Terri stepped onto the sidewalk. Michele looked at her funny and, for a moment, she thought she'd been talking to Gary aloud. She'd had a lot of different conversations with Gary on this curb, over the years. In retrospect, she could see he'd been trying to be supportive without being left behind. There'd been tears, angry words, numb good byes, and an assortment of soft kisses through the window of his Camaro.

Instead, Terri realized the look was because her bald head was going commando. She'd left her wig in the car.

She chuckled softly. Michele had bought her a nice blonde WASP wig, skeeved out that her mother had been wearing various wigs that had belonged to her mother's dead lover. "Normalcy is a luxury, not a requirement," Terri responded when Michele had clucked over Diane's wigs.

Michele had responded by buying her a wig as an early Christmas present. It was a very nice, boring wig made from human hair (which didn't skeeve out her daughter, somehow). The brand name was even Wasp, which tickled the dying woman's fancy a bit. Still, the only reason Terri had even worn it was that Michele had flown it in from London at what Terri imagined was a great expense.

Michele held her hands out, going through where she thought the door must have been. The "female revue" had been a long time gone before she and Gary had entered the place for the first time and yet still pictures of the dancers from the late sixties had graced the walls. There were even a few photographs of what Terri had been sure were drag queens.

Here was the coat check. They'd take your coats and occasionally sell you coke.

Here was the dance floor.

Here was the bar.

Here were the tables.

Seems like such a small space now, with all the walls gone. But it had been a whole new world for her. It had been a scary time and it was, surprisingly, the end of an era for her. Things would never be the same again.

Another line crossed off the bucket list.

Terri was vaguely disappointed. She'd expected something to happen. She didn't know what, but something.

No, I know what I expected.

Since Diane's death, she'd never really felt her presence. Not that she believed in ghosts or even an afterlife but, after Gary's heart attack, she'd always felt him with her. That connection had remained.

Not so with Diane.

Looking logically at it, Terri knew it was the way they'd been torn asunder at the end. Diane had gone to North Carolina to visit her family and Terri hadn't been invited. In point of fact, she'd been specifically excluded. When Diane had been pulled over and then shot when she stepped out of her rented car, Terri had to hear about it from Fox News. She was less welcome to the funeral than the Westboro Baptist Church.

She learned from CNN that Diane's family had been mixed race. As out and in your face about her sexuality as she'd been, she'd never once mentioned that she was half black.

It didn't matter; I wasn't a Breeder.

Diane's voice stopped Terri dead in her tracks. She became dizzy with a sudden spell.

When you next see me again, I won't be any of that.

Terri felt suddenly unsteady on her feet. She had to be remembering something her lover had said once; some forgotten argument or drunken confession. She wasn't hearing things; this was a snippet of dialogue bouncing off the cutting room floor of her mind.

"Mom?" Michele was at her side suddenly, supporting her. She staggered, spinning her daughter in a little half circle as she tried to regain her balance and her bearings. Terri came to a stop next to something that looked like a teal rabbit's hutch, an elevated box on four spindly legs. Still, it appeared solid enough. Terri latched onto it and steadied herself for a moment.

It proved remarkably solid. Michele fluttered and hovered, as if concerned someone might accuse her of attacking some poor old lady if she moved too quickly. The thought made Terri smile for the brief instant before she realized that she probably did look quite ancient.

"Are you ready to go, Mom?"

"Just give me a minute, Michele," Terri said. She'd been more than ready to go the second that voice had been in her head, but unless her daughter was willing to drive over the curb up to this strange quadruped box, she wasn't going anywhere. The obvious, sad truth was that the monster in her head was tormenting her with promises of madness. She wished she could believe in ghosts. She counted to ten, feeling the strength returning to her legs.

Terri opened her eyes, and the world spun. She tried to focus on the green grass, but it was wild and uncut. It had a mind of its own. A teddy bear walked up the sidewalk from the east, the boardwalk area. He swayed slightly as the cement rippled under his plush brown feet.

As he came to the teal box, Terri saw that he wasn't a teddy bear. Nor was he a boy in a bear suit. He was something alive and not alive. Like a cartoon bear, he seemed flat and without dimension. Yet, he seemed awfully realistic.

The bear smiled at Terri and stood on tip-toes to open the foot wide doors on the street side of the box. With a wordless grunt, the little bear-thing leapt and wiggled and twisted until it was inside the box.

The most outrageous part of all this was that Terri's heart was nonchalant as the box vibrated with the struggles of a small anthropomorphic bear. What was this? A bear trap from Tiffany's? She pushed herself off the box, her legs wisely deciding to support her full weight.

She walked around the box and found two little red wooden doors with glass inserts.

Terri had trouble focusing for a moment on the words over the door.

"Little Free Library. Take One; Leave One."

As if she'd spoken some magic phrase aloud, the monster in her head let go and the mundane world snapped back into place without smiling bears and magical boxes. Just like that, delusions gone.

Except, the teal box remained.

*Is **this** what I came for?*

"Is this what we came here for?" Michele asked curiously. Quietly.

She hadn't told her daughter what this old address had meant to her. How she had met Diane here and how they became lovers. It was all so terribly complicated and, truth was, Terri had felt guilty and remorseful about some portions of it. Just not enough to wish it had never happened.

She just wanted a connection, some small token, beyond the Mini, that Diane's family couldn't begrudge her or take away when so much was already taken away.

She opened the doors to the teal box and stared at the dozen or so books inside.

"I heard about these," Michele said. "They are like little pop-up libraries. Bird feeders for bookworms."

It had seemed to pop-up, Terri thought. She certainly hadn't noticed it when she'd gotten out of the Mini. But then, she'd been too busy looking at the empty lot and staring into the eighties. Suddenly, her eyes were drawn to a placemat sized children's book.

She pulled out the thin, glossy tome. The cover was a colorful assortment of cartoon animals drawn in a strange mixture of water colors and colored crayons, not unlike the Little Golden Books of her own youth. A dozen different fully clothed animals capered in front of a white castle. Little yellow pennants fluttered from its towers and each flag had a little black bird, rising up from the flames.

The title of the book was *Castle Phoenix* and in the lower right hand corner of the cover was a little bear in a row boat, waving upwards to the reader. Waving at her.

"Yes," Terri said. "This is what I came for."

***

Terri called off the rest of the "bucket list drive" for the day. It wasn't a very ambitious list, things she wanted to see again before popping off. Places she associated with Gary and/or with Diane. But she'd forgotten how much walking was involved in those shared pleasures. The Collingswood Flea Market had nearly killed her. The bear episode was nothing but a dehydration induced vision.

She napped on the drive home, clutching the book.

She dreamed of Diane drawing. In the dream, her lead pencil bled colors across the paper. Rainbow streaks that Terri thought might stain the couch danced off the paper. She said she was drawing them: Terri, Gary, and Diane. And on each new page, she drew Gary further and further away. Terri tried to stop her, but she laughed, not unkindly, that "that ship had sailed."

The last tiny drawing of Gary floated away and Terri cried, furious, that he never got angry about being sent away. He was just a little blob of lead etching that could have been anything, and Diane held her as the tears ran dry.

***

"Grandma! Read to me!"

Terri smiled at the bundle of energy that was her only granddaughter. Wrapped in a costume that was a microfiber fluffy white unicorn bathrobe, Amitola pushed *Castle Phoenix* into her hands. Her father's Amerind skin and deep dark eyes made her the prettiest child she'd ever seen. Her grandmother admitted that she was biased, but didn't give a fig.

"Amy," Michele made scooting motions with her hands, giving Terri a look and a smile. She was sending them both to bed. Terri and Amitola giggled into the bedroom, although standing had depleted a portion of her energy.

There was very little fussing. Amitola got into her *Adventure Time* pajamas and had crawled into her Adventure Time bed linens by the time Terri had settled into her recliner chair. It matched nothing in the child's room. It didn't matter; it'd be here a year at the most. In the meantime, a rainbow throw blanket helped it to blend in.

Amitola stared at her prematurely aged hands with the greatest patience a seven-year-old could muster. She, too, had learned Grandma needed a moment alone with the words in her head before speaking.

"Do you want to read about Flynn, instead?" Terri asked, hinting. The truth was, *Castle Phoenix* made her slightly uneasy.

Terri fingered the smooth, glossy cover and wondered if a child had ever read *Castle Phoenix*. It was almost too perfect. There was at least one page missing, Terri figured, as she'd never been able to find a copyright or publishing information. There wasn't even an author name or artist credits given on the remaining pages (she'd looked, because she'd half expected to see Diane's legal name… the art was in the same style as Diane's… just not as adult).

Amitola shook her head vigorously. She saw the book as a delightful present and her grandmother's duty was to read it to her. It was hard to argue with the Princess, even if she was sure her granddaughter could have read the book herself.

"Start with the Bear In the Boat."

The Bear in the Boat was the first story of several in the *Castle Phoenix* book.

So, Terri read the story of Barry the Bear aloud.

Barry ran the ferry across the river. He rowed some, but mostly he pulled on a rope using a science that fascinated his passengers. Barry went back and forth and helped people on their way. But Barry dreamed of bigger things, of pushing off with the currents and watching the wind collect in his sails. He dreamed of waves instead of wakes. He didn't necessarily want to go to places other than the other side of the river, but Barry's river was much too tame. He wanted it to be more of an adventure.

Then one day, Princess Puss-Puss showed up. She was lost and being chased by monstrous Dhouts. She needed to get to Safe Harbor. Barry did not know where Safe Harbor was but he knew of a Safe Haven. Maybe they were close together? In either case, his heart recognized that this was his chance at adventure.

For the first time ever, when he landed them on the opposite shore, Barry got out of his boat and never turned back. He left a note for his brothers, took Princess Puss-Puss' hand in his, and helped her forge a path into the unknown (to them) forest.

By the end of the story, Amitola was asleep, cuddled up with a familiar looking toy bear.

Terri, however, was too anxious to sleep. She was pretty sure she'd never seen that toy before.

Except, tottering along on a sidewalk in Asbury Park.

***

Wigless and on the floor surrounded by photographs from a half-forgotten cookie tin, Terri was having a good day. She was helping Michele pick photographs to be scanned for an Internet tribute for her father, Gary. Her job was mostly to give context to the photographs.

This picture was from Carlsbad Caverns. This is you at The Land of Make Believe. This is your father at work. This is a picture of his boat.

"Dad had a boat?" Michele asked with a spark of interest.

Terri nodded. "My parents had no money to spend on our wedding and his parents never approved of me. So, Gary sold his boat to pay for it and our honeymoon."

Michele smiled seeing the romance in the gesture (as Terri had also), but then she seemed suddenly flustered. Terri thought Michele was going to ask why he never bought another boat, when things got better. Financially. Instead, she asked (bravely for Michele), "Did his parents know? Is that why they didn't approve?"

Terri laughed, knowing what she meant. Her daughter had never really liked talking about her sexuality, but she liked talking about the cancer less. On this, mother and daughter agreed. "I didn't know. I don't think they even knew bisexuals existed." In point of fact, even some people in the community still refused to believe in bisexuals. She herself occasionally doubted that she was anything more than a lesbian. Being with Diane had so been liberating and their love so strong that she wondered on the bad days if she had simply wasted her years with Gary.

But on the good days, Terri knew she had loved Gary. There was no doubting that he had loved Terri, too. Still, even on a good day, Terri did not feel like sharing all this with her daughter. "I think I would have loved Diane even if she had had different plumbing."

"Wouldn't that have been awkward with Dad?"

Terri snorted. "Trust me, it was almost always awkward." Then they both blushed and looked away. Michele had hinted more than once that she was curious how often the three of them had been "together" over the years. Yet, it was really none of her business. Terri always assumed, "Just once, sober, on the night you were conceived," was so very much **not** the answer her daughter wanted.

Terri sought to change the subject. "You know that book I found? *Castle Phoenix*? Amitola has a teddy bear from it."

Michele thought for a moment, obviously welcoming the new topic. Her child had a lot of toys, so it wasn't too simple a matter. Then her eyes brightened and she reached for one of the few physical pictures she and Enyeto had ever taken. In it, Gary held little Amy in his right arm. She was maybe a month old and fit in the crook of his arm like she had grown there. In his left hand, the teddy bear, twice the size of his grandchild, was playfully dangled over her head.

Terri was startled and wondered where she was when the picture was taken. Seeing the bear in the picture, however, satisfied her. She wasn't going crazy.

"This goes in," Terri smiled and put the 3x5 into the approved pile. There was no need for a post-it; Michele knew what it was.

When they finished sorting the pictures, Terri had a small pile of pictures of Diane. Some alone, some with Terri. She screwed up her courage. This was another "bucket list" moment and it made her feel a bit like the roles were reversed. She was the child asking the parent to do something nice for the child's friend that the parent had disapproved of. "Could you scan these for me and post them to Diane's Obituary Page?"

Michele looked as uncomfortable as Terri had expected, but her daughter's words surprised her. "I already tried that. Not these pictures. Mine. The few I had with her and Amy. They deleted them. They deleted everything from her friends in the North. They sent me nasty emails. I assume they sent everyone the same hellfire and brimstone."

Michele looked at her mother and, for the first time in weeks, felt like they were on the same level. Like they were friends. "I loved her, too, Mom. I just didn't want her to... replace my father."

Terri felt tears forming in her eyes. "She never wanted to replace Gary."

"No crap," Michele then wiped her own tears from her eyes. They laughed at themselves and the situation and all the emotional bullets they had suddenly stopped dodging. "You're right, it's always awkward."

"Not always," Terri amended. "But love gives you the strength to leave your comfort zone."

***

"Read to me, Grandma," Amitola pleaded, but Terri begged off. The picture project and crawling around on the floor had tired her out something fierce. Michele intercepted before the child could escalate to wheedling. Or the dreaded tantrum.

Once they were in the bedroom, Terri picked up the phone to give it one last try. She dialed the long distance number and hoped they wouldn't hang up on her again. It was 9pm, it wasn't too late. The phone was picked up on the third ring. They'd never gotten caller I.D… there were a lot of things in the 21st century that they hadn't bothered with.

She heard the elderly voice of Marsha Freeman and rushed in, "Mrs. Freeman. Don't hang up. I wanted to let you know that I was dying. Of brain cancer."

There was silence and a sound that might have been a long sigh. "Mrs. Winkle. I'm terribly sorry to hear that. I never wished that… or any kind of curse upon you. I know you might think so; I know that your exclusion must have hurt you so much, were I in your shoes, I might hate me also. All I have ever wanted was for you to find your way back to God and Jesus. No more and no less. I want you to believe that."

Terri choked up, all her practiced words forgotten. "But I loved your daughter."

"Love without God means nothing; forgive me for saying so, but what you two had was but a mockery of the righteous love my Diane was entitled to. Good night and, please, pray for God's forgiveness."

Terri pleaded and cried. Diane's mother hung up and the dial tone was unmoved by her words. Eventually, even the dial tone stopped its patient hum and screamed stridently that Terri was to hang up now. Right this minute.

Terri did not hang-up until she heard the garbage cans falling over. Raccoons. She forced herself up and went outside to chase them away.

She did not expect to see the huge black bear picking through the trash. She stared at it, startled, but not afraid. It would leave her alone if she didn't try to mess with it, but her head calculated how much quicker it would be. To be mauled to death by a bear. It cast sidelong looks at her and eventually turned to face her as it chewed a ham-bone it had found.

She felt very brave. Until it spoke to her.

"You should have read to Amitola," it said. "She's playing a very important role in all of this, you know. Diane's mother, not so much."

Terri's bladder instantly lost three pounds. "Gary?"

The bear blinked and sniffed at her crotch, suddenly next to her. "Yes and no. Identity is somewhat fluid here. But call me Gary if you want."

Terri took a careful step back. "Gary?"

"Seriously, you don't believe in an afterlife, a here-after, a paradise, Puss-Puss. That makes coming across a little harder. Or, let's use the phrase of the day… *it's awkward.* Go back inside and read to our Starchild. Let her at least believe in a Paradise."

"She's asleep," Terri said, moved by the vividness of this delusion in spite of herself. She took refuge in anger. "Gary, you're not real. You're the product of a brain eating cancer growing within my skull."

"Perhaps. We work with what we have." The bear licked a yogurt container clean and tossed it in the blue recycling bin. "But if you think Amitola slept through her grandmother crying in the kitchen, then that cancer is way ahead of schedule. Go read the next story to her."

The bear lumbered away, his little speech completed.

Terri went inside, annoyed to discover that she'd wet herself during… whatever that was. She cleaned herself up and put on her bed clothes. She picked up the book and looked at the bear in the boat. Feeling guilty and foolish, she snuck into Amitola's room.

The girl was awake and sniffling into her pillowcase. The dying woman turned on the light by the chair. "I couldn't sleep," she told her granddaughter and read the next chapter/story in the book.

This was about White Horse. Will was a white horse, but he wasn't. He was a Gray Horse. Everyone agreed; there were No White Horses. No matter how much he bleached his coat white, it was never white enough. He would always be called a Gray Horse. He tried paint, but then they called him a Painted Horse and NOT a White Horse. He wasn't even sure what white meant anymore; he became so confused. He tried pink contact lenses, and some people thought he was a White Horse, but most called him an Albino. His hooves scraped up the contact lenses something fierce. If he dropped one of the lenses, the chickens would eat it.

The Pharm Farmacy never carried his brand of cleaning solution, either.

Before long, his friends fought with each other over his "antics." He left his farm to find a place where people could just accept that he was a White

Horse, no matter the color he seemed. He met Barry the Ferryman and Princess Puss-Puss on his way.

He accepted that Barry was a ferryman, even if he didn't see the bear with his boat. He accepted that Puss-Puss was a princess even though she had no tiara and no kingdom that he could see. For their part, they accepted that Will was a White Horse, for the road had left them all dusty.

It was almost like Paradise, being with them.

Then one day it rained very hard and the dust washed off all of them. While neither Barry nor Puss-Puss liked being wet, it was Will that cried and hid in the bushes from them. Between the two of them, they figured out Will's issue. They told the horse that it didn't matter what color he was; he'd always be a White Horse to them.

That was almost enough to make Will happy. He walked along with them again, but he needed more. He was tired of pretending to be a White Horse, especially when he was a White Horse on the inside. Barry remembered a wizard he'd once helped across the river and he brought the merry trio to visit him. The wizard instantly saw the problem and stuck a horn on Will's forehead.

Suddenly, rainbows shot out of Will's body and, on the very next page, a brilliant white unicorn stood in his place. He still looked like Will and his coat was still basically the same color, but the rules for unicorns were different. Will licked them all happily and galloped back to his village to show everyone what he'd been trying to tell them all along, but hadn't had the words.

After all, no one ever believes there's a unicorn inside of them until they find a way to let it out.

***

Wilma Einhorn did not make a pretty woman, but she made a very passable woman. Very professional looking. She looked more in command than Willy had ever looked; but years of success probably figured into that as much as anything.

Terri hadn't thought about Willy for years but she had spent a sleepless night thinking about the chef all the same. He'd been Gary's friend during the years Gary had managed the Landmark Seafood Restaurant. They'd lost track as people do, but the fine dining circles were small in this part of New Jersey. Terri made a few phone calls and, on the power of being a widow looking to reminisce about her dead husband, she tracked him down.

She'd been warned that Willy wasn't the same person that he used to be, but she was still somewhat surprised when Willy answered the phone and gently corrected her, that Willy now preferred to be called Wilma. Yet, at the same time, she had suspected something of the sort because of that stupid children's book. They arranged a dinner date at his new place in Belmar, The White Horse Stables.

"I was very sorry to hear of Gary's passing," Wilma said, touching Terri's hand gently after suggesting that she start with the house special, she-crab soup. "And Diane's. I wish I had been more supportive at the time, but…"

Terri waved him off, resisting the urge to straighten her wig. "I wish I had known that you were having an identity crisis of your own."

Wilma shook her head. "I didn't know what I was having. I didn't have the words. And you have nothing to apologize for. You and Gary were an… I don't know… an affirmation once I made my decision. Gary kept loving you… and you kept loving Gary, even if things were changing between you."

They had a long talk, and they promised to keep in touch. She was a good conversationalist and she made all the old days new again. Wilma drove her home, disappointed to see she was living with her daughter and son-in-law in a ranch house. "I needed to sell my house for medical expenses," Terri explained. "I'm avoiding hospice until the last possible minute. I'm lucky, my cancer isn't often very painful. If I'm luckier still, I'll just be walking along one day and keel over, dead."

"Oh, don't say, that."

"It's true, I'm already having hallucinations and day dreams and magical thinking on a daily basis now."

Wilma turned sideways in her seat, her breasts falling almost naturally within her pink blouse. She gave Terri a frank and direct look. "What do you mean by magical thinking?"

"You know, I've always been a devout atheist," Terri explained. "But for the last few weeks I've been… hearing Gary's voice. Once Diane's voice. And I know it's them. I believe it's them. Not them haunting me, just them… comforting me. And you know what… I like it." Terri began to sweat and she ran her fingers through her wig. She laughed. "Even now, I'm running my hands through this wig, and I feel Diane is here with me and I'm stroking her hair for comfort."

"Well, it is Diane's wig." They both chuckled nervously.

"She did have some pretty distinctive wigs, didn't she?"

Wilma stared at her through the shadows and then tenderly placed a few twists back into place on Terri's hair. Although, they'd just eaten, she looked a bit hungry.

After a long awkward moment of them just staring into each other's eyes, Wilma said, "For the longest time, I didn't believe... couldn't conceive of the idea that there was a woman in me, trying to get out. I liked girls too much. Oh, and I was always so very attracted to you. Did you know that?"

Terri gave an awkward nod, not knowing if it was true or not. The days when she had inspired lust seemed a lifetime ago.

"Some days," Wilma said softly, urgently, "you just wake up and you realize that one of your assumptions was just flat out wrong. There wasn't just a woman inside of me... there was a LESBIAN inside of me. A hundred years ago, maybe that might have been magical thinking, too. But now..."

"Shut up and kiss me," Terri said with the demanding purr that had given her the nickname of Puss-Puss. "Life is too short."

In a moment, the car began rocking gently and Terri ignored the squeaking sound, convinced that if she looked up, she'd see a bear on a unicycle, in the middle of the street, juggling little red balls.

***

Amitola giggled to know Grandma took a long time to say good bye to her friend. Michele frowned a lot but seemed to take some pleasure in her mother dating again. The doctors had repeatedly stressed that a positive attitude could only improve her chances of a longer life. Never mind that, at this point, a longer life could mean months instead of weeks.

She took the book and her position at her granddaughter's beside. She read the next story, arriving at the Castle Phoenix with a grand ball in full swing. Amitola had fun naming all the animals.

Terri's mind became filled with scenes from a cartoon gala. No doubt, some of it was the classical music put on when Enyeto came home (he abhorred television), but she was transported to the ballroom in the book.

A little dogsbody in a dog's body, sneaked them into the cloak room where she and Barry found costumes set aside for just such an occasion. Weasel Thieves attacked travelers and many visitors often had their outfits stolen on their way to Castle Phoenix. Everyone treated each other like royalty, because they all dressed like royalty, so even the thieves seemed to serve a purpose in the world of *Castle Phoenix*.

Here was the ballroom, where polished marble floors were so shiny no one danced alone.

Here was the bar, where bartenders handed out candy bars and sparkling water. (The water sparkled in little rainbows).

Here were the seats all along the walls where animals rested (some panting) and sipped teal root beer.

Seems like such a large space now, within the book. It was a whole new world for her. Yes, it was frightening, but she could still feel Wilma's warm, gentle kissing on her lips. Things were forever changed now, and their ardor had surprised them both.

Princess Puss-Puss tugged at the ferryman's Bear hands and pulled him in close. They stared into each other's eyes as they joined the dance. She felt her tail slipping out the slit in her dress as she spun. Her tail reached for the stars the disco balls cast among the rainbow pop-fizz of all their sparkling drinks. The Bear smiled at her tail as it danced into a happy question mark. What a team they had made, they both thought.

Princess Puss-Puss leaned in to kiss Barry—

"Gary."

Suddenly, Terri was back in her granddaughter's room. The stars fell from the sky and Terri was alone in the room with Amitola. Tired brown eyes sleepily stared up at her from yellow cartoon bed sheets. She clutched the toy bear and was fighting sleep.

"I'm sorry, Amy?" Terri asked with a start.

"Gary," the little kid said plainly. "The bear's name is Gary."

Terri looked down at the bottom of the page. Beneath the explosions of colors and the main characters embracing in fancy clothes, there was a block of text.

Gary the Ferry Bear danced with his Princess.

Gary danced with his best friend, his companion, and the Cat Girl he loved above all else.

He danced among many for hours. He danced with just one girl.

Gary danced with Puss-Puss like no one else was in the room.

They danced for so long, all the other dancers fell asleep in the chairs.

They danced so long, the Dhouts finally caught up with them.

What do you know? Amitola was right, but the kid was asleep and Terri couldn't tell her.

Terri left the room and realized the music had stopped. In the living-room, John Oliver was on the television making a very good argument against reality. Enyeto's car was not in the driveway.

Michele turned away from the television as if she could sense her mother with her. Terri hoped that, with any luck, she would for many years to come.

"I love you, Michele."

Michele smiled, "I love you, too, Mom."

On the television, a bear in an Orangina commercial blew her a kiss and Terri blew a kiss back before heading back to her room, almost asleep on her feet.

Gary had always known subtlety was lost on her.

***

Monday turned out to be a very bad day.

Immediately, Terri woke up uncertain about her medicine. The letters on the little plastic timing calendar lost all their meanings. The letters, in fact, had become strange foreign glyphs. She took her best guesses and stayed in her room for most of the day.

She felt sorry for herself, as dying people do when forced to get through another Monday. Luckily, Yeto was off from work today and he got up early (for him) to spend time with his daughter. Amitola came with a breakfast the two of them had made together. Terri forced herself to eat a forkful of eggs before explaining how terribly sick she felt. After Amitola left, Terri vomited up the mouthful of eggs, some of last night's dinner, and something that felt like it might have been her spleen.

The bed rocked and swayed and Terri cried softly, ignoring the bear in the room.

Late in the afternoon, when the sky darkened with a storm to better suit her mood, she tried talking to the bear. Her "Leave Me Alone" came out all wrong. The only Gary left to her belonged in her head. Outside her head, sitting in her last and final bedroom, watching her, wasn't just unnatural; it seemed to give the brain eating monster free range.

She cried, feeling her words betray her. She did not want to become a voiceless victim. She had been willing to die; but with dignity. She did not want to become a mindless animal in the the end, or worse, a whining vegetable.

She feared the worst the most; a sort of sanity cut off from reality. To become unfamiliar and unrecognized within the meat of her body. A living ghost unable to even fully understand her living hell.

She tried not to dwell. She could see that, with a little effort, she could imagine a fate worse still. Terri tried not to think about that, but it was like trying not to think about pink elephants.

The bed squeaked as a great weight settled upon it. Giant, sharp bear claws stroked her hair, with an amazing amount of tenderness. She allowed herself to be petted. She allowed her mind to become still. She felt a warmth, eventually, and stared at the hands of an old woman until she realized that they were hers.

"I'm not wearing a wig," Terri muttered, a little crankiness in her voice. An immense feeling of relief surged through her. She had a voice. She had her words.

The bear continued to stroke her imaginary hair. "You pick the strangest things to complain about, Puss-Puss."

"Who are you," she asked without looking, enjoying the grooming, even if it was pure madness. It was comforting madness. "You are not really Gary."

"I am," the bear said. "And I am not. I am your guide, your companion, your guardian."

Terri turned her head towards her "guardian." It was dark and massive, a bulking shadow looming over her. She felt no fear of it. Whatever it was, it was bigger than Monday. Massive bear claws reached up and pushed its hood back, allowing light to shine onto the bleached bear skull. It was awesome and majestic.

Then those claws pulled at the skull and it popped off with a mechanical click. A smiling bear with golden corn colored eyes stared back at her as it tossed the mask aside. "My gosh, the thinks you think." He took her prematurely old hands and rubbed his muzzle against them until the wrinkles were smooth. "You've got a little more ways to go to get to Safe Haven, and you're exhausted. Rest."

"Why are you a bear?" Terri refused to be distracted by her young looking hands.

"We often get to choose our roles, Puss-Puss," Gary/Barry/The Bear said. "We almost never get to pick our forms. You should know that by now."

Giant, deadly bear claws pulled her eyelids down, gently as if they were made from cotton balls. She slept until dinner, knowing a formidable bear kept guard over her from the worst Monday might bring.

***

Michele made something with rice and beans and almost no spices, which Terri was silently grateful for. Enyeto offered her some chicken, but she wanted to be careful. The bad day felt over. Yet, she expected a bad turn could come easily and start her off on a new bad day.

The mineral water she drank cast no rainbows.

Amitola was on her best behavior. Terri wanted to ask what they had done today, but maybe later.

The hand of an old crone went for her water glass and it took her a second to recall that it was her hand. She almost cried.

Her emotional reserves were gone and she wondered if maybe her bad day wasn't over yet.

She skipped dessert and plugged her cell phone into the charging base. It looked like she had missed a phone call. She was curious, but needed her rest.

"Spoiler alert," the bear said from the top of her dresser. "It's Wilma."

Despite herself, Terri smiled at Gary. "You're a silly old bear."

"We've got a little more bad weather ahead, Puss-Puss. If you push through it, we'll be in the mouth of the Safe Haven by tomorrow."

***

She stared at the white ceiling and imagined it as a blank sheet of paper, rolled into the typewriter of her life. Her death. Whatever.

She wondered if the words to be typed on that page were new and fresh. Or perhaps she was a just a transcriptionist, working off a tape recording from a lifetime or from a hundred years ago.

She would not be surprised to look at the floor and see quick brown foxes jumping over lazy dogs, the way things were going. Confusing one's imagination with earth-shattering revelations depressed Terri. It was so very belittlingly human of her.

What depressed her further was that she knew she was still having a bad day, of a sort. It was a purely biochemical reaction to what her body was going through. Soon, she'd feel elated (soon being a relative term). It all meant nothing. Just a series of long, slow-motion homeostasis adjustments as her body began to shut down.

Somewhere in her head, the monster was typing a new script. She could almost see the final act being revised as she stared at the giant blank page in the sky.

Bastard was using invisible ink.

A tentative knock on the door. She looked at the clock. She hadn't slept much. Just a nap. It was her grandchild's bed time. Unless it was Tuesday morning, already. "Amitola?"

Amy was wrapped in her unicorn towel again and Michele hovered behind her to make sure it was all right. "Read me another story, Grandma Terri."

Terri found that she had the strength to get out of bed. She paused as she noticed the mess on the floor the same time that she noticed the smell. Michele showed her cleaning supplies and motioned that Terri should change rooms. "Of course, Amitola… I could never resist a unicorn."

She quietly thanked Michele as she passed.

In the room, in the easy chair, Terri settled in. She opened up the book and flipped past the earlier pages. The drawings, she decided, were flat and even the colors seemed a bit muted. She double-checked that her granddaughter still didn't want to visit Princess Bubblegum or any of the other Princesses in *Adventure Time.*

Terri began on the penultimate chapter in the book.

The Dhouts, which had long pursued Princess Puss-Puss, finally caught up with her. They attacked the Castle alone and in waves. Both Amitola and Terri were fascinated by the Dhouts. They were drawn in a similar style, but different. Instead of bright, gaudy colored pencils and pastel watercolors, the Dhouts were drawn in simple charcoals. Dhouts were people.

No door could be barred to them. Walls did not stop them for long.

When a Dhout attacked a talking animal, the animal turned a little grey. Rainbows fell from the ceiling like dead leaves. One poor pig was reduced from a poetry spouting Earl to a little naked piglet under their onslaught.

Gary began hitting them with an oar. Where the bear had gotten it, no one knew, except the bear himself. Dhouts avoided him almost immediately. "I am a ferryman! I know what I am," the bear bellowed, "You have no power here!"

Princess Puss-Puss was frightened. Her claws were out but these Dhouts were the darkest things she'd seen at the Castle. She had a hard time denying them or even crying defiance. She was too afraid of getting hurt and there was something about these Dhouts that made it seem like they too wanted to keep her from harm. They didn't want to fight. They wanted to argue. They wanted to convince her that they only wanted to keep her safe.

Isolated from the others in the castle, the Dhouts hugged her. The Dhouts petted her fur, softly. She whimpered, trapped. They were trying to, she saw, rescue her, by their lights. Only their constant contradiction of each other kept her from surrendering. She did not know how long she would last, nor did she fully understand what she'd give up if she did surrender.

The next page was black and Princess Puss-Puss was gray. Her ballroom dress was two sizes too big for her and Dhouts were eating her alive. Terri sniffled as she read aloud and Amitola cried silently into her stuffed bear.

A realistic (yet still a cartoon) bear arm pierced the walls of the abyss. It grabbed Princess Puss-Puss by the scruff of the neck. As it pulled her out of the darkness, the Princess became more real. Puss-Puss reached for Gary the moment her thumbs came back and gripped his brown furry wrists desperately. They both pulled for her life. The Dhouts tugged back, hard, and the Princess feared they'd grab and capture Gary, too.

She began to let herself slip from his grasp.

Suddenly, another furry arm shot out of the darkness. This one was yellow with a few brown spots. It wasn't quite as muscular as the Ferryman, but it was stronger than Puss-Puss!

They pulled her out, together, and Princess Puss-Puss was restored almost the instant she was free.

Yellow arms wrapped around her; a massive spotted body clutched her. Protected as she hadn't been since she was a little kitten, Princess Puss-Puss cried with relief and joy. The castle dwellers had rallied with the arrival of the yellow warriors and they pushed the Dhouts from the castle and then, from the kingdom.

The battle was the strange mix of cute and serious that they'd become accustomed to during the course of the book. Gary moved on to save others and Princess Puss-Puss… did nothing but stare up at the strong, wild face of the Hyena who had saved her. Male or female, she could not discern.

"Is this Safe Haven?" Princess Puss-Puss asked softly. "Is this Safe Harbor?"

The Hyena smiled. "No—"

Teri was suddenly thrown from the book. The mundane walls of her daughter's daughter's room clamped down on her. Muscles complained. Joints rebelled. Even the electric colors of *Adventure Time* decorations dimmed around her.

The words the warrior spoke were unreadable.

Amitola had fallen asleep, so Terri relaxed, back into the seat.

Diane's voice said, "You're home."

Terri did not see the ghost of Diane. She did not see anything that might even be speaking for her dead lover. After a moment, Terri decided that it was nothing more than the monster in her head. Nothing more than that.

Sleep claimed her in this confused and uncomfortable state with the book left open in her lap.

The Hyena Warrior looked up from her flattened world and watched Terri sleep, with a knowing look.

***

Terri hadn't meant to count the number of times she and Wilma had smooched during this little date. Five. Well, she was dying and all the rules were off. Wilma was wearing a floral sun dress and Terri was wearing an *Adventure Time* t-shirt Amitola had "bought" for her last Christmas. It was a little tight, then. Embarrassingly so. But now it was very loose and, if she lived long enough, it would be embarrassingly loose in a few months.

Something to look forward to.

"You could still outlast us all," Wilma chided her when she'd started to get morbid again. She suddenly swerved her van into the right lane so she wouldn't miss Exit 100A.

Terri bit down on the bile from the sudden vector change and clutched the book tighter. "Perhaps," she said as lightly as possible under the threat of self-explosion, "If you keep driving like this."

"The meds?" Wilma asked as they merged into local traffic. Michele never took this way. Terri gathered her words even as she was appalled by how many acres of woods were missing from this part of Tinton Falls. Worse still were all the old, vacant office buildings that sprawled over huge tracts of land rather than being built up. The world moved on. It always did.

"Maybe," she answered. She hadn't been able to read in the morning again. It was really hard to be sure what she was taking and how much. Habit should have carried her through; after all her eyesight wasn't affected yet. Or, rather, she wasn't color blind yet. If anything, she might have been the opposite of colorblind today. All the colors of the world danced before her eyes.

They drove in silence for a few blocks, the one lane traffic improving Wilma's driving. "So, did you want to talk about your Lisa Frank inspired nightmares? Because I can pretend it's perfectly normal to drive into another county just to throw a book away. I have those skills."

"I'm not throwing it away." Terri snapped softly. She shook her head, "I'm not sure what it is I'm doing. I just… I just don't want to read the last story. I don't know…" She looked at Wilma and tried to put on a brave face. Or at least not cry. "I've never been… superstitious before."

Wilma nodded and met her eyes in a quick glance away from the road. "Is the bear here in the car now?" He had accepted her visions with an ease that Terri found almost condescending. She wanted to be talked away from this mystic mumbo-jumbo. But then why had she asked Wilma for this favor? She should have known Wilma would encourage it.

Despite herself, Terri found herself looking around for the bear. "No, and I don't get why Gary is a bear and I think the last chapter is going to be about how I've betrayed Gary. And I… just… don't… I just don't want that."

"We could go to the beach and I could just read it for you?"

She hadn't told Wilma that she'd lost the ability to read. Nor about the pain just above her ears. "Honestly, I'd be afraid that the stories I've been reading wouldn't be the stories you'd find in there. Or worse, you'd make up the last story or change the ending so I wouldn't feel bad."

"You're wrong." Wilma merged into a two lane highway and drove between two massive malls. When it was clear they'd survive that, Wilma continued. "I mean, yes, I might have done that, you know. But you're wrong. You never betrayed Gary."

Terri remembered that night so hard, yet it was just shadows of sensation in her mind. Not the night of sex that knocked her up after years of trying, but, the look on Gary's face as he watched the look on her face lighting up when Diane walked into the room to see their child. When she had thought the word "their," she'd only been thinking of Diane and herself.

She cried huge, hacking tears the rest of the way to Asbury Park.

***

They both stared at the vacant lots. To Terri, the teal book case seemed closer to the road than her last visit. Wilma was able to verify that there really was a strange, four legged teal hutch just standing in a random spot. They both agreed there were no bears on the street.

"Do you want me to put it back?" Wilma had noticed that Terri hadn't tried to open her door.

Terri shook her head. "I just feel like this is something I should do."

Wilma smiled and gave her a gentle push and then a soft kiss on the cheek. Terri turned to her, looking a bit like a little girl lost. They kissed on the lips then, Terri's right hand actually letting go of the book long enough for Terri to caress her cheek.

Kisses six and seven. Mild ardor brought her back to the present, such as it was.

I should leave her my Mary Kay make-up, Terri thought, feeling Wilma's cheap foundation under her fingers even as her friend left her lips tingling.

Wilma gave her a sly look as they pulled away. "Just so you know, I don't open doors for my lady friends anymore." Wilma was not shy about taking charge. Terri was grateful for that. "Why don't you put that book back and then we can go to the Korean burger place for lunch?"

Terri felt the stirrings of love and affection in her heart and soul. Stepping out of Wilma's PT Cruiser was easier than climbing out of her own Mini. The walk to the teal box wasn't so bad. She didn't have to lean on the box at all. She opened the red doors. Some of the same books were there. Some different one.

None of them had bears on their covers.

She looked at the cover one last time. Had the characters moved since she'd first touched this book? Did the little brown bear look crushed? Did the hyena look up at her like she knew the secret of the universe? No. No. And no.

The title swam back into words and a warmth escaped the book and the world centered around her. Everything was normal again. Terri had no idea how long it would last, but it pleased her to know that once this was done she could go off to Mojo's as if they were just two normal people flirting with love.

She had lived to see the day Asbury Park had becomes a little bit of Paradise.

No longer feeling the dread or superstition, Terri flipped to the final page of the book. It was just one line on a white page without any illustration. It made Terri smile.

…And they lived HAPPILY FUR-EVER AFTER.

With her decisiveness restored, Terri put the book in the box. She closed the red doors and stood up in the sunshine of a warm summer day.

The bear stepped in front of her, casting the world into shadow. It spread short furry brown arms apart until they stretched across the horizon and then it engulfed her with its dark, musky mass.

***

The End.

***

Puss-Puss?

***

Terri stood up from the grass, surprised to find herself in a yellow sun dress. The cartoon bear in a tuxedo, of all things, helped her up. The sky was teal, the grass was green, and the path was white dappled gray paper in a fresh, virgin coloring.

All that paled before the massive structure that stood beyond the bear. Castle Phoenix was a massive fortress flying a rainbow assortment of pennants. It was more fantastic than any children's book's cover could have done justice to.

Terri forced herself to look away after a moment and pay attention to the bear in front of her. The tuxedo was giving her a great deal of pause and distress. The bear looked down on himself and laughed. "Oh, no! You're not marrying me."

Terri felt guiltily, relieved. "Why…?" There were too many questions.

"The part of me that was Gary… and vice versa," the bear said, "loved you for the journey you shared. He never stopped loving you, and vice versa. But I am the Ferryman. I am about the journey. If Gary had been a braver man, or a stronger man or a more selfish man, he might have left you when you found home. But he did enjoy seeing you happy and he did enjoy watching you be happy."

"I made a home with Gary… with my husband… for years," Terri stated more out of confusion than protest.

"You did. And you built a family and they will remember you with love and get you into the afterlife."

"Why here? Why animals?"

Gary laughed and pulled the wig from her head. He tossed it behind her. She looked back and saw that it had landed near her prone human body. Wilma was out of the car and doing a quick, panicked walk to her corpse. It was like watching something on Youtube. It seemed like it was happening to someone else.

"This was a place I could bring you to. This was a place that Diane could meet you again. Most importantly, it was a place Amitola the Unicorn could understand and believe in." The bear took her hand and pulled her towards the red metal drawbridge that crossed the moat. "To a child, Paradise is an adventure land where the best of all impossible things happen. It's that simple. It's that complicated."

Something like a giant bird fluttered in her chest. Her free hand reached up for her bald scalp and stroked the softest fur. Giant cat ears twitched as her claws brushed them lightly. She licked her thin lips with a rough tongue. Her tail danced up.

It took her a moment to recognize hope.

"Diane?"

The bear nodded and smiled.

Then a huge muscular warrior stepped out from behind the red doors. "Princess Puss-Puss, welcome to Castle Phoenix. Welcome home."

Princess Puss-Puss ran the rest of the way to her lover's arms. "Home?" she asked as they embraced.

"Oh, yes, Home is where the heart is."

There were so many questions she wanted to ask that she did not know where to start. Gary was leaving. She was staying. What sex was this version of Diane? The hyena smiled and looked down on the little cat-woman. "For a princess, you sure like other people to take charge."

Diane the hyena guided her through the red doors.

"What did he mean, that you had to find a Paradise that Amy could believe in," Terri asked as she looked at all the anthropomorphic people in the castle and the monstrous version of Diane shut the doors behind them.

"Atheists don't always get an afterlife." The strong warrior took her tiny hand paw in her more massive hands. "Sometimes, they just get to be right."

"But," the cat started to protest and the hyena silenced her with an impossible kiss considering the shape of their muzzles.

Princess Puss-Puss began to purr in the throaty way that had given her the nickname.

And if it was a death rattle in the world that she'd left behind, what of it?

There may be no better preview of the peace and contentment of paradise than the blissful grin of a cat who has found the perfect patch of sunlight.

Kypris' Kiss

Slip Wolf

I'm in a small part of heaven. My delicate feline nose picks apart what my eyes already feast on; inside the glinting glass hull of the French press, the coil-rimmed filter, carrying grounds from the toasted gold above, descends. A caramel head of froth crowns the results. I pick up the press by its warm stem, pour with care so no drops escape the bone-white mug with its silver-leaf logo reading Kypris on its flank. Steam rises as I set the press down and stir the cream upward. I delay the moment with bated breath, then another. In heaven there's no need but I do this because savoring is no less wondrous than having. Then a Moroccan kiss touches my lips and passes on. I love this place. I savor my solitude amongst kindred but separate souls and feel the sands of time settle as they always do here. This is a small part of heaven.

A Madeline cake would be wonderful right now. My loving coffee shop dotes on me, the sea-shell confectionary on my plate spongey and fragrant as my coffee. Crossing lanes beneath my nose I can move from baked sweetness to off-bitter bite. The coffee is exquisite. "I love this place." I say to the shop. "I love you." Is there sugary perfume on the napkin that I dab at my lips? I finish the next page in my book and set it down. It will be here when I return through the red door frame onto these ebony, ivory tiles. Everything is where you leave it here. I wander the streets, my shoes scuffing the cobbles under a perfect dusk.

Home is an apartment that is a cloud that is a cradle in the sky, glass walls that see for infinity in every direction. Slumber finds me if I want it, but mostly I get to meditate on all the others milling below on their way to and from whatever enclaves of heaven wait for them. A movie house, a painted cave, a parlour of flattering mirrors, a lush lick of wild jungle. There's a slice of heaven carved out for everyone. Nap time.

I was somewhere else once. The end was irrelevant, as the beginning of what came next was enrapturing. The blue sky became a pale iris, the pink dusk a rose garden under clouds. I don't remember the cat I was before I came. To do so would, I suppose, recall some pain or shortcoming. I danced from cradle to rest, bright in my moment, hopeful for the next day, but alone. I remember that much. A solitary creature, my happiness or lack of it was in books and tuna and grooming. I think. These are all inseparable parts of me in some way. I don't remember what I toiled at or what reason I had for doing so. I could have walked or I could have loped on all fours. I don't remember that either. Did I wear these clothes? These off-whites and meditative greys? My fur is the same color so maybe this is an extension of me. I'm lithely naked whenever I feel like grooming, clothed again when I follow certain paths, seeking the perfect flower to adorn my breast pocket as a corsage. Whatever I need to be to be happy, I am, as I suppose I was where I came from. And what I am now, as I'm sure I was then, is alone.

I pass a braided coyote on the way into the coffee shop, tail swaying, teeth shining above a caftan that looks like a Navajo sand-painting unfinished with itself, winding in an unfelt wind. Her claws click on the polished tile as she passes me with kind eyes and leaves through the same red door frame through which I enter. A rabbit, a lion, a dolphin, a horse. In duos or trios they occupy their spaces inside the café. My space waits for me, single chair drawn back, book open face down. The press and mug wait empty. When I sit, they are ready. My coffee shop has ticked the seconds off till I return. The press descends and the pour is perfect. How well Kypris café knows me.

I sit; I read my Proust. Laughter and talk around me is musical as a brook. There are no distractions in heaven, well, none that aren't welcome. The draperies framing the window behind me brush my back and cool air breathes a caress into my shoulder, like the coffee shop's very soul is teasing me in affection. "I love this place," I repeat behind closed eyelids, and then, to the walls and windows and tiles and brass and wood collectively, "I love you." It feels good to say that, to acknowledge how much a part of me this place is, this oasis of calm in eternity, this space of repose and rejuvenation. This must have been an important part of what came before, wherever that was. It doesn't matter.

Coffee replenishes. The currents of surrounding chatter wind round one engaging topic after another. I stay alone. Then I leave. My return to the cloudy domicile this time is naked, slinking and leaping from high rooftop to rooftop. The ghosts of caffeine have my tail in the air the whole way. Slumber finds me in perfect peace once again.

Next day the coyote is back, this time in a black kimono, white paint stark against the red on her toothy lips, black lining her wise eyes. She gazes at me for some time as I seat myself, book and press at ready. There is an empire cookie on the plate, tart and sweet, icing like a wink.

My mind is absconded by the words on the page, but only momentarily. I realize the coyote is talking to me.

"What?" It's been some time since my voice was used with another here. I squeak, mouse-like.

"I'm saying your proposal has been accepted," the coyote says in the manner of congratulations.

I fidget a moment, having lost my place on the page. I look over the black nose on that painted white muzzle and cock my head. "I'm not sure what you mean."

"Of course you understand. We all have someone for us here, someone who shares us, completes us. You found yours," the coyote said as though pointing out the obvious.

I know of course of the trickster dispositions of coyotes, of the way they wind you in wiles. She's having fun at my expense, obviously. "I don't know what you're speaking of," I mutter, ears swivelling in confusion.

"Always alone," the coyote says. "Or so it seemed."

"I like the freedom solitude affords," I answer honestly and she clicks her long tongue.

"But you love," the coyote grins. "Just like the rest of us. Love brought you here again and again. And that love was accepted. Now it is done."

"What is done? I've accepted nothing."

The coyote rises gracefully and begins to glide to the door. "Everything is where you leave it here, especially your affection."

I wrinkle my nose. The other mammals in here regard one another over the waft of java's team, paying us no mind. She lowers a paw to my shoulder and the bracelets chase each other to her wrist like an abacus adding the universe up. "You and Kypris are married now."

"What?"

"I will leave you alone." The coyote does, sashaying out the door frame which shines its crimson shine.

I am left with my coffee and my questions. My coffee wafts strong. The sun is warm on my shoulder. The drawn drapes tickle my neck.

Soon enough I'm home. I don't have to sleep. So I don't, unthinking.

Next day I hurry back, and linger in the open doorway of my coffee shop. The coyote is there again, dressed in a blue cloche and a flapper dress. She smokes her cigarette through a lacquered stem and stares off into space. So I settle in my seat, resume my book and sip my coffee. There is a sense of peculiarity in the air, as though I'm missing something important. The white frosted cake is exquisite, soon gone to the last spongey crumb. I read my novel as it spools the woe of a love unrequited, and I wonder with amusement at the needs of creatures to find affection for themselves in others. Such a strange predilection to thrive in such a way. Whatever wants I was once slave to, such was not it. Chimes sing above the distant cash register which itself rests un-manned and has never rang once in all my time here. The chimes are either in agreement or chiding me. I know this is for me alone. I am the only creature who listens and I laugh when I remember yesterday. "Can you imagine being married to anyone?" I ask nobody in particular. I sip my coffee again and something brushes my lips. I look into my cup and see a small fragment of something floating in there. By the glint of icing sugar I can see its more cake.

I feel the coyote at my side even though she casts no shadow. "Happiness where you least expect it," she laughs. "There are still surprises, even here."

My ears swivel. "What surprises?"

"I told you. You are married. You and Kypris. This is the first day of a honeymoon that may never end."

I could laugh, but I can't. I could sputter, but the sweetest caffeine ambrosia in heaven isn't for the most startled throat to choke on. "You can't be serious."

"You found its kami. It found your heart. That was enough."

"I can't love a coffee shop enough to marry one."

"Have you never loved a place before?"

"Before here?" I frown. It's a strange feeling to frown, no less than feeling confused. "I don't remember exactly who I loved."

"Who. So you believe that true affectionate love is only granted between people like us?" The coyote is even more amused now as she sits across my small table from me in the space that up until a moment ago needed no chair nor had one.

"I don't know," I say, feeling consternation that has become alien to me. "I never thought of love that way at all. This place is important to me."

"And you love it for that reason. I've heard you say it. So did Kypris. What's to deny? Love brought you here. Love keeps you here. It always does. I've got to go." The coyote rises.

"Who are you?" Different feelings are pulling me from different directions, and everything feels a mess. My throat is dry and the dark potion awaits, but it has become suspect. "Did I know you before?"

She doesn't meet my gaze. "Everyone knows someone like me from before. It's not important." She puts her paw on the red door frame as she passes through, patting affectionately as though on the shoulder of a friend. "I'll leave you two."

"Where are you going?"

"To play billiards. Or roll in a meadow. There's quite a few options." And she is off.

I frown into my coffee, which hasn't cooled from the way I like it one bit. Reading my books and drinking my ever-filling mug. Nothing about it needs to be personal. My solitude, in and of itself, is the whole point.

More white cake has appeared, this time with a tiny frosting rosette in red. I regard it for a while before I go back to my book, reading more about a man who sought love where it was not to be found and failed to learn. Fools are so much more interesting to read about than the wise. No interesting surprises ever befall them, do they? I'm having trouble paying attention to the book in front of me, glancing back to the rose-bejeweled cake and back. I'm not hungry. When I leave through the red door, I leave it behind next to my book.

I wander alleys back, tail twitching. Night passes, then a day and I lay in my cloud, thinking on the details of my coffee shop. It wasn't made for me. Too many others share the space for it to be just mine. They are as real as I am; I know it. Life has a gravity, a warmth that you can sense. None of us here are shades of a life, but the purest essence. All Kypris café's other patrons are paired, or trioed, or collected in larger groups. Is that why the shop has given its love to me, the solitary visitor? Or are there others who share it? I don't recall there ever being love like this in what came before this place. Is it good that I don't remember?

Perhaps it is all a lie. Perhaps the coyote has spread this to others and there are several of us, each assuming Kypris café has given its love to us and us alone. What a trick that would be. But the whole idea is senseless, making fools of so many people. Just me then.

I am seeing a half truth, tying myself in needless knots. It makes no sense for paradise to allow such a thing.

The next day, I am unable to focus on my book at all. I look up and study all of Kypris' furnishings and decorations collectively and separately, all organs of a whole. The shop has the aged appearance of something musty and lived in, but conversely spotless and highlighted with bright spots. Stained-glass chandeliers, brass fittings and wood panels, and here and there frames of red, highlighted by the prominent hot-red door frame in which the French-glassed oak door rests, eternally hinged inwards. There is no sense of a closing time. I would imagine there are nocturnal souls who visit when heaven's lights are low and licks of sodium and neon create beckoning beacons all up and down this street. So strange that I am so rarely nocturnal, and never here. But then I remember; I can't read clearly at night.

Nor can I now. I'm barely another paragraph ahead in my book before I'm drawn up anew by some crackling of presence around me, not just in occupied, warmed chairs all around me filled by cheerful bodies, but in the empty corners, the details of my world drunk in and absorbed and taken for granted.

The treat today is an almond croissant. I take a few bites that tingle my senses, but something doesn't feel right. There's a cloying sense of deliberation in the air around me. I'm being crowded with sightless intent, doted on by dextrous hands unseen. I'm being smothered by an attention that is at once invisible and ever present.

I close my book and leave feeling uneasy, but break from tradition. The croissant receives only a few bites, but the book comes with me. There's a distinct cold stirring in my wake as I leave, no words spoken to myself, the other patrons, or anyone in particular. I'm home soon enough, on my cloud, book open but too tired to read now. Slumber gauzes the eyes and the senses and another day has passed.

The next begins with trepidation. My book is under my arm, poking at a lilac corsage I've picked along a garden path, and as the red portal of Kypris café appears, the well-worn fragrance of ground coffee bean and spongey, desert decadence entice me in.

But the uncertainty is still there, that feeling of disturbance deep within. Entering suddenly entails more than I can comfortably fathom.

I move on, avoiding the wet shimmer on the window panes as my passing reflection ripples across them and out of sight. Out in the endless light I walk the thoroughfare of heaven, into the throng of other souls in joy and repose, passing other waystations of their amusement. Jazz and toasted tobacco smoke rolls out of a club with doors wide and no lineup and a snap in my step that urges me to smooth down my lapels. A bakery tickles my whiskers with scents that dab my tongue with marzipan and sugar icing, and I see cakes filling a frosted window that stands the fur on my shoulders on end, countless exotic offerings sampled by gourmands of every species. All the while the disturbed goods bake themselves back into replenishment with fragrant splendor on their azure cornflower pedestals. I sidle up to the open door, as all doors in heaven necessarily are, and rub my narrow flank along it to gather a bit of its scent. Then, perfumed in sweetness, I'm up a drain-pipe and sneaking past a soft-shoe dance chorus of multiple mammalian species of matched grace at a rooftop garden party, stopping momentarily to drown my confusion in a sip of sweet bubbly from a champagne pyramid at the shindig's edge. Soon I leap back to heaven's side-walked earth and come face to face with another open door on an open portico and familiar signs with universal symbols. A ring-handled cup on a saucer lets off steam in rough gold-leaf filigree. The sign above the door says, rather tacitly, Angel's Gin and Java.

I check and see that the book I'd lost track of during my flight from Kypris is still under my arm, a part of me in that strange alchemy of paradise, but still something to be set down. I enter the coffee shop, smell unfamiliar smells, and take a seat at an empty booth near a window. The vibe in here is wholly unfamiliar, not welcome, nor exclusionary. Wallpaper and tryptychs of pastoral landscapes with hedge-leaping horses and parasol bearing foxes glint in oily light. The clientele is thick, but isolated and among the teapots and mugs I see sporadic beer pints and highballers, along with a martini-glass borne by a lizard who sips away in an opiate torpor. The coffees are spiked by liqueurs and the teas are paired with mustily strong edibles that overwhelmingly stain the air. I find a seat and take it, reading my book. Nothing manifests at first as I read, then finally I look up and see a coffee. Angel's has seen me at least, and read my simplest of desire. I sip. The coffee isn't bad, I don't think, a bit over-sweetened. I settle in against the plush cushions, which are soft and lose myself in the sensation of welcome solitude. No mis-requited love from a place that holds any power over me, nor uncertainty at its proximity. I can get my bearings again in this place, just another building in paradise's endless playground. No bizarre shade of needy affection chases me.

The light is just bright enough to see, then just enough to read comfortably. Stupid coyote. Feed me a line and think I can't get away from your manipulations, or the manipulations of whatever tried to hold me to Kypris café. In paradise we are bound by nothing, our memories sifted for the most fleeting joys, made eternal as we desire. This cat walks eternity in the grasp of no love that can bind it. The very idea is treason to all I am. My dues to mortality are paid. I demand little of the universe and it demands nothing of me. What an absurd imposition of my identity the whole idea is; that one can love any place in the manor of another soul. Especially when you don't want another one.

It's hard to concentrate on my book, with its lost subject scattered into the machinations of others' desires and repulsions. Such a reminder of the world I must have left behind in these pages, such a warning as to the follies that could have beset me had my heart lay unguarded. Now, having nearly succumbed again, I've proven with a simple traipse down heaven's artery that I will never be tied down by the ensorcellment of any bosom of flesh or wood. I've gotten bored; I've stepped out. Commitment isn't for me, sweetie. The décor in my peripheral sight appears slightly lurid in a way I like.

My coffee spills. On its way to my lips I lose my grip on the mug stem and coffee that isn't quite scalding but not cool either splashes onto my chest and lap. My clothes, for I need clothes in this moment, absorb the spill and its halo of drops.

Well damn. I sit there in my booth, drops of coffee all over my front, spread across my lap and sprinkled on the underside of my muzzle. A moment passes, then a second, and the café-bar carries on as normal, none of the other raucous creatures noticing my clumsiness.

I blink. The spill cleans itself up from the table and floor. But not from me. I'm wet and dripping. Even my book has been dabbed in liquid, the page bubbling up under the spots of moisture. Well why not? If what I read is a part of me and not of this place, it wouldn't stay intact.

One never has to change clothes or fur or skin in paradise, for all that affects what we are is with consent and as desired. Like the gravity of other places, this is a rule universally known and everywhere unspoken. I can't think of why I would desire a soaking. Even a cool rain here is just neutrinos of tingling refreshment that fades with sensation. Most often it is the lullaby of thunder beyond Kypris' window while I—

No. I won't ponder her here. I escaped that place for a reason, namely the absence of reason brought on by the coyote, the trickster. My hackles, wet and dry rise and fall. She sowed the discord that chased me away. I decide I hate her.

I am still dripping with coffee and uncomfortable, so I rise and head deeper into Angel's. I know what a restroom is though I don't recall needing more than a mirror in one for all my time here. I gaze in the mirror, willing the dark stain to dry and recede into memory, but it doesn't happen.

The thick scents that permeate this whole place have become a miasma, a low hanging smoke like cloudy dread. One should not feel this sensation in heaven. I wrinkle my nose at the stale headiness of it and realize I need to clean myself. I run water under the tap, and from icy cold the water turns to scalding hot. I draw my paw back from the torrent with a yowl and feel the sting throb and then subside. A bang takes me off my feet as a stall opens and a goat shuffles out, horns crooked, sniffing, foul smoke curling from a mouth without a cigarette. "You don't know why you're here either," he wheezes and holds up an open pack of what looks like tobacco-stuffed finger-bones. "May as well light up and stay awhile. Maybe longer."

My whiskers twitch as my gaze falls to the pack in his bony hand. The bones in the pack are moving, whispering things I can't quite hear.

"No. We have to go." A paw wraps round my elbow and squeezes my forearm. The coyote narrows her yellow gaze at the goat, leads me away as the ragged figure backs into the dark of the stall and seals the portal with a click.

I frown as I'm led back to the door, close to the mirrors, far from the other stalls, most open and innocuous. The coyote answers my unasked question, the filigree on her golden sari catching gaslight. "Wherever you lose yourself, you'll find one like him. Yes, even here. Keep walking."

In a moment, we're back in the café proper, my sense of unease still present if subsided. My book is still on the table where I spilled the coffee, still bubbled on the open page. But I myself am dry now, just like that. I return to the table and the coyote comes with me, takes an uninvited seat. I'd bristle, but I'm not sure if I should be grateful or not.

"You followed me," I say sourly.

"I was going to ask if you followed me," the coyote says. "We don't all have one place here that's chosen us. Some move around."

"Places don't choose us." I fold my arms in defiance and glance longingly down at the wrinkled page of my book. Will it be eternally maimed in the part where Swann laments his time wasted with Odette? I am thankful the story has so many separate, pristine volumes. Had this happened to Tolstoy's *War and Peace*, I would probably weep. "There are places where we're comfortable. That's what I want. Comfort and solitude."

"And what makes you comfortable?" The coyote's paws grasp mine, the shock of warmth on my paws sending a shudder through me as thumbs wrap over my palm. Direct contact has eluded me for so long. Who in heaven even desires such fleshy, foolish things?

"The quiet. The solitude."

"You can have that anywhere. Go deeper. Details, please." Her golden eyes look up from her bowed head, ears wide and receptive. "Please."

"I love the simple décor. Much nicer than this place."

A badger knocking back a pint at the bar gives me a glare over his shoulder, more pitying than annoyed. I ignore him. "I like the way the sun dapples on the tables through the French glass in the transoms. I love the simple elegance of the cloth-covered tables and wicker-backed chairs. I love the coffee, the confectionaries, the way the place always knows what my mood wants before even I do." I think back to the rose-encrusted cake. "Well, most of the time anyway."

In a corner two wolves call out a cheer in a language I don't recognize and slam their pints together hard enough that one breaks and sloshes suds. The one with his back to me has a battle-ax affixed to his back and is nearly naked. I think I'm glad they didn't hear me putting this place down.

"Valhalla isn't the same for everybody," the coyote says, following my gaze with a shrug before looking back. "It sounds like you love Kypris café. So why are you here instead of there?"

I don't quite know why, so it takes some time to collect myself. "Marriage, I mean, whatever game you were playing in there, I didn't appreciate it."

The coyote turns her head sideways. "What game? You're attached to that place, more than any other here. The café is attached to you, more than any other patron. What about the profession of love disturbed you?"

"Besides it not being possible?" I want another coffee and I have one, black as night and bitter when I steal a sip. This place doesn't know me, but that's just fine. Maybe it takes a while. "Kypris is a coffee shop, a place, an inanimate space."

"No, it's not." The coyote wants to frown, I can tell, but smiles with a patience I find unnerving instead. "Here everything has a spirit, a force, an emotional agency. A place called Japan called it *kami*, while far North in the colder climes of the world before, Araniit, the breath of all things, affected people's lives. We all came to know the world we exist in now in different ways, just bits of truth, gleaned or guessed while we were still wandering around wherever we were before this. Much of this is a surprise, and that's part of the fun when you think about it. I mean why would you want to move onto a world where you already know everything, right?"

I don't know what to say to that. The coyote's tail wags as she waits for me to agree, then slows and rests out of sight. "You don't have to understand everything to enjoy paradise."

"I want to enjoy it by myself. It's just how I am. Is that bad? I don't love a coffee shop."

The coyote swallows, and her enthusiasm slackens as though coming to accept what I'm saying. "You don't have to love Kypris back, not in that way. But we all love something, if not someone, in some way. We couldn't live otherwise. You could love a mountain top, or a wind-swept plain or a subway stop. The only difference is that here, it can love you back." The coyote shifts in her chair. "Here, everything and everyone can love you back."

I look into my coffee, take a sip. It's still bitter and I miss the coffee at Kypris. Dammit. "So what do you do with four walls and tables and chairs that love you? I mean... this whole thing feels absurd."

The coyote laughs and I sense that its slightly painful. "You consummate that love with your presence. That's all it requires. Understand, cat, everyone is given the gift of knowing, even if just once, what their heart really wants."

"But it isn't real." I think of the tickle of the drapes, the unceasing warmth of the sun through her windows, the perfected sensation of every bite and every sip in those walls. "I don't know what love is, but I know this isn't it."

"You don't have to know," the coyote chides with a smile. "Love is confusion, and yearning, and often unrequited. Your mistake is to assume it is somehow weaker for all that. Giving it with no expectation of its return is where its strongest." She stops and takes a breath, then sips from a cool glass that has manifested in her paw. Maybe it's gin and tonic, maybe it's water. I don't ask. She stares into her glass for a moment. "Kypris loves you even if you decide to avoid her and never see her again. Her kami, like all spirits, is for you and you are for her. You only need acknowledge that whether in an oasis, or a café, or in another's arms, you find love for something, if not someone…" The coyote stops and sets down her glass. "… outside yourself."

She turns away and scans the crowd of souls congregating in the Angel pub, together, apart, content. As she turns back to me, her fidgeting stops for her to wipe a tear away. "Just let it happen. You already have."

"Who are you?"

The coyote lets boisterous celebration and laughter from all corners drift into our small realm of quiet. She holds her muzzle straight and dries her last tear away. "You don't know me. You never did. I'm just someone who sees what is. No tricks. I was never one for tricks."

I curl my tail around myself, and sigh, my dry chest fur rising and falling as I lean back. The coffee isn't working. Something is missing. I stare down at the dried book, pages wavy and rippled from water damage, willing order to return to them. This is what paradise is supposed to be, the order that follows the messy chaos of the outside, the preamble, the intro. Doubts shouldn't torture anyone here and it's for that reason that so much is swept from memory, consigned to insignificance. Loneliness never plagued this cat. So what plagues me now?

I look up at the stuccoed ceiling past the slow turning, brass-plated fan, and with just a slight change in focus that alters perception, even past that barrier through to the blue eggshell skin that surrounds the vast heart's locket of this heaven for all of us. Focus again, and then one can see past it into the nameless dark.

Love put me here, safe from oblivion, and the very same found my tiny crèche in heaven, my place of comfort. What else would possibly take the one thing that mattered most to me in the mortal coil and put it here for my enjoyment, as part of my sense of self as the tail raised behind me or the whiskers that sample every wondrous sense ahead.

"I'm a fool," I say glumly.

The coyote's soft paw rests upon mine again. "We all are. It's our most endearing quality, don't you think?"

"I didn't ask your name," I realize as I rise.

"No you didn't," she says as she gets up with me, adjusting her sari. "It's Cloud. Walk back with me, will you?"

I nod, not needing to ask where.

My walking stick clicks the cobbles and I tilt the bowler I've adopted above my pinstriped suit. Her sari has given way to a satin gown that follows curves from sinewed limb to cobbled ground. In another life, under other circumstances, I'd want to see how her hips sway. Here and now, I appreciate the warmth of her paw and feel the giddiness of her lively heart as we stop at Kypris' red arch and part ways with respectful bows. Cloud's parting is silent, but reluctant. The coyote fades into the crowd of another cross-thoroughfare of heaven and I rifle the rippled pages of my book as I feel the electric charge of my café, welcoming me in. I can't remember if I was gone hours or millennia. As Cloud said, it doesn't matter. The cake waiting for me next to my French press is the most delightful, airy slice of culinary sugary joy I think I've ever sampled. The coffee is a lively melange of Moroccan warmth and spice. I know now I can go anywhere, but my joy will reside right here.

It may be that to be happy, even in heaven one mustn't fully know the self, why we're at peace with the people or things we were close to or apart from. Love is the most confusing element of any life. I'll never fully pierce the fog of the world before this one, where joys and pains brought me to struggle as we all did in some way. I'll never seek out the reasons for my self-proscribed solitude, never deeply wonder if doubts were insects in my stomach. The faces that occasionally flash before my mind's eye with dips of madeleine cake or sips of coffee or glimpses of dusk along heaven's distant edge will never resolve back to knowledge of family or acquaintance, friend or foe.

And I'll never turn and see the coyote who called herself Cloud, decked just once, fleetingly, in a smudged coffee shop owners apron with the Kypris silver-leafed logo, looking longingly and lovingly across the sea of content regular patron souls, picking mine out of the throng as she had countless times before in a world all but forgotten. She'll ache once more with curiosity and affection and a love of the kind that even when fate leaves it unrequited, fills us, grows within us and creates a place in paradise for us all.

The journey may never end.

Behesht

Dwale

When father died, I cleansed his remains and wrapped them in a sheet, then secured them in a sling I'd fashioned ahead of time. His thirty-five-kilogram corpse strapped to my back, I made the long climb up the dusty steel ladder of the surface access tube. The rungs were cold on the pads of my hands and feet. My efforts, my breath and heartbeat, the chimes and dings as I climbed, all resounded in the narrow confines.

Up above, I checked my compass to make sure his head would be facing the holy city, then said prayers and buried him in the sand. There were no animals or people to disturb his remains, which would quickly mummify once the sun rose, but it was our tradition to bury the dead in this way.

I thought of smashing the only solar array with the shovel while I was topside. Father's last words were, "Farad, my son, you must leave this place. Get married and, God willing, have children. You should not have stayed so long." I had told him to go to sleep and kissed the top of his head.

But in spite of my father's wish, I was tempted to spin out the rest of my days sustained by the hydroponics and insect farms that my great-grandfather had scrabbled together. I thought smashing the solar panels might hasten me along, until I imagined some desperate caravan would come hobbling into town only to find the pump inoperable and the water beyond their reach. So, I left the panels as they were and made my descent, back to the home where I had grown up, where my supplies were already packed.

The backpack was heavier than my father had been, but less bulky and therefore easier to handle, so my footsteps should have been light and quick, as a Jerboa's ought to be. But the further I walked, the more some vague unease stirred at the edge of my consciousness. The boulevard had

253

been a quiet place even in my youth, when we had boasted a populace twenty persons strong; now it bordered on silence. As I passed the empty houses and storefronts where once we had played as children, the hairs on my back and ears stood on end, as though thousands of eyes were peering out from the dark and dusty windows on each side. I told myself it was only my imagination, a nervous response to being the only person within a hundred kilometers or more, but I quickened my pace nonetheless.

There was only one sound on the streets which did not originate with my person: the hiss of falling sand. It worked its way in through the old ventilation system, covering everything I had ever known. Now the dunes finally encroached on the last of the unburied structures. The sand would swallow everything in the end. Perhaps that was for the best.

A short time later and the maw of the underground highway loomed before me, the beam of my flashlight vanishing into its depths. As I steeled myself and stepped over the threshold, tears began to flow. I was the last inhabitant of New Fatimabad, below the ruins of Ardabil, and I was leaving forever…

Or so I thought.

I ran into the caravan mere hours after my journey started, a handful of individuals whose appearance reflected an assortment of cultures and phenotypes. Their leader, a short man of vole genetic stock, offered that I should join them before he even asked my name.

"Peace, my brother," he said. "Come with us, and leave these wretched places behind. Where we are going is far better."

When I inquired as to where that might be, he smiled and said a single word: "Behesht." Their destination was nothing less than Heaven itself, the hidden garden which is the reward of believers.

We ended up going back into New Fatimabad for water and the food I had been forced to leave behind. What we could not carry, my new half-starved comrades jammed into their mouths until their bellies were distended. While that was going on, I gathered up paper and ink from my father's articles. I had lived my youth in his books and reckoned it was time to try writing one myself. So, after traveling with the caravan and interviewing its members, I have set out to chronicle those stories which best reflect the world in which we find ourselves. It seemed the proper thing to do since we might be among the last people who will ever walk this earth.

The Clergyman

Their leader was a man named Shapur, a vole with a greying coat. He dressed in the simple fashion of desert nomads in times past, a knee-length shirt with a robe over it, and a turban, one wrapped in such a fashion as to expose his rounded ears. He approached me during our meal at the end of my first cycle with the group, there among the ancient vestiges of transports that would never again run on this road, what had once been a major thoroughfare but now aboded dust and silence.

"Peace," he said, smiling and taking a seat on the ground before me. His movements were stiff and abrupt, as though taken with a perpetual nervousness. His nose and whiskers wriggled in spastic contractions spaced some four or five seconds apart. "I wanted to welcome you formally to our group."

"And upon you, peace. May God reward you," I answered. "I wasn't sure if I would ever meet another person."

At that he laughed, and the laughter rang warm and earnest in my ears, such a strange sound as I had not heard in years, since before my mother died.

"You'll come to know all of us in time, and more people besides, once we get there." He must have read something in my face then, because before I could say anything, he added, "You have doubts. Do you lack faith?"

"I have faith in God. I have less faith in men. Do you truly believe we will make it to paradise?"

He smiled and said, "Paradise is always just around the corner for the righteous."

But of course, I could not be satisfied with that for an answer, so he continued.

"Tradition holds that the tomb in the holy city is considered a part of Heaven. You have heard this, no doubt?"

I nodded, remaining mute but seeing where this was headed.

"Then you must also know that a prayer made there is always answered."

"My great-grandfather's father was the last of our line to attempt the pilgrimage," I said. "He spent four years trying to find a tunnel westward that hadn't collapsed, and came home with nothing. So, what do you mean to do, sir? Will you build us a ship? Will you march us overland without environmental suits?"

My color must have risen, because his tone took on a conciliatory inflection when next he spoke.

"He would have checked the major roads, but could he know of every subway, access tunnel or pipe? Just because he could not find a way doesn't mean the way is lost. We have maps. It will not be easy, but we will get there."

The thought sparked a glimmer of hope in my heart, only to be snuffed out by the one that followed it.

"But what if the city is gone, what if the sand- "

"Brother!" he said, not shouting, but more than a little firm. He shut his eyes for a moment, and when he opened them again his smile had reconstituted. "If God, praise to Him, should so will, surely He could cover even the tops of the mountains. But should we believe His holy places are no more before we have seen it with our own eyes? Think about it for a while."

With that, he yawned and excused himself, the irony in his final question gleaming like chrome, but eluding him all the same.

The Newlyweds

Babak and Nadia were rabbits draped head to toe in bright clothes printed with intricate, spiraling vine motifs, such fine stuff as I had only seen before in books, but which must have been common in their oasis for them to put together entire outfits from it. Babak's shemagh had slits cut in it to admit the passage of his lanky ears, which was not uncommon; Nadia kept hers folded back and hidden beneath a scarf. But it was not their ears which most drew attention, but rather Nadia's protruding belly.

She noticed my staring and smiled.

"God has willed it," was what I said, referring to the kittens she carried. But I couldn't make myself smile. How could she think of bringing a litter into this dead world, to struggle and suffer in privation?

"Praise to Him," Babak addended. "Peace. I'm Babak and this is Nadia. Come, sit down." He took my hand and all but pulled me onto the large carpet he'd been spreading out.

"We found a little powdered tea," he said. "You must drink with us."

I refused five times, and still ended up with tea.

We talked for a while on small matters of personal history, our hometowns, our families. It may have been that they sensed my alarm and wanted to put me at ease. Babak and Nadia were from the same oasis, only three-hundred kilometers or so from my own, to the south, which was closer than I had expected. They were cousins.

"You're too gracious," I said after he forced a peach candy into my hand. My eyes kept wandering over to Nadia's bulging abdomen, however much I might try to stop them. I had never seen a pregnancy before.

"You are wondering," Babak said, changing the subject with a delicate air, "why my wife and I are... baking."

"Baking?"

"Yes. You know, the sort of baking for which rabbits are so well-known."

"Ah! Yes, of course," I stammered. He didn't seem offended at my curiosity, though other men might have been.

"When a doe is under stress, the bread…" he paused here to search out a word, "*returns*. The oven gives you nothing. My Nadia is the first in many years to come so far along. That's why we joined this caravan."

"You believe Shapur." I thought of the greying vole, the holy man leading this expedition, with his wary eyes and constant twitching, and did not see how anyone could be convinced by him. But then, I hadn't needed convincing to join; it could have been the same for them.

"I don't *not* believe him," he said, and laughed. "But about that, I have a theory. What if the world isn't ending at all? What if far away from us, who are isolated here in this tunnel system, the world continued on as it had before?"

The notion had occurred to me in idle moments over the years. The surface world, all sand and lethal heat in our region, might yet sustain survivors closer to the poles.

"Much was lost when the bombs fell," he said, his voice dropped down almost to a whisper. "It may be the case that this entire sector, or parts of it, were written off as a loss. We were cut off. Why would outsiders suffer the cost to excavate a wasteland? They forgot about us, and vice versa."

"Then you think we can reach it?"

"God willing," he said. "If we can, we will, for the sake of our children."

They were a charming couple and I often spoke with them when we encamped. Like her husband, Nadia was most cordial, but she rarely said more than a few words. Babak confided in me during our march one cycle that bandits had attacked her family's caravan and killed her parents when she was only a child. Her eyes, though, were clear and watchful. I sometimes wondered what went on behind them, and what she beheld when she lapsed back into her customary silence, staring off into the dark.

The Beekeeper

Ruzba was an oddity: a chimera with a reptilian phenotype. We shall assume his gender as male for the purposes of this story, but I couldn't be certain. He wore a white thawb, the ankle-length shirt which was not unusual for territories near the western mountains, and a plain white shemagh on his head. I would guess his weight at close to 60 kilos, which was a lot more than I had. He was only a bit taller than me, but stocky and powerful for his size. It was hard not to stare at his eyes, which were huge in proportion to his skull.

I think it was the jerboa DNA in me, but I was never entirely comfortable around Ruzba, which was unfair since I know he never willed me any harm. It must have been his teeth, which were not sizable , but were pointy, like his jaws were lined with stout ivory needles. Or it could have been his eyes. Unlike most geckos, the "leopard" variety possesses functional eyelids. More the pity, then, that Ruzba did not often think to employ them. The vertical pupils made his gaze even more unsettling. None of this was helped by the fact that his fingers ended with brutal hooks: claws like the blade of a jambiya.

There were two carts in our caravan, the labor of pulling them was distributed in shifts. But poor Ruzba, Shapur had explained, was, for all the human DNA in him, still too much a reptile for sustained physical activity in the cool temperatures underground. He could not even digest food without the aid of a heater. Whenever we went near a tube accessing the surface, he would always make the effort to go topside and bask, even during the day, which was flirting with death. We all understood, though no one ever mentioned it, that he wouldn't live long if he were to be cut off from surface access, and the batteries on his portable heater were exhausted.

But for all his woes, Ruzba would still take a short turn pulling one of the carts, then clamber on top of it to become part of the load. At first I could not understand why we would take the effort to haul him around when he was good for so little. But he was simple in manner, and quiet, bothering no one, and it was the charitable thing to do. And at dinnertime, he doled out a spoonful or two of honey to each of us, which inclined no few of us to favor him.

I had been with the caravan two days when we spoke. He had just finished his ephemeral turn hauling supplies, when I stepped in to take his place. He greeted me.

"Peace," he said. His mouth opened when he spoke, but his lower jaw didn't bob up and down. It was as if the sounds he made were produced all in his throat, and the mouth was only a channel for them. The words were distinct, but off, as though they were being played from a recording device rather than originating from his person.

"And upon you, peace. It's good to meet you, brother," I said, forcing myself to be civil. "I hear you were a beekeeper."

"Aye," he said, and licked his eye clean. I had begun to pull. The cart was not so bad once you got it going. I didn't begrudge his rest.

"You can keep bees underground?"

"We bring sunlight down for the plants with fiber-optic cable, same as any farm. Used to be a cable factory nearby, we had so much of the stuff we used it as rope. And our bees were specially engineered for that kind of life."

"I see." Even then, I had the thought that I would write this story someday, so I had a look around to see if anyone was in earshot, then put the question to him.

"Brother," I said, "Do you believe we will get to paradise?"

He didn't answer for some time and I began to think he had fallen asleep.

"What is paradise?" He asked dreamily, startling me back to attention. "For me, it's a warm, shady place with plenty of water and lots of food to eat. That's all I've ever wanted from life, and it would be so easy for God. It's not too much to ask, is it?"

The Djinn

We came across an abandoned oasis, the sign at the edge proclaimed it "New Doroud." The main transit tunnel we'd been following up to this point had suffered a cave-in some years before, so we were forced into the auxiliaries. When we emerged from one of these into a park or public square, our immediate response was to locate the residential area and fan out to scavenge for supplies. Most such localities were picked clean before any of us were even born, but there was always a chance some things might have been hidden or overlooked.

It must have been a thriving community at one time. It was by far the biggest city I had ever seen and must have sheltered two-hundred families or more. Judging by the four-centimeters-deep layer of dust on the floor, it was safe to say no one had been through for a long time.

As I searched a house, I became aware that my companions had spread out so far that I was quite alone. I held my breath and turned my ears this way and that, but heard only the slow passage of a draft, and the faint hiss of shifting sand. Then I caught movement from the corner of my eye.

I was not at first alarmed, but thought it was one of my fellow travelers come looking for me. I called out a greeting, to no reply.

"Who's there?" I asked.

Nothing.

I wanted to convince myself that it was only my imagination, but I was certain of what I saw. I slipped out the back entrance and found myself in an alleyway. A disused ventilation shaft had dumped sand onto the path to my left, blocking the way. Could they have gone back, taking care to duck under the windows so that I didn't see? But even if that were the case, why should anyone wish to move about in secret like that?

A chill ran up my back and every hair on my body stood on end. My hand wandered down to the jambiya on my belt; the blade sang a muted tone as the tip scraped free of its leather sheath. It was the first time I'd ever exposed the knife in a public place, as this was only permitted in our culture by the needs of self-defense. If ever there was a time, I thought, that time had come.

"Sir?"

I just about jumped out of my skin, but my composure returned at speed. It was a child's voice I had heard; I was certain. Taking care to replace my jambiya, I turned around. There was a chimera child standing in the middle of the road. I say "chimera child" because I could not, still cannot, identify her phenotype. She most resembled a jackal, sleek and fine-boned, but her coat was mottled shades of yellow and brown like the lifeless desert up above, which had once been scrubland, and her ears more resembled those of a ground squirrel, with tufts on the ends. Her tail was long and broad, like that of a skunk. At the time I took her for a hybrid, though of what, I couldn't discern. She was naked and smelled of ash and smoke.

"Hi, I'm Atash," she said.

"Girl, what are you doing? Put some clothes on!"

She ignored that and ran around me, out of the alleyway, into the road.

"Let's play! Come get me!"

Three seconds in and I already had enough of her. I prayed for patience and walked after her.

"Where are your parents?"

She went so still that if she had been lying down, I might have thought she died.

"They're gone," she said. "Long ago. The others, too. All gone."

"Well," I said, almost caught up with her, "I'm with a group. Poor thing, have you no clothes? Come with me and we will give you something."

"Where?" she asked. I pointed and we started to walk back together with me looking straight ahead, as much from embarrassment as from a concern to protect her modesty. She asked a few questions about the group, how many people, what sort, our method of transport. I answered her, but she continued uninterestedly, so that I was not sure if she was listening.

"You should all stay here," she said. Something in her speech had changed. It wasn't an issue of timbre, but of feeling. It was the same voice, but as though it issued from one who had already been on this world a hundred and more years, all of them weary. "You will never reach your destination."

"Ah," I said, unsettled by her change in tack, but still taking her for a child and willing to indulge her little game, "but you don't know our destination."

"Of course I do. You mean to go to the holy city and pray for paradise."

I stopped and whirled around in surprise. She had vanished.

"I'll show you…" she said, her words issuing from everywhere at once, and the world around me began to spin. How can I describe that feeling? It was like I had rollers on my feet, and the earth spun beneath me while I remained fixed in place. I was of a sudden on the surface, the multitude of stars shining down on the endless expanse of desert.

"Here is your refuge," she said, her words acidic, taunting, "Blasted ruins buried thirty meters deep."

Then the world rolled back over and I was standing in the ghost town, as I had been a moment before.

"We are the last of our peoples," she said. "Stay here. You will find only death out there."

Folks may berate me for this, but I ran away as fast as I could, and I didn't stop until I found someone. I didn't speak of the incident at first; I was afraid they would think I was crazy. There was talk of setting up camp there, but I wouldn't hear of it. I babbled on until Shapur relented and agreed to set up in the tunnel past the edge of town.

A week passed before I shared this story. It made its way around the caravan. Some said I must have dreamt it, others smiled and nodded but I knew they thought I was making it up. I guess I wouldn't have believed me either. I was surprised that Shapur did.

I found him sucking on a tube of fifty-year-old nutrient paste near the front of the caravan and poured out the whole story. He listened with a passive face until I was done.

"That was a djinn," the vole said, "in a child's form. Even as we were made from clay, so were djinn made from fire. The smoke and ash smell must mean it is near the end of its life. It would seem they are dying out along with us. Pay no mind to the vision it showed you. It was only an illusion meant to bring you to despair."

"Might it have been an angel?"

He scoffed and we left it at that. At times, I was not sure myself whether it was a dream, but I took care not to stray too far from my companions. I often thought of that girl, djinn or not, dying all alone in the dark, in that immense, inexorable stillness, and I pitied her.

The Highwaymen

We found the first body outside a formidable-looking structure that must have been a bank or government office in times past, which had been hollowed out of the living rock. Such architecture had been easier to produce with the assistance of machinery than it had been back in the days where it was all done by hand, but was still a colossal, labor-intensive sort of project spanning years. As such, there were not many of them.

The dryness and cool air had mummified him, this mole, who was shriveled but otherwise intact. He had a pistol in his hand and a wound in the side of his head. Near to his remains we found a shallow pit filled with bones, which were scattered in such a way that we could only discern how many people were involved by counting the skulls, of which there were three. Their teeth suggested they were all moles like their mummified friend. To judge by the holes, they'd been killed each with a shot to the back of the head. Everyone must have noticed, though we did not mention it, that the bones were covered with bite marks, and had been cracked open to extract the marrow.

There were bullet-holes in the door of the stone building, which wouldn't open. Circling for an alternate means of entry, we discovered that the windows had been blocked with piles of heavy furniture. We had just about resolved to give up and move on when I decided to throw my shoulder against the door to see if it would give. I am neither large nor strong, so this gesture was symbolic, yet, there was a crack and the door swung open, catching me so unawares that I almost bowled face-first onto the floor with all the excess momentum.

The door had been barred with a slab of some composite material which must have been rigid enough for the task when it was new, but had degraded with the years and become brittle. There was another mummy in this first room, this one laying prone with a pistol in its hand. The holes in the back of the shirt left little doubt as to the cause of this fellow's demise.

The last of them we found not far from that front area, sitting with his back to the wall, legs stretched out in front of him. He'd been shot three times in the upper torso. Stains on the floor indicated it had happened in the other room, after which he had dragged himself in here to die. He was clutching a pair of bags about the size of pillow-cases, full of canned food. We were excited about that until noting the way the cans had swollen up from bacterial activity inside.

Shapur insisted that we give the remains proper burial rites even though he conceded that these men had almost certainly been a family of highway robbers squabbling over the last of their stores.

"Murderers? Cannibals? Why should we?" I wasn't angry at the suggestion, but perplexed.

"God can forgive any sin if we turn to Him in sincere repentance," he said. "Only He knows what is in the hearts of men, and only He is fit to judge them now. Desperation can drive the best of people to an evil path. No man has the right to say who is or is not worthy of Behesht."

The Nomad

We lucked upon a caravanserai that had a pump in good condition. We believed we might top off our supply of water if only the power might be restored, so we made to locate a surface access to see if anything could be done for the solar panels. While engaged in this, however, the overhead lights sparked to life. There was only one conclusion: that we were not alone in this place.

It may have been a group like our own, but then it might also have been persons of less than noble intentions. A moment's talk and we took up a defensive position in the room with the pump, watching the doorway and waiting. Those of us with pistols had them ready. We did not have to wait long before the stranger made her appearance.

She entered the room with her head down. Chimera, being based on the human genome, fell within the limits of the human range of sizes, with those of smaller phenotypes tending towards the low end, and those of larger phenotypes tending towards the high end. But these tunnels and buildings had been made by and for chimera derived from slight, burrowing creatures, and this woman was a camel. We weren't in doubt about that, the famous hump, though reduced compared to that of their four-legged counterparts, was in evidence. She was well over two meters tall, the ceiling was just shy of it.

When she saw us, she startled and bumped her head, then clasped her hand over her heart.

"Peace," the she-camel said. "By God, you scared me!" To say her voice was like a man's would have been wrong. It was far deeper than that, a rumble that was felt as much as heard. She wore a long, white, hooded robe with trousers underneath, all made from some shimmering material I could not identify beyond saying it was no natural fiber that I had ever seen. There was a pistol at her waist but she made no move for it.

"Peace, sister," Shapur said. He gave us a look and we holstered our arms.

I was not privy to the conversation which followed, as she and Shapur went to speak in another room while I was summoned to assist in getting the pump to run. It was not until later that cycle, when we were encamped and taking our meal, that she came to me and exchanged greetings. Shapur must have sent her for me to interview, but whatever the case, I invited her to share my carpet.

"I was surprised to see a camel," I said. "I thought your kind was lost."

"My kind shall walk the earth until the final day." There was pride in it, but she could not conceal a twinge of sadness. She knew, as we all did, that day could well be imminent.

"Will you be joining us, then?"

She shook her head. "With these," she indicated her attire with a hand wave, "and our genetics, we can survive on the surface for days. It is dangerous, but because we can circumvent obstructions in the tunnels, we are able to range far when we scavenge."

"Ah." I thought about the civilization that had once graced the overworld, the great cities with buildings that seemed to touch the sky. "You must have seen so much."

She shook her head again and smiled. "Only sand, from horizon to horizon. We have been farther than you can imagine, and found nothing."

"You keep saying 'we,' do you have a herd?"

"Oh, yes," she said, confident. "We were attacked and became separated, but I'm sure I'll catch up with them soon."

"And when was that?"

She looked up at the ceiling, her lips moving as she performed the calculations.

"About ten years ago."

"I see." I didn't say what I was thinking, that her fellows were long dead. The both of us were chasing ghosts, and differed only in direction. "And is that why you won't come with us, because you're looking for them?"

"No," she said, and laughed. "I already told you, there's nothing out there. You fools are going to get yourselves killed."

The Executioner

Amir the hare stood out from the rest in many ways. He was just over one-hundred and eighty centimeters tall (not counting the ears), by far the tallest in our group. In dressing he was utilitarian, favoring slacks and baggy pullover shirts, eschewing traditional styles. He was the only male in our party who didn't wear any sort of head covering, and the only male to wear his hair long, which was not forbidden, per se, but so far removed from contemporary mores as to be peculiar. But the thing that stood out most of all was that he carried a shamshir. Swords had not been used in war for centuries, so I was curious as to its purpose.

But Amir was a hard person to approach: he took his meals alone and always sought the fringes whenever we encamped. It wasn't that he was rude when spoken to, people said, but rather that he preferred his own company. It wasn't until I had been with the caravan two weeks that I got a chance to speak with him in private.

It was our sleeping period and I was losing a battle with insomnia, so I decided to see if anyone else was conscious. Living almost all one's life underground bestows a certain awareness; we become accustomed to feeling our way along, seeing with our ears. I found the wall and followed it, not wanting to wake anyone with my lamp. I had the sense that a sleeping bag which had been occupied earlier was now empty, and a moment later I heard the clink of glass on glass and moved towards it.

A little while and I could see a glow emanating from a house we'd searched earlier that cycle. I'd always been told that it wasn't right to spy on people, so rather than creep up on whoever this was, I cleared my throat. The light inside the building changed, like someone wearing a lamp had turned their head. Then the light moved towards the doorway and there I met Amir.

"Ah," he said, and went back inside. I followed him.

Further in, he had pried up a piece of the floor, revealing a crawlspace. That was presumably where he had found all the bottles of liquor he had set up, and from which he was so nonchalantly sipping. My first reaction was to peek behind me to be sure I hadn't been followed, then to ask him a question.

"Are you crazy? Shapur will have you whipped if he finds out."

He smiled and shook his head, indicating his sword. "Let them try. The one who puts a hand on me surrenders it forever."

"They have guns."

He shrugged. "I never said they wouldn't shoot me. But you are right, if it pleases them to whip a dead man, they're welcome." That settled, he tipped the bottle in my direction, offering.

"No, thanks."

"Suit yourself."

As he did not appear to mind my presence, and would be more talkative on account of his inebriation, I decided to stick around. I had nothing better to do.

"So..." I began, but he never let me get started.

"You want to know about my shamshir." It wasn't a question.

"Yes. Yes, sir."

"I cut people's heads off for a living. Or at least I did. No courts anymore, that means no sentencing. Used to be, folks would catch a robber now and then. Bandits are parasitic, you know, but now there's no one for them to feed on. No host, no parasites."

"Oh. How did you get into that...."? I trailed off in thought, trying to find a tactful word, and came up with, "occupation?" He had already said more than I had ever heard him say. The liquor seemed to be doing its work already.

"You're born into it," he said. "One of my ancestors was a criminal, probably, who got stuck with it. From then on, his genealogical line became an 'executioner family.' That means we can only marry among other executioner families. How many of those do you think there are? God only knows how we made it this far. It stops here, though. No one for me to marry, executioner family or otherwise."

He took another drink and we were content to let the thread of conversation sleep a while. When he continued, he did so with a smile.

"The work is not so bad," he said. "The day before, I go to the aggrieved family and beg them to grant clemency. I beg mercy for murderers! If they don't forgive him, then at the beginning of the next cycle I sharpen my sword. It's just like swinging a pick, easiest job in the world."

I tried to imagine myself decapitating someone and decided I couldn't do it. By then, I was ready to change the subject. I asked him if he thought we would reach paradise, as I had done with the others, but he seemed not to understand that the talk had moved on.

"Well, why shouldn't I?" he asked, ears flat, his tone agitated. "God saw fit to have me born into this position. How, then, am I tainted? I'm just like this sword, an instrument for someone else's use. If the sentence is wrong, then that wrong falls on the authorities. And if a sentence is just, then what sin transpired?"

"Brother, I apologize, I didn't mean that. I'm asking if you think we'll ever escape these tunnels, if we'll ever reach the holy city."

Now that he understood the question, he settled back into thought, and his bearing softened. Then he laughed and gave me the answer for which I had been looking.

"I don't have any idea about that," he said, "but what would you have us do, sit on our hands?"

***

As I write this, the supplies are running low. Shapur pores over his maps and makes promises, but I felt it prudent to commence this project. Two cycles ago, Ruzba went on to his reward. His scales had gone from yellow and black to a greyish brown. We think it was the lack of sun. If you should stumble across this record, I hope you will pray for him, and for us.

So now I commit these pages to posterity. With this cool, dry air, they should last for many years. If you read this far, you have my thanks. Please return them to the box you found them in.

I had thought to write a warning here urging you to go back, but the fact is, you're going to die either way. You may not reach Behesht, but you definitely won't if you never make the attempt.

It's strange, but the more we search, the more certain I become that we will arrive in paradise. We are very close, I think we will find it any time now.

There is nowhere in the universe from whence the light and hope of heaven shine brighter than the darkest depths of hell.

Hope For the Harbingers

Allison Thai

"God creates out of nothing. Wonderful, you say. Yes, to be sure, but what he does is still more wonderful: he makes saints out of sinners."
~Søren Kierkegaard

The tethers binding his soul were warm yet firm, pulling him up from the bowels of Hell. Impossible. Nothing could escape the downward pull of a fiery eternity, just as nothing in the physical world could defy the power of gravity. Still, somehow, he felt lighter than he ever had before, buoyed by a force that took him past the fire and muck filled with screaming, cursing sinners. Shadows of the damned wallowed in never-ending rounds of punishment, dealt out according to their vices. To be freed from such torment made him gasp in relief. What could he have done to gain this sweet release? Was he being saved?

Suddenly he found himself on water, standing on it, as the ocean heaved and bucked all around him. A storm brewed overhead, gathering, rumbling, and tumbling in swells of dark clouds. A beam of sunlight peeked through. He shuddered from the warmth, frightened at first, then quickly found it pleasant on his skin. He looked down, caught sight of his reflection, and gasped.

A horse stared back, one with a withered build, bones jutting out to form odd tents and hills of skin here and there, with off-white hair to match an off-white coat.

"Where am I? *What* am I?"

"You are Death, one of the Four Horsemen." A little lamb, riding down the beam of light, had hailed him.

Though the reply was no more than a whisper, hardly heard amid the waves, the one called Death felt his knees buckle and heart race. The lamb exuded a blinding white halo, stronger than even the sun, and Death had to lower his eyes and muzzle lest he go blind. His voice dipped low with awe. "The Lamb of God."

The animal he had been, the name he once bore—he could not remember, but nothing in his past life mattered now. Death looked around. "You say four. Where are the other three?"

"They will join you soon."

True to the Lamb's word, more horses burst through the ocean's surface—one in red, one in black, and one in white. Blinking, gasping, and stumbling on the waves, they along with Death formed the quartet the Lamb had expected.

The Lamb of God addressed them in order of appearance, giving each a cordial nod. "War, Famine, and Pestilence, welcome."

These horses too ducked their heads, more out of fear than rudeness, and quailed at the face of overwhelming power.

The one called War, blood-red and rippling in muscles, was the first to muster a response. "You called us, Lord?"

"Indeed."

The water bore a reflection distilling some of the Lamb's light, and from this Death took notice of the Lamb's somber face.

"The Last Judgment is at hand. I have broken the four seals, as it was foretold, and hereby bestow upon you the task of destroying the world."

Death exchanged looks with the other horses, and they mirrored his disbelief.

"Why us?" Famine asked. "Why appoint souls of the damned? Why not trust your own angels to do it?"

"You have been in Hell for some time," the Lamb replied, "and because of that, memory does not serve you well. In your past lives you have made names for yourselves from the deaths and suffering of others. This world remembers you as warlords and monsters. You had been punished accordingly." The Lamb's voice did not ring with accusation, like a judge sentencing criminals, but was soft and sad, more like a father pining for his prodigal sons. "I chose you four out of many because you have the experience. Now I've raised you to be agents of calamity once more, this time in my name."

The Lamb of God lifted an arm, summoning an array of tools from the water. "Take these before you go. War, you will bear a sword to sow the seeds of violence and discord. Pestilence, spread disease far and wide with the bow and arrow. Famine, with the weighing scale you shall run the world's food thin. And Death, use this scythe to reap the harvest of souls."

Death closed his hooves over the staff of the scythe, and its weight made veins stand out on his skin. He felt honored to earn the privilege of this task, grim as it may be. Anything was better than going back to Hell. He bowed even lower, till his muzzle almost brushed the water. "By your grace you brought us out of eternal flame. For that we shall carry out your will."

Despite including the rest in his declaration, reactions among the other Horsemen varied. From the corner of his eye Death saw Famine rendered still with reluctance, Pestilence struggling to comprehend, and War squinting against the light.

"What will we get in return for completing this task?" Famine asked.

Death cringed at this bold inquiry, but the Lamb of God's reflection rippled as he shook with gentle laughter.

"Hungry for more now as you were in your past life—I should have expected as much, Famine. I will say this: you are in no position to make any bargains. But I do everything for a reason. Just do your duty, Horsemen." With that the Lamb departed from them, his coat of white wool one with the light.

Death nodded at his newfound equine brethren. "After you."

The Four Horsemen shot off, surging with power that bore them before the wind, over land and sea, through the four corners of the world. Entire nations buckled under the tide of the Apocalypse. Even before the Four Horsemen were called, world leaders had their teeth bared and hackles raised at one another, unable to reach any kind of agreement or settle for peace. The air crackled with tension. All War had to do was strike a match with his sword. For all his bulk and redness, War cavorted across continents unseen, jabbing his blade here and sweeping it there to ignite the flames in people's hearts. Animosity among species spiked. Even the meek and gentle, those less inclined to start fights, flew at each other like rabid beasts. War, always holding his sword aloft, saw to it that no alliances were formed. Not even among those of the same species. Camaraderie be damned—it was everyone for him or herself.

Famine played a part in fostering these schisms. Rivers ran dry, meat spoiled, and greens withered under his influence. What was scarce became sacred. People groveled and scrabbled for these necessities, and quickly resorted to looting and killing just to fill their bellies and live to see another day. Famine soon found himself in good company, surrounded by gaunt, stick-thin victims whose meat and fat wasted away from lack of nutrients. Famine viciously dismantled the Interspecies Protection From Consumption Act, as carnivores were driven to break the law by sinking their teeth into herbivores—fellow citizens, sometimes their own friends. The number of bodies climbed, but no one thought to keep track. The weak became meat, snatched up and swallowed down to feed the strong.

Such disregard for morals and sanitation gave way to disease courtesy of Pestilence. The Horseman slung his arrows far and wide, each riddled with every kind of poison and plague to send people by the hundreds and thousands to their graves. For a horse weighed down in boils, hair broiling with flies, and limbs weakened with rot, as arguably the slowest Horseman of the four, he did not have to run very fast or far at all. His joints, knobbly and frail as they were, could still bend the bow and that was enough. His arrows did much of the terrible work. They worked best on herds and packs, striking through many victims at once. Coughs and moans from the sick thickened the air. Contagion spread like fire, with no way to be extinguished except for the utter annihilation of those it consumed.

The Lamb of God had chosen well to bring them back as horses, for no other animal was more hardy and swift of foot to carry out the Apocalypse. Wherever War, Famine, and Pestilence went, Death was never too far behind, almost always on their tails. What else could follow such calamity but the end of one's life? The harvest of souls was plentiful, ever growing. Death thought he would have found this somewhat enjoyable, if his past life held any indication. Instead, the sheer magnitude of souls to collect overwhelmed him. If he had an earthly body that breathed and bled, the work would have easily killed him. He had already died once, so no need to fear a second death.

Fear—the Fifth Horseman, Death liked to call it—proved even swifter and more terrible than his comrades as it drove hordes of people to take their own lives. Mass suicide became a common sight for Death, the most common source for his harvest of souls. Death watched how disaster and doom brought out the worst in people, with many cursing the end times and even more still resigned to forfeiting their lives in order to forego the slow agony of disease, starvation, and bloodshed.

Many met their deaths with despair. Only a few faced theirs with dignity. One such fellow was a young rabbit named Viktor, one of many brothers and sisters constituting a poor warren in Russia.

Death took great interest in this little rabbit, constantly looming over him, for Viktor teetered on the edge of life and death with his weak heart. Viktor was the smallest and weakest of his siblings, a classic case of the runt of the litter. Often short of breath, he was red-faced under his thin fur as the *borscht* his family was so fond of eating. He could hardly venture out of his home, and his family sheltered him for good reason—he'd be torn apart in a blink of an eye. Death drifted closer and closer; never before had he been so intrigued by the life of any mortal. For all his frailty and bleak future, Viktor held onto life stronger than even the fiercest lion or tiger. Out loud and in his heart, he gave thanks for every breath he took, every moment he could spend with his parents and siblings, who fretted over him and saw to it that he always had his needs met. He gave thanks for the food he was given, grown and salvaged though carrots would never be as crisp and fresh as before. He was grateful for the blankets and toys his siblings gave up to keep him comfortable and entertained. Death could not help admiring this young rabbit, who seemed to live in defiance of the depravity around him.

One night, alone in his bedroom, Viktor craned his head up to meet Death's eyes.

"Hello there."

That took the Horseman aback. "You can see me?"

"I've always known you were watching." The rabbit did not scream or bolt out of his room. Instead he climbed onto his bed and wiggled into the blankets, like he would for any uneventful night. This amused and baffled Death.

"Do you know who I am?"

Viktor frowned, studying Death from head to toe. "You don't look like a guardian angel. You don't have wings."

"You're right. My name is Death."

"Hello, Death," he said, as if making a new friend. "I'm Viktor. Call me Vitya, if you want."

"Are you afraid?"

Viktor shook his head. "I know you'll come for me. I've known since I was very little, when I realized I could never run as fast or jump as high as my brothers and sisters. Everyone will find you at the end of the road sooner or later. I don't have long, but I'd like to be with my family for a bit more, please."

Death nodded, impressed with Viktor's courage and touched by a politeness that he had never before received in all his time as a Horseman. Most people feared him and hated him. He, like time, never stopped for anyone, but somehow he could not find it in his heart to go against the rabbit's wish. After all, Viktor's soul was not for the taking just yet. For someone terminally ill and on the verge of death, Viktor still had some life in him.

"I'll leave you alone, then," Death said, "and come back for you when you're ready."

"You're welcome to come back before that," Viktor replied, "just to relax, if that's possible. You look tired and lonely. I don't think the rest of my family can see you, and for most of the day they're out foraging, anyway. I'd like a friend to keep me company."

Death tipped his muzzle at him. "I appreciate the offer." And he took it whenever he could, for his duty proved very taxing and draining, indeed. After rounds of collecting souls and witnessing all manners of terrible deaths, the Horseman liked to visit Viktor and take his mind off the strain, if even for a moment. They spent most of their time together over open storybooks, fairy tales with happy endings, or silly stories that would make Death whinny and snort and break free of the somber frown that seemed to have set in his muzzle permanently.

"I love to read," Viktor said. "It's my escape. It takes me to faraway places and lets me be the hero I've always dreamed of being."

"You're already a hero."

"How? I don't swing a sword." Viktor tilted back to behold the scythe that loomed over him. "And I'm very sure that thing would crush me if I tried to lift it."

Death let out a rueful chuckle, hefting the weapon for a moment. "You don't need anything like this to be a hero." He rested a big, worn hoof over Viktor's head, dwarfing it. "I mean that you are strong and brave in ways you can't imagine. Believe me, I've killed—er, met many, many people around the world, and no one's quite like you."

The rabbit's ears stood rigid and fluttered a little. His cheeks flushed, making his face even redder, and bunched up below his eyes in a wide smile. "You may not look it, but you're very nice."

Time was not so kind. Viktor grew more sick and frail with each passing day. He was confined to the bed and could not even risk a venture to other burrows in the warren.

Death knelt over the little rabbit's bedside. "It's almost time," he murmured.

Viktor closed his eyes. "I understand."

After supper, he asked for the attention of the entire family. Of course they were all ears, wide-eyed and curious, wondering what he had to say. Death also listened in, invisible to the rest, wondering how they would take the news.

"Everyone…" Viktor paused. His nose twitched and eyes blinked rapidly as he struggled to collect himself. With great effort he sucked in a deep breath, and went on, "Please don't be upset, but I think now is a good time for me to say good-bye." Stunned silence all around met him.

Finally, his father asked, "What do you mean?"

"Vitya, don't say that," his mother cried. She reached out to take his paw into hers. "We're doing everything we can to care for you—"

"I know, and thank you." Tears welled in Viktor's eyes. "I feel I can never thank you enough. But you've seen the world around us, outside our warren. Even the world's coming to an end. I am going to die, and I know you're just trying to protect me, but you will have to let me go." Viktor offered them a wide smile. "Don't worry. I will see you all on the other side someday." He bid his family good night, for the last time. He gave each sibling a long, earnest hug, while they restrained the urge to pile up on him all at once. Finally he was enveloped in arms and tears by his parents.

The lights went out. Viktor's body went still and slack, his voice no more than a whisper. "I'm ready, Death. Take me away."

His passing was a painless, peaceful one—the only one Death carried out alone. He had insisted on acting without the aid of his fellow Horsemen. With a pull of Death's scythe Viktor's soul slipped free, and without a weak earthly body to bind him, he sprinted out of the warren and floated well above the Muscovite landscape. Death followed him up, and Viktor turned to him with wide, searching eyes.

"Are you coming with me, Death?"

The Horseman gestured to the desolation below them. "I'm afraid not. I still have work to do down here."

"Will we see each other again?"

Death had to be honest. "I can't promise anything, but I hope so."

"I hope so, too." Viktor waved a little white paw. "Good-bye, for now."

Death watched the rabbit's soul drift—up, up, up—along a stairway to Heaven the Horseman could not see.

Parting ways with Viktor weighed down his heart. At the same time Death rejoiced that the young rabbit could leave this crumbling world after a proper farewell to his family and end up in a better place. If anyone deserved that, it was Viktor.

Death tore his eyes from the sky, a glimpse of Heaven, and turned back to search for more worthy souls to send into God's kingdom. Unfortunately, the Apocalypse produced few instances of enlightenment and mental fortitude. Death grew weary of his work again, wondering if there would be an end to it all. In the constant accompaniment and teamwork with his fellow Horsemen, Death took it as a reprieve to strike up conversations with them.

"What is God's plan for us after this?" Death had to raise his voice, on account of howls and screams from the mobs of starving, disease-ridden people fighting over scraps. Such an event called for a group effort, the presence of the other three Horsemen.

"You mean what's after the *Last* Judgment?" War folded his arms over his huge chest. "A foolish question, Death."

Famine's dark eyes glittered. "On my way here I caught a glimpse of Heaven, maybe even Empyrean. I've never wanted anything so badly before."

Pestilence's ears, riddled with holes, perked. "You've actually seen it?"

War's muzzle stretched from a frown. "We're damned, anyway. God's sending us back to Hell after we do our part."

"Why would he do that if we are following his orders?" Death asked. "Surely he will reward us." He paused to scoop up souls who had lost their bodies to bloodshed.

"What reward? After what we've done?" War snorted. "God said so himself: we'd been punished accordingly. Hell is final."

Death shook his head. "Christ went down and came back up for the third day. He broke open the bolts binding the gates of Hell. Bolts that even Satan could not pry out. Even now the gates are left open."

War waved a hoof in dismissal. "The Harrowing of Hell. It happened, yes, but everyone down there just takes it as hope, a chance, for a way out. Well, false hope and fat chance. Christ descended into Hell only for the righteous, anyway. We are sinners. There's no freedom for the likes of us." He reached down to thrust his blade into the hearts of those too tired to fight, making them spring back to their feet and rejoin the mob.

Death knew better than to fuel War's ire, but he felt inclined to disagree. God had already done the impossible: bring up the damned from Hell. Not up to Heaven, of course (a ridiculous stretch), but onto the physical plane. That was a miracle in itself. God made use of even sinners to do his good work. Deep in Death's unbeating heart, he felt that God would not toss them away like trash. At the same time he felt he did not deserve redemption.

"The Lamb is too detached for my taste," War went on. "Maybe he's making us do his dirty work. He wouldn't soil his wool for this. And he's hiding things from us. He gave me this sword but not my memories. I'd very much like to know who I was and what I did."

Famine cracked a grin—a rare act, considering their line of work. "Well, I'm quite sure that even at your prime, you hadn't started up this many wars." Then he craned his narrow muzzle back as he pondered, as if weighing the scales in his head. "I must have wanted a lot of things in my past life. Even if I remembered them all, they don't matter anymore."

Death followed Famine's gaze upward, searching for an inkling of light amidst the storm. "If God isn't telling us everything, I believe it's better that way. I don't want to know what I've done to earn a place in Hell. I think

God made us Horsemen to give us a second chance." His grip tightened over the scythe. "Forget the past. Trust in God to lead us to a better future."

War doubled over guffawing. "You should hear yourself. Have you gone mad?"

Pestilence did not respond with scorn as War did. Sunken eyes peeked through a matted forelock, making him look like a lost child. "Do you really think there's hope?"

"Yes. Hope for the harbingers." Death wanted his comrades to believe that, too.

"Whatever put that idea in your head?" Famine asked. "That little rabbit, am I right?"

Death conceded with a smile.

War chuckled. "You must have taken a real liking to him. You wouldn't let the three of us get anywhere close to that warren."

"I do not like giving children terrible ends," Death admitted. He remembered the fairy tales Viktor would read to him. "I like happy endings."

"I doubt it will end well for us." Pestilence heaved a sigh, the huge boils sagging with his shoulders.

"That's fear talking," Death said. "You have to believe with all your might that God will forgive you. Forgive us." He did not believe he deserved such a thing, but yearned for it all the same. He began to take inspiration in how Viktor led his short life on Earth, making it a habit to thank every moment he spent out of Hell, even if he stood far from Heaven. Fear of going back down there fueled his gratitude. He encouraged his comrades to do the same. As they gathered together and shared stories, Death found that War, Famine, and Pestilence had found their own Viktors in the midst of strife and suffering.

"I have found peacemakers," War told them. "My sword can't cut them."

"I met givers," Famine said, "who gave all they had when they could have helped themselves."

"I might have produced the finest physicians the world has ever seen," Pestilence said.

These stories pleased Death greatly. This cemented his belief that he and his fellow Horsemen were doing good work, after all. There was something to be learned here.

Finally, after what seemed like ages, the Last Judgment drew to an end. Every soul was sent up, or down, and accounted for. The Four Horsemen joined forces, combining their strength, to deliver the blow that would send the world into oblivion. Death lifted his scythe, adding to the steeple formed by War's sword, Famine's weighing scale, and Pestilence's bow. They swung down together, and remnants of a sinful, imperfect world gave way before their very eyes. A huge wave of light blinded them. Death expected the downward tug, the return of his soul to Hell, now that his work here was done.

He felt no such thing. He dared to blink his eyes open, and the other Horsemen followed suit, their stances tense and unsure. What Death saw next took his breath away. Before him stood the Lamb of God, heading a multitude of angels and souls, innumerable beyond measure and compare. Death's legs buckled and he sank to his knees.

The Lamb smiled. "Please rise. You are in good company."

Death obeyed, exchanging wide-eyed confusion with his comrades. He certainly did not remember Hell looking like this.

"You have done as I have asked, and you did well. My tests are never easy, and I must commend you for passing the one I imposed on you. For that you will be rewarded."

Pestilence's mouth hung open, then worked like a fish out of water, and finally he shut it and lowered his head out of embarrassment over looking ridiculous before the Lord of all creation.

Famine managed to spring out the question. "This… this is Heaven? We made it?"

The Lamb nodded. "I'm afraid I must save a proper warm welcome for another time." He turned his muzzle downward, and amid the light a spot of darkness remained, where an ugly serpent writhed and hissed below the heavenly host. "There is still the Enemy to vanquish once and for all. Only in his defeat can we rejoice in the founding of New Jerusalem."

"We will help," War said. With his ears tucked back and head bowed, he looked sorry to have doubted and spoken against God at all. Clearly he sought to make up for it.

Famine, Death, and Pestilence nodded in agreement.

"Thank you," the Lamb replied. "Now, I can't have you go into battle unprepared." With a sweep of his arm, he sent up a great wind that peeled away every blight on the Horsemen's bodies, granting them pure white coats and builds that brimmed with health and vigor. Then with another wave of his arm, he substituted their Apocalyptic instruments for blades forged in the brightest holy steel. Death embraced this new identity with open arms, thrilling in the divine power that coursed through him.

Then something else hit him—something white and soft. Death drew back and gasped. "Viktor!"

The rabbit, who had tackled the former Horseman with a fierce hug, pulled away and grinned. "I knew you'd come."

Death drew him back for another hug. "I didn't think I would, but here I am."

The Lamb of God gave them a warm smile. "It seems I have given you two the happy ending you've wanted."

"I would not have it any other way, Lord." Hell seemed nothing more than a bad memory now. Death felt he could burst, overjoyed to know that he was given another chance, that his hope and faith bore fruit. Fruit he had shared with his fellow Horsemen.

Viktor clasped his friend's hoof with both paws. "Come on, let's go slay a dragon together."

ABOUT THE AUTHORS

Madison Keller is the author of the *Flower's Fang* series of young adult fantasy novels, the new adult *Dragon Tax* novella series, as well as numerous short stories. Madison originally hails from the great state of Utah, but for the last eight years she has made the Pacific Northwest her home. When not writing Madison enjoys bicycle riding, knitting, and playing Dungeons and Dragons with her pals. She lives in Portland, Oregon with her husband and an adorable Chihuahua.

Jelliqal Belle enjoys writing. Her favorite aspects are imagining the new worlds and the people in them and researching to make it right and realistic. She earned a double major in Psychology and Theatre with a minor in Studio Art and an MFA in Theater Design. She is a lifelong gamer and reads science fiction, fantasy, and mystery stories voraciously. Jelliqal Belle resides in Metro Atlanta with her menagerie of one husband, one son, one dog, and three cats. Jelliqal Belle is the writing facilitator for Furry Weekend Atlanta 2017. Follow her for random thoughts on Twitter @Jelliqal.

Tim Susman has been part of the furry fandom for over a quarter century now. He co-founded Sofawolf Press and has edited the *New Tibet* anthologies and many novels for them. His short fiction has appeared in *Apex, Lightspeed, Yarf!, Mythagoras, Anthrolations, ROAR*, and *New Fables*, and has won one Cóyotl Award. His latest novel, *The Tower and the Fox*, is coming out in 2017 from Argyll Productions. You can find out more about him and his work at timsusman.wordpress.com.

Frances Pauli writes speculative fiction and has authored over twenty novels, most of which have at least one animal character or another. She's recently focused her attention on anthropomorphic stories and is fairly certain she'll never go back. Adding the many-layered aspects of furry characters and species has put the spark back in her pen, and driven her to begin her first completely anthropomorphic novel. Her short furry fiction can be found in various anthologies.

She posts free stories, excerpts, serials and previews of the upcoming *Hybrid Nation* books on social media sites as Mamma Bear, and a full list of her publications can be found on her website: francespauli.com

She lives in Washington state with her family, four dogs, two cats and a variety of tarantulas.

E. S. Lapso is a furry author from the cornbelts of Illinois. The E. S. In her name represents Elijah and Skylar, the twin fennec foxes that make up her singular fursona. Currently studying Zoology, she finds inspiration in the beauty and science of the natural world.

Amy Fontaine received her bachelor's degree in wildlife biology with a minor in English writing from Humboldt State University in 2015. As a wildlife biologist, she has studied wolves in Yellowstone, hyenas in Kenya, and fishers (basically big tree weasels!) in the northern Sierras. She draws inspiration for her writings from her experiences in the wilderness with animals.

Amy writes fantasy, science fiction, and poetry. Her work often involves strange creatures of one kind or another. Her short stories have been published in *Bewildering Stories*, *Fossil Lake IV: SHARKASAURUS!*, and *ROAR Volumes 6* and *7*. Her poems have been published in the *North Coast Journal*, *WEREWOLVES VERSUS: FASCISM* (a charity anthology supporting the American Civil Liberties Union), and *Civilized Beasts*, an anthology of animal poetry which donates its profits to the Wildlife Conservation Society. She is a proud member of the Furry Writers' Guild.

Amy's fantasy novel, *Mist*, will be released by Thurston Howl Publications in August 2017:

In a misty forest where no one remembers their past, five young shape-shifters are compelled by the struggles they face to transform their minds and hearts as well as their forms.

You can find more of Amy's writings at her website: https://amyfontaine.wordpress.com.

Priya Sridhar a 2016 MBA graduate and published author, has been writing fantasy and science fiction for fifteen years, and counting, as well as drawing a webcomic for five years. She believes that every story is a journey, and that a good tale allows the reader to escape to a new world. She also enjoys reading, biking, movie-watching, and classical music. One of Priya's stories made the Top Ten Amazon Kindle Download list, and Alban Lake published her novella *Carousel*. Priya lives in Miami, Florida with her family and posts monthly at her blog *A Faceless Author*.

Mark Blickley is a widely published and produced New York author. His latest book is *Sacred Misfits* (Red Hen Press) and his latest play, *The Milkman's Sister*, recently concluded its run at the 13th Street Repertory Theater. He is a proud member of the Dramatists Guild and PEN American Center.

Christopher Shaffer (a.k.a. "Mythic Fox") discovered the furry fandom via an anime magazine's letter column in the late 90's. While he'd been writing before that, mostly trying to shamelessly ape Stephen King, finding the fandom helped focus him. His biggest influences are, in no particular order, the aforementioned Mr. King, William Gibson, S. Andrew Swann, and Kyell Gold. He's also an avid tabletop gamer, and has freelanced for *White Wolf* and *Onyx Path*. His RPG writing, fiction and otherwise, has primarily appeared in both the *Werewolf: The Apocalypse* and *Werewolf: The Forsaken* game lines, as well as *Mage: The Awakening* and the upcoming *Trinity Continuum: Aeon*.

"Bite the Apple" is his first published writing credit within the fandom. More of his writing, much of it in the same setting, can be found at FurAffinity and SoFurry under the username 'MythicFox.'

John Giezentanner lives in Lafayette, Colorado, removes invasive, nonnative plant species in Boulder and writes sci-fi, fantasy and horror stories in addition to being an aspiring dinosaur. He found "paradise" to be a challenging theme to write on but ultimately very rewarding. "Lonesome Peak" was a joy to write because—spoiler—paradise is mostly about hanging out with your best buds. John's stories have also appeared in *ROAR Volume 7* and online in *Fantasy Scroll Magazine*. John needs to start being mindful of what he puts in author bios in case a family member randomly googles his name, but he is also informed that this short bio can be up to 200 words long, so PUNCH NAZIS, PUNCH NAZIS, PUNCH NAZIS, PUNCH NAZIS, PUNCH NAZIS, PUNCH NAZIS, PUNCH NAZIS, PUNCH NAZIS, PUNCH NAZIS, PUNCH NAZIS, PUNCH NAZIS.

And, also, RESIST, RESIST, RESIST, RESIST, RESIST, RESIST, RESIST, RESIST, RESIST, PERSIST, RESIST, RESIST, RESIST, RESIST, RESIST

Searska GreyRaven is a dragon of the noodly persuasion who makes her home in South Florida. When she isn't chasing some shiny new idea, she can be found reading, tending her bees, or basking in the Floridian sun.

Matt Doyle lives in the UK and is the author of multiple books, including *The Spark Form Chronicles*, a science fiction series about five card players and a holographic anthropomorphic wolf/rabbit hybrid that claims to be alive, and *Teller Tales*, a middle-grade fantasy/horror series about a twelve-year-old gamer, a teenage girl, and a six-foot-tall fennec fox.

When not working on fiction, Matt spends his time working on his pop culture blog, planning and building various cosplays, and designing a variety of t-shirts. If you want to know more, you can find him skulking around the internet in the following places:

Website: www.mattdoylemedia.com

Twitter: @mattdoylemedia

Facebook: https://www.facebook.com/MattDoyleMedia/

Thurston Howl is the editor-in-chief of Thurston Howl Publications. With a BA in English from Vanderbilt University and an MA from Middle Tennessee State University, Howl now pursues his PhD in English and Sociology with a concentration in Animal Studies at Michigan State University. He is the author of four novels, and his works have appeared in *Civilized Beasts*, *Purrfect Tails*, *Dogs of War*, and *Seven Deadly Sins*.

Nicholas Hardin has been involved in the furry fandom for well over a decade, but only recently stepped into the world of publication (after far too long, he says). His first published story, "Guardian Angels," appeared in FurPlanet's *Inhuman Acts* anthology. Prior to that, he had stories in numerous conbooks as well as the first two annuals of the *Extinctioners* comic. He is also in the process of submitting his first full novel for publication, with more on the way. Aside from writing, he enjoys making art of his characters and stories when he isn't lost in a book or video game. A librarian by day, Nicholas is constantly surrounded by literature, and hopes to one day have his own works on display among esteemed others.

Bill Kieffer was born in Jersey City, NJ. He never fully recovered.

A brain injury at an early age left him with some mild issues and just enough aphasia to be amusing at parties. He tries to be very open about these. He doesn't drink, having the bare minimum of inhibitions to begin with. His only admitted vice is being himself. He is ever-so grateful to his wife and the day job for putting up with him and his unadmitted vices.

When he is not looking in the mirror, Bill Kieffer is actually a 6 foot tall gray anthropomorphic draft horse that types as Greyflank. Past writing credits include comic books like "Billy Joe Van Helsing: Red Neck Vampire Hunter" and "Great Morons in History, the Dan Quayle Bio." More recent publications include short stories in *Roar 7*, *Bleak Horizons*, and *Seven Deadly Sins: Furry Confessions* and the novella *The Goat: Building the Perfect Victim*. He is a member of the Furry Writers Guild and a columnist for *Underground Book Reviews*. In the near future, Jaffa books will release COLD BLOOD: *Fatal Fables, a collection of furry noir stories*.

Slip Wolf has been brewing up tales in the furry community for about five years now, and has found he's unable to stop the clumsily slow pour of stories that spill now and again out on the coffeeshop tables of the collective literary Valhalla. In trying to be a good soul, he's sought zen with Sofawolf Press, peace with Furplanet, introspection with Rabbit Valley and composure with Weasel Press. Despite his best efforts he's made a mess or two with sinful transgressions in just about all of the above. No sense in a wolf trying to get to heaven if the trip can't be fun, right?

Dwale is a semi-sapient congerie of dross and shadow play who walks the path illumed wherever the moon touches the sea. Its works examine moral and/or spiritual matters through a gritty fictional setting readers may find all too familiar. You can follow it on twitter: @ ThornAppleCider

Allison Thai is a Vietnamese-American pursuing a career in medicine, hoping to work either in the operating room or a lab. When she's not studying and delighting in all things science, she likes to read, write, draw, and swim. Disney movies, Redwall books, and the Sly Cooper games were her first glimpse into the furry/anthropomorphic world. Her stories usually involve one or more of the following: Asians, Russians, made-up worlds, the military, talking animals, monsters, robots, neuroscience, or body horror.

ABOUT THE ARTIST

Teagan Gavet is a professional illustrator, graphic novelist, and freelance rambler. Find more at: http://www.teagangavet.com
  http://www.furaffinity.net/user/blackteagan

ABOUT THE EDITOR

Mary E. Lowd, your fearless editor, is a science-fiction and furry author in Oregon. She's had more than eighty short stories published, as well as several novels through FurPlanet. She's been editing ROAR since Volume 6.

www.ingramcontent.com/pod-product-compliance
Lightning Source LLC
Chambersburg PA
CBHW051638050726
47502CB00011B/1087